A Mercedes in the Sand

A Mercedes in the Sand

A NOVEL BY
LEON LEVIT

Praise for *A Mercedes in the Sand*

"A generous, thought-provoking book, epic in scope, overflowing with humor, wonderful storytelling, emotional range and surprising depth. The story deals with identity, nationalism and racism in an impossibly playful, and sadly relevant way."

David Sachs, bestselling author of *The Flood*

*

"The story of *A Mercedes in the Sand* is a captivating one. It is in turns foreboding, comical, and romantic. And in all cases, it is a heart-warming story. Even as it wrenches on the heart strings at times. *A Mercedes in the Sand* tells a story that should be told, that needed to be told.
The author's sense of narrative flow is simply extraordinary - every page turned as easily as the last led me to expectations of more intriguing and evocative moments to come."

AJ Sikes, author and editor

*

"This wonderful novel based on the authors own life experience is both fascinating and poignant. A many faceted story told with humour and charm, set against a sorrowful era – becomes a plea for tolerance and civil courage. I highly recommend this book and believe it will have a wide readership."

Dr. Susan Glickman, author and editor

*

"A beautiful and colourful account of life in Germany and Palestine. The subtle and brilliant style will resonate with every reader"

P. Elwood Enns, Ph.D.

FIRST PUBLISHED IN GERMAN IN 2002 BY EDITION BUCHERGILDE

Copyright © 2016 Leon Levitr

COVER ART BY MARTIN GOMEZ
TRANSLATED FROM THE GERMAN BY PETER HESSEL

MANDOLIN PUBLISHING

ISBN-13: 9780995812314
ISBN-10: 0995812314

DEDICATION

This book is dedicated with much love to the memory of its author, our father Leon Levit and to the memory of our mother Rivka Levit.

To my sister Daphna Levit whose efforts resulted in the publication of this book in its original form in Germany.

Ruth Levit Miller
Ottawa, summer 2016

BERLIN IN THE 1920'S AN EXCITING CITY OFFERING MANY DIVERSE ENTERTAINMENTS. Albert Berg- the pampered son of a factory owner fully enjoys the life and the women of his city. He refuses to acknowledge the signs of growing anti-semitism and why suddenly he is "less German" than before. Though a proud German and never a religious Jew- he is forced to emigrate to Palestine in order to survive. In Palestine, he encounters a hot-bed of Arab and Jewish communities, the British Police, and many arriving immigrants who like Albert feel lost and alienated by the only country willing to take them in. From service in the British Army, to battles on the hills of Jerusalem for Israel's independence, Albert's adventures, loves and disappointments form an exotic colorful novel. "A Mercedes in the Sand" takes us through some of the most dramatic and beautiful moments of the twentieth century. Originally written in German it has at last been made available in English.

Attempting a Foreword

THIS BOOK IS FICTION. I⊤ therefore contains many indecent stories. It also contains many indecent thoughts because besides the stories of many people, it contains the thoughts of a single man. And this particular man, like many people, can be indecent.

Above all, this is the story of a human life. The life of a German Jew who lost one home in the land of his birth and who found another elsewhere after many internal and external struggles.

Whose fault were these struggles? His own. Although this story deals with Jews and with Germans, it isn't really a tale of the pursued and their pursuers, but rather an expression of the author's belief that people are responsible for their own lives. It is also a testament to his conviction that no nation is free from intolerance and prejudice, and that the victims of such prejudice don't become better people just because they have been persecuted.

If in the course of telling this story I step on some people's toes, and some of God's Cossacks with beards and side-curls feel insulted, I can't help it. The Holy One hasn't appointed any people on earth to be His exclusive bodyguards, and He hasn't chosen any nation for special treatment, not even the Chosen People.

The Jews are a comical and difficult people, and a very miserable people. Almost as miserable as other people. The specimen of that nation which my story introduces are all based on truth, and what happened to them is true also, right down to the smallest detail.

Those who object must argue with the facts, not with me. The whole story is none of my contriving. I only wrote it down. I hope not too badly.

Tel Aviv, May 1965

I
1914

— ◆ —

"DAMN, DAMN, DAMN!" IT FELT wonderful to curse outside where his mother couldn't hear him. At home he wasn't even allowed to say a single *damn*! But out here, on Dönhoff Square, Albert could curse as much as he wanted. Mademoiselle didn't understand German anyway. She'd only ask, *"Albair, qu'est-ce que tu dis, Mon petit?"* If his nanny hadn't been so pretty, Albert would have been embarrassed to be out with her in public.

Albert steered his four-wheeled cart over the cracks and crevices of the sidewalk with difficulty. At this point in the story, his cart represented an express train. Little Albert served as engineer, conductor and stationmaster. A lot of responsibility for someone eight years old. He devoted himself to all three jobs with earnest dedication. His train station was the pedestal of the monument to the Baron Vom Stein.

Albert didn't know why this larger-than-life bronze statue had been erected on Dönhoff Square. He wasn't aware that the Baron had been a famous Prussian statesman, besides which, this fact has nothing to do with our story. But Albert was fascinated by the look on the Baron's bronze face: a look which seemed to extend right across Leipziger Strasse to the Aschinger Pub where a pretty waitress with enormous breasts was busy serving beer. Other pedestrians might not have noticed the direction of the Baron's gaze, only that the sculptor had marked his face with a certain severity and vacuity of mind, two attributes typical of the Prussian aristocracy.

There may be people – in Cambodia or Alaska – who have never heard of Dönhoff Square. For those poor underprivileged creatures, here is some useful information. On the Berlin city map of 1914, Dönhoff Square appeared as a small yellow-green spot in the city's business district. For the children of that neighbourhood, it was the only piece of nature for miles around. There were a few stately trees, some carefully tended and fenced lawns on which it was strictly forbidden to walk, and symmetrically arranged flowerbeds in which each little bulb had been planted precisely, if not lovingly. They had probably been told, "Now behave yourself, and flower according to the rules!"

There were benches under the trees. Albert's Mademoiselle sat on one, weeping. Albert, who had just brought his express train to a halt in front of the bench, was worried. His feelings for Mademoiselle were not particularly warm, but he did not dislike her. He had nothing against her personally since she was usually nice and friendly with him, and she laughed readily. What he resented was the institution she represented. None of his friends or fellow students had to endure a French governess teaching them the nasal sounds of her idiotic language. *"C'est ne pas le chemang, Albair, c'est le chemin – in, in!"*

Despite his ambivalent feelings about his governess, when he saw her crying he was shocked. So shocked, he forgot that Mademoiselle always had to be spoken to in French and shouted in German, "What's the matter? What has happened? Why are you crying?"

Mademoiselle continued to sob, but tried to pull herself together.

Albert finally remembered his French. *"Pourquoi vous pleurez, qu'est-ce qu'il y a?"*

Mademoiselle regained control. *"Rien, rien de tout. Viens, nous quittons."*

If any answer was designed to deepen his worry and heighten his curiosity, it was that 'nothing had happened'. Therefore he kept on questioning her until she slowly revealed what had upset her: The war, which had begun against the Russians, was now also a war between France and Germany.

"Ma patrie et la votre sont en guerre."

So that was it. Mademoiselle was now an enemy of the state! Albert felt as if Mademoiselle had suddenly contracted an infectious disease and he would have to stay away from her. Or should he point the tip of his sword against her and demand that she surrender herself to his mercy? But he didn't happen to have a sword handy, and besides, it didn't make any sense. Could people tell just by looking at Mademoiselle that she was French? Would the crowd on Dönhoff Square come and beat her up?

Albert didn't know what to do. He hardly protested as Mademoiselle stood up to go home and told him to come along. But he refused to let her hold his hand.

I I

"*OUI MADAME, JE LE GARDERAI* bien," Mademoiselle assured Albert's mother, placing her arm protectively around the boy's shoulders. He didn't understand what was happening. His mother stood there in tears, with a little suitcase in her hand. His father hadn't come home at all. Minna, the maid was holding the door open, crying bitterly. Only Mademoiselle, who had already wept on Dönhoff Square, was keeping her cool.

"Damn it!" he shouted. "What has happened?"

His mother ignored his cursing. "Papa and I must go away for a few days, Albert. Be a good boy and listen to Mademoiselle," she said in a weepy voice. She hugged him as if she were saying goodbye forever. She nodded to the young governess and quickly patted Minna's cheek while the girl kept howling like a siren. Then Albert's mother hastily walked out the door.

Albert could see Johannes, the factory porter, waiting outside. He took Mama's suitcase and ran down the stairs ahead of her. Minna locked the door, wiped the tears off her face with her fist and said, "Such a thing in my worst dreams I never could have expected." When Minna was angry, she reverted to speaking her native Low German. Then she wondered why the French *Mattmoisell* understood her even less than when she addressed her in High German.

Albert looked expectantly at his governess, hoping for an explanation. At the same time, he had the inexplicable feeling that Mademoiselle had suddenly grown older and demanded more respect. He couldn't understand it. Why of all people she, an enemy French woman, was suddenly supposed to have authority over him? It wasn't the first time his parents had to go away unexpectedly, so why was everybody crying? He'd never seen Minna so upset. He decided that unless he got an explanation right away, he would start screaming.

But Mademoiselle's face was very serious. Realizing that she was preoccupied with something important, Albert decided to postpone his temper tantrum. They went into his father's library where Mademoiselle took a seat in one of the deep leather chairs. She had clearly reached some kind of conclusion. Against his mother's advice, she decided to tell him the truth.

"Of course, you don't know, *mon petit*," she explained with a gentle smile, "that the two of us, you and I, are in the same situation." Albert's face showed that he had no idea what she meant, but she just kept talking slowly, using easy French so that he would have no difficulty understanding her.

"You see, I was born in France, so I feel French. You were born in Germany, and therefore you feel German."

Albert nodded. That much he understood, and that much he could accept.

"My mother was also born in France just as your mother was born in Germany. Yet my father is not from France but from the Alsace. That's why my father and my mother, and I myself, have German citizenship. Do you understand that?"

No, Albert didn't understand. "Don't you always have citizenship of the country you're born in?"

"*Mais non, mon petit*. A man's wife and children are always given his citizenship, which is why you're no better off than me. Your father was born in Russia, and for that reason you and your mother are Russians too."

"What?" Albert cried in horror. "But the Russians are our enemies! That's impossible."

"Impossible? *Peut-être, mais vrai*," Mademoiselle said. "Since Germany is now at war with the Russians and the French, the police have arrested your mother. But we hope they will only hold her for a few days. Your mother told me that your uncles, who are already serving as soldiers, are doing everything they can to vouch for your parents. So have no fear."

Albert sat at the edge of the sofa, stunned. He knew that Mademoiselle was telling him the truth. She had never lied to him. His mother sometimes answered evasively when she didn't feel like telling him whatever she felt he didn't need to know. But Mademoiselle had never equivocated – she either gave him straight answers or none at all.

He could no longer hold back his desire to shout. "But Mama and Papa haven't done anything wrong. Why have they been arrested?" he cried. "Mama is not a Russian, and neither is Papa. He *hates* the Russians. None of us speak a word of Russian, and my grandfather received the Iron Cross . . . ." He began to sob so much that he couldn't speak anymore.

Mademoiselle stood up and took him in her arms. His outburst had been in German, so she hadn't understood much except that he needed consoling. But he was soon pulled from the soft arms of his governess by Minna, who stood before him with her sturdy legs planted like the Pomeranian grenadier whose daughter she was.

"Young man," she said, "let me tell you something. If those fool police don't bring your folks back by tomorrow, I'll knock their stupid helmets off their thick heads. So quit the crying already, okay?"

Albert didn't doubt that Minna would be ready to do as she said. Her statement consoled him more than the nebulous prospect of help from his uncles. Drying his tears, he sat down at his father's desk and accepted his fate: the difficult and unpredictable conjugation of the French verb "*être*." But he added something, just to tease Mademoiselle a little. She began the dictation with "*je suis*." He wrote down "*je suis Allemand*."

She looked over his shoulder at the page, but didn't say a word.

Minna muttered something before leaving the room and slamming the door. He wasn't sure what it was, but it sounded like *shit*.

Albert had a good and legitimate reason to be convinced that his father wasn't Russian, although he didn't know it, just as he didn't understand terms such as *passport* and *citizenship*.

Mademoiselle's explanations had given him an idea of the situation, but the reality was that, in spite of all the official paperwork, his father was not, in fact, a Russian.

What Albert had shouted – that his father hated the Russians – was quite true. His father hated Tsarist Russia, which he regarded as an evil state with an atrocious form of government. His father was a Jew and in the small Lithuanian *shtetl* where he grew up he had only been exposed to his own culture: to Jewish history, the Hebrew language and its literature, the philosophy of the Talmud and Rabbinic law.

These areas of knowledge made him a whole person, proud of his origin and his national heritage, not torn asunder by contradictory influences. He was neither a Russian Jew nor a German Jew, but just a Jew. There had never been any doubt in his mind that the first language his son would learn – after the local parlance – would be Hebrew.

But Albert's mother wouldn't allow it. "Hebrew is a dead language," she declared. "He can learn it later if he is so inclined. At school, he will have to learn Latin and Greek – also dead languages. What he should really learn, as soon as possible, is French, the international language of good society."

That had been the reason for Mademoiselle's appearance in Albert's life. Papa had capitulated.

"Maybe you're right," he told his wife. "At this point Albert has no idea what it means to be a Jew".

"And what does it mean?" asked Albert's mother.

Max Berg looked at his wife with concern. He rarely found himself unable to answer a question.

But a clear definition of this particular term was difficult, even for him.

The young official who had to conduct the interviews with enemy aliens in Berlin's police headquarters on Alexander Square had no trouble at all finding a definition. He only entered a few lines in the Berg Family file: "Apolitical, emigrated from Russia twenty years ago due to persecution of Jews. The wife is of German origin. No concerns."

So Albert's parents returned before noon the next day, and Minna didn't need to attack the helmets of any Prussian policemen.

It didn't cheer Albert up in the least that in the afternoon Mademoiselle made him conjugate "*vouloir*," a more regular verb. He had already learned all the forms of "*être*." He didn't know how to express the thought, but he was convinced of a basic difference between *vouloir* and *être*, between *to want* and *to be*.

III
1917

———

THE BOYS IN THE SEVENTH grade at the Royal Friedrich Wilhelm Gymnasium were at the age in which, according to experts, they had the greatest capacity to acquire knowledge while simultaneously offering the greatest resistance to it. Their class had never been a showcase of academic magnificence, and this winter term was no exception.

The classroom was unheated. Ice crystals in interesting shapes had formed on the windows, inspiring the physics teacher to enthusiastic explanations. But that was the only use these crystals had. The boys sat in their overcoats, listlessly tapping the floor with the wooden soles of their shoes to keep their feet warm. Neither rutabaga soup and sawdust bread, nor the disgusting new artificial sweetener called saccharine could provide the energy they needed.

Professor Stender, who taught mathematics, didn't even attempt to instil the basics in his restless pupils. Albert tried to find a spot on his desk where he could carve his name with his pocket knife. Generations of students had immortalized themselves that way. Once he found room for his name, he encountered another difficulty: his name had far too many round letters, which made the knife skip in the grain of the wood. He noticed his seat-mate smirking at his efforts, wearing a superior grin on his face. "I'm going to fix him," he thought. "I'll carve my name in Hebrew letters." And he did. Almost all the letters of the Hebrew alphabet are angular with straight horizontal lines. The letters are also extremely patient, having survived many thousands of years, and therefore submitted to his efforts uncomplainingly.

"That Jewish boy has a lot of nerve, defacing a German school desk with Hebrew letters!" the other boy thought, but his good upbringing prevented him from saying it out loud. Nonetheless, Albert knew exactly what was going on in that blond head next to him. The boy had been raised according to the false elegance of convenient prejudices. One of them was that you ought not to associate with Jews. Unfortunately, a perverse teacher had seated him next to one of the three Jews in his class, and the most aggressive of them to boot. You couldn't sit next to a boy and never speak a word to him. However you didn't have to continue the relationship outside school.

Albert recognized these rules but didn't like them. He would have preferred to be friends with his seat mate, and with a few of the other Christian boys, instead of being forced to hang around with the only other two Jews and with that Socialist, Borck. But there was an invisible barrier between him and the Christians that he couldn't cross. One thing was certain: If he had been accepted by the *upper ten* in his class, the boys he felt were his equal in knowledge, looks and academic performance – the things he was really proud of – he wouldn't have even mentioned that he was a Jew.

At home, the long-discussed Hebrew teacher had arrived after Mademoiselle left. He didn't live with the family the way that Mademoiselle had, but he visited three times a week, which was bad enough.

When the Hebrew teacher, Mr. Werba, first arrived, Albert thought he was a boy his own age because he was so short.

"Shev," Mr. Werba said.

Albert had no idea what that meant. "Shev," Mr. Werba repeated, pointing at a chair.

Albert deduced that *shev* must be the Hebrew word for chair, so to show that he understood, he pointed at the chair and also said, "Shev."

But Mr. Werba was not pleased. *Shev* is the imperative form of the word *Shevet* and it means sit down. Gradually, the Hebrew language revealed its secrets to Albert. Although he wasn't very motivated, he learned it in spite of himself because he had an extraordinary teacher, tremendously enthusiastic about the language.

However, Albert opposed this indoctrination with all his might. He hadn't been born in a ghetto nor had he ever lived in one. He couldn't understand why he should value his Jewish identity above everything else. He understood even less why he should feel closer to a Jewish boy in Poland or Lithuania, a boy whose language he didn't understand, than to classmates he had known since the first grade.

Why did everyone want to force him to be something he didn't want to be? Those snobs in his class on the one hand, and Mr. Werba, the Hebrew teacher, on the other. Who the hell cared whether someone was a Jew, a Catholic, or a Protestant? And how could you even tell what religion someone belonged to just by looking at them?

Albert went to the kitchen to ask someone who would know.

"Tell me, Minna, can people tell that I'm Jewish? Do I look Jewish?" he asked.

Minna thought hard. Then she said, "Yes."

"But how?"

"No way I'm telling you that, kiddo," Minna said, blushing.

He couldn't get any more out of her.

IV
NOVEMBER 1918

———◆———

THE CROWD PROMENADING BACK AND forth on Unter den Linden Street was in a festive mood. Those who could afford it wore red carnations, while others had to be satisfied with scarlet ribbons. Men who had until recently been sporting monocles now walked around with red neckties flaming under their stiff collars. Soldiers still in their field-grey uniforms had torn the national insignia from their caps, replacing them with red buttons or red pieces of fabric. Officers couldn't be distinguished from enlisted men since all signs of rank had been removed from their uniforms. Older married couples wore holiday attire: the men in frock coats, and the women in dark suits, all decorated nicely with rosy artificial flowers. They laughed, waving at friends and relatives, and walked about aimlessly. At Café Kranzler, all tables were occupied.

This was the German Revolution.

Albert had already recognized that something was afoot before his parents were aware of it. School was an accurate political barometer. For about a month now his classmate, Wilhelm Count of Gladen-Zellerlinde, had been unusually friendly towards him and Borck. He couldn't think of anything better than to play handball with them or walk with them in the Tiergarten. Other formerly unapproachable boys also sought companionship with former outsiders, including the three Jews in the class.

"Man, they're shitting in their pants now," declared Borck, the great politician.

"But why?" asked Albert.

"Don't tell me you don't know!"

"I don't."

"Oh man, are you ever retarded!"

Albert grinned. Politics had never been of any interest to him so he had no idea what Borck was hinting at.

"Every baby in diapers knows that we've lost the war, right?" It gave Borck special satisfaction to make that statement. The year before, he had paid a heavy price for echoing his father's opinion on the subject. Professor Binderlein had been using maps projecting the future configuration of Europe to make strategic predictions in geography class. According to him, the western borders of Germany would run from Basel in Switzerland north through Épinal, Nancy, and Verdun to Maubeuge, and from there via Namur to Maastrichtand into Holland. He was generous enough to leave Brussels and Antwerp to the Belgians, but he wasn't quite prepared to let the French keep Reims and Lyon. He had justified similar geographical changes for the eastern territories, using the Daugava River as a *natural* division between Slavs and Germans.

Borck – instead of obediently tracing Binderlein's borders with carbon paper and thus fabricating an image of Germany that resembled a circus elephant with an outstretched trunk pointing east – had dared to ask, "What would happen, Professor, if we were to lose the war?"

"A German boy isn't even allowed to *think* something like that, let alone say it!" Binderlein scolded him.

To atone for his heretical thoughts, Borck had to enter all the rivers, mountains, cities and lakes of Europe, Asia, and Africa on a blank world map. He was lucky that Professor Binderlein was unable to forgive the Americans for entering the war on the enemy side and that he also recognized that even after a German victory it would be unlikely for Germany to occupy America. For these reasons, he was as little interested in it as he was in Australia, so Borck only had to deal with three continents. Still, since he was doing poorly in geography, he made many mistakes and earned an F for the assignment.

In recent months, Binderlein, like the other professors, spent less time urging the boys to hang in until victory came. Ollenberg, the Professor of Latin, who had always been more interested in classical antiquity than in the present, even said, "The only war whose purpose was clear and understandable was the Trojan War.

It was all about Helen, a beautiful woman. At least there was a valid reason for that conflict."

Borck, as a pacifist and social democrat, agreed with that analysis. In September and October, when the teachers and the aristocratic boys were going through their strange transformation, he explained to Albert what was happening.

"Wilson has offered his fourteen points, but the Emperor doesn't want to accept them. Now he's pulled Prince Max of Badenout out of mothballs, thinking that he'll fix things for us. But the war's gone on too long. We have no more food on the table, and my old man says we won't have the Emperor much longer either. All those guys who are suddenly sucking up to us must have heard the same thing at home. That's why they suddenly want to lick our boots. But they can kiss my ass."

Albert admired Borck. An outsider, though not Jewish, he had the guts to stick to the convictions he had learned at home, in spite of the influence of his teachers and classmates. In this dark old school built of gray stone, where everything else was gray as well, right down to the boy's caps, Borck was the only spot with any colour – his colour was bright red.

But now red flags were flying from houses on every street in Berlin. However, the traditional flag of the German Empire still flew from only one building: the university.

Albert and his father stood in front of the university gate and looked up at the windows. Albert's father wasn't wearing a red flower.

"What do they want? Are they against the revolution?" Albert asked.

"Everywhere else in the world, students have always been the first to fight for freedom and democracy," his father answered. "But in Germany, it is the students who are the backbone of reaction and class ideology."

"Do you think they'll shoot those rifles at the crowd down here?"

"I think it's very likely. The young gentlemen up there have an exaggerated opinion of their own importance. They believe people want to storm the university. That's why they're holding their rifles at the ready."

Suddenly, there was movement behind the Arsenal. A small group of soldiers with red armbands pulled two heavy machine guns right up to the steps of St.

Hedwig's Church, where they brought the weapons into position. "*Tak, tak, tak!*" Their shots were aimed at the university windows. The students themselves were firing at the soldiers the whole time, to no effect.

"They must be law students," Albert's father said. "Only lawyers can miss the target that often. Come, we should leave before a more accurate profession takes up the gun."

Albert was sorry not to witness more of the fighting, but his father pulled him along with the fleeing crowd. His last impression of the German Revolution was an act that was almost symbolic, although it hadn't been planned that way: A woman, apparently much affected by fear, pulled up her skirt and relieved herself in front of the monument to Frederic the Great.

Sic transit gloria mundi.

V
1925

———◆———

THE FACTORY HAD PROMISED TO drop the kayak off at the bridge at nine in the morning Manfred and Albert had already been waiting for an hour. Increasingly nervous, they kept looking down the street – Heerstrasse – but there was no sign of a delivery truck.

"Did you pay for everything? The shipping as well as the kayak?"

"To the last penny," Albert said.

"In that case, they're just making you wait."

"I've never been treated like this before."

"I don't want to stick around for more than a half hour, otherwise the whole day will be wasted. I promised Erika I'd take her out tonight," Manfred said.

"There is no telephone here, so I can't call to check when they are coming. I don't know what else to do. What time do you have to be back home?"

"Around seven."

"Well, even if these guys don't arrive until eleven it will only take four or five hours to paddle to the boathouse, so you can still be back in the city by seven," Albert said.

"Do you have any plans for tonight?"

"Not yet."

"Tell me," his friend pestered him, "don't you have a steady girlfriend?"

"I do. Eva."

"She's not what I'd call a girlfriend! I can't imagine Miss Eva allowing you to – you know what I mean."

Albert had the decency not to brag and ruin the reputation of innocent little Eva. So he just said, "Of course not!"

"So who else is there?" Manfred wanted to know. "Tell me honestly: have you ever fooled around with a girl?"

"Of course I have," Albert lied. So far, an inexplicable fear, comprising both embarrassment and the possibility of being rejected, had kept him from attempting sexual relations. He didn't know whether he was more afraid that a girl would turn him down or that she wouldn't and he would have to admit his own lack of experience.

Besides which, he had nowhere to take a girl. He couldn't bring anyone back to his parents' house. Hookers filled him with fear and disgust, as did one-night-stand hotels. That's why he was so eager to own a boat. It wasn't merely an end in itself but a means to another, more desirable, goal. A boat, supplemented by a tent and camping equipment, would give him the opportunity to combine a healthy outdoor sport with healthy indoor activities.

But he had to find a girl first. What was the matter with him? Everyone he knew had a real girlfriend, even Manfred, while he was stuck with what his mother called *fine young girls from good Jewish homes*, girls with whom he could talk about Schopenhauer and Spinoza, but who offered him nothing else. On the other hand, a saucy noodle like Manfred's Erika wouldn't suit him either. She was vulgar, and it was impossible to have a decent conversation with her. He would be bored to death with such a *shiksa*.

As if Manfred had guessed what his friend was thinking, he said, "Listen! Erika knows this girl who doesn't have a steady boyfriend right now. She's a good athlete. You'll need a crew for your luxury liner. Maybe we should introduce her to you."

"Thanks a lot, but I'm not hiring galley slaves. Eva and Lilly will be happy to come aboard my kayak if those crooks ever deliver it. It's almost eleven. Do you think we should wait any longer?"

"Let's hang around till eleven o'clock, since we've already waited this long. But to return to the subject of your crew: Eva and Lilly are not built for water sports. They look very well on *Kurfürstendamm* but otherwise they're good for sweet bugger-all."

"Nonsense, you don't even know them."

"I've seen them often enough in your company. But do as you please. Why didn't you ask one of them to pick up the kayak with you? Why did I have to waste my Sunday?"

"Four hours of paddling requires two strong men. Not even Erika and her athletic friend would be able to manage that."

"You have no idea. You don't know those two."

"Here they come!"

"Who?"

"The truck! Man, he's carrying six kayaks."

The truck slowly approached the bridge and came to a halt. The driver and his helper got out. Albert and Manfred ran across the street to meet them. The driver pulled some papers from his leather jacket and said, "We have a kayak to deliver here. Are you Albert Berg?"

"Yes."

"Do you have your receipt?"

"Yes, but you were supposed to be here two hours ago."

"Sorry, but the truck broke down."

They lifted the kayak from the truck and set it down on the narrow sidewalk.

"Sign here that you received the craft in good condition."

Albert accepted the sheaf of papers and pen from the driver. He signed his name as clearly as he could without a firm support for the papers, then handed the whole mess back to the driver.

"Thank you, and we usually get a tip."

Albert looked at Manfred, then back to the driver, who clearly expected something for his trouble. Albert shrugged. The driver sniffed his disgust, then waved at his helper to get back into the truck.

As the truck coughed smoke and pulled away, Albert and Manfred picked up the kayak, one at the bow, the other at the stern. They carried it carefully down the narrow path from the bridge to the water and sat it down on the shore of the Havel

River where they had piled a big bundle of their supplies. The package held kapok cushions, an old blanket, sandwiches, a thermos and some nautical instruments. The first thing Albert took out was the flag he had prepared for the boat. Manfred walked around the kayak, examined it with the eyes of an experienced mariner, took the paddles and assembled them, fitted the backrests into their tracks and pulled a line through the brass ring at the bow. Suddenly he stopped short.

"You must be totally off your rocker!" he scolded. "You want to go out on Lake Wannsee with that written on your kayak?" He pointed at the name that had been enscribed in gold paint, in stylized Hebrew letters, on both sides of the bow. "Who painted that?"

"I did, when I was at the factory," Albert replied. "When it was dry, they lacquered over it."

"Almighty God, why are you planning to steer a Jewish boat through Potsdam? You can tell right away that the letters are written as if they were Hebrew. And what on earth does *Heruth* mean?"

"Freedom."

"Man, you're really asking for trouble. You'll be mugged."

"I don't think so," Albert said. "On the contrary, I think you'll discover that everybody will respect a Jew who respects his own nationality." Albert unfolded the little flag while making this proclamation. The flag was blue and white, with a superimposed yellow Star of David. He had used a chocolate bar to bribe Anna, the new maid, to sew the star – made from narrow gold braid – over a reversed Bavarian flag. It hadn't turned out very symmetrical, but that wouldn't be noticed when the wind was blowing.

"Do you want that thing to be stuck up your rear end?" Manfred asked.

"It's not for my stern; it's for the kayak's!"

"Do me a favour and only put that flag up when you're paddling by yourself, or with somebody else. The name already makes me worried enough. You're *meshuggah*, Albert. Couldn't you come up with a something else?"

"What, for example?"

"A normal name. Like Eva or Lilly, or whoever you fancy," Manfred said, carefully pushing the stern into the water while Albert lifted up the bow. They had taken off their socks and shoes, rolled up their pant legs and waded into the river, which was still quite cold. It was May, but so far the spring had been very rainy. They sat down in the kayak and began to paddle with regular strokes. Manfred sat in the forward position and determined the speed, while Albert operated the rudder with his foot from the aft seat.

Albert talked to Manfred's back.

"What you call a 'normal' name is extremely pedestrian. Besides which, if you give a boat a girl's name, you have to change the name whenever you change girl-friends. Have you ever counted how many *Lolas* and *Inges* and *Hildes* and so forth are floating around on the water here? When I was at the boathouse to rent a spot, I saw a little dinghy named *Kunigunde II*. Presumably its owner had tired of his first *Kunigunde*! In my opinion, the name *Heruth* isn't any worse than *Kunigunde II*."

"I wasn't talking about phonetics," Manfred said, "but about your bragging 'I'm a Jew! Do you know my colours?' Sometimes I can't understand you at all. When old Flanter took us out of religion class, you didn't want to be a Jew, and just two or three years ago, you made fun of your Hebrew teacher. But these days you are determined to build your own little ghetto and segregate yourself in a blue and white non-existent fatherland. You don't associate with women. I suspect that you're still a virgin. Man, you should be sent to the mental asylum at Dalldorf. You're just not normal."

"I'm more normal than you, Manfred. At least I'm trying to live in accordance with my own conscience. I'd rather segregate myself than allow others to segregate me. You're in the same ghetto as me, despite your Old High German looks and your Brandenburg attitude, only you don't want to admit it."

"You are really crazy! How do I live in a ghetto? Explain that to me!"

"How many Christian friends do you have?" Albert asked. "Can you name a single one – except for Eva? Maybe your friend Horst Birken, who wanted to re-cruit you for the National Socialists because you're such a nice Aryan type? As far as I know, he was the only Christian boy who wanted to be your friend. And you slapped him in the face; shame on you!"

"I didn't slap him because of his Hitler mania but because he was gay."

"What? You never told me that before."

"I was embarrassed."

"So there you are. A nice Christian boy offered you his affection, and you separated yourself from him. It appears that Sir Manfred, Knight of Lady Erika and of the black, red and gold banner, is living in the same ghetto as the rest of us."

"What do you have against the black, red and gold?" Manfred was angry now, and he showed it by paddling irregularly. A strong wind drove the kayak off course. Albert used the rudder and paddled on one side only, trying to redirect the craft in the direction of Lake Wannsee. The Havel had developed waves as powerful as those on a much bigger river. Water flowed into the low-lying boat, and the two friends collided with their paddles as well.

Albert hadn't answered Manfred's question. He felt that pursuing this conversation might jeopardise their friendship.

Manfred also wanted to end the discussion, but not before explaining himself. "One thing I need to explain clearly to you," he stated. "I am a German above all else, so *my* boat flies the flag of the German republic. Nobody can persuade me to do otherwise, whether they're anti-Semitic or Zionist or whatever. Just remember that!"

"With pleasure," Albert said. "Let's just hope that the republic is as loyal to you as you are to it. When those pigs murdered Walter Rathenau, his sacrifice for Germany during the war and his service afterwards didn't mean anything to them."

"You can't blame an entire nation for the actions of a handful of crazy fanatics," Manfred countered.

"Yes, you can. And you must, if the people don't speak out against them. Just look around you, even here on Lake Wannsee. What do you see on all those beautiful big yachts and motor boats? Only black, white and red banners. Swastikas too are becoming more and more frequent. Their crookedness represents their ideology perfectly. What you called a 'handful of crazy fanatics' is actually quite more numerous than you like to think."

"Whatever! But nobody has the right to badmouth my fatherland or try convince me that I don't belong to it just because of my Jewish faith. That's silly. There were Jewish communities in Germany long before there was a German nation. Do you think all those families with Polish-sounding names, or with Kashubian and Wendish names like *Ruschke* and *Piefke*, *Lobke* and so forth are Germans, and we're not? You're out of your mind."

"Just a moment," Albert shouted, "I can't debate when my ass is wet. I'm sitting in a puddle of water."

"Your weight is pulling the boat down even more. Man, this kayak is leaking!"

Either the two eager sailors had forgotten or they didn't know that the wood of new boats must swell up with use before the planks can become water-tight. They had nothing to bail with other than the small cup of their thermos.

"What are we going to do now?" Albert asked.

"First of all, we take our pants off," Manfred said.

"And sit here bare-assed?"

"No one can see us, but we have to get rid of the water or this crate will be so heavy that it will sink. Then you'll really be remembered in history as the captain of the first Jewish submarine since King Solomon's fleet."

"He didn't have any submarines."

"But I'm sure he had leaking ships."

The young men used their sopping pants and underwear to soak up the water and wrang them out repeatedly over the sides of the boat. It was a tedious process, but at least the water was no longer rising. It was also very cold, but neither of them wanted to put their wet pants back on. So as they approached the bridge over the juncture of the Great Wannsee and Little Wannsee, they placed their underpants over their laps so that they weren't exposed from above. Finally, just before Lake Stölpchensee, they arrived at the boathouse. The brisk wind drove the clouds away and the afternoon sun came out.

"I'd like to know how we're supposed to get out of here," Albert said. "I can't even get my pants over my feet."

"I guess we'll have to parade around bare-assed," Manfred pronounced, in the tone of a man who had experienced everything in life already.

"Are you out of your mind? Don't you see all the girls running around here?"

Indeed, many boats had arrived at the dock at the same time, waiting to be pulled up by a cart that went into the water on tracks. Among the people around was one young man about Albert's age, who took great interest in deciphering the writing on Albert's kayak.

"What does the word *Heruth* mean?" he asked.

"Freedom."

"Oh, you're nudists?"

"What do you mean?"

"Well, you're not wearing anything below. So I thought maybe that's the freedom you mean."

"No, it's just that our pants are completely soaked. Maybe you could call Mr. Gundermann, the owner of the boathouse, and ask him to lend us two blankets or something. Would you do that, please?"

"Of course."

Instead of Mr. Gundermann, Mrs. Gundermann appeared with two blankets. Mrs. Gundermann was a typical woman of Berlin, whose sense of humour was far greater than her sense of decorum. She threw the blankets into the boat and doubled up with laughter.

"Guys," she said, "you didn't have to take off your pants to prove you don't have the rental money today. Besides," she added with a twinkle in her eyes, "I already knew that you two boys was Jewish."

Now, Manfred and Albert had to laugh at themselves. It wasn't easy to climb out of the boat with bulky blankets wrapped around their waists.

Mrs. Gundermann stretched out a bony hand to help and then said, "Give me them wet pants for pressing. They'll dry under the hot iron. Meanwhile, go and tie up that leaky boat. You can bring it up after, but don't just stand around here half-naked or all the girls will fall in love with you. Now off you go!"

An hour later, they left the boat house with dry and neatly pleated pants. They went to the Wannsee train station, then separated at the Zoo. Manfred went off to see Erika, but Albert didn't know where to go. He wasn't in the mood to go home. His parents had gone to visit friends in Dresden for the weekend and wouldn't be back until Tuesday. So he decided to explore some areas of Berlin he didn't know, rather than walking in familiar west end neighbourhoods where he wouldn't dare to talk to any girls he met. He boarded a bus without knowing where it went and got off at Alexander Square, where it was a little brighter than in the surrounding streets.

Without any plan or goal in mind, he circled the Berolina statue. Then he did some window-shopping at the Tietz department store. Girls walked by, laughing, shouting all kinds of important things to each other, but he couldn't find the courage to address any of these inaccessible creatures. He had seldom felt so completely lonely in the city of his birth. Conceding defeat, Albert took the first bus back to the west end.

V I

ELEGANT YOUNG LADIES WEARING BLACK Persian lamb coats don't belong on the open top of a rattling bus. They should be seated in a fancy private car or at least a taxi. It was natural, therefore, that when two of them boarded the bus at the corner of Friedrichstrasse and Unter den Linden, they attracted great deal of interest from the other passengers, especially the men.

It is sometimes worthwhile watching other people. For example, here is a row of men standing around with sullen faces. One's impression is that they get no fun out of life whatsoever. Psychologists and sociologists wrack their brains to find ways to remedy mankind's general apathy. They write volumes, which people – being apathetic – won't read anyway. At the same time, the medical profession conducts all kinds of experiments to fight melancholy and fatigue with pills.

And then, something happens to such a group of tired and grumpy men. As Christian Morgenstern notes, "A pretty knee walks through the world." Let's say, the shapely legs of two pretty girls, in fashionable stockings, climb up the winding staircase of a bus to the top deck. Immediately the psychological state of the men changes. Dim eyes become shiny. Grim lips turn into smiling crescents. Hands holding on to the brass rods as if they were wilted twigs suddenly recover their muscle tone and develop a firm grip. Men who had idiotic faces before still have idiotic faces, but they're friendlier now.

Once the passengers were awake, they could tell by the light of the street lamps that the two young ladies wore matching fur caps with little veils. Underneath were two not overwhelmingly beautiful but quite pretty faces. Perhaps they wore a bit too much lipstick and other makeup, but that didn't diminish the girls' generally attractive looks. Since they called each other by name, telling each other where to find a better seat, where to hang on and not to fall, to be careful not to tear their stockings, the whole bus soon knew that the blonde with the lively grey eyes and the well-rounded figure was called *Henja*, while the name of the taller dark-haired lady with the broad shoulders, narrow hips and slender figure was *Edith*. Of course, the phrase *well-rounded* is a hypocritical euphemism designed for the purpose of flattery. A woman is either slender or not. *Well-rounded* means that her slenderness is so round that the slightest weight gain would make her too round. So, Miss Henja was well-rounded.

The other passengers were very sad that they couldn't make out the rest of the conversation due to the humming of the motor and noises from the street. Thus, they couldn't quite figure out what kind of people these young ladies were. Were they dancers or actresses or girls from good homes on their way to a party? It was difficult to tell.

"Did you have to slap his face, Edith? Couldn't you have controlled yourself?" Henja asked in an angry tone.

"I don't allow anybody to treat me like that."

"But you silly goose, now we're as broke as ever. For a hundred marks – in such a lousy season – a little perversity is not the end of the world."

"We'll find somebody else," said Edith.

"I hope so. Otherwise we'll have to be satisfied with twenties like the street hookers. Quite frankly, I'd be happy to get a twenty today. I have to pay Krupnick something on my rent."

"And how much will that leave you for food?"

"I still have six marks and a few pennies, enough for tomorrow. Then I'm going to call some of my steadies. Otherwise I'd have to pawn something again. It's enough to make you throw up."

"But Monday is always a slow day. We should still be able to turn a trick tonight. It's such a pity that the Bellevue has closed down. All our friends will go looking for us there. How about the Barberina instead? The barman there knows me. He once got me a fat john."

"Who was that?"

"A corset manufacturer from Cologne. He could only get it up in the morning," said Edith.

"That's what happens with a lot of nice old gentlemen. They have to get their sleep at night while we just lie there like unclaimed parcels," Henja quipped.

"Yes, but my corset manufacturer was truly strange. He wanted me to stand around naked in exactly the same pose as the gal in his ads. That's what made him horny, just imagine! I told him I didn't wear a corset. Thank God I don't need one. He told me women like me were ruining his business, but he still liked me. 'I'm a professional, you understand? A professional!' he repeated over and over again. And then he left me two hundreds on the dresser top. Quite generous, don't you think?"

"He would have had fun with me," Henja said. "I would have asked him for a couple of corsets to boot. Oh, we're already at the Memorial Church. I think we better get off here."

"Out you go!"

"Don't look around right now, Edith. The young man who was sitting behind us is getting off too."

"Good God, such children are the worst thing that can happen to us. Too bad we can't wear a sign that says NO MINORS ALLOWED – like in the movies. Please get rid of him."

"Wait. I'm going to look in my makeup mirror."

"Can you see him?"

"Yes, he is still bravely marching behind us. He's no older than twenty. Looks dreamy. The romantic type."

"So let's walk a little faster. He's not my kind of merchandise," Edith said.

"Actually, you never can tell," Henja said. "Sometimes those fat wallets and fat stomachs make me sick. The men who tell you their wives don't understand them. The guys with the stereotypical question, like 'How come a well-educated young lady like you is in a racket like this?' I often long for something fresh."

"You just finished crying about your finances, and now you're suddenly going all romantic on me? If you can afford it, go right ahead. You have my blessings."

"Oh, I'm only talking. Sometimes I think of home and my parents. If they knew what I was doing, my father would kill me."

"You're twenty-one, so you can do what you want. But don't get run over! There is so much traffic here. Wait! Did you see the guy in the red sports car? He looked at us."

"A lot of guys are looking at us. Now we can cross the street. It's much too early to go to the Barberina. Let's have a coffee. They already have tables outside at the Café Vienna."

"The way our finances are?"

"We have enough for a cup of coffee."

"Look how busy it is! So many people pass by here," Henja remarked, after they sat down at a little round table.

"The bus kid just passed," Henja laughed. "Would you object if he paid for our coffee? Such a lonely boy wouldn't ask for more anyway. He just wants company; he wants to have a conversation and feel grown-up. I'll get him to join us."

"You're out of your mind. As long as a child sits here, no real man will come over to talk to us."

"Do you have a better prospect? I didn't think so."

"There he is, passing for the third time. His eyes are soon going to fall out. Henja, no! Jesus, Mary, and Joseph, now you've done it. I'm washing my hands of this."

Henja ignored her friend's advice. When the young man from the bus began passing the café for the third time, she turned her face towards him and looked at him with her big grey eyes. Then she gave him an artificial smile that showed all her regular white teeth. She bent her head in a gesture that could have been interpreted various ways. It could have been a hello among old friends, or the request, "Won't you join us?" At least, that's how the young man interpreted it. Politely lifting his hat, he asked, "May I join you? I believe I have seen you ladies somewhere else before."

"Yes, we're bus buddies, aren't we?" Miss Henja said.

Edith sat as stiff as a rod, saying nothing, while Henja looked the young man over without shame. He felt awkward under the probing regard of such an elegant girl. He touched his necktie, thinking that it might not be quite straight. Then he looked at his fingernails to check whether they were clean. But he couldn't think of what to do or say now that he had joined the two girls.

God, I'm such an idiot, he thought. *First I behave like a man of the world and sit down with two nice young ladies, and then I can't think of anything to talk about. What the hell does a man do in such a situation? They're both staring at me, and they're not saying anything either. I think they're making fun of me.*

That's exactly what the two girls were doing, but they weren't letting on. Finally Henja said, "May I adjust your necktie? You've messed it up a little. It was fine before."

Grateful that she had broken the ice, the young man bent forward. Miss Henja, who had taken her gloves off, straightened his tie with skilled fingers. He noted that she had very pretty hands that were obviously not accustomed to manual labour.

"I would like to order a coffee and some cake," he said. "May I invite you to join me? I see you have already finished your coffee."

Before Edith could say that she didn't want a second cup of coffee and didn't eat cake, Henja answered, "We'd be delighted. One can always use some more coffee, and we both have a passion for cake."

Edith gave Henja a razor-sharp look but she didn't say anything.

Slowly, the young man seemed to find his confidence again. Now that he had become the host, he lost some of his fear of the two girls. He felt that the tall slender young woman didn't like him or she would have talked with him, too, so he turned to Edith and asked, "Perhaps you'd like to order something else? We can think about it before the waiter comes."

"No thank you," Edith said. "Coffee is enough."

"Oh, excuse me," the young man said. "I completely forgot in all the excitement. My name is Berg."

"What excitement are you referring to?" Henja asked, with the most innocent face in the world.

The young man felt so stupid. How could he tell these girls that just talking to them was a great adventure? What would they think of him? He considered inventing something about an accident he had seen on the way over to the café, but then Edith started to laugh hilariously.

"Obviously Mr. Berg got excited when he heard of your passion for cake," she said after she had calmed down a little.

Henja was annoyed, and gave Edith a reproachful look as if to say *Don't be so mean*. Then she said kindly to the helpless boy, "You don't have to be embarrassed. I get somewhat excited, too, when I meet new people. You never know what strangers are going to be like, do you?"

"That is so true!" the young man said, in a tone expressing both gratitude and respect. "However, I did have a very exciting day today. I went down the Havel River in my new boat for the very first time."

"You have a boat?"

"A motor boat?" Edith asked.

"No. It's a kayak, but it's also equipped with a sail. When there's a good wind, it'll sail very well."

"What's a kayak?" Henja asked.

"It's a small paddle-boat where one person sits behind the other," Edith said. "The advantage is that girls always sit in front, so they don't have to look at the dumb faces of the boys."

"Edith, you are really being mean," Henja said. "Now you torpedoed Mr. Berg's nice new boat. And he might think that you're talking about him, too."

"I'm just making a general statement. Personally, I really like watersports."

Henja thought the boy would get the impression he was being teased. She didn't want that. What she really wanted was to prove to Edith that young customers could be worthwhile. But the naivité of this particular boy provoked her to go beyond a mere business strategy and to assume a kind of protective role.

"You know what?" she said, "when we're finished with our cake, we should go for a stroll. Would you like to come along?"

"With the greatest pleasure," he said. He kept wondering why such independent girls were wearing matching clothes – the same fur coats, the same little hats – since they looked too different to be sisters. He wanted to invite the blond one home with him but felt it would be rude unless he asked both, even though the other one, despite her good looks, was so unfriendly and was also taller than he was. If they walked together it would look ridiculous.

"We haven't paid yet," said Edith, interrupting his meditation.

"Good God, I completely forgot," said the young man. "Waiter! I want to settle the bill. I almost got away without paying."

"'Almost' is right. You wouldn't have got very far," said the waiter.

The girls walked quickly to the exit while he settled the bill.

"What would you like to do now?" Edith asked.

"I think, in the end, the boy will come home with me," Henja answered.

"And what about trying our luck at the Barberina?"

"You know, better a bird in the hand than two in the bush ..."

"But I don't think this bird has any money or that you have him in your hand. The moment your bird realizes what game is being played, he'll fly away for sure. Never in my wildest dreams would I have expected you to be interested in childcare."

"By the way," Henja told the boy when he joined them. "My name is Henja, and my friend here is Edith."

"So you're not sisters?" he asked.

"No," Edith said. "Only Henja is playing the sister today, not me."

"Sorry, but I don't understand what you mean."

"It's not important," Henja said. "You know, girlfriends sometimes have little secrets and jokes between them that nobody else understands. Since we have told you our first names, what's yours?"

"Albert."

"Many thanks for the coffee and cake, Albert.," Henja said, "but I've been thinking, you must be very tired after such a busy day. Perhaps we'll meet again another time instead of going for a walk right now."

Edith, who was just as surprised as the boy by this sudden change of plans, stood still. But when she looked up at her friend and colleague under her eyelashes, she saw a coy look that she recognized. Henja was manoeuvring him so that he would beg her to stay with him, and then she could play the passive girl so that he wouldn't be able to accuse her of soliciting. She admired Henja's audacity but worried that she would lose the game, because the boy might simply give up and then they'd get no money from him. It might be a lot harder to seduce this child than the regular johns they had, who knew how to play the game.

She watched Henja with curiosity, wondering how she would proceed.

"But Miss Henja," the boy stuttered. "I'm not tired at all, and I thought you wanted to go for a little walk. Let's not waste the evening."

"I'm a little tired myself," Henja said, "and I know Edith is too. Isn't that right, Edith? Aren't you too tired to go for a walk this evening?"

"What a question," Edith said. "If I didn't have such long legs, I could hardly keep upright."

Henja gave her a nudge, worried that the boy would notice that they were making fun of him. But the boy noticed nothing. He was disappointed, and preoccupied with what he had said or done wrong to make the nice blond girl not want him around anymore. Clearly she was too elegant and clever to be interested in a boy with a paddle boat. If only he'd had a motor boat things might have worked out!

"I'm really sorry," he said. "I had hoped to ask you to come home with me and listen to some fantastic new records. But since you're too tired today, I hope we will meet another time. Would it be possible, Miss Henja, to have your telephone number?"

"What kind of records do you have, Albert?"

"Anything you like: classical, foxtrot, whatever. Oh, will you come? It's not far. If you can't walk, I'll call a cab. Really, it will be fun."

"Where do you live?"

"Near Wittenberg Square, across from the KaDeWe department store. It's very near. Please come, even if it's only for an hour!"

"What do you have there, a room?" Henja asked. "You know, it isn't proper for a girl to go to a young man's ..."

"Oh no," Albert interrupted. "I don't mean that. I live with my parents, but they're away, and we have the whole apartment at our disposal."

"Alright, we accept your invitation, but only for an hour, really," Henja said and smiled at him. Looking at his beaming face, she realized that she hadn't made anybody so happy for a long time.

"I'll say goodbye," Edith said promptly. "I'm not that interested in records. And you don't need me to help you listen to them."

Albert felt he had to protest just to be polite because really he was happy the other girl wouldn't be joining them, but Henja beat him to it.

"Please, Edith, I will accompany you where we have to go afterwards. Don't be a spoilsport! I don't know Albert that well yet, so I can't go to his home alone with him."

Albert gave an embarrassed laugh, but he understood. Miss Henja was behaving very correctly. He was a bit disappointed to find that she was such a good girl, because he already knew so many good girls and thought maybe he needed something different, but he didn't want to be pushy.

Edith still didn't understand exactly what her friend was up to. But she was curious, so she said, "Alright. The things we do for friendship! I suppose I can tolerate the music."

"You don't like music?" Albert asked, incredulously.

"Don't you let my friend fool you," Henja laughed. "She is a wonderful pianist, and she even plays the cello if she isn't busy with ..." Henja wanted to say *Something else between her legs*, but at the last moment she changed her mind and ended the sentence with, " . . . something else."

Albert didn't notice.

—•—

He turned the light on in the wood-panelled hall. Then he turned it on in the living room and in the library. The oil paintings his father had collected with good taste glowed in the dim light. To improve Edith's mood, he went over to the Blüthner grand piano and opened the lid.

"Please, will you play something for us? Unfortunately we don't have a cello."

Henja hadn't lied. Edith really could play the piano. She didn't feel like demonstrating, but no one who plays the piano – even badly – can resist a concert grand. She sat down and played some chords which developed into a mazurka by Chopin. She played it well. Albert looked at her hands. Strong hands with long fingers and with spade-shaped nails. Not soft lady's hands but the hands of a musician. He didn't have the courage to ask her directly, but he whispered in Henja's ear: "Your friend must be a professional musician."

Henja didn't want to answer when Edith couldn't hear her, so she pretended that she was deaf to everything but the music. Still, Albert's remark had given her an idea.

The girls had taken off their fur coats and hats. They wore elegant evening dresses which took the young man's breath away. They looked very different now. Henja looked younger without the fur coat and hat while Edith looked older. Henja was the prettier of the two. Her soft blond hair fell to her shoulders. How old could she be? Certainly no older than he was himself. But Edith must be over twenty. On tiptoes, not to insult Chopin, he went to the bar, took out glasses and a few bottles of liqueur (*Something sweet*, he thought), and set them on the coffee table. In a cupboard he found some chocolates and other sweets which his mother hid there. He set them out as well.

Edith ended the mazurka and stood up. "That's a wonderful instrument," she said.

Henja said nothing. Slowly, she walked from one painting to the other in the living room, from one silver bowl to the other. She looked carefully at the crystal and china vases. Albert felt it was his duty to comment but she didn't respond, nor did she ask any questions. He turned the light on in the large dining room and she looked around there, too.

Meanwhile Edith had sat down on the sofa in front of the coffee table. She seemed to be in a better mood than before.

"Is there a kitchen in this establishment?" she asked.

"Of course," Albert said. "Unfortunately our cook has Sundays off, otherwise I would have offered you something more substantial than chocolates. It's almost ten o'clock, and I've had no supper today. So may I offer you some sandwiches? I would be very happy to make them."

"Just show me the kitchen and the pantry, young man, and I'll find my own way around."

Albert was delighted. Things were going better than he had expected. Both girls were fabulous. Edith was much nicer than he had first thought; probably she just wasn't attracted to him because he was shorter than her. Henja, on the other hand, was exactly the right height.

He went ahead to the kitchen and turned all the lights on.

Henja said, "Albert has guessed that you're a musician, Edith, and that you play the piano in a ladies' band."

Edith swallowed hard on her advocaat liquer. "You're an absolute genius," she said. "Did you also guess what Henja plays?"

"I bet you have," Henja said.

"No, I haven't," Albert said. "Are you a musician too? I wouldn't have thought so."

"Why not?"

"Your hands look so soft."

"I play the drums, including the bass drum: boom – boom – barroom."

"Now it all makes sense," Albert said, thinking about their elegant evening dresses and the fact that they had some kind of an appointment later in the evening.

The kitchen wasn't very tidy. After he'd made his breakfast that morning he'd left everything lying around. His dishes still sat in the sink and the pantry door had been left ajar. He apologized.

Edith went to the sink and began to do the dishes.

"But please!" he said, "that's not necessary."

"If the kitchen isn't tidy, I can't cook anything," she said. "You two please leave now. In ten minutes, I'll serve you scrambled eggs with ham. Also some toast and tea."

Henja, who had been quiet for a while, laughed and said, "When Edith gets into her housewife mood, it is best to get out of her way, otherwise she'll get nasty. What's that room in the back of the hall?"

"That's my room," Albert said. "It's not very neat because the help has the day off."

"Please show it to me anyway," Henja said.

He did.

"You know, your room looks exactly like my little brother's room. He also leaves his books lying around and doesn't hang up his pants."

"Does your family live in Berlin?"

"No, they live in Bavaria. I haven't seen them for a long time, but now I'll probably have to go back there," Henja said. She sat down on his bed. Albert was disappointed. In his mind, he saw his new friendship with this nice, attractive girl break up and his new flame disappear into the primal forests of Bavaria.

"But why would you want to leave Berlin?" he asked.

"It's not a matter of what I want," she replied. "The establishment we have been working for has gone bankrupt. We didn't even get our last pay-cheque, so I can't pay my rent. My only choice is to go back to my Papa. We want to talk about a new contract tonight, to people in another establishment, as you have already heard, but even that wouldn't bring money in right away."

"But surely another solution can be found," said Albert, who didn't doubt the truth of this story in the least. "Wait, I have money. I would like to lend you some until you can earn something again. I don't have much on me, but you would do me a great favour by accepting it." He looked in his wallet and counted out a bit over thirty marks – that was all he had.

"No way!" Henja said. She had the courage to add, "A decent girl doesn't accept money from strange men."

"But that's precisely it. I don't want to be a stranger. You know, when I saw you, I thought, that's the kind of girl I would like to have as a girlfriend, someone as smart as you. Couldn't we become friends? So take this money – it's only a few marks – as a token of our friendship. You can repay me later."

"Does it mean so much to you that I don't leave Berlin?"

"Honestly, yes," answered Albert.

"Are you trying to tell me that a young man built like you, living in a home like this, doesn't have a girlfriend? I'll bet the girls are just lining up for you."

"Frankly, I don't have a real girlfriend."

"Good, then I'll take the loan, but next week I'll pay it back, and you must promise to accept the repayment and not try to play the cavalier with me. Promise?"

"Yes, I promise!" Albert shouted with great enthusiasm.

To her surprise, Henja didn't feel the least bit of satisfaction about the flawless execution of her strategy. Everything had been too easy. She didn't have to stay in his room a minute longer or give him the fictitious address she and Edith had invented, an address which had already come in handy from time to time. She could just leave whenever she wanted, without supplying any kind of service in return, and the boy would still be so happy.

But she wasn't happy. The Bergs' apartment made her feel sad because she had run away from a similar home herself with her first great love six years earlier. When he abandoned her she took to the streets, and had never dared to go back to her strict religious father. For six years she had lived in bars and places of amusement, in furnished rooms and – when she was with a well-to-do man for a while – in classy hotels. However, she hadn't been inside a beautiful, upper middle-class home since her childhood.

That's why her heart filled with sadness when she saw the familiar objects in the apartment. And the innocent boy next to her – how happy he was to help her! Her little brother would look something like him by now. She had always been clever, but now she had become hard and calculating. Her friend Edith was also well-educated, intelligent, and a loner. Edith didn't have a pimp; she wouldn't let anyone use her. Henja was determined not to fall into the hands of a pimp either so she relied on Edith, who was as strong as a man, to be the physical protection she needed occasionally.

Henja was still sitting on Albert's bed, turning the bank notes in her hand instead of putting them in her handbag. Albert had no idea what was going on in her head.

"Do me the favour and put the money away. Really, Miss Henja, I beg you," he said.

Henja smiled. Suddenly she had tears in her eyes. He assumed she was regretting that she needed to accept help, and realized that he had fallen in love.

Henja stood up, put her arms around his neck and gave him a kiss. "You're a nice boy," she said.

Blood rushed to his face. She addressed him with *du*, the familiar *you*, and she had kissed him. With the furious wildness of shy people who suddenly feel liberated from their inhibitions, he flung his arms around her and covered her mouth with kisses. He threw her back onto his untidy bed. Henja pushed him away with all her might, and he stood up, ashamed. He looked so crestfallen, and his face seemed so unhappy that she laughed.

"You're a very dangerous man," she said. "Now turn around please!"

Albert didn't know why he was supposed to turn around, but he obeyed. He heard the rustling of silk and shoes falling to the floor. A slight hope arose in him.

"Now come here, but don't be so rough," Henja said.

From his excited clumsiness, she recognized immediately that she was dealing with a novice. She felt pity for him, but also a tenderness that she hadn't experienced for a long time. "Not so hasty, my boy." She said. "Let me do it. Here, I'll help you."

Albert was grateful to let her take the lead.

———•———

Edith was sitting in the salon. She had eaten and was therefore in a good mood, although she had waited for almost an hour. "Your ham and scrambled eggs are cold now, but the tea is still hot," she said. "The kettle is on the gas stove. I'll go to get it."

"You didn't call us, so we've had a long conversation. I'm sorry you had to wait here all by yourself. Why didn't you tell us the food was ready?" Albert asked, in an attempt to behave as if nothing had happened.

Edith had a quick-witted answer at the tip of her tongue, but she stopped short of blurting it out. She got the kettle and poured the tea while Albert and Henja looked on in silence.

"I wanted to ask you," Edith said, "who owns the mandolin-banjo that's lying on the grand piano. Do you play it?"

"Yes. That's how I could afford my kayak," Albert said. Both girls looked at him quizzically. He explained. "I don't like to ask my father for money all the time, so I play the banjo in my cousin's band. We're only amateurs, playing at a wedding here and a small private party there, maybe once or twice a week. Our saxophone player organizes the gigs for us and we each earn about twenty-five marks an evening. Of course, when we have to study for exams or go to lectures the next day, we can't go to bed at five in the morning. But this winter was pretty busy. That's why I could buy the boat from the money I earned myself."

"So that makes us sort of colleagues. You play in a band and we play in a band. Isn't that right, Henja?" Edith said, grinning. She was playing with her gold necklace while she said it. Albert noticed that a small golden crucifix hung from it.

"I can't compare myself to you. We're only amateurs but you're professional musicians, aren't you?" said Albert.

"Yes, which reminds me that we must leave," Henja said, in a very somber tone of voice. The girls got up and walked down the hall. They put on their coats and examined themselves in the mirror.

Albert pulled Henja a little to the side and whispered, "When will we see each other again? What's your telephone number?"

"I don't have a telephone in my room," she lied, "but I'll call you."

"When?"

"Thursday or Friday night."

"What? I won't see you all week?"

"I'm going to busy over the next few days. You know that we must find work."

"Alright, but no later than Thursday. Promise?"

"I promise."

She went to the mirror and pulled a lipstick from her handbag. In the mirror, she saw a Hanukkah candlelabra with eight branches standing on a small carved dresser. It looked exactly like the one at her parents' home. She turned around, touched the menorah and said, "This is exactly the same shape as ours at home."

Albert was startled. "You know what that is?"

"Oh, you're already using the informal *you*. That's nice," Edith said.

Henja disregarded the remark. "Of course, I know what it is. A Hanukkah menorah."

"You're Jewish?"

"For sure," she said and turned back to the mirror.

Albert would have never guessed. His face clearly showed his surprise and Edith had to laugh. Now that they were leaving, she didn't see why she should keep up the pretence that she didn't know what the two had been up to in his room for an hour.

"Oh, you don't like that, Mr. Albert? You didn't want to commit a sin with a Jewish girl, eh?"

"Edith, you're really impossible," Henja said. "How dare you? Albert, don't you listen to her. She has had a bit too much to drink. Catholics always have problems with alcohol."

"Good bye, sweetheart, and thank you."

"I thank you. You know it."

When the girls had left, Albert still stood at the door with a somewhat perplexed look on his face. Then he turned all the lights off and went to sleep. It had been quite a day.

———◆———

After the girls had left the building Henja hailed a taxi.

"What?" Edith said, "You made him give you enough money that we can go by taxi? I've never seen such nerve. Where are we going?"

"To the Barberina. It's better to arrive there by taxi."

"All right," Edith said, "since we can afford it now. So pleasure first, and business after. Is something rubbing you the wrong way, Henja?"

"Something awful happened to me today," she replied. "I had feelings."

"Seriously? Holy Mary! With that Boy Scout? He's such a child."

"That's probably why I like him. But it must never happen again."

"Better not," Edith said.

———◆———

"The way you tell the story," said Günther Kirschbaum, Albert's best friend, "the only logical conclusion is that those two girls are prostitutes."

"You're out of your mind!" Albert said.

"On the contrary, it's you who has lost his mind. It's possible that they're a better class of hookers, but I still say they're whores."

"Impossible."

"Why impossible? Let's assume she is really making *boom-boom-barroom* with drums and trumpets in a cathouse establishment. So what? Those ladies' bands are usually made up of girls who will only give you joy when they stop playing their bad music."

"Just as there are good and bad male bands, there are good and bad ladies' bands. But let's talk logic. Hookers take money, right? But Henja didn't want to take my money. That's already proof that your logic is wrong."

"But she did accept it in the end, didn't she?" Günther mocked him.

"Yes, but only because I agreed to make it a loan. Otherwise she wouldn't have accepted it at all. Besides, she is a charming girl. There is just no way she is what you think she is."

"In that case, everything is tickety-boo and I don't understand why you're so nervous because she hasn't phoned yet."

"She promised to call me on Thursday, or Friday at the latest. Since it's already Saturday, I'm a little worried. Of course, I wanted to go boating with her tomorrow, and now, I don't know where to find her. That's what makes me nervous, not your ridiculous speculations. Prostitutes! What next? Didn't I tell you that she is Jewish?"

"What does that have to do with anything?"

"Have you ever seen a Jewish prostitute?"

"Just because I haven't met one doesn't mean there aren't any. Maybe I don't move in the right circles. My acquaintances in the demi-monde are limited. Perhaps you can introduce me now."

"What is that supposed to mean?"

"It means that I stick to my opinion," Günther said, "and that you're a blockhead. If you haven't picked up a disease from her, you've paid a very low price for a valuable lesson. But I guarantee you'll see neither your money nor the girl again."

"On the contrary—" Albert started to say, but Günther interrupted him:

"I'm not done yet. Let me finish. You say the idea that she's a prostitute is ridiculous, but what's actually ridiculous is to say that a Jewish person can't be a hooker. You're always insisting that Jews aren't a weird religious sect, just ordinary people. If we're ordinary people – which I personally reject – you should admit that there must be Jewish murderers, prostitutes, streetcar conductors, garbage collectors and so forth, and not just doctors and lawyers, merchants and scientists. Anyway, if I'm proven wrong about what I think of your friend with the bass drums I'll eat my hat. I have spoken."

"You have spoken well," Albert said. "It's too bad such a speech can't be preserved for the— Yes, Anna, what is it?"

"Mr. Albert, you're wanted on the telephone," Anna said, standing in the doorway.

"Günther, that's her! I am sure. Anna, find Mr. Kirschbaum's hat!"

"I wish my hat were made of chocolate," Günther said

———

Mrs. Emma Krupnick wasn't satisfied with her bundt cake. It hadn't risen as well as usual and she couldn't take it to Mr. Krupnick on Sunday; that was for sure. Krupnick would throw a fit if she brought him such a pathetic offering. Now that the two years were almost over and Krupnick was about to return from his *health resort*, she would have to keep him in good spirits. She'd bake another cake, but this time cover the dough snugly under a pillow first so the yeast would work properly. In the meantime, she thought she might make coffee for the girls. They wouldn't object to the droopy state of her bundt cake.

Mrs. Krupnick rented out three of the five rooms in her apartment. After Mr. Krupnick's sudden departure, she only kept the master bedroom and the living room for herself. The rent each of her three tenants paid her for their rooms paid for the whole apartment. Because of that, she didn't care what went on in their rooms. If anyone had accused her being no better than a madam running a bawdy house, she would have declared indignantly that her tenants were not paying her any commission, and that it wasn't her business what they did. And her tenants were really nice girls. Mrs. Krupnick was always a little afraid of Edith and Henja, who sometimes talked about things she couldn't understand. They were so well-educated! But Lola, she was all right. She was exactly the way Mrs. Krupnick had been in her younger years, before she was married.

Emma Krupnick put the coffee on and set the good cups on the round table in the living room.

"Kids, come here, all of you, and have some coffee and cake," she called. "I'm sure you're not asleep with that caterwauling going on." What she called caterwauling were the sounds of the cello coming from Edith's room. Edith was practicing the "Ave Maria". The cello had often been the cause of bitter quarrelling. "If you had a piano here, I wouldn't play the cello so often," Edith had declared. "Fine," Emma had answered. "I'll tell Krupnick to swipe a piano next time."

Saturday afternoons were always dedicated to quiet before the storm of the evening. Saturday evenings were the busiest of the week, involving two shifts of visitors whenever possible.

The girls came out of their rooms in their dressing gowns and sat down in the living room, the *salong* as they called it. The artistic centrepiece of the living room was a large portrait of Paul von Hindenburg, the new President of Germany, in his uniform of a general field marshal.

"Why is he hanging here anyway?" Lola asked.

"Can't you tell? He looks just like Mr. Krupnick when you take away the moustache," Henja said.

"Don't talk nonsense," Emma said. "My husband served under him, that's why the picture's here."

"What? Hindenburg was in prison, too? I had no idea," Edith said sarcastically.

"Now stop that! Have a piece of cake and pour some milk into your coffee, it's healthier," Emma said.

"Healthier than what?" Henja asked.

"Healthier than all the liquor and the cocktails you're going to have later," Emma said.

"Henja doesn't drink. She always has the barman pour her tea and tells her john it's cognac. The john pays, and she gets a commission," Lola said.

"Miss Charlotte Katharina Louise Benzig, also known as Lola," Henja said. "Mind your own business!"

"This week you've worked harder than ever," Emma said. "I couldn't help noticing. What's gotten into you, Henja?"

"You have to get rid of your debts sometimes, don't you? Also, I want to create some capital to cover the summer doldrums."

"You're going to make yourself sick," Emma warned.

"Nonsense, I'm as healthy as a horse." She sang the first line of a popular German folksong: *Freut euch des Lebens …* 'Enjoy life as long as your candle is still burning!' "Apropos burning," she said. "I almost forgot this burning issue: I still owe someone thirty marks. I have to pay him back. I'm going to do that right now."

"Have you gone mad?" Edith said. "That thing from last Sunday?"

"Yes, my dear, exactly that," Henja answered, and walked over to the telephone in the hall.

Edith jumped up, placed one of her large strong hands on the receiver and grabbed Henja with the other.

Henja felt like she was caught in a vice. "Let me go!" she shouted.

"No," Edith said. "Be quiet and listen! That whole thing was a colossal joke and I enjoyed it as much as you did. But if you want to go further with it, you are completely out of your mind."

"You don't understand me," Henja said. "And you're hurting me. Let me go so I can explain it to you."

"Fine. Come back to the living room."

"Good," Henja said, going back to the salon and sitting down on the sofa, where she lit a cigarette. Lola and Emma had watched the scene with open mouths. They looked at Henja expectantly, wondering what was going on. Henja was silent for a few minutes and then said: "Every profession has its own ethics. Edith, explain to Lola what the word 'ethics' means. I doubt she knows it."

Lola protested, but Edith told her not to interrupt.

Henja continued. "We have chosen a job, or have been forced into a job, that doesn't have a particularly good name. But that doesn't mean that we must be heartless bitches through and through. When I'm with a man who knows that his pleasure is going to cost him money, I don't have the slightest hesitation about making him pay for my company. But when it happens – as it did last Sunday – that an innocent boy ends up in your arms, a boy who respects you as though you are a fine lady, you mustn't destroy his illusions. He might suffer emotional damage, and that would be on your conscience."

"This is complete nonsense. I don't believe a word of it. You're just itching to play the role of the decent girl for a while, but don't play games with us. And there is something else itching you; you know what I mean. And that can ruin your whole life," Edith said.

"Well, what kind of life is this anyway?" Henja asked.

"Would it be better to sell shoes all day and smell all those stinky feet?" Edith said, referring to her friend's previous attempt to return to respectability.

"Anyway," she continued, "if you must, give him back his pocket money, but don't get involved with him any further."

"What kind of a guy was he? I've never seen a girl give her hard-earned money back to a john," Lola said.

Emma Krupnick was even more surprised. "Only thirty marks? Since when has Henja charged so little? Has she gone crazy?"

"Do you think I can understand it?" Edith said.

"What kind of guy was he, really?" Lola repeated her question.

"A completely green, stupid Jewish boy," Edith answered, though Henja hadn't revealed that he was a virgin.

"Oh, he was a Jew!" said Emma Krupnick. "Now I understand."

"You understand what?" Edith asked.

"Henja is attracted to her own *mishpoche,* as the Jews call it. They stick together like a cluster of flies. There is nothing you can do about it," Mrs. Krupnick said.

Henja hadn't heard any of this because she was on the telephone. She came back to the salon and said, "Auntie Emma, I'd like another cup of hot coffee."

"Did you reach your minor?" Edith asked.

"Yes," Henja said, laughing at her own behaviour. "Tomorrow morning we're going paddling on the Havel River to see the cherry trees in bloom in Werder."

Edith just said, "That takes the cake."

VII

———

ALBERT STOOD UNDER THE CLOCK at the Zoo railway station. Thank God, the weather was fine. If the weather report on the radio could be trusted, it should stay this way all day. But where was Henja? She still hadn't told him where she lived, so he didn't know which streetcar she would be arriving on. Eight o'clock had been too early for her. She wanted to sleep longer on Sunday. But still, she did promise to be on time when he insisted. He had been firm and commanding which was good, because women expected men to be forceful. So he would excuse her if she were a quarter of an hour late, but any later than that and he intended to give her a piece of his mind.

He noticed a taxi pulling up beside him but ignored it, knowing she had no money. Then a voice broke into his meditations.

"If you make me get up in the middle of the night, you should at least say 'good morning' to me."

Albert was dumbfounded. In her sporty trench coat, a beret on her head at a smart angle, Henja looked like a new woman. He hadn't recognized her. Now he found her even prettier than last Sunday, when she had been in an evening dress and a fur coat.

"You look so different," he apologized. "But I like you a thousand times better this way. I'm so happy!" What a pity that Günther couldn't see Henja now. He would have to eat ten more hats.

No one would have suspected that Henja had sent Saturday night's last john back to his wife at five that morning. Wearing a thin, tight-fitting sweater whose simple cut revealed her figure, she impressed the young people in the boathouse, and Albert was proud. She traded her skirt for a pair of white shorts and tied her hair back with a broad red ribbon that matched the colour of her sweater. Her whole appearance was perfectly athletic. The sun shone on her naked legs, and in the kayak she stretched out in the pleasant warmth, finally acknowledging the fatigue in her limbs.

A slight easterly wind drove the boat. Albert had set up the mast and hoisted the sail so they didn't have to paddle. Henja felt lucky that she didn't to have to paddle on a day when she was so tired. Edith was right. She was crazy. But surely a single day out in the fresh air with this boy scout couldn't do any harm? It was so beautiful and quiet here, where trees covered with fresh green leaves lined one side of the river, and impressive villas with large gardens the other. She let her hands slide in the water, feeling the speed with which they were moving. The boat had started going faster since they had passed the bend in Lake Griebnitz. The sail billowed in the warm breeze.

Then, ahead of them, she saw a group of ten boats lying close to the right bank. On each boat, a red pennant with a swastika fluttered in the wind. Henja wondered whether Albert would steer away from them. That would be the smartest thing to do if he were the coward she suspected he was, especially given the proud little flag with the Star of David flying from the stern of his boat.

"How do you like those guys ahead of us?" Albert asked.

"I don't like them at all," she said.

"So let's bother them a little," Albert said. He pulled the sail tighter, setting the course of his boat directly into the middle of the group. In daredevil fashion he headed right at them, only avoiding a collision by frantically paddling out of the way at the last minute.

The men in the boats screamed in outrage even before they spotted the Hebrew writing and the Jewish flag.

"Look, it's the Jewish navy!"

"You dirty Jewish pig, we're coming to get you!"

"Let's go, boys! After him!"

"He has a blond German girl with him. She should be ashamed."

"At least he's sailing under his own flag."

The pursuit didn't succeed. Albert's lead was too great. With the full wind in his back, he sped away twice as fast as the paddlers behind him.

Henja turned around and declared, "That was the dumbest, most unnecessary display of bravado I've seen for a long time. It was dangerous, too, especially since I can't swim." But she was also quite pleased that she had jumped to the wrong conclusion. Albert might not be that bright, but he wasn't a coward.

"You'll have to learn it now, though," Albert said.

"What do I have to learn?"

"To swim."

"I see," she said. It was her fault that he regarded her as his girlfriend, and she had no clue how to get out of the situation without hurting him. The truth was, she wasn't sure she wanted to get out of it. Her high school home-room teacher had once told her mother, 'Mrs. Bach, your Henriette is the smartest girl in my class, perhaps even in the whole school. But she is lazy, and doesn't know what she wants.' Nothing had changed. Henja still didn't know what she wanted.

If she could keep this boy for a few years, he would have a good career and make a good husband. She could have a home and children and she'd be good to him. Such wishful thinking! Still, he was in love with her, and must never know what she did for a living.

What should she do? Nothing. What will be will be.

"Tell me, Albert," she said, trying to get away from her thoughts. "What do those guys with the swastikas have against us anyway? Did some Jews hurt them or something?"

"That's a question that could take me ten hours to answer, but let me try."

"I hope it doesn't take ten hours, or I'll grow old," Henja said.

"How old *are* you, by the way? I've been meaning to ask you that for a while," Albert asked.

"You should never ask a woman her age, but you may try to guess."

"Twenty at most, but I would say nineteen."

"So what's your last estimate, nineteen or twenty?"

"I can't tell," he said.

"You're not exactly a flatterer, but you're forgiven. How old are you yourself?"

"Twenty," Albert lied.

Henja gave him a penetrating look with her grey eyes. It was a long-practiced trick of hers that confused even experienced men. Albert succumbed immediately.

"To tell you the truth, I'll only be twenty in six months," he corrected himself. "And now you must tell me the truth too."

"My boy, I'm afraid you will be so shocked, you'll make your ship capsize. I've already turned twenty-one." It wasn't a lie. She just didn't tell him that her twenty-first birthday had been more than a year ago.

"I wouldn't have guessed, but I'm certainly not shocked," Albert said.

"Don't you think I'm much too old for you?"

"Nonsense! That little difference in years is negligible. The main thing is that we get along so well in every respect, and anyway …"

"Anyway what?"

"Anyway, I can talk with you about everything, and you seem to understand my problems."

"How do you know that in such a short time?" Henja asked.

"I'm a quick thinker, sweetheart," Albert said. "And I can judge most people correctly."

"A valuable gift," Henja said, trying not to laugh. "But now we have digressed from the subject we were discussing. You were about to explain anti-Semitism to me."

"I will, but I must start by telling you that these aren't original conclusions. I've been reading a lot about the subject."

"Excuse me for interrupting," Henja said, "but where exactly are we? What is that dome over there, to the right?"

"May I present to you the city of Potsdam. The dome is the Garrison Church, where King Frederic II is buried. And closer to the front, also to your right, ladies and gentlemen …" Albert enjoyed taking on the jargon of a tour guide, "You see the building with dark brown scaffolding on the roof? That's the brewery where the world-famous Potsdam beer is brewed. The sorry-looking body of water we're on now is a miserable branch of the Havel River upon which we'll travel the rest of the way to Werder, after we pass under a bridge. We'll point out other sights during the course of today's cruise, at the end of which your guide would be grateful for a little token of your appreciation."

Henja had to laugh. "Good, Mr. Tour Guide, we won't argue about your tip. Is lunch included in this Havel River cruise?"

"Yes, Miss, but it is still too early for any food other than food for thought. So do you want to hear my lecture or not?"

"Of course I do. And I couldn't think of a more fitting background than the city of Potsdam for a lecture on anti-Semitism. I'm not going to say another word."

Albert had picked up his paddle to propel the boat through the narrow waterway. He cleared his throat and began. "Your remark about the city of Potsdam, symbol of the spirit – or dispirit – of Prussia, was excellent, but there is another city that would be an even more suitable background for a dissertation on anti-Semitism, and that is Jerusalem. That's where two thousand years ago the inhabitants delivered one of their own to the gallows. First, because they regarded him as a traitor to their national struggle for freedom, and second, because they saw him as an element destroying and corroding their religious and national unity.

"Now we can think what we want. Whether the Jew called Jeshua, son of Joseph the carpenter, had a right to preach that his people shouldn't rebel against their foreign rulers, or whether he had the right to criticize and publicly insult the authorities of his people – who can judge this today? The only thing we can say with certainty is that it was a completely internal affair of the Jewish nation in the land of Israel. However, it so happened that many heathen people adopted the teachings of this man without being aware that they were the traditional wisdom of his religion, Judaism. Instead of going down on their knees to thank the Jewish people for giving them such a man, they refused to give the Jews credit as his people of origin, and his spiritual source. They saw the Jews only as descendants of the villains who had delivered him to the executioner. That is the very first basis of animosity against the Jews."

"I didn't want to interrupt you," Henja said, "but I think you overlooked something, namely the divine birth in which the Christians believe."

"Oh my God, that idea came much later, from the Greeks, the first people who turned the belief in Jesus into a separate religion. They couldn't divest themselves of their own mythology overnight, so they transformed Jesus into one of their own gods, complete with a supernatural birth and a divine parent. Pallas Athena had sprung from the forehead of Zeus, and so had Artemis. Therefore, Jesus also had to be given a noble birth certificate. How else could they have worshipped him? Do you worship the sons of carpenters?"

"Do you really believe that anti-Semitism began for religious reasons? As you say yourself, that would be completely illogical."

"Of course it is illogical, but it is historically true. Especially in the late Middle Ages, when the Church couldn't tolerate the fact that the only people who refused to worship the cross were the Jews. But other reasons contributed."

"Namely what?"

"Well, those obstinate Jews who kept on rebelling and resisting the Romans were expelled from their own country and settled in small groups elsewhere in the Roman Empire. They were a minority everywhere. Nowhere could they be masters of their own destiny. In every country they were subject to the whim of the majority, and of the rulers. But they still didn't assimilate. That, incidentally, is the eighth wonder of the world! A people scattered into small groups across the globe for two thousand years managed to keep its identity and culture and even its language; a language it isn't permitted to speak. And it even maintained its national aspirations. There is no parallel in history."

"You're really proud to be a Jew, aren't you?" Henja asked.

"I'm not so certain about that myself," he answered. "No one should pride himself on his origin – nor be ashamed of it. But I do find it interesting to be a Jew."

"What's so interesting about it? And it seems to me that you don't suffer from an inferiority complex. I'm not certain whether your theories are correct. All I know is that I'm starving, and I need to get out of this boat as soon as possible."

"Do you see that restaurant on the shore over there? The terrace with boats moored in front of it? That's where we're going."

They had left Potsdam behind them but now they had a headwind and the fluttering sail interfered with their progress. Albert told Henja how to pull down the sail since he couldn't reach it from the back. Then he began paddling. She took the other paddle and plunged it into the water.

"Don't dip it so deeply," he told her. "Keep it flat; it's easier that way."

She didn't find it easy; the damn paddle felt as heavy as lead. But if she gave up after the first three strokes, Albert would be disappointed, so she resolved to keep paddling until she dropped dead. She'd survived worse things in her life.

"Hey, Henja, stop splashing!" he cried out. "You're drenching me from top to bottom! Don't pull the paddle so hard. I didn't realize you were that strong; those arm muscles must come from playing the drums."

"Of course," Henja said. She was glad to be reminded of her cover story.

"Look who is here!" Albert said, pointing at another kayak moored at the restaurant's dock.

"Who is Erika?" Henja asked, reading the boat's name.

"The boat belongs to Manfred, my old school buddy; Erika is his girlfriend. Sometimes I don't know which Erika he likes better."

"Probably the wooden one; that's what you men are like. But now you must excuse me. While you're busy mooring your frigate here, I need to go somewhere," Henja said. "Sit wherever you like, and please order me something to eat; anything at all as long as it's not pork. I'll find you."

Henja ran up the little stairway from the dock and disappeared between the restaurant tables. Albert tied up his boat with loving care then went to look for Manfred and Erika. He spotted them without much trouble. Having already noticed his boat with its distinctive blue and white flag, they had pulled two more chairs over to their table.

"Welcome!" Erika said. "When we saw your boat, we told the waiter that we were waiting for friends. That's why we haven't started to eat yet."

"That was really nice of you."

"Nice of me, because Manfred wanted to go ahead and eat without you."

"I was hungry, and couldn't be sure you would stop here. Who's the girl? A new acquisition?" Manfred asked.

"Yes," Albert said. "You'll meet her in a minute. She's a wonderful person."

The waiter came and took their orders. Albert ordered veal schnitzel for himself and the same for Henja. She hadn't shown up yet, and he kept looking around to make sure he would see her when she came out.

"Albert," Erika said, "you must like variety."

"Why?"

"Your Lilly is a brunette, Eva is a redhead, and the new one is golden blond. I saw her briefly when she ran through."

"What's her name?" asked Manfred.

"Henja."

"I see that you've abandoned all your principles," Manfred said. "You're accepting the colours of the national flag, black, red and gold, eh?"

"Mannie, I'll die laughing at your jokes one day. Albert, is Henja's hair colour natural?" Erika asked.

Albert was offended by her tactlessness. "You can ask her yourself," he replied.

When Henja finally appeared, Albert suspected that she had spent most of her time in front of the bathroom mirror. She had fixed her hair, put on a necklace and matching bracelet and done something to her makeup as well. Whatever it was, she looked most elegant in spite of her sporty clothes.

"May I present Henja. Erika – Manfred."

"Delighted," Manfred said, rising halfway from his chair.

Erika, still seated, smiled and said, "How do you do? Please have a seat."

The two girls scrutinized each other. Henja, who was almost obsessively neat, noticed immediately that the bra covering Erika's somewhat flat breasts was held together with a safety pin, and her blouse was askew, baring a shoulder that was much too muscular to be feminine. That amused her, but otherwise she liked the girl. She wished she could advise Erika how to put some glow into her dull brown hair and teach her not to dress so tastelessly.

For her part Erika – as is often the case when one woman recognizes that the other is prettier and more elegant – decided at once that she didn't like Henja.

"Don't you find your sweater much too warm?" she asked.

"Not in the least."

"It's kind of tight, isn't it?"

Recognizing the aggression in this comment, Henja replied with her most charming smile, "You mean that the contents of my package are visible? Yes, that's the way it is with sweaters worn by women who have something to show."

Manfred and Albert were amused, but they didn't understand that hidden inside this harmless conversation was a declaration of war.

"You haven't known each other for very long?" Erika asked.

"Not long, but well," Albert said and believed that he had given his friend Manfred the necessary message.

Henja understood him immediately and was angry about his silly boasting. She turned to Erika and said, "We don't know each other that well. But you have known Albert for some time, so tell me, can we trust him on the water? Or is he a danger to us poor defenceless girls?"

"You don't give me the impression of being quite so poor and defenceless," Erika said. "But Albert is quite a nice guy even though he doesn't like me."

When Albert politely protested, she continued, painfully aware of how neglected her own hands were by comparison with Henja's manicure. "You can try him for a few weeks. If he doesn't suit you, just trade him in."

"What do you mean by 'trade him in'? Are you suggesting we swap? You'll take Albert and I take Manfred?"

"Terrific idea," Manfred declared. "Miss Henja, shall we make a date for a dress rehearsal?"

"You'd like that, would you? But there's no way it's happening," Albert laughed.

"Don't you even think of that, you bad boy!" Erika said.

Laughter brought on a truce. Meanwhile, the waiter had brought their meals, as well as large glasses of Berlin wheat beer. Albert and Erika poured raspberry juice into their beer, a practice that Henja, used to Bavarian drinking traditions, regarded with distaste. They wolfed down their food.

"How's the kayak? Is it still leaking?" Manfred asked.

"No, it's completely dry now. Gundermann charged me twenty marks to seal it last week."

Erika said, "I was very mad at you, Albert, when you took Manfred away from me last week. But he told me all about your adventures. You're quite the pair, you two."

"What were they up to?" Henja asked.

"Should I tell?"

"Why not?" said Manfred.

"They paddled with bare *tochuses*." Erika loved to use Yiddish expressions she had picked up. Like many other non-Jews, she found them funny.

Henja played the fine lady and asked, "With bare what?"

"Well, how do you say it? They had no pants on."

"Well, I'll be …" Henja said naively, acting astonished.

Manfred thought it might be better to change the subject. "Did you have a good trip today?" he asked.

"Wonderful," Albert said. "We had a first-class wind. No effort at all until Potsdam."

"Only mental effort," Henja added. "Albert gave me a lecture on the background of anti-Semitism. However, he didn't get to the end. That's why I'm still uneducated."

Manfred laughed. "To what chapter did he get? I already know the record by heart."

"Don't act so smug," Albert said.

"Do you also dislike the Jews?" Erika asked. Albert started to laugh. He was just about to say that Henja was Jewish when he felt a kick against his shin. Startled, he fell silent. Then Henja looked at Erika with wide-open eyes and asked, "Why do you say 'also'? Are you anti-Semitic yourself? I think your boyfriend is a Jew. Or am I wrong?"

"No, it's true. Manfred is Jewish," Erika said. "But thank God you can't tell. I must admit: except for Manfred and Albert, I can't stand Jews. Manfred knows how I feel, but it doesn't bother him. Right, Mannie?"

Manfred didn't reply, a sign that he was very angry. He found this conversation extremely unpleasant, especially in front of Albert and his new girl. He was ashamed of Erika's stupidy, knowing that she didn't really mean what she was saying and was only trying to sound interesting.

Henja had the same impression but nonetheless was determined to destroy Erika. She put her knife and fork aside, placed her hands flat on the table, and then said very slowly, pronouncing every word clearly, "You know, that's the most terrible thing I ever heard. You have a boyfriend who thinks highly of you, yet you tell him right to his face, 'I gladly accept your friendship and what it offers me. But I want nothing to do with your people, your friends, your parents, your brothers and sisters. Them I can't stand. In fact, I only associate with you because you don't look like them.'

"I assume that must be what you mean when you say 'Thank God you can't tell'. What is it that you can't you tell? That he's Jewish? How does a Jew look? I wonder what Greeks and Spaniards and Italians look like according to you. I suspect you believe that Jews must look like the caricatures anti-Semites make of them. Do you think all Germans look like the caricatures the French make of them, with bulging beer bellies, goggle-eyes and square heads? I doubt it. But even if there were such a thing as a Jewish appearance, is that something indecent in your opinion?"

Erika was stunned. She hadn't meant what she said that seriously. In fact, she had only wanted to offer another Christian woman some kind of justification for her relationship with a Jew. She had also intended to diminish the bad impression she thought she had made on the elegant girl by using a Yiddish expression like *tochus*. Manfred, who was such a kind person, was probably furious at her now, and Albert – for him, this was oil on the fire. She started to stutter:

"I, I only w … I wanted to say that generally people don't like to see … when we Christian girls go out with a Jew, and that's why, only that's why I thought it is better that Mannie doesn't look so Jewish."

You're quite right in a sense,' Henja said. "Because Jews always regard it as a great misfortune when their sons have anything to do with Christian girls – or their daughters with Christian men."

"The Jews do?"

"Oh, didn't you know that? Go and ask Mannie's mother. Strangely enough, they are convinced that most non-Jews are morally and mentally inferior to them. This is just as silly and the same kind of prejudice as anti-Semitism, but still, that's no excuse for you," Henja continued mercilessly, "because you said that you personally didn't like Jews and yet you don't even know any others besides Manfred and Albert." This was a shot in the dark, but Henja was sure of it, and she proceeded with the coup de grâce. "If I were a man and your friend, I would break up with you right here in this restaurant."

Erika was red in the face with shame and anger. How could she defend herself against this horrible person who Manfred seemed to regard with respect. Desperate tears came to her eyes. "Oh God," she sobbed, "I really didn't mean it like that, Mannie; I never intended to insult you. Please don't be mad at me."

Manfred, who knew her good qualities and her decent character, was much too easy-going to be seriously angry with her. He put his arm around her shoulder and said, "I'm not mad at you. You're not responsible for your narrow-mindedness. But it's good that somebody gave you a piece of her mind. Maybe you'll learn to think before opening your mouth and not to say things you don't mean like a silly goose."

Erika calmed down. His affectionate insults reassured her. She felt that he had forgiven her, and she gave him a kiss. Under different circumstances she would have never had the heart to do this in a public place and in front of so many tables filled with strangers.

During this scene of tenderness, Henja stood up and gave Albert a sign to follow her. "Now don't you dare tell them that I'm Jewish," she said.

"Why not?"

"Because that simple-minded person thinks that I'm a *shiksa* like her. She is very ashamed right now but if she finds out that I'm Jewish, the medicine I gave her won't work at all. On the contrary, then she'll really hate Jews."

"You're right. You're a clever child," Albert said. They went back to the table, and Albert declared, "We didn't want to disturb you while you were celebrating your reconciliation."

They demolished the remainder of the dessert before saying goodbye. Henja asked how far they still had to go to reach Werder and the cherry blossom festival. When she heard that it would take almost two hours, she didn't want to go. The return trip would end so late at night it would interfere with her evening program.

Albert suggested that instead they head to the other shore where they could pitch the tent under the trees and rest a little. "The railway track is close by, but who cares?"

"You know," Albert said when they were back in the boat, "you would make an excellent lawyer. You should study law." Just this week, an older man had told her the same thing. That's why she had made a little bit of money again in the days past. She had paid more attention to conversation. She had also increased her fees. She would no longer do anything for less than a hundred marks. Men paid her that without complaining. On the contrary, she was suddenly much in demand. If she charged that much, they assumed that she must be better and more skilled than the others girls. Exactly the same tactic lawyers used.

"Unfortunately I can't go to university since I never graduated from high school," she said. "Are you studying law, Albert?"

"No, economics."

"Is that interesting?"

"So-so. I'd prefer philosophy."

"Why aren't you taking it then?"

"Unfortunately, there aren't too many career prospects."

Henja was silent. She didn't feel competent to discuss the subject.

———— ◆ ————

Albert took all the pillows from the boat and distributed them about the floor of the tent. Now that she had eaten, Henja recognized how tired she was. She lay down inside the tent and closed her eyes.

Albert sat outside the flap, smoking a cigarette. They could easily stay till four or half past four, he thought. He was glad they hadn't continued on to Werder; there would have been no opportunity to pitch the tent there. But how could he take advantage of the situation? Henja hadn't been encouraging him at all, neither in words nor in body language. She kept treating him as if he were nothing but a friend, despite the fact that last week she had been so passionate. He had to admit that too had been strange – becoming intimate right after they had met for the first time. He was sure that Günther was wrong about her being a hooker, but obviously she must have had a boyfriend before. It was clear she'd had experience.

The thought occurred to him that she might even have another boyfriend right now. That would be a catastrophe. He would never find another girl like Henja, and yet he knew so little about her: where she lived, where she worked, or even much about that ladies' band she played in – as Günther had suggested, not a very classy profession. He could only imagine his mother's face if he introduced her future daughter-in-law as someone playing the drums in a band. Good lord! But of course, she earned a lot more money that way than she would working in a store or an office. If he could earn twenty-five marks an evening with his amateur banjo-playing, the girls must get at least that much, which would make more than seven hundred marks a month. As a salesgirl or clerk, she wouldn't even earn half that much.

That also explained how she could afford a fur coat. Yes, she knew what she was doing. She was clever; after all, she'd impressed Manfred. He'd been blown away. And the way she'd demolished Erika was something to behold! He'd actually felt sorry for her. Henja was fabulous.

Albert threw his cigarette butt into the water, then quietly crawled into the tent. Carefully, so as not to wake Henja up, he stretched out beside her, but the tent was too small. He involuntarily bumped into her but she didn't move. Looked at the sleeping girl he became so aroused he only restrained himself with difficulty from jumping on her. Instead he stroked her hair, then gently caressed her breasts. They were as firm as grapefruits. His hands were on the way to her hips when he became aware that her eyes were open and she was looking at him.

"Don't," she said.

His desire grew, but he felt he'd been caught red-handed like a thief.

"Please don't be angry. I thought you were sleeping, and I only wanted to caress you."

Henja didn't say a word. She only turned to the side, away from him. Albert tried to lie down again, but he couldn't hold back.

"Have I done anything to displease you?" he asked in a whiny tone, feeling sorry for himself. "I love you so terribly much."

Henja turned around, sat up with a jerk and whispered very softly, bending over him: "You silly boy, that's all I wanted to hear. You should have told me first that you love me. Do you really, really love me?"

"Yes," he almost shouted. "I love you like crazy!"

She laughed and then helped him to get his pants off.

He had no idea how long he slept afterwards, but he felt an unaccustomed peace and contentment. It had been completely different from last week. Much, much better. Did she feel the same? She was lying on her back again, her arms folded under her head.

"Awake again, my boy?"

"Yes, sweetheart."

"Would you please get me my handbag?"

She rummaged around in the handbag trying to find her balance again. She had never felt this way while doing the work with which she earned her living. Her body had made the decision for her; reason was useless in this case. She took three ten-mark bills from her bag and said gruffly, almost as if she were angry, "I want to pay my debt back to you, as we agreed."

She was prepared for a fight, but under no circumstances would she accept money from a man who caused genuine feelings of love in her. That would be against all decency. It would be a real sin.

Albert took the thirty marks without any comment. She was flabbergasted, and for some reason, disappointed. He opened a small suitcase he had brought to the tent from the boat, deposited the money into it and then turned toward her.

"I would also like to give you something," he said, with some embarrassment. In his hand was an oblong case containing a dainty watch, not the cheapest, but not a particularly expensive. He had bought it on instalments.

"Last Sunday, I noticed that you didn't have a watch. That's why – after your call last night – I went to buy it before the stores closed. I hope you like it."

She couldn't tell him that in her jewellery case were a gold watch with rubies and diamonds as well as a platinum watch with diamonds. Because here, in this little box, was the first untainted gift she had received since childhood. And with that gesture he had captured her. She, the hard-nosed expert on all kinds of men, was spellbound by this innocent child.

A terrible fear rose up inside her. *This can't turn out well. I will destroy him, and myself, too. Oh God, help me*, she thought, and then she broke down. She hugged him, crying, and kissed him like a lunatic. "You devil, you nasty rascal, you rotten bum!" she sobbed between kisses.

Albert was in seventh heaven. He didn't have the faintest idea why she cried so much and why she called him a devil, a bum, and a rascal. But he didn't care. The main thing was that she belonged to him, for real. Nothing else mattered.

It was very late in the evening when they got back to the boat house.

"Your Ma already phoned a few times, afraid you drowned. I think she already called the cops. Go phone her and tell her you're still among the living," Mrs. Gundermann said.

"What do you mean 'still among the living'?" Albert sang cheerfully, emphasizing the word *still*. Falling into Mrs. Gundermann's dialect, he said, grinning broadly, "It was only today I started to live!"

Mrs. Gundermann and Henja looked at each other knowingly. Both women laughed.

VII
1926

———

MAX BERG'S MASSIVE HEAD BENT over the desk where he was busy drawing geometrical shapes on a sheet of paper. He should have been an architect; he had an extraordinary talent for designing buildings. However he was not concentrating on his drawings. He was worried, extremely worried, about the son who was slouching in a soft chair in the library.

"The Talmud says that every human decision derives from two causes, one overt and one hidden," Mr. Berg said. "I have heard the obvious, plausible, and logical reason for your decision, but what's the true reason, the reason that's hidden? That's what I'd like to know."

"Don't you think it's possible that the obvious reason could also be the true reason?" Albert asked.

"It's possible but it's not likely. It's logical that you want to earn money. It's logical that you want to be independent. It may even be logical to argue that these goals will not be easy to accomplish while you're a student. But I don't believe any of these are the true reasons. The truth is still hidden." While Mr. Berg spoke excellent German and had an extensive vocabulary, he had retained the harsh Baltic accent that barely distinguished between short and long vowels. The word *truth* sometimes sounded like *trruss*, and *logical* turned into *loggikle*. But he became irritated when someone corrected him, so Albert had stopped doing it long ago.

"Do you think I'm lying when I repeat how unpleasant it is for me to have to ask you for every penny I need? Especially since I know how bad business is right now."

"Have I ever complained about how much you spend or even that you cost me money? On the contrary, my main goal in life is to send my only son to university, something I could never do myself. In Russia, few Jews were allowed at universities. We weren't even permitted to attend secondary schools. So for the most part, we became shopkeepers and peddlers and tradesmen. But you have an opportunity to make something of your life and now you want to throw it away to become just another shopkeeper. This is nonsense. Absolute nonsense!"

"Excuse me, dearest Papa, but no one would ever call you a shopkeeper."

"It's is only a difference of degree, not in kind. Do you think that I'm satisfied or happy being a merchant? Besides, I'm a very bad merchant, and you, my boy, would be an even worse one. You have no talent at all for business. My educated son, who can already speak three languages, wants to become a shopkeeper! I just can't understand it."

"Precisely because I speak three languages, I could be successful in business," Albert argued.

"But why? My God, you're only twenty years old. Are you planning to get married and support a wife already?"

"No, of course not," Albert said, feeling uncomfortable the way everyone hiding something does when other people get too close to the truth.

"Then I can understand this decision even less. No one can force you to stay in school. But you have a roof over your head, you have enough to eat and everything else you need. There are students who must earn their daily bread as well as their tuition. They have to work in the daytime and study at night. They may have to study in unheated rooms but they don't give up. I could understand if you wanted to switch subjects or if you wanted to emigrate to Eretz Yisrael to become a farmer. All that I could understand, and agree to. But dropping out of university to become a shopkeeper? Don't do that to your parents!"

"That's interesting. If I wanted to be a farmer in Palestine it would suit you, even though my education would still prove to have been a waste of time and money. But to be in business would be a disaster? That doesn't make any sense to me," Albert said.

"To be a farmer in Eretz Yisrael – that, at least, would make sense. If my son made that commitment, I would be proud. He would be helping to establish our national home, which theoretically, the Balfour Declaration has already given us, and for which we have never summoned up enough people and energy."

"Who is this 'we'?"

"The Jewish nation," his father replied.

"I see. And you are quite certain that all Jews share this opinion and regard themselves as a nation, with their very own national obligations?" Albert asked.

"Would you like to give up those obligations along with your studies?"

"I can't because they are too deeply engrained in me, but lately I have had the feeling that it has all been unnecessary."

"What is unnecessary?" Mr. Berg asked. Now he was really upset.

"Jewish nationalism, this exaggerated self-consciousness you brought me up with. We live in Germany, and Mother is German in every fibre of her being. German is my mother tongue. My schooling has been in German. My friends, who are also all Jews, feel like Germans first and foremost. But you have raised me so that ever since I was born I have felt like a foreigner in my own homeland. A father shouldn't have the right to indoctrinate his children with his political opinions. Nor do you have the right to force me to waste two more years of my life so that you can introduce me some day as 'my son, the doctor *rerum politicarum*.'"

"You think that's really what I want?" his father asked. "If so, what do you plan to do to make amends for my sins, and those of your ancestors?"

"Two things. First I want to make myself economically independent. Secondly, I want to feel at home in the country of my birth, in my language and my culture."

"Alright, my son, I wish you lots of luck, and I hope you won't be too disappointed. Now please go away and leave me alone."

After Albert closed the library door behind him, his father sat behind his desk for a long time and cried.

———

At the Butterfly Bar, Henja gave her evening dress and a little white ermine cape, neither of which Albert had seen, to the cloakroom attendant. "Rosie, store them somewhere safe. I'll be back by eleven or so. I'm expecting a man from Paris today; if he shows up before I do, tell him I'll definitely be here. He can order some champagne for us and put it on ice. I'll change into these clothes when I return, but now I must run, or my boy will be mad at me."

Rosie, the cloakroom attendant, Hans-Friedrich the barman, and all the ladies at the bar knew about Henja's romance. It had been going on for over a year. For two summers she had travelled with the boy, first to the island of Norderney in the North Sea, and then to the Tyrol. She had told them about these holidays like a bride coming back from her honeymoon. And she still refused to work on Saturday nights so that she could spend all day Sunday on his boat, or go skating with him.

At first they had been convinced that he would get wind of her professional life in a matter of weeks, but now they were accustomed to her situation. It was incredible how cleverly she had managed it! In addition, it was miraculous that she had never picked up anything and got him infected. Of course, she ran to the doctor every week and had herself examined. She always came to the bar late, and when no one was there she liked, she went to another where they understood her priorities as well. In fact, more than her professional skills, it was how she had negotiated her private relationship that invested her with fame and prestige among her colleagues.

She had made Albert promise that he would never follow her to any of the places where she allegedly played in a band. She had told him that she was ashamed of her profession, and that he must never see her behind her drum set. He had kept his promise. But even if he had been inclined to visit one of the places she claimed to be working, he wouldn't have gotten far. She was better protected by the camaraderie of her milieu than by the police. Albert had no idea that Henja had distributed photos of him so that his face was familiar to all the girls, barmen, and bouncers. He wouldn't have been allowed in anywhere before the proper preparations had been made. A plan was in place for such contingencies. Edith would sit at the piano and Henja at the drums, whether the band playing that day was actually a male or female ensemble.

At the beginning of their relationship Albert kept asking why she wouldn't look for different work, and she had told him quite truthfully that she had tried to find a better job, but without letters of recommendation from former employers, she had been turned down everywhere. She could have worked as a waitress at two different restaurants but didn't think it was worth leaving a much more lucrative job for that.

"Don't you realize that it's impossible to find work these days? There are three million unemployed in Germany, half a million here in Berlin alone. Just be happy that I'm not a financial burden for you, my sweet. And be happy that I'm earning my keep."

About a year ago, Albert had asked whether there were any prostitutes frequenting the places she worked.

"Professionals or amateurs?" Henja asked.

"What do you mean by amateurs?"

"Upper-class ladies looking for adventure, or secretaries and clerks who want to amuse themselves and dance in expensive places. They get laid so they can afford to buy clothes and jewellery, and provide competition for the professional girls," Henja said.

"Are there any Jewish girls among what you call professionals?" The question had occupied his mind ever since his conversation with Günther.

"Of course," Henja had replied bluntly. So much for his idealism.

From the bar, which was still closed – only Rosie and the cleaning lady were there – Henja ran to the subway station. She had promised to meet Albert in front of the Great *Schauspielhaus* Theatre, where he and Günther would wait for her. She had begun to like serious plays. Now she could talk about Max Reinhardt, Erwin Piscator, and Leopold Jessner with the understanding expected of cultivated women

They also went to concerts and to the opera. In the beginning they only bought the cheapest seats, since Albert was always short of cash. But then she started purchasing more expensive tickets, telling him that, as a professional musician, she got free tickets. That's how they enjoyed Bruno Walter at the philharmonic and Leo Blech, who Albert called 'the baptized Jew', at the opera. That these important icons of German art, music and theatre, such as Reinhardt, Jessner, Weill and others, were born Jewish was extremely important to him. "It shows you," he said, "that we are the intellectual yeast in the heavy dough of German culture."

Henja had also become good friends with Günther. He liked her and was a little envious of Albert. She always sat between the two quietly and listened to them argue. When Albert became excited, she intervened by placing one hand on his thigh, which took his mind off the subject, and the other on Günther's hand. He couldn't talk at all when someone held down his hand.

It was really too bad that she had to go back to the Butterfly Bar after the performance, but her customer was expecting her. Though he was old enough to be her father, he was a good man. And he wanted to marry her.

———◆———

Watching *Julius Caesar* at the Great *Schauspielhaus* made Henja feel like she was a Roman woman and part of the action. Once the players took the stage, Henja was at the Forum in Rome and not in the theatre. Intermission destroyed that illusion and much more.

"I had a terrible argument with my father today," Albert said to Günther. "I told him I want to quit university to go to work. He thinks I'm crazy."

"I think you're crazy too," Günther replied.

Henja felt the veins in her neck throbbing. "Are you doing this for me?" she asked, digging her fingernails into Albert's arm.

"Yes, Sweetheart. We have to start saving some money. I can't wait another three years until I'm old and grey."

She was horrified by his decision, knowing she would never be able to marry him.

"You better think this over again carefully," Günther said.

"I agree," she said. "Albert dear, I don't have time tonight to discuss everything thoroughly with you, but please give me your word you won't do anything foolish, at least for another week. Günther, please help me persuade him."

"Of course, I completely agree with you," Günther said.

"You two are funny," Albert said. "You''e acting as if you were my executives. Henja the president and Günther the secretary general. But you have to allow me to live my own life."

"Can't you wait a few more days before doing something so irreversible?" Henja asked.

"All right, I can wait for a day or two. But I don't understand why you are making this out to be such a tragedy."

Because she knew it would be. If he abandoned his education she would blame herself for the rest of her life, and she was convinced that he would too. These thoughts ruined the performance for Henja, and led her to a long-deferred decision. When they left the theatre, she said goodbye to the two young men and then gave Albert a lingering kiss which took his breath away.

"Hey," he said, "why so passionate? And why do you have tears in your eyes? Did you get carried away by Marc Antony?"

"Yes," she whispered, and ran off.

As Günther saw her disappear, he told Albert, "You have more luck than brains."

———————

It was the third time he telephoned. Yesterday, only Mrs. Krupnick had answered and said that Henja wasn't feeling well. And yet she had been fine at the theatre just two days earlier. Today he was told again that she couldn't come to the phone. What was the matter with her? He was worried that she was seriously ill.

"Krupnick," a man's voice said.

"May I speak to Henja?"

"I think she ain't home," Mr. Krupnick said, "but hang on."

"Albert?" it was Edith's harsh voice.

"Edith, what in God's name is wrong with Henja? Is she sick? Should I come over right away?"

"No, don't get so excited. Henja had to leave town suddenly."

"That's impossible. Leave for where? Did something happen to her family in Bavaria?"

"I can't explain it on the telephone. Where can we meet?"

He arranged to meet Edith at the Romanisches Café, but was only somewhat relieved. At least she wasn't ill. Yet why hadn't she told him herself what was going on?

———————————

Edith sat down across from Albert. She was wearing a dark suit and, as always, she looked very sophisticated. Even in those first few minutes, as nervous and distressed as he was, he was aware of what a strange impression the two of them must be making. He, a young man of medium height in very sloppy clothes, opposite this tall, well-dressed, older woman. Edith didn't meet his eyes but kept watching the street.

"The time has come, Albert," she said, "to explain a few things to you. I don't relish the job but I'm Henja's friend. And if there is any human being I love, it is Henja. I have to say that first."

"For heaven's sake, talk! What has happened? Henja isn't dead, is she? Edith …"

"No, but as far as you're concerned, Albert, she might as well be."

And then Edith told Henja's story from beginning to end. She glossed over nothing, even things about herself. Albert remained silent. The shock, the horror, the disgust and shame about his own stupidity overwhelmed him so much that he wasn't able to say a word. At the same time, he had the sense of an enormous loss. He loved Henja, and nothing could change that. Even when Edith told him that Henja had decided to marry a gold merchant from Paris old enough to be her father, Albert listened only with half an ear.

"You must understand, Albert," Edith said, "that Henja has given up on everything."

"So have I," he whispered, the first words that had crossed his lips since Edith started talking.

"Nonsense, Albert. You are young, you still have a future. You'll soon get over her. I have to go, but before I forget, here is a letter for you."

She opened her handbag and took out an envelope. Albert quickly tore it open. Across the paper was Henja's meticulous handwriting.

Goodbye, my darling. Farewell and don't be mad at me. I always wanted the best for you and still do, even with this terrible goodbye. It is better this way. Pray for me sometimes, as I will pray for you.
Henja.

The signature was almost illegible. Recognizing that her hand must have been shaking while she wrote it, Albert broke down, sobbing uncontrollably. The other guests in the café wondered what was going on. While Edith hadn't expected such a collapse, she immediately took charge of the situation. She paid the waiter, who had come quickly, and then she took Albert by the arm and supported him until they had hailed a taxi. It was clear to her that she couldn't take Albert home in such a state.

"Take us for a little ride in the *Tiergarten*," she told the cabbie.

Albert kicked his feet as if he were suffering from cramps and kept swallowing compulsively as though he couldn't breathe. She slapped his face twice, trying to shock him out of his fit, forgetting the very reason she had ended up in Berlin and in her profession in the first place – her conviction for aggravated assault the last time she had had tried this old remedy for hysteria.

When Albert came to, his face was lying on Edith's lap, and the taxi was driving down *Siegesallee* – Victory Avenue – for the third time. Albert's cheeks were swollen, but his head was clear again.

"I beg your pardon," Edith said, "but you were hysterical. Where should I drop you off? The way you look now, you don't want your parents to see you."

"It would be best if I could go to my friend Günther's place," he said, giving her the address.

———

Henja tried to make herself presentable though she looked pale and run-down. "How did he take it? Did it hurt him a lot?" she asked.

"He didn't exactly jump with joy," Edith replied. She didn't tell Henja about Albert's breakdown or her response to it.

There was a ring at the door. Both girls assume it must be Henja's betrothed.

"Let him wait a while. I have to put on some more colour," Henja said. "I don't like him, but he is intimidated by me, which is good. I can manage his business and he knows it."

"You'll get used to each other."

The bell rang for the second time, and Henja opened the door and accepted a huge bouquet of red roses from a courier. There was no card; none was necessary because she knew whom had sent the flowers.

Her fiancé, who was indeed coming up the stairs, was surprised. There was his future wife standing in the door, holding a bouquet of roses against her breast, crying her heart out. He was holding another bouquet in his hand and didn't know what to do with it.

"Give those flowers to me," Edith said. "I've earned them."

But Henja's assumption was wrong. Günther had sent the red roses, not Albert.

I X
1930

———◆———

MAX BERG LIFTED UP THE plate of matzos, the flat, almost paper-thin unleavened crackers. "*Ho lachmo anyo, d'akhla avatana …*" he intoned the two thousand-year-old formula of the Passover Seder like Jews all over the world, commemorating the liberation of the ancient Israelites from slavery in Egypt.

"This is the bread of affliction that our fathers ate in Egypt. Therefore, whoever is hungry shall come and eat, whoever is needy shall celebrate with us: This year here, but next year in the land of Israel; this year as slaves, but next year as free people."

However, none of the assembled friends and relatives had any intention of celebrating the feast in the land of Israel in the coming year. These poor slaves in their bondage all looked well-rested and well-fed, while the news from the land of Israel made it clear that those living in freedom still had to slave away very hard. Contributing to their reluctance to follow this pious wish, no doubt, was the fact that none of those present – with the exception of Mr. Berg and his son Albert – could understand the text in its original language.

The company at the table that evening was more numerous than at previous Seders. New faces included a tall Englishman, the employer of the youngest Berg brother, an engineer, and the only one of the family who had been sent to university in England, where he'd stayed. Also at the table were two married couples whom Mr. and Mrs. Berg had met last summer. One of the husbands was Christian while his wife was Jewish; with the other couple, it was the other way around.

There was another face that didn't belong to the family and its closest friends. It was a quiet face, neither beautiful nor ugly. The nose was perhaps the most piquant feature, but all parts together looked to be in harmony, radiating calmness and fortitude and making the face most attractive. Surrounded by brunette hair and terminating in a round but strong-willed chin, Marion's face attracted all eyes, Mrs. Berg's critical eyes in particular. Mrs. Berg hated the idea of a daughter-in-law, though she had to admit that Marion made a very good impression, despite being taller than Albert and hardly speaking a word. Still, she considered that a boy of twenty-four was far too immature to think about marriage.

Mrs. Berg didn't realize that Marion's shyness was caused by the scrutinizing looks of her future mother-in-law, but Albert knew exactly what was going on in the minds of his mother and his prospective bride. He pressed Marion's hand to give her confidence. She thanked him with a little smile, happy that the ceremony made it impossible to have a loud conversation.

Albert's father didn't tolerate private talks while he was singing the traditional melodies from the *Haggadah* in a loud, off-key voice. He observed that Albert and the girl beside him whispering something to each other so he increased the volume, having just arrived at a suitable passage: "And if the Holy One, blessed be He, had not taken our fathers out of Egypt, we and our sons and the sons of our sons would have remained enslaved to Pharaoh. Even if all of us were wise and learned, all of us authorities and scholars, it would still be our duty to tell about the exodus from Egypt ..."

Albert held his index finger to the passage his father had just sung with so much emphasis. Marion became absorbed in studying the poor translation of the text that read so majestically in the original. Albert kept holding Marion's left hand in his right. From her counter-pressure, he knew that she liked it. The girl he had met without any illusions or expectations had somehow become his greatest love.

After Henja, he met many other girls. His boat and his bachelor pad at the back staircase had seen a lot of action, but he soon realized how much Henja had spoiled him. Other girls expected to be pleasured in bed without doing any pleasing themselves. Unused to their passivity, he found them boring, his passion subsiding as quickly as it caught fire.

The previous winter, one particular girl had represented a more dangerous adventure. He had returned home late one night, having spent the evening with Günther at an English conversation group conducted by a nice old lady in her over-decorated home. Albert found it interesting, not only because he wanted to improve his English, but also because the American and English participants in the group had very different values than the young Germans. They didn't pronounce their opinions with the same energy or volume, and they never tried as hard to convince their listeners to adopt their perspectives. Albert admired the easy and relaxed manner of those foreigners as compared with the stiff German decorum he had been brought up with. He often tried to imitate them.

He and Günther were discussing these issues on the way home, new snow crunching under their feet. They didn't notice the bitter cold, they were engaged in such heated conversation. When Albert finally arrived home it was after midnight, so he decided to use the back entrance to avoid waking his parents. He had just turned on the light in the stairwell when he saw Anjuschka, the seventeen-year-old daughter of Jellinek, the janitor, sitting there. Jellinek was a shoemaker by trade, and occasionally repaired soles and heels, but usually he sat in his concierge cubicle, drinking.

To Albert, Anjuschka was still a little girl with a runny nose in dirty blouses, a girl he sometimes saw jumping rope or playing ball in the back yard. When he was sixteen, he had won a doll at a fair, a beautiful doll who could open and shut her eyes. Since he didn't have a sister, he had given it to ten-year-old Anjuschka. Ever since then Anjuschka had secretly worshipped him from afar.

Surprised, he asked her, "What are you doing here so late at night? Why don't you go home?"

"I can't. My mother is in the hospital because Papa has beaten her up. He's over at the pub now, and he has the key to the apartment. I'm really afraid of what he'll do when he comes back."

Albert was shocked. "But you can't sit on the stairs all night. It's cold, and you'll freeze to death wearing such a thin coat."

"So what. I wish I was dead," Anjuschka said dully.

"Don't talk nonsense," Albert said. Impulsively and without giving it much thought he suggested, "Come upstairs with me. Our place is warm."

Anjuschka nodded and obediently followed Albert. He had no idea what to do with her. When he suggested she sleep on the living room sofa, she replied that she would be afraid to be alone in such a big room in a strange apartment..

"But where will you sleep then?"

"In your room."

He put some bedding on his bedroom sofa, then picked up his own pillows and blankets to go sleep in the living room.

Anjuschka looked at him with big expressionless eyes. "Don't you like me?" she said.

He couldn't imagine that such a child could have indecent thoughts, so he just assumed that she must be afraid to be alone.

"Alright," he said, "I will sleep in my own bed, and you can sleep over here on the sofa."

But when he woke up in the night, Anjuschka was lying in bed beside him, naked. She was asleep, or at least pretended to be. Fearful of going to prison for molesting a child, he turned his back on her. At dawn, he shook her awake and ordered her to get dressed and go home immediately.

"But you didn't even touch me," Anjuschka said.

"Of course, not. You're still a child."

"If I'm such a child, how come you wanted me to come to you?" she asked, and for the first time there was expression in her voice.

"Because I felt sorry for you sitting outside in the freezing cold, you stupid brat!" he shouted.

She looked at him with incomprehension, love turning to hate.

A few weeks later, Albert saw her wearing a brown blouse with a swastika badge. She had joined the Hitler Youth. And a swastika had been painted on the white door of the back entrance, in brown paint that smelled of shoe polish. Underneath it were the words *Juda verecke* – Jews drop dead. There was an *r* missing in *verrecke.*

"Who could have done such a thing?" Mrs. Berg asked Albert. He kept his suspicions to himself.

———

"At least the girl has a goal in her life now," Günther had said, when Albert had related Anjuschka's story.

"A glorious goal dedicated to noble ideals," Albert said.

"That's not the point. What else does she have in her life? Beatings from a depraved father at home. Disregard and discrimination outside. She feels that you rejected her as well, so she wants revenge."

"I could understand if she wanted revenge against me, but why against all Jews? What the devil drives a girl of average intelligence to such insanity? That's what I'd like to know."

"Probably she – like many other people – has an inferiority complex. She wants to feel superior to someone and learns from newspapers like the *Stürmer* and *Völkischer Beobachter* that she is innately superior to Jews because she is Aryan."

"If it weren't for the fact that many people in this unfortunate country believe in such ideas, I would laugh my head off."

It wasn't long after this that Albert decided that looking for girlfriends wasn't worth the effort. Henja had been his great love, but now that was over. His life was botched and finished. Had it not been for the fact that it looks strange when a man always sits by himself in the theatre, or while eating a huge banana split with whipped cream and chocolate sprinkles at the American Bar on *Kurfürstendamm*, and had he not wanted company on his boat in the summer, he would have given up all thought of female companionship. But there were certain things one needed that he resolved to accept without sentimentality and without any effort.

One day, when he was feeling like a fifth wheel, as usual, with Manfred and Erika, he intoned tragically, "Is your girlfriend still available, Erika?"

Caught off guard, she responded, "Yes. In fact, I keep telling Manfred that the two of you are so well-suited to each other."

But at his first meeting with Marion, the first Christian girl he had ever been involved with, things got off to a very bad start. Albert found her boring and behaved artificially in her presence. She, on the other hand, found him aggressive, arrogant and boastful. After an hour at the dance hall the four had gone to, Marion declared that she had a headache and wanted to go home. Albert offered to accompany her. She declined politely but very firmly. More to keep up appearances rather than with any real interest, he asked her where she lived. He also learned her full name: Marion Goldstein.

"You're the first non-Jewish Goldstein I've ever met" he said, surprised.

"What gave you the idea that I'm not Jewish?" she asked.

Manfred and Erika burst out laughing. "I guess Albert can't imagine that my best friend is Jewish," Erika said.

Manfred added, "Or maybe it's because Marion doesn't make as much of a fuss about being Jewish as you do."

Albert felt like the butt of an April fool's joke. To escape the laughter of the other couple, he asked Marion for one more dance. Erika had advised her to wear shoes with low heels, which meant that her eyes were level with his. Unintentionally, they looked at each other long and deeply. Albert wasn't the worst dancer, though not the best, but they danced easily and harmoniously together. He felt that the unnatural tension and nervousness had left him, giving way to a happier mood. He hummed the refrain of the dance tune, "Yes, we have no bananas," which a band member was singing in a hoarse voice.

"An awfully stupid song, isn't it?" Marion said.

"Yes, but I think from now on I'll be fond of it," he answered with a grin.

She lifted her head to see if he had meant what she thought by this remark. He no longer seemed so disagreeable. Her headache disappeared, and she stayed for the rest of the evening.

When Albert accompanied her home later, he unintentionally addressed her with the informal *you*, and she responded the same way. Neither was certain whether it would make sense to continue their acquaintance, but they made a date to visit the wave pool in Halensee on the weekend, Albert's routine with every girl he met. That place provided a discrete opportunity to observe the ladies.

He had never realized what a poor impression he made upon the women he'd brought to Halensee. Although he had well-formed shoulders and strong arms, his stomach protruded more than his age warranted. Marion patted his belly lightly and said, "You have to get rid of that paunch, young man." Before he could answer, she ran to the diving board and performed an elegant, first-class dive. She was an excellent swimmer. With some discomfort, he realized that he would never catch up with her in the water.

On their way back to town, he noticed her shoes. "Do you always wear such low heels?" he asked.

"No, I borrowed them from my sister," she said.

"Why?"

"Because people say that a man always feels uncomfortable with a woman taller than him," Marion said. She could never tell a lie, something Albert had yet to discover.

"Would you be comfortable being seen with me if you wore high heels?" he asked provocatively.

Her embarrassed smile illuminated her face. "I wouldn't rule out that possibility."

Her openness made Albert embarrassed in turn. Though he had initiated their relationship, Erika's talk about her friend had never really interested him so he'd asked nothing about her before they met. But apparently Marion had been fully informed about him.

"In that case, my Aphrodite arisen from the foam, please wear your own shoes in future. Any man who gets an inferiority complex from two or three centimetres isn't worth much."

"Don't be such a show-off, with your classical education," Marion said, and Albert deflated like a tire with a leaking valve.

Marion was sitting beside him now at the Seder table, but the question prescribed by the Passover ritual, "Why is this night different from all other nights?" had acquired a new meaning. How strange it was that his original aversion to her had ended the moment he had learned that she was Jewish. It was completely absurd; he could not understand it. If he could be prejudiced towards Jews, he had no right to blame anti-Semites for feeling the opposite. For what were the Jews, really? A race? But there are at least twenty different races among them! A nation? Maybe so. Was this why people like him felt this exaggerated feeling of community? Or was it merely the result of persecution and slander? What had Heinrich Heine called it? "The thousand-year family malady, the plague carried along from the Nile Valley." Heine – now there was a torn human being, with his love for Germany and the intellectual heritage of his Judaism.

Like Heine, Albert kept trying to find a synthesis between his homeland and his heritage. No one else around this table, including the two interfaith couples, seemed to be perplexed the way he was. On the other hand, except for himself and his father, none of those present had the distinctive Mediterranean looks which Germans commonly associated with Jews.

Mr. Chessman was a tall, lanky Englishman. Had he not asked for *chrain* when he wanted the horseradish, no one would have thought that he was Jewish. Uncle Bruno, with his light-blue eyes, blond moustache, and ruddy complexion looked like the driver of the brewery wagon in the *Schultheiss* beer ad. Professor Levy looked like *Turnvater* Jahn, the founder of the patriotic gymnasts in the nineteenth century, and Mr. Goldschmidt had the oriental visage of Sun Yat-sen. Marion gave the impression of being exactly who she was – an athletic German girl – while Hilde looked more like a Swede or a Dane than a Berliner. Nothing set these people apart from any other race. Albert was absorbed in thought as he dipped two hard-boiled eggs in salt water and ate them.

"Don't stuff yourself with eggs," Marion admonished him. "Leave some room for the other courses."

He woke up and picked up some fragments of the conversation which had begun around the long table.

"I always said that it was Chancellor Stresemann who made us socially acceptable in the world again," said Zuckermann, the crate manufacturer. Albert recognized at once that by *us* he meant Germany.

"Yes, if only he hadn't died in September we could have avoided the latest crisis."

"What do you think of the new man, this Brüning?"

"He's a Papist, and I never expect anything good from the Papists," Mr. Karsten said. He was a Protestant.

"But on the contrary, the Centre Party people are the only ones not leaning towards extremism," Mr. Goldschmidt said.

Professor Levy declared, "At least they don't like to go in for adventures."

"Who?" one of the ladies could be heard, "Marlene Dietrich? She speaks volumes – just with her legs."

The conversation was interrupted when the doorbell rang. It kept on ringing loudly. Anna ran to the hall and opened the door. Then she cried, "Help!"

All the men got up and ran to the hall. The ladies followed. A man was hanging onto Anna's shoulders, swaying like a reed in the wind. The Bergs recognized Major (retired) von Müller. Major von Müller was dead-drunk.

"But Major, you're on the wrong floor. You must go one storey higher."

Anna, frightened but giggling, was released from the arms of Major von Müller. But the Major didn't budge.

"Lemme go," he yelled. "Go away, everybody!"

Waving his arms about, he looked at the people around him with dazed and expressionless eyes. Eventually his confused brain realized where he was. "Damn pack of Jews!" he yelled, stomping out through the door. In the stairway, just behind the door he had slammed, they could hear him vomiting.

The only person who was really disturbed by the scene was Mr. Karsten. The others resumed their seats and continued with the Seder.

Two days later, the von Müllers' maid arrived with a business card and the message that the Major wished to talk with them. Von Müller appeared wearing a frock coat, transformed back into a perfect gentleman, a well-educated officer of the Old Prussian school. He clicked his heels.

"Wanted to apologize for the day before yesterday. My nerves, you know, my nerves. Never know what I say or do. Think I disrupted a family celebration. Most embarrassing. Extremely unpleasant. Sincerely beg your pardon."

"It's a pleasure," Mr. Berg said, who was amused by it all. "I only have one request. If you should have another bout of … nerves and wish to vent your feelings, could you do it in two parts? For example, would you say 'Jews' and 'damned pack' separately rather than conflating them into a single term of abuse? You see, the word 'Jew' is not an insult to me. I'm very proud to be a Jew. It's the combination that makes the word seem unattractive."

"Did I say something like that?" Major von Müller went as pale as the wall. "That's impossible. Totally against my nature. Could never forgive myself. Owe my whole existence to a Jew. Can't live on my pension. Wife and two sons. Officer, you understand? Can't sell shoe-laces. Wine sales rep more appropriate. Boss in Mainz, a Jew, very nice gentleman. Has introduced me. Never had such thoughts. Most embarrassing. Am ashamed. Please forget it. Once again, apologies."

"What did the Major have to say in his defence?" Mrs. Berg asked her husband.

"He explained to me where he gets his alcohol. He's a sales rep for a Jewish wine merchant. The bottles are his samples."

"Actually, I feel sorry for the man," Mrs. Berg said, "He can't cope with life since there isn't a real army anymore."

"Is that why he must get drunk all the time?"

"What else can he do?"

"Write his memoirs," Mr. Berg said.

———•———

The residents of the Bergs' apartment building had two inducements to regard themselves as aristocratic. One was the statue of the Venus de Milo, which stood in the middle of the garden separating the front and rear residences. The other was the elevator. While one might argue that reproducing such a famous statue as a lawn ornament was tasteless, there could be no argument about the elevator, even though its existence mainly served the purpose of justifying higher rental fees. That's why it was mahogany-panelled, with plate glass mirrors in all three walls, and equipped with an upholstered bench covered in red velvet. The bench reduced the space for the conveyance of passengers to a minimum.

In addition to Mr. Jellinek, who had to operate the elevator, there was room for only two slim people.

Mr. Jellinek pulled the wire cable that set the water pressure mechanism in motion and also served as a brake. Albert and Hans-Ulrich von Müller went up with Jellinek. Twenty-year-old Hans-Ulrich was the older of the two sons of Major von Müller. When he was still a boy, he had always greeted Albert, who was four years older, with a polite "Good day." Now, he couldn't very well greet a Jew with "Heil Hitler!" so since he was wearing his brown Stormtrooper uniform, he treated Albert as if he didn't exist. Given the lack of room in the elevator cage, this was a remarkable achievement.

There was a bang, and a sudden jerky downward movement. The grinding sound of the safety system was heard for one moment and then the car stopped between the second and third floor, immobilized.

"The cable she's busted. Now we are trapped," said Jellinek, whose German lessons under Emperor Franz Joseph had cost him a leg, which he lost on the field of honour in Galicia along with most of his regiment. His wooden prosthesis gave him chronic pain, which he tried to kill with liquor; it also hurt his wife and daughter, whom he would occasionally beat with it. On the other hand, it earned him money when he used it to polish hardwood floors for the building's tenants.

"Why aren't you pressing the alarm button?" the von Müller boy asked.

Jellinek muttered something in Czech. He didn't think that stupid question deserved an answer.

Albert answered on his behalf. "The alarm rings in his cubicle. Since he's not there now, no one will hear it. We must wait till someone is going up the stairs, and then we'll have to shout."

"Quite a mess," young von Müller said.

"Yes, *Gruppenführer*. Prepare to starve to death in the company of two inferior races," Albert said, gratified to see Hans-Ulrich blushing.

Jellinek felt obligated to give young Mr. Berg an explanation. After all, the Bergs tipped him better than all the other tenants. "My Anna also listened to them people and joined up, but I polished her behind, so now she stay home. I tell her politics is only for rich people, not the poor."

"What I don't understand," Albert said, "is how your daughter was accepted into such an exclusive club of Germans. You are Czechs, which means Slavs. Since Mr. von Müller and his friends have promoted themselves into the master race, Anjuschka doesn't belong with them."

Hans-Ulrich struggled hard with himself. In the stuck elevator cage, he couldn't apply his natural talent for fist fights. Moreover, they were two against one, and the brave militant spirit of National Socialists worked best in groups. On the other hand, he couldn't allow himself to endure these insults silently, although everyone except his father knew it was a waste of time to get involved in discussions with Jews. He had even gone down to those people to apologize for a little episode after he had a few drinks. How could an aristocrat and Prussian officer lower himself to that level? It was a disgrace.

He decided to address Jellinek instead.

"You can be sure, Jellinek, that we checked Anna's background very carefully. Your family comes from the Sudetenland, and that is a land of German heritage. Anna is blond and blue-eyed and of pure race in every respect."

Albert nodded. "She is certainly racy but there are people around who are even blonder and have even bluer eyes. For example, a certain Miss Levy I know."

Hans-Ulrich ignored the heckling. He wasn't finished.

"Your conduct towards Anna and your refusal to let the girl fight for the liberation of Germany has been noted, Mr. Jellinek. You will be sorry. That's all I can say."

"You can kiss my ass," Jellinek said.

"From whom do you want to liberate Germany, Mr. von Müller?" Albert said

"From you and your kind," Hans-Ulrich said, biting his tongue because he had allowed himself to answer the damned Jew.

Albert wanted to get to the bottom of this disease. Young von Müller had always been a nice boy and had turned into a smart, good-looking young man. Günther's theory about racism being due to an inferiority complex surely couldn't apply to such a fellow.

"I am not aware," he said, "of having occupied Germany in any way. Perhaps you could explain this to me."

Having started the conversation in such close proximity, Hans-Ulrich saw no alternative but to continue it. "I don't mean you personally," he said, also trying to remain calm and objective. "But the Jews are a foreign people that have plunged us into disaster. The Jewish Bolshevist conspiracy is trying to bring Germany under its rule before taking over the whole world. That's what we're fighting. Jewish power in Germany must be broken."

"This rhetoric is commonplace. But be completely honest: Do you believe it?"

Albert was appalled. He sometimes bought a copy of the *Völkischer Beobachter* to inform himself of what the Nazis espoused, but he had been certain that normal people would not take such fantasies seriously. Intelligent people, educated people, couldn't possibly believe such nonsense. *The Jews* and *Bolshevism* were diametrically opposed worlds. Jews didn't produce conspiracies and did not constitute a power. In Germany, they represented a very small part of the population and wanted nothing more than to live in peace. But here was a well-educated boy of average intelligence from a decent home. His father hadn't always been a drunk. How could such a boy regurgitate meaningless slogans with the power of genuine conviction?

"Whether Germany is facing disaster is obviously a matter of opinion. My father concurs with that, though he wouldn't agree with your theory as to the cause of this process of deterioration. Also, his idea of 'deterioration' wouldn't be the same as yours. But leaving that issue aside, I can't see what it has to do with the six hundred thousand Jews who form less than one percent of the German population."

"Germany's misfortune is that this small group of people has captured top positions everywhere and has corroded the essence of Germany with its Jewish character."

"I don't understand your logic. On the one hand, you say that Jews are an inferior race, and on the other hand you argue that they have captured influential positions."

"It is a fact that Jewish influence is making itself felt everywhere," Hans-Ulrich insisted.

"In my opinion, such influence would be very good for the German people. Sadly, that is not true, with the exception of the fact that the foundations of Christianity are in fact Jewish."

"Very true," Hans-Ulrich said. "You see, there are things on which we both agree. Christianity has softened up the Germanic nature of our people—"

"Perhaps civilized would be a better word," Albert interrupted him.

"No, I say softened up, and that we intend to change as well."

"Is that right? Then you should start with your own name. 'Hans' comes from the Hebrew name 'Johannes' and means 'God is gracious'. I suspect you will need a large portion of God's grace!"

"Oh, I never knowed that," Jellinek said. He had been listening silently but wanted to contribute something himself to the conversation. At that moment, steps were heard on the stairs. The three trapped passengers knocked on the walls of the elevator and shouted.

"Go get the fire department!" Jellinek yelled.

"Why?" the man on the stairs asked. It was Dr. Schneidel, the dentist. "There is no fire. A mechanic would probably be better."

"It take hours for a mechanic to arrive," Albert said. "The fire department will be quicker."

"Alright," Dr. Schneidel said, "I will telephone right away."

It still took a quarter of an hour before the fire department came. They broke open the door to the elevator shaft on the third floor and pulled the elevator up with two thick ropes, allowing the captives to crawl out. Then Jellinek went to fetch a mechanic.

X
1931

———

A RAILWAY STATION REPRESENTS SOMETHING final, either a conclusion or a new beginning, a port from which one sails off into the distance or into which one arrives
from a distance. Any station that doesn't symbolize a new beginning or an absolute
end, that has trains rolling through in both directions and is only an intermediate
point for boarding and disembarking, has failed its calling. *Friedrichstrasse* Station
was such an interlude on rails. Albert couldn't conjure up a feeling of departure,
not even a temporary one, when he leaned out of the window to press Marion's
hand once more when the first tiny jolt indicated that the train was starting to
move.

How sentimental women are, Albert thought, noticing that she had tears in
her eyes. "Surely you'll manage without me for two months. Stay true to me, I beg
of you," he said.

"You monkey," Marion laughed, despite her tears. "Don't you fool around with
any English girls, and write to me as soon as you get there. Alright?"

"Will do. Good bye, darling!"

"I wish you success, my sweet boy."

Their hands parted. The train's speed increased as Marion stood on the platform, waving her pink handkerchief. Albert pulled his own handkerchief from
his pocket and waved back. When they lost sight of each other, he closed the
window. He carefully folded the white square to ensure that the corners peeking
above his pocket would not reveal the bright-red smudges from Marion's lipstick,
then he looked around at his fellow-passengers. All six seats of the second-class
compartment were occupied. Marion had been right, as usual. She had insisted

that he reserve a corner seat in advance, which guaranteed him a comfortable place at the window.

The elderly lady with the unfriendly face directly across from him was obviously English. This was apparent not only from the *Daily Mail* she was holding but also from her posture and her clothes. More interesting were the two bearded gentlemen beside her, both of whom wore turbans. They talked with each other in a language he didn't recognize, laughing frequently. Albert caught himself grinning in response.

The young girl sitting beside him made him uneasy. She had hands with protruding knuckles and thumbs that bent backwards, a physical trait he found disturbing. Those hands constantly wandered around the clasp of her handbag, as if a valuable treasure or a great secret were hidden there that required constant safeguarding. They made him nervous. He compared them with Marion's beautiful, expressive hands whose firm pressure and tender touch he would be missing for eight weeks. All he could see of the final passenger was a big stomach and plump thighs. The head of the man who owned those ample features was hidden by the upholstered headrests, and also by the young lady with the ugly hands, who was bent forward, staring at the handsome Indian across from her. The Indian's beard failed to disguise his youth. He looked back at the girl with large dark eyes under heavy eyelashes. Albert wouldn't have been surprised to see the young lady start swaying from side to side like a hypnotized cobra, but the spell was eventually broken.

To Albert's amazement, the unfriendly English woman addressed him. "Do you speak English?" When he said yes, she asked him to change seats with her. Albert had no objection because he was going against the direction of travel, but he was puzzled because most of the ladies he knew complained bitterly when they had to sit backwards. Then he learned the real reason for her request when the young Indian said, "I hope you don't mind sitting next to a primitive coloured man."

Albert was taken aback. It hadn't occurred to him that the woman objected to sitting next to his neighbour from the shores of the Ganges River. When the colour flared in her pale face he realized that the Indian had hit the nail on the head.

Anger and indignation rose up inside him against her narrow-minded contempt and he answered with more emphasis than necessary, "The only primitive people are those who fancy themselves to be better than others."

Albert introduced himself to the young man, Ranjit, and shook hands with him ostentatiously. The two turbaned gentlemen each produced business cards and presented them to Albert with polite smiles. Albert in turn offered the card of the company that was sending him to England, a card on which his own name appeared only in the bottom left corner. Mr. Berg's illness had obliged his son to enter in his footsteps, finding work with the same firm. Albert had become a *shopkeeper* after all.

The vessel travelling from Hoek van Holland to Harwich might have been called a ferry but it rolled and rocked like any other ship. Albert felt as sick as a dog. He had the lower bunk in the narrow cabin where he lay awake; Ranjit had the bunk above him. Albert wondered whether his companion was seasick too. If it hadn't been such a cold rainy night he might have found relief on deck so he wouldn't have had to worry about vomiting in the airless cabin. But eventually he must have fallen asleep because the next thing he knew, a chubby English stewardess was shaking him awake.

"Your tea, Sir," she said, putting a large stoneware cup in his hand. It was filled with very black steaming liquid. On the saucer was a big round biscuit. Albert looked at his watch. It was only a few minutes before five. He could imagine many urgent reasons for waking him up at five in the morning but hot tea wasn't one of them.

"Good morning," Ranjit said, bending down over the edge of his upper bunk. He also had a cup of tea in his hand.

"Good morning," Albert answered. "Did the stewardess wake you up with tea also? Silly, isn't it?"

"Indeed, the customs and traditions of the British Isles seem very strange at first. But you will discover that some are very useful. This tea, for example, will alleviate your nausea, and you will hold out much better till breakfast."

"When is breakfast?"

"There is no breakfast on the ferry," Ranjit said. "You'll have breakfast on the train from Harwich to London. It is still two hours before we're in Harwich. I've done this trip twice already."

Albert drank his tea. It was strong, sweet and bitter at the same time. He also ate the biscuit. To his surprise, he actually did feel better. The Indian with the light-blue turban dangled his long dark-brown legs, which stuck out of his pyjama pants, over the edge of the bed. He seemed to be too tall for the short bed.

"Tell me," Albert said, "do you wear that thing on your head all the time?"

"Yes, my religion demands it. I'm a Sikh."

Albert had read something about Sikhs. He remembered that they also kept daggers in their turbans, under which their hair is very long. He would have liked to learn more about the stranger's own customs and traditions but he was reluctant to ask him about his religion, so he changed the conversation to a more general topic.

"Was this your first trip to Germany?"

"Yes," Ranjit answered. "My friend and I spent time in both Germany and Austria. We were thrilled by your country."

"In what way?"

"The friendliness of the people and the beauty of nature."

"You found the people friendly?" Albert asked, surprised.

"The atmosphere is very different in Germany from Holland, Belgium and Switzerland."

"What do you mean?"

"There is no prejudice in Germany. Nice young girls in the best hotels were happy to dance with us. We spent some very pleasant days and met good people. That would be impossible in England."

Albert suspected that those 'nice young girls' had really been fifty-mark hookers but all he said was, "I saw from your business card that you live in England. Are you studying over there?"

"Yes and no," Ranjit said. "I mean, officially I'm a student. At least, that's what my father believes. My father is a Sardar, which means he is nobility. We live in

Gujranwala, which is in the Punjab." He pronounced these names as if assuming that Albert would know exactly where they were.

"And what do you do unofficially, if I may ask?" Albert said.

"I'm learning to fly," said the son of the Sardar from Gujranwala in the Punjab.

"I beg your pardon? Do you mean you're learning to fly an aeroplane?" Now Albert was really interested.

"Yes. You see, soon the time will come when my homeland can dispense with the nobility. But then it will need a lot of good pilots."

"You mean for an air force, if I understand correctly?" Albert asked.

"You understand correctly. We will need airmen to fight against the Brits."

"Isn't that a little unfair, to have the British help you acquire skills you intend to use against them?" Albert hadn't meant to say what he was thinking out loud but the words just slipped out.

"Unfair? How can any action against the British be unfair when the future of India is at stake? And when have they ever treated us decently?"

"To be honest," Albert said, "I'm not very knowledgeable about this subject. You're probably right."

He got out of his bunk and began to shave, using the small wash-basin, pondering the young Indian's indignation. If pompous Englishwomen like the one on the train didn't behave so rudely, or if British girls were more generous and if the British in general weren't so arrogant, perhaps he wouldn't hate them so much?'

Albert got dressed and said goodbye to the Sikh, who urged Albert to visit him in Welwyn Garden City. Albert promised that he would and then went up on deck.

It was still raining, but it was no longer torrential. It had already become an English rain: light, thin, and civilized. It was no longer cold, so Albert's hardy raincoat kept him warm and dry enough, but his thoughts were as gloomy as the weather. Seagulls accompanied the ship, the only white spots in a completely grey symphony of water and sky. He could only assume that if English seagulls weren't brave enough to venture out in the rain they would forget how to fly. The sun had to be out there somewhere, but he found it impossible to tell the four cardinal directions. A dark stripe on the horizon must be the coast of England. It didn't look very inviting, but why should it? No one had invited him.

Albert stayed on deck, brooding until the ship entered the port of Harwich. The wooden planks laid from the dock to the ferry, to allow passengers to disembark, ended right in front of the long train waiting to be boarded. Albert didn't see any porters; instead the passengers lugged their baggage themselves from the ship to the train. Because he had checked his heavy baggage straight through from Hoek van Holland before he had boarded the ferry, Albert just picked up his suitcase and joined the queue. This railway station, or port, or whatever it was, had neither barricades nor wickets. There were no officials or uniforms to be seen and no one asked him whether he had a ticket. He boarded a shabby compartment marked Smoking. In Berlin the word *smoking* meant something much more elegant: a tuxedo jacket. The whole train looked as though it were about fifty years older than the German railway. So far England, centre of an enormous empire, hadn't impressed him at all.

He wondered why he was alone in the compartment. A few suitcases filled the luggage racks, and two coats had been laid on the seats. No one could be seen on the platform, so he concluded that his fellow passengers must be in the dining car. Albert asked a gentleman standing in the aisle where it was. "Either way," the man answered. The train must have more than one dining car. In Germany, there would have been a bell notifying passengers to take their seats for the first breakfast serving, then for the second and third. Perhaps the practical English had enough dining cars to feed all the hungry mouths on the train at the same time.

For the first time in his life, Albert ate fried sausages at seven o'clock in the morning. In the midst of his enormous breakfast he didn't even notice that the train had started to move; the English wheels might be old, but clearly they were well lubricated.

Liverpool Station in London also seemed to be old, but with such a crowd of people rushing about it seemed like a public assembly. A porter finally showed up and addressed him in Chinese. At least, that's what he thought at first, hearing "*Hairsyaluggitch.*" Albert thought he spoke English fluently, yet he had no clue what the man was saying. An older lady who had been in his compartment came to his assistance, explaining to him slowly and clearly that the porter wanted to know where his baggage was. He gave the man his baggage stub as he'd seen other passengers do. Then he waited to see what would happen next.

He didn't have to wait long. In one third of the time it would have taken at a German railway station, the porter came running back with all his baggage on a cart and pushed it to the taxi stand. Albert was already resigned to the fact that his English comprehension was insufficient to penetrate the mysteries of the Cockney accent. Therefore, he decided to take a handful of coins from his pocket to present it to the porter. There was no point in asking how much he owed the man. The porter and the taxi driver had an animated conversation. Judging by their laughter, it must have been hilarious; sadly, Albert didn't understand a word. Then the porter took a few coins from Albert's open hand, threw the last suitcase into the baggage space next to the cabbie's seat, and closed the door.

The cabbie turned around and asked in reasonably good French, "Where should I take you?"

Albert was flabbergasted to learn that London taxi drivers spoke French, but he responded in the same language. "I want to go to the Regent Palace Hotel near Piccadilly Circus. But why are you speaking French? And where did you learn it?"

"Four years in France with the British Army – that's where I learned it," the cabbie replied. "Aren't you French?"

"No," Albert said.

"You look like a typical Frenchman," the cab driver said.

That's funny, Albert thought. *In Germany, I'm a Jew. In England, I'm a Frenchman.*

The taxi drove through the city. Gradually the streets became wider, but traffic still moved very slowly and the taxi had trouble getting through. With great interest, Albert looked at the crowds milling about the streets in the light drizzle. There were more men wearing uniforms here than in Berlin. The men not in uniform all wore dark suits, Khaki raincoats or black overcoats, and bowler hats; most carried umbrellas. All things he didn't own. His beret made him feel almost exotically dressed when the cabbie dropped him at the hotel's revolving door.

After the receptionist had found his name in the list of reservations, he glanced at Albert and said in French, "Please complete the registration form."

Albert shrugged, resigned to playing the role of a Frenchman until he bought himself a bowler hat and an umbrella.

———

Following a classified ad posted two months earlier, a Mr. Henry Bradd-Smith had responded with impressive bank references. He was interested in representing the Berg firm in England, Scotland, Wales and Ireland. Max Berg had decided to leave the decision up to his son. He wanted to see whether the boy could act independently and prudently.

In his own mind, Albert had dubbed Henry Bradd-Smith – with his distinguished double-barrelled name – "Mr. Bratwurst." The man turned out to be "nonexistent in the sense of bourgeois convention," in the words of Albert's favourite poet, Christian Morgenstern. Following a short telephone call during which neither party understood the other very well, Mrs. Bratwurst hurried into the hotel room on the afternoon of Albert's arrival like a four-masted schooner in full sail, pulling a little rowboat named Henry behind her. And after Henry Bratwurst sat down in the only comfortable chair in Albert's hotel room, his wife Ethel did all the talking.

Since she couldn't find a seat that accommodated her girth, she planted herself on the bed. She was tall, broad, and fat everywhere. Only her face was elongated, with a sharp nose between watery-blue eyes. In contrast, Henry was short and skinny, though he had a round baby face. His crescent-shaped moustache looked as if it had been glued on. He wore thick glasses through which his wide eyes stared out innocently at the world.

"We need a trial run to see whether it is worthwhile for us to go into business together," Ethel said. Albert wasn't sure whether this was the royal *we* or whether she just used the first person plural to be polite to her husband.

"We need to consider the situation first," Ethel said, without waiting to see whether Albert had anything to contribute to the conversation. "Unfortunately, you've brought your collection here at the worst possible time. September is too late for showing winter models but too early for the summer season. We could still try to offer something for Christmas if your factory can deliver on short notice. Another problem is that you're from Germany, and there is still a lot of consumer resistance to German products. So we must describe your merchandise as coming from the Continent, not from Germany."

"More than twelve years after the end of the war?"

"Yes, Sir," Ethel said, adding, "It is good that you look like a Frenchman – that may help us, although the French are not that popular either."

Albert wondered who the English liked, if both the Germans and the French were so unpopular.

Ethel continued implacably. "We will look at some of the samples. Then we can tell what stores and what price categories they will suit. But to show them properly, we must book one or two models. You didn't bring one with you, did you?"

"No," Albert said. "How much does one have to pay here for such a lady?"

"A guinea a day."

"A guinea? What's that?"

Her husband made a movement as though to say something, but she cut him short with an abrupt, "Be quiet, Henry." Henry immediately shrunk back like a little boy who had been disobedient. Had she used a vulgar expression such as *Shut up*, or raised her voice, it wouldn't have been as embarrassing as this almost incidental proof of her absolute dominance over the man.

"One g-u-i-n-e-a," Ethel spelled out the word, "is one pound and one shilling; that is to say, twenty-one shillings." She added, "We shall meet tomorrow in our office to get things organized. Henry will pick you up at ten o'clock. By the way, our commission is seven and a half percent of all sales."

Albert considered. How should he figure out seven and a half percent of all those pounds, shillings, and pence? Mathematics had always been his weakest subject. Ten percent he could calculate with ease, but that would be much too much commission. Half of ten percent would be easy enough, but seven and a half was just too complicated. More for that reason than for any business consideration, he said, "Five percent would actually be much more appropriate."

Ethel, who had just taken one of the samples from the wardrobe and was holding it against her own massive body in front of the mirror, turned around. "You're not as stupid as you look." Apparently this was her idea of humour. "We'll talk about this later, but first we must see whether we can do business at all. Come on, Henry, we're leaving. We'll see you in the morning, Mr. Berg."

Albert stood up and shook Henry's pale, flaccid hand, and Ethel too shook his hand briefly. Albert wasn't a weakling, but it seemed as if his hand had been caught in a punch press. He felt unspeakably sorry for Henry Bratwurst.

At ten o'clock sharp next morning, Henry showed up and skilfully directed Albert and his suitcase into a taxi. Albert was surprised first of all that Henry could talk, and secondly that he could understand every word. On the other hand, he had also understood every word Ethel had said the day before, so things were not as bad as he'd feared where English was concerned. Perhaps his ear just had needed to become accustomed to the London dialect.

"Mrs. Bradd-Smith has already arranged an appointment for you," Henry said. "At twelve o'clock we will call at one of the largest department stores in London." Albert thought it comical that a husband would refer to his wife by her surname and wouldn't simply say *My wife.*

Their taxi passed a magnificent park set back from a wide street. On the opposite side the houses were twice as high as houses in Berlin.

"We're going to Kensington. That's where we live, and the office is in our flat," Henry said. Albert said nothing, absorbed in the sights of London. Last night he had been too tired to leave the hotel.

"Do the girls in Germany still have thick legs?" Henry asked, smiling under his moustache.

Albert was so surprised he almost fell off the seat. Skinny Bratwurst noticed girls and their legs, and he had once been to Germany. If Ethel heard him, she probably would have grabbed him and put him across her knee.

"When were you in Germany?"

"Right after the war, with the army. I was a captain in the paymaster corps. I only resigned three years ago."

Albert thought, *Resigned is the right word. He is still resigned. With that wife of his, he has no other choice.* But he couldn't imagine the man as an officer. Perhaps he had married that mountain of a woman after his military service ended, no longer interested in the legs of young girls.

"You found the legs of German girls too thick?" he said.

"Oh yes, but I love plump women."

Albert looked more closely at Mr. Bratwurst. The man wasn't unhappy at all. He probably needed to be dominated by a woman mentally as well as physically. Perhaps he adored her strength because of his own weakness. He might even enjoy getting a spanking from her!

As if Henry had guessed that Albert was thinking about Ethel, he said, "You don't know us well yet, but I can assure you that you'll not find any better agents in England. My wife" – this time Henry didn't say Mrs. Bradd-Smith – "is just phenomenal. You'll see."

"Yes, I have already seen some evidence of this," Albert said.

The Bradd-Smiths had a fifth-floor apartment. In the room they had made into an office, Ethel was on the telephone. She seemed to be working on introducing Albert to another firm that afternoon. Albert overheard part of the conversation and had to admit she knew her business. A tall, slender girl stood by a window. She had a splendid figure and the stupidest face Albert had seen for a long time, except on a window mannequin.

"This is Gladys," Ethel said after she put the receiver down. "I have asked Gladys to help us today. We must hurry because we have to be on Oxford Street at twelve. Gladys, get undressed and try on this red suit to start with …."

Ethel took a woollen suit from the suitcase which Henry had already opened. Everything happened so quickly that Albert had no chance to say anything. Gladys undressed in the middle of the room. Albert knew that she was a professional model, but he still couldn't understand why she was not embarrassed to stand in the front of two men wearing nothing but a bra and a girdle. But perhaps Albert couldn't be taken for a full man.

Ethel seemed to be of a different opinion. She suddenly said, "Henry, turn around, my dear."

Henry did a military about-face, pulled a chair into a corner and immersed himself in a magazine. Albert couldn't tell whether he was concentrating more on the horseracing pages or the photographs of young girls.

———

Albert received his first orders. He knew that he would be given credit for his proficiency at home, but he had done almost nothing himself. Mrs. Bratwurst had conducted the whole thing. Gladys and Agnes, another young lady with a good figure, had stalked around with choreographed movements in various buyers' offices. Henry had done the pricing calculations and the currency conversion. Albert had just stood around with a bored face. Instead of thinking about how important the British market was to the company to which he had owed his daily bread ever since he was born, he let his mind wander over all kinds of irrelevant subjects.

Glad that they were looking after his business with such energy and enterprise, he signed a three-month contract with Mr. and Mrs. Bratwurst. Henry had assured him that it would be extremely easy to calculate a commission of exactly seven and a half percent on all direct sales. So Albert had ultimately agreed to that percentage, which he recognized that they deserved. By the time the contract had been signed, his own uselessness had become quite evident.

"You know, my dear," Ethel – who called everybody 'dear' or 'love' – said to Albert, "Why don't you explore London? We can manage without you. You should go to the theatre too. After all, no city has such plays as London."

Albert wanted to answer that other cities in the world had also heard of the theatre but during the three days of his stay he had made an odd discovery. Everyone he was introduced to seemed to be convinced that nothing in the world could be any better, more solid, more perfect or more beautiful than what existed in England – except for the weather. Conversations always went the same way.

"Is this your first visit to England?"

"Yes."

In any other country, the visitor would have been asked how he liked it. But such a question was never asked. The British didn't care whether visitors liked their country or not.

"And where did you learn English?"

"In Germany."

"Are you German?"

"Yes." It had taken a trip abroad for him to become a German. When Ethel had asked him the same questions during their very first meeting, his answer had been different. He had explained that he was a Jew born in Germany. Ethel had looked at him with big eyes and said, "But that means you're German. We have Jews here, too and they're all British. Disraeli was a Jew, and he was the greatest British statesman of all."

Henry had nodded and allowed himself to remark, "We could use the likes of him now, instead of Ramsay MacDonald."

"Henry, my dear, one doesn't talk about politics in the presence of foreigners," Ethel had admonished, silencing him as always. This short conversation had taught Albert more about the British than he could have learned by reading volumes.

The fourth and last question he was usually asked depended on whether it was a man or a woman he was talking to. A man usually took a pack of cigarettes from his pocket and asked, "Do you smoke?" A woman, on the other hand, wanted to know whether he had already seen one of London's famous tourist attractions.

"Were you already at …" followed by a place which allowed Albert to guess what the woman's personal interests were. In this way, he had been informed of all the most important sights: Buckingham Palace, Whitehall with the Royal Guard standing around like their own monuments, the Houses of Parliament, Westminster Abbey, the British Museum, St. Paul's Cathedral, Hyde Park, Soho and many other places. But no one would have asked him whether he had been to Whitechapel. His visit there happened by accident and on his own.

After Ethel had given him leave, he did indeed look around in London. Had anyone asked what impressed him the most, he wouldn't have been able to answer. He came from a big city himself, yet he felt there was a significant difference between London and Berlin, which he described in a letter to Marion: "Berlin is a city of bourgeois background that has become wealthy and would like to imitate the nobility. But London is an aristocratic lady. She used to be wealthier than she is now but she has kept all her somewhat outdated jewellery. She imitates no one, not even when it would be advisable."

In Soho, Albert had been spoken to in French, Italian, Spanish, Greek and other languages which he didn't recognize. It was great fun to move about as though he was at a masked ball – without a mask, yet unrecognized. On the first Sunday of his stay, he wanted to see and hear the famous speakers on the soap boxes in Hyde Park – 'the symbol of our democracy', according to Henry. When he put his shoes on in the morning, both shoe laces broke.

The importance of shoe laces is not in proportion to the few pennies they cost. One never thinks of them until they break, which is usually at the most inconvenient time. Then even these worthless strings can play a remarkable role. Albert tied a few knots in them before walking downstairs. In the hotel lobby, he asked the concierge, "Would any shoe store be open Sunday?"

"Everything is closed here," he answered. "But in the East End, at the Jewish market, things are still open. From shoes to bicycles, you can get anything you want." He explained what bus Albert should take.

Albert boarded the double-decker bus. From the top he had a wonderful view of streets and squares, which were completely without activity on Sundays, whereas during the week the ground couldn't be seen, the spaces were so crowded. London on Sunday was a city on holiday. But the Jews in the East End could keep their stalls and shops open Sundays because they were closed on the Sabbath. The speakers at Hyde Park weren't the only symbol of British democracy.

The bus went to a part of town that looked poor. Small stores, poorly dressed people, many sailors and merchant seamen. Suddenly signs and posters appeared in Hebrew writing, so he got off. He saw a long row of market stalls on both sides of the street offering a huge variety of goods. He wandered past the stalls, looking for shoe laces. At the same time, he was amazed by the diversity of people: Chinese, blacks, women with little children in their arms, sailors, and other characters he wouldn't like to meet alone at night. They were bargaining, laughing, shouting and fighting with the vendors.

"Do you want to buy something or are you only sightseeing?" The vendor had addressed him in Yiddish, having had a brief look at him. Albert didn't speak Yiddish, but it was close enough to German that after some pondering, he got the meaning of the question, "*Villt ir eppes koyfn, tsu seyd ir a kibbitzer?*"

He thought it curious that the man had immediately recognized him as a Jew, not as a Frenchman or Spaniard or Italian or anything else.

"How do you know I'm Jewish?" Albert asked in English.

"A Jew shouldn't recognize another Jew? Where are you from?" the vendor replied.

"From Germany."

"*Oych mer a medine,*" the man said, again in Yiddish. Albert translated it correctly as 'also some kind of country'. He had to laugh. Then, pointing at his shoes he said, "I need shoe laces, as you can see."

The vendor looked at the shoes, then pulled two pairs of brown shoe laces from his cart.

"How much are they?" Albert asked.

"Nothing. With the compliments of the management."

Since Albert didn't want to take something for free he bought a silk scarf, probably of Chinese origin, to give to Marion, and strolled on between the stalls and hand carts. He came to a stand full of dozens of umbrellas. It happened to be a day without rain but the sun was reluctant, and one could always use an umbrella in London. The vendor was busy selling umbrellas to three short Japanese tourists, trying to match their size. When he saw Albert, he interrupted the English conversation with his customers for a moment and said, "*Dervayl seecht sish oys aleyn.*"

It wasn't difficult to figure out what it meant, namely, "In the meantime, look around on your own." Albert was once again surprised at how quickly he had been recognized. He rummaged around in the umbrellas. As soon as the Japanese had left, he asked the man, "Tell me, why do you assume that I can understand Yiddish? You can't possibly know whether I'm Jewish or not."

"I can't know for sure but I can guess, and in such cases I address my customers in Yiddish. If they don't react, I know I've made a mistake."

On the way back to Piccadilly Circus, loaded down with his umbrella, another pair of shoes and some other trinkets, Albert considered that he had no way to know whether he had been taken advantage of. Since the vendors had all been Jews who had recognized him as a Jew, he had simply trusted them blindly. Perhaps he should have tried to bargain with them, but he'd never been able to do that, unlike Henja. Whenever she bought fruit or flowers, she always got them a bit cheaper than advertised.

He wished he could stop thinking about Henja. Just the night before he had written a long letter to Marion, but as soon as it was finished, he no longer thought of her. He worried that he would grow tired of her because of her good character; maybe even cheat on her. Indeed, he felt like he was already cheating on her by thinking about Henja! Resolving to remain faithful to Marion on this trip, Albert went through the revolving door of his hotel. Immediately, he saw the tall Sikh from the train approaching him with a grinning face. "I've been waiting for you for an hour. I've come to pick you up. We're going to Welwyn Garden."

"You didn't telephone me, so how could I know you were coming?"

"But you had promised to call me," the Sikh said. "Good thing I remembered which hotel you had mentioned."

It had never occurred to Albert that the man would take his promise to call him so seriously; certainly not in the first few days of his sojourn in Great Britain. He wasn't too keen to spend his first Sunday away from London visiting some village, but he didn't have the heart to turn down his new friend, concerned that he would misunderstand a refusal. So he gave his purchases to the elevator boy and asked him to put them in his room. Then he followed his turbaned friend out of the hotel.

Ranjit led him to a rickety old Ford, got behind the wheel and took off. He didn't drive, he flew. He raced through the streets of London as if they were his personal domain where no one else had any business to be.

"Not so terribly fast, please," Albert called, almost shouting to be heard over the noise of the old jalopy. "I'm my parents' only child!"

The Sikh laughed and glided through a red light. It was lucky that it was Sunday, with not much traffic.

"That policeman's face wasn't a very friendly face just now," Albert called.

"That's understandable. They don't like it when a dark-skinned native is at the wheel."

Although the Sikh drove like a madman, never used his horn or his brakes, and ignored the rules of the road, he assumed that the policeman was only mad at him because of his skin-colour. His attitude reminded Albert of an old joke about Little Moritz, who comes home from school with a poor math mark and claims that his teacher is anti-Semitic.

They drove north, going through endless streets where the houses were all the same monotonous reddish-brick with pathetic little gardens.

"Who lives in these depressing little boxes?" Albert asked.

"The rulers of the universe," the Sikh said. "England's lower middle class, the electorate that decides our fate, feeling they're the summit of civilization. Cute, aren't they?"

"They might have two storeys, but they're terribly narrow. How many families occupy each building?"

"You don't think for a minute that a true Englishman would give up his privacy and share his residence with anyone else, do you? Each house belongs to a single family. All the houses are alike inside. The kitchen is down below, the parlour or living room is on the ground floor, and the bedrooms are upstairs."

Ranjit explained this with expressive movements, taking his hands off the wheel. When the car didn't show enough sense to continue racing straight-on, but veered off in another direction, he put his hands back on the wheel. He almost hit a dog.

"That was close. You have to be careful with dogs here, you know. If you drive over a person, that's not as tragic as killing a dog. The English respect human beings, but they love dogs. Is it like that in Germany?"

"Not quite. In Germany, we don't respect human beings," Albert said.

———— ◆ ————

Against all odds, they arrived in Welwyn Garden City in one piece. Albert hadn't eaten anything since breakfast and it was past two o'clock. They had been on the road for almost three hours but his new friend seemed to have boundless energy. Immediately after their arrival at his house, which was surrounded by a pretty little garden, he suggested that they drive to the nearby airfield.

"Let's go on a plane ride," he said. "I want to show you what I have learned."

"My esteemed friend," Albert said. "If you fly the way you drive, it will be too much for my nerves today. Also, I read somewhere that you shouldn't fly on a completely empty stomach."

"Oh, you poor man, I forgot that you Europeans can't live without your lunch. Come on, we'll still get something to eat, I hope."

They went to a one-story eatery, a mix between a soup kitchen and a university cafeteria. It was very simple, but also very clean. Albert had mutton in a green mint sauce. It tasted as green as it looked, but he was hungry. Ranjit had a giant serving of salad. Then they walked through beautiful garden paths, fragrant lawns and trellises of wild roses to his house.

Ranjit said, "I have been here for more than two years but I still can't get used to European cooking."

"If you regard English cooking as typical of European cuisine, I'm not at all surprised," Albert said.

"Isn't it strange how little imagination and romance the English put into the preparation of their meals, even though they are a very imaginative and romantic people?"

"The English are romantic? That's news to me."

"You just don't know them well enough yet. I have studied them thoroughly, both in India and here. For example, consider my landlady. She is the widow of a sea captain and has decorated her house like a museum. The living room, which you will see in a minute, displays a collection of Dutch china. The old lady's bedroom is in the Chinese style. She sleeps in a Chinese bed, and probably has Chinese dreams there. The room she rents to me is in a Turkish or Persian style. She rents another room to a Russian baroness, and that one is as Baroque as a Viennese palace. But however much imagination her decorating suggests, apparently the old lady can't cook."

"What do you mean, 'apparently'? Have you never had a meal with her?"

"Oh, yes, I have. But I can't judge English food. It all tastes terrible to me. But the baroness assured me her food is definitely inedible."

The living room of the landlady was indeed a china museum, but it was tastefully arranged. Two ladies were sitting in comfortable chairs, knitting. One was a short white-haired woman dressed in black, with a surprisingly fresh face without a single wrinkle and a pair of light-blue eyes that gazed happily at the world. The other lady was young and blond. Her eyes were a darker blue. The Sikh introduced Albert first to his landlady, then to the baroness.

"I'll go make us some tea," the sea captain's widow said.

"Wait, I'll help you," the younger woman said.

"No, my child. You stay here and entertain the young men," the landlady said.

The conversation was as civilized as the furnishings, but as soon as the old lady had left the room Albert felt a hint of tension between the Indian and the young Russian woman.

"You can talk your own language with Baroness von Goldberg," the Sikh said.

"You speak German?"

"A little. It's my mother tongue," the young lady said.

"You're not from Russia?"

"I'm a Russian émigré, but we're from the Baltic region."

A female specimen of the famous and infamous Baltic barons, whom his father hated with such a passion, Albert thought. His father held the Baltic barons responsible for the Tsar's hostility towards the Jews. Once Albert had suggested that the Russians were quite capable of being anti-Semitic without the Baltic barons' influence, but his father didn't agree. And here was an offshoot of that caste, looking quite normal. But of course, one couldn't go by looks. Surely there were people committing robbery and homicide who looked like pastors.

"Ranjit, your friend Arjan was looking for you. He has a letter for you from India," Miss von Goldberg said.

The Indian jumped up. "Excuse me for a moment. I'll be back right away. I must see my friend."

"I didn't know that the mail was delivered on Sundays in England," Albert said in German.

"There is no mail today, and who knows how long his friend has had the letter in his pocket," Miss von Goldberg said. "You're the young man who was so pleasant to Ranjit, right?"

"I don't know when, where, or how I was pleasant to him," Albert said.

"Weren't you on the train with him?"

"Oh, is that what you mean, the incident on the train? That really wasn't anything special."

"You don't know Ranjit. A little impulsive friendliness and he is your friend for life. But hurt him with one thoughtless word and he becomes your enemy. I believe all Indians are the same way."

"I don't believe that. I believe that such sensitivities only develop under particular circumstances," Albert said.

The young lady looked anxiously at the kitchen door, behind which the old lady was rattling dishes. Then she spoke rapidly. "I like Ranjit a lot; he is a wonderful person. But we're in England, and I can't be seen with him here. He refuses to understand that. Here in the house, I can sit with him for hours and talk about anything in the world, but I can't go out with him. He will have to be made to understand that, so perhaps you could do that for me. If I told him directly, he would be very hurt."

"Just a minute. You said you like him. Does that mean that you could love him if you were in different surroundings?"

"It's not impossible."

"Then I don't understand you. Why don't you ignore petit-bourgeois prejudice and go out with him in public? After all, he is kind of an aristocrat himself, as befits your rank."

"I don't like being looked at with contempt by other people. And unfortunately, I'm no longer financially independent. I'm working here as …"

"Where is Ranjit?" the old lady asked, as she pushed open the door and returned with a silver tray prepared for the ceremonial ritual of afternoon tea.

"He will be right back. He is picking up a letter."

"Then we'll start without him," the old lady said, as she set the narrow Dutch table. Its inlaid Delft tiles represented a windmill landscape in the Netherlands.

"You have some very beautiful things here," Albert remarked.

"My late husband brought most of the objects in this house back from his journeys. He liked beautiful antiques."

She poured steaming dark-brown tea from a pretty antique silver teapot into white and blue china cups. When Albert carefully lifted his cup together with the saucer, as his mother had taught him to do, the lady of the house gave him a look of approval. There was silence for a few minutes, during which time the reason for Albert's presence in this house became less and less clear. What had Ranjit intended by bringing him all the way from London to have tea with an English sea captain's widow and a Baltic baroness in a Dutch china store?

Finally the Prince from the Punjab came back, bringing his friend along. It was the same young man who had been with him on the train. The lady of the house welcomed both men very cordially. Perhaps with too much cordiality, Albert thought. This observation proved to be correct, because, on their way to the airfield in the rickety car, Ranjit asked him, "Did you notice how hard the old lady was struggling not to reveal her deeply-rooted prejudice?"

"Would you have preferred her to show such prejudice, assuming that she has any?"

"Oh, she has. The baroness has the same hesitations against people with dark skin unless it is late at night when colours can't be distinguished very well," Ranjit replied, with a bitter laugh.

Albert thought, *Et altera pars auditor*, as the Romans put it, but aloud he only asked, "What is a Russian emigrant doing in such a small town?"

"She works as a secretary in a laboratory. I'm very fond of her."

"My impression was that the feeling is mutual."

"Really? Do you think so? I don't know. Sometimes she treats me like a dog and sometimes she is very nice, but even when she is friendly I feel an undercurrent of animosity."

"Ranjit, please excuse me for asking a very indiscrete question, but have you ever told her that you love her?"

"Oh, yes, many times."

"Have you also told her that you want to marry her and take her to India with you?"

"No. Not that. That would be impossible."

"Why?"

"It's hard to explain," Ranjit said, somewhat taken aback. When Albert remained silent, Ranjit added, "My father would never welcome a European in his house; I mean, as a daughter-in-law. Sikhs are a proud people and we have a very strict religion. In India, I was in love with a very nice, well-educated young girl from a good family, but my father didn't allow us to marry because she was a Moslem."

"The young lady you're talking about is Indian and speaks the same language as you?" Albert asked.

"Of course. We grew up together, in spite of the traditional hostility between Sikhs and Moslems," Ranjit said.

"So please allow me to think out loud, Ranjit Singh. You feel hurt when you encounter aversion to you here, an aversion which may be nothing more but the insular British dislike of all foreigners. You regard this as an arrogant prejudice of the white race. On the other hand, you find it quite natural and perhaps even justifiable when a similar Indian prejudice destroys your dreams and makes it impossible to have goals that are outside the prescribed limits of your caste, religion, or status. My friend, it is said that charity begins at home. So does the fight against prejudice."

"In India, we have already begun the fight. Surely you have heard about Mahatma Gandhi, who has just been jailed again by the British?"

"Yes. I read that he organized a march to the sea to produce salt in protest against the government monopoly. But isn't that more of a political protest than a fight against an internal bias?"

"It's all interconnected. As long as India is under British rule, the caste system of the Hindus and the enmity between Hindus and Moslems and between Moslems and Sikhs will never end. We have to liberate ourselves nationally first, and I'm telling you that as a Sikh even though we Sikhs are treated preferentially by the British."

Having said that, he pulled the emergency brake, which failed to engage. Albert realized they had arrived at the airfield. The car eventually came to a stop anyway and they got out, then went through a small door into a hangar that housed a few single-engine aircraft with exposed pilot seats.

"This is my machine," Ranjit said, pointing at one with obvious pride. "Now we have to find the mechanic who has the key for the fuel pump."

It transpired that the mechanic had already left for his well-earned Sunday rest and couldn't be located anywhere, and Ranjit's plane could not be motivated to fly without fuel. The two young men sat around on the airfield and talked till dusk. There was only a single bus leaving for London this Saturday night, and Albert didn't want to miss it, so Ranjit drove him to the bus stop.

"It was a great pleasure to have you here. You are the first European with whom I could discuss such intimate personal questions. I hope we meet again soon," he said and helped Albert to climb up the steep steps of the bus as if he were a fragile old man. Then he asked the driver to make sure to let the young man off at Piccadilly Circus.

"I'll do everything in my power," the driver said. Albert laughed, but Ranjit seemed to be somehow offended, because he gave the driver a dirty look. Apparently humour didn't travel well between nations.

———

Two months later, a young man wearing a bowler hat stepped off the train at the Zoo railway station in Berlin. He had travelled via Hoek van Holland, Rotterdam, and Hannover. He held a pipe between his teeth, which he kept smoking in a masculine way although it made him nauseous. In one hand he held an umbrella; in the other hand a light-yellow, very English-looking suitcase. It was covered with hotel stickers from London, Liverpool, Brighton, Sheffield, Glasgow, Rotterdam and other cities in Britain and the Netherlands. No one could doubt that the suitcase was widely travelled.

The young lady waiting on the platform wore a warm woollen overcoat. November had started out cold, and there was already snow on the ground. She looked around frantically, but couldn't see the young man she expected anywhere.

When he suddenly confronted her in his unfamiliar apparel, she was so surprised that for a moment, her good manners gave way to the Berlin vernacular.

"They made a monkey out of you over there?" Marion asked, and burst out laughing.

"I'd call that a cordial welcome," Albert said dryly, trying to keep his quiet English composure. He had anticipated that Marion might be surprised by his London outfit and would criticize it, but he hadn't thought she would make fun of him. Her response hit him like a cold shower, especially after the elevated emotion he had felt when he saw her standing on the platform, constant, tall, solid and reliable as the White Cliffs of Dover or the Rock of Gibraltar. But he was much too glad to be home again to let his hurt feelings last very long.

"You're not offended that I laughed, are you? But have you looked at yourself in a mirror? With that hat, Sweetheart, I almost mistook you for a younger version of Charlie Chaplin," Marion giggled. But since she pressed herself against him at the same time, he was placated, and admitted that his apparel was perhaps a little silly.

"How was it?" she asked as they walked downstairs.

"Horrible."

"Really? But why? Your letters and postcards were written in such high spirits."

"That's true, but it was still horrible. I've never been as alone as I was in England, in spite of all the many people I met and their polite friendliness. It's a meaningless friendliness, as lukewarm as the English weather and just as foggy."

"Were you invited much?"

"Invited by whom?"

"By the people you met."

"No, honey, there is no such thing in England. You probably have to be friends for years before you're admitted to the castle of an Englishman. I was invited for meals but only in restaurants, so now I'm an expert in Chinese, Hungarian, French and Italian cuisine."

"They have all of that in London?"

"Yes. London has everything," Albert said, emphasizing the word *everything*.

"Girls, too?"

"Oh, yes, girls, too, and boys who dress and behave like girls."

"So?"

"So what?"

Marion was looking for the right words and finally asked, "Did you conduct any experiments?"

Albert decided that lying to her in order to show off made no sense. "No, gracious lady, I walked through the desert like a camel, holding my own water supply stored up inside me. But now, I'm rather thirsty. You'd better believe me."

Marion blushed. Then she smiled and said: "I can only answer with a verse from the Bible. What did Rebecca say at the well? Do you remember the passage?"

"Yes, but I wouldn't have expected you to know it. 'Drink, my Lord, and I will even water your camels.' That's what she said, really only thinking of water."

"I'm also only thinking of water, or did you assume something else?" Marion said, grinning.

When they got home, Mrs. Berg was very offended. "You sent Marion information about what train you were arriving on, but you didn't even tell your own mother," she said, and gave the girl an accusatory look, as if Marion were responsible for her son's omission. But then her motherly feelings took hold, and she saw to it that the poor boy, who had probably starved in England, was served a decent meal.

"Did you tell Albert what happened to Günther?" she asked Marion.

"No. I didn't want to give him bad news right away," Marion said.

"What happened?"

"Your friend Günther is home now, but he was in the hospital for two weeks."

"Why?" Albert said.

"One evening he was accosted in the street by a group of Nazis, who beat him up badly. He had a concussion and his right eye was injured," Mrs. Berg said.

Marion said nothing. She was annoyed that the cozy evening she had been looking forward to for so long had already been spoiled.

Albert threw down his napkin. "I had almost forgotten the poisoned air of our dear fatherland. This scum of the earth, this swastika riffraff that is spreading out everywhere! Why did those bastards have to pick on Günther, of all people?

I would like to go and visit him right away," he said, pushing his chair back from the table.

"Can't it wait till tomorrow?" asked Mrs. Berg.

"No, I have to see him right away, otherwise I won't be able to relax."

"At least wait until your father comes home, so you can say hello to him after such a long absence. You owe him that much."

He stayed till Mr. Berg arrived, grateful that his father wasn't a man of extravagant temperament who would blurt out everything he felt. When he was younger, Albert had often suffered from his father's outwardly cool matter-of-factness. He had mistakenly regarded it as indifference toward him. But now he liked it.

"Excuse me if I leave now, but I want to visit Günther."

"Just be careful that nothing like that happens to you, God forbid. It's very dangerous to walk on unlit side streets these days," his mother warned him..

"Your son has always said he feels at home in his fatherland, the land of his language and culture. So he'll just have to learn to tolerate this German culture," Albert's father said.

Albert wanted to respond to this provocative comment, but Marion pulled on his sleeve and told his mother that she would be going along to protect Albert.

"Then I have nothing to be afraid of," Albert laughed.

"It's no joke! I'm better at ju jitsu than you are," Marion said. And arm in arm they walked along poorly-lit Fasanenstrasse.

Günther lived with his widowed mother in one of those old houses, which – like their tenants – kept trying to maintain their original refinement in spite of poverty and advancing age. There were two important institutions in the neighbourhood. One was the large Kempinski restaurant at the corner of Kurfürstendamm. The other was Berlin's most modern synagogue. To outsiders, the connection between the synagogue and a restaurant that wasn't even kosher might have been incomprehensible. But those who happened to be walking on Fasanenstrasse at noon on Yom Kippur – the holiday which demands strict fasting for twenty-four hours – would have discovered the connection quickly. The faithful, who usually had eaten a forbidden breakfast already, would all be flocking to Kempinski. Without a good lunch, they could hardly muster up enough energy to continue fasting in the afternoon. Indeed in terms of religious devotion, it was questionable whether Kempinski or the synagogue achieved better results.

Wanting to express his thoughts about the two hostelries, the physical and the spiritual, Albert remarked, "It is just as ridiculous as it is immoral that the majority of people go to churches, synagogues, temples or mosques when they neither believe the commandments of their religion nor adhere to them in their everyday life."

"But there are people who are really religious," Marion said.

"What do you mean by 'religious'?"

"Those who sincerely believe in God."

Albert shrugged. "If you are honestly convinced that there is a God who has created this whole universe, wouldn't it be blasphemy to tell this God which special religion and laws he must reveal himself to? Did you ever read Thomas Paine's book?"

"No; who is he?"

"He was a co-founder of the United States of America. He wrote a book called *The Age of Reason* about a hundred and fifty years ago. I bought it in England, and I'll lend it to you."

"Is it in English?"

"Yes."

"I'm afraid my English isn't good enough for me to read serious books. What's it about?"

"It's about the various religions. Such a book should be given to schoolchildren. They would develop more acute judgment from it than from all the religious writings of all the different faiths."

"It's obvious from what you say is that this Mr. Paine was not a friend of religion. And although you apparently agree with him about the hypocrisy of religious people, you still call yourself a Jew. How can these two points of view be compatible?"

"They're not compatible, that's the trouble," Albert said, as he rang the doorbell of Günther's house.

Mrs. Kirschbaum opened the apartment door. "What a surprise, Albert! When did you return home?"

"Just a few hours ago."

"And you came to visit right away? That's very nice. Günther will be so happy."

She ran down the hall to announce the visitors. Rosa Kirschbaum was a kind-hearted woman who suffered a great deal from the way her witch-like appearance frightened little children. Günther was oblivious, thinking the problem was that she just talked too much.

Marion gasped when she saw Günther. The young man lying in bed was not a pretty sight. Both of his hands, his head, and one eye were bandaged. His bluish-black stubble made the white bandages appear even more gruesome than they were.

"They did quite a job on you," Albert said. "Did the police at least catch the criminals?"

"I don't think they're even looking for them," Günther answered. "But frankly, I no longer care. What worries me more is that I'll probably lose my job because I can't go to back to work for another few weeks. My firm has already hired a substitute."

"But surely that's only a temporary measure," Marion declared.

The non-bandaged part of Günther's face grimaced. "Marion, my angel, the most permanent things in the world are the so-called temporary and intermediate measures. How was England, Albert?"

"Very interesting. They have a lot of unemployment there as well, but the people don't go insane because of it like they do in Germany."

"Yes. You know, since I have to lie here doing nothing – I can't read much with one eye, I can only listen to the radio and think – a lot of things have been going through my head. And I have to conclude that your father's judgment of Germany may be correct."

"Which judgment are you talking about? My father has many very different opinions from many points of view. Sometimes he may use hindsight, but the only view he never employs is foresight. Speaking of sight, how is your eye?"

"The doctor says it will heal and I won't have worse vision than before. I have to wear glasses anyway. But don't change the subject. What I was referring to was a conversation we once had with your father in which explained that there were decent and honest people everywhere, just as there were coarse and mean people everywhere, and that the distribution in Germany is no different than in other countries. Where Germans differ from other nations, he said, is that they leave it up to their government to decide what is decent and what is indecent. As a result, citizens have no obligations at all.

"That's what I thought about when I was attacked. Dozens of people walked by but it didn't occur to anyone to come to my assistance. One old man wanted to intervene with his umbrella, but his wife pulled him back and said, 'Don't get involved in political fighting; that's for the police.' They call it political now, do you understand?"

"Did the police show up, at least?" Albert asked.

"I think so. When I came to in the emergency ward, two policemen were present who seemed to have brought me in."

"You know, Günther, my father is lucky. Living here, he has a box seat at a play; he feels like he's in the audience while you and I are on the stage. When people in England said that they disliked Germany, I was insulted. You and I are connected to our home country, whether we like it or not."

"Sure. I'm only bitter when I remember that although my father died a hero's death in the war, I was beaten up by brutal thugs because they imagine themselves to be better Germans than me," Günther said, trying to sit up higher in the bed.

Marion stood up and skilfully fluffed up his pillow for him. "I believe you're getting yourself too worked up because of this conversation, and that's not healthy," she said. "Albert, can't you talk about something else?"

"For example?"

"How about your travels? I haven't heard anything yet myself. Tell us something amusing."

Albert took the hint and started telling them stories about England. Then Mrs. Kirschbaum appeared carrying a tray with tea and sandwiches.

"Children, you have to eat something, and our patient too must be hungry. Also we shouldn't stay too long here with him; the doctor said he still needs a lot of rest."

Marion was in a hurry to leave anyway, and not only out of consideration for Günther. She had been thinking things over during her weeks alone, and also had many conversations with her mother. Her mother told her that no man ever wants to get married on his own, so women have to withhold sex until after the wedding – advice which had come too late for Marion and which she probably would have disregarded had it come earlier. Still, she didn't want to continue living the way they were, with Albert's furnished room costing almost as much as a small apartment big enough for both of them. Since they earned enough to make ends meet, she wondered what they were still waiting for. They were treated by everyone as if they were engaged, even though they hadn't had a real engagement party. When acquaintances asked her when they would be getting married she always replied, "Probably in the spring," but Albert wouldn't commit to anything.

It was not a good situation.

They had turned onto Kurfürstendamm and now walked to the Uhlandstrasse subway station. It was raining and Albert's proper English umbrella provided only insufficient protection. Cars drove by without regard for pedestrians on the asphalt, which resembled a wet black mirror. They went charging right through the puddles, making the water splash up on both sides.

"My shoes and stockings are soaked through. You're lucky that men wear pants," Marion said.

"I have been told that in some families the women wear the pants."

"Metaphorical pants don't keep the rain out, but otherwise it might be better for me to wear them," Marion said, pinching the arm holding the umbrella between them.

"Oh? How would it be better?"

"Then you couldn't treat me however you wanted to."

"Why would you say something like that? I've never done anything to you that you didn't want, nothing you fought against. Besides which, considering your muscles, I doubt whether I could win such a fight."

The yellow and red cars of the subway were warm and nearly empty. Albert reflected on how much the scene differed from London, where you have to descend to the centre of the earth to reach the trains and then you're jammed in like sardines in a can. Here, the subway resembled a toy train set. Sometimes the trains traveled above ground, sometimes below. Wondering where they were going, to Marion's home on Wittenbergplatz or to his room, he suddenly recalled that he hadn't paid the rent for two months. As they took their seats, he said, "Do you know that I forgot something important?"

"No. What?"

"The rent for our secret hideaway."

"It's been paid," Marion said. "If you can, pay me back."

"Of course. You always think of everything, don't you?"

"Not everything, but practical things," she said, and grinned.

The practical things she had thought of included clean sheets, which she had taken to the narrow, dark room a day before his return and in which they now lay. She had imagined that after such a long separation, their first night together would be so different. But Albert seemed to be bored or preoccupied. What was the matter with him? He hadn't even kissed her properly! Visiting poor Günther had been a mistake. She had known it right away.

Albert lay silently in the crook of her left arm. With her right hand, she tenderly stroked his naked body in the most sensitive place. When she felt no reaction, she pulled back as if she had been struck.

"What's going on? Don't you love me anymore, Albert? You've been away for so long, and now you're completely absent," she whispered, tears in her eyes.

"I am just dead-tired, sweetheart. You forget how long my journey was."

Hoping that was the only reason for his listlessness, she felt her way back to his manhood and held on with light pressure.

What soft skin this beautiful narrow hand has, Albert thought. *And yet she has at least as much strength in her hands as I do.* He turned towards her and felt his self-confidence rise as well as his member.

"No, you need your rest. Go to sleep for a little while," she said, and pulled her hand back. But he was wide awake now and wouldn't be turned down. She was glad that he didn't want to listen to her and embraced him. They melted into each other, then Albert fell asleep, the full weight of his body on top of her.

I seduced him today. I believe I must take things into my own hands in other respects as well, she thought. She worried about waking him up if she moved him, but he was snoring in her ear, so she carefully pulled her shoulders sideways, placed her arms under his body and lifted him up a little. Then she moved to the side and let him roll over. He didn't wake up for several hours. First he released two sharp snoring notes like the shifting gears of a decrepit old car. Then he inhaled one deep breath like the howling of a dog.

"You are really an expressive sleeper," she remarked.

"What do you mean?"

"You sing in your sleep, and when you wake up you make a racket like a factory."

"I don't believe you. What time is it?"

"Not very late. It's not even ten yet. Strangely enough, I'm hungry."

"That's a good sign. You're always in good spirits when you're hungry. I still have British pounds and Netherlands guilders on me, and I expect they'll exchange them with pleasure. So get dressed! We're going out to a restaurant."

———◆———

"*Grüß Gott*, Sir! *Küss die Hand*, Madame!" the old waiter said with traditional courtesy. All the regulars of the café on Nollendorfplatz had declared him to be a true Viennese, Vienna being the largest city in Europe, its borders extending from Czernowitz to Prague.

"You haven't been here for quite a while," the waiter said and started to direct them to a table that was a bit apart in a sort of grotto meant for lovers. Then he stopped. "Oh, no, my apologies! You're a married couple," he said, and took them to a less isolated table.

Marion gave Albert a wry look. "You see?" she said after they had taken their seats, and the waiter had taken their order. "Everybody thinks we've been married for years."

"Why? We don't look that old and decrepit yet."

"Here's why. You never fuss over me; in fact, you're not attentive at all. People notice it. When the flower girl passes the table, you never buy me a bouquet. Sometimes you even read the evening paper when you're in a restaurant with me. No wonder the waiter thinks you're a dyed-in-the-wool husband."

Albert was perplexed. Marion hadn't made such a long speech for a long time. But everything she said was true. There hadn't been the slightest undertone of an accusation. She had made her statement very soberly and almost cheerfully. That made her observations even more impressive. He clearly ought to treat her better. Yet he felt he had to defend himself.

"You may be right, but then I can't understand why women always want to get married if a butterfly – the breathless lover – only turns into an ugly caterpillar reading the newspaper."

Marion giggled instead of answering. She didn't want to say the wrong thing now, so she kept playing with her napkin and twisting the ring on her finger, turning the little diamond inside so that the band of gold looked like a wedding ring. Finally she said somewhat reluctantly, "Albert, girls are much more courageous than you think. We know that you can't be passionately in love forever, but we hope – at least I hope – that you can always … that you can love someone always. I also don't want that we're … so endlessly and aimlessly … you know very well what I mean. Albert, why don't we get married now?"

He had seen it coming. This was the question to which he had no answer. How had his father expressed it? Every human decision has two motivations: a good and plausible one and a true one. He hadn't decided *not* to marry Marion, but he wasn't certain that he was head over heels in love with her. He worried that he would become bored with her in the long run. But mainly he wasn't sure about what kind of future he wanted for himself.

"Everything is so uncertain now, Sweetheart. I don't know where I belong. I'm scared to think that my only purpose in life is to take over my father's business. And then there's the current situation in Germany. I feel so outraged. I really believe that any person with self-respect must emigrate. We can't think of marriage until I have reached a decision about that. Where would we go? How could we make a living somewhere else? Furthermore, my parents are too old to start over in a new country. It has to be thoroughly worked out. So have some more patience. I won't be unfaithful to you, if that's any consolation."

"That is a consolation," Marion said and smiled. After some thought, she declared, "I'm convinced your sudden desire to emigrate was influenced by Günther's bad luck. Unfortunate events happen in other countries, too."

"True, you can get mugged in other countries by hooligans and drunks. But elsewhere, such violence isn't systematically controlled and carefully channelled into hatred, the most unfounded hatred in the world. Only in Germany is hatred turned into a science, is prejudice and a nebulous vision turned into a theory. It makes me puke. If I had any idea where to go, I would pack my bags and leave tomorrow."

"Not without me. I would never let you go away alone," Marion said. "But anyway, you won't emigrate, my boy. You are much too spoiled and much too lazy to start over somewhere else. And why should you? Because there are rowdies here? That's ridiculous. There are more decent people here than you admit and besides, Germans are so cultivated, they will never allow thugs and fanatics to take over. This is our homeland. I speak no other language. So stay at home and be content."

"And marry Marion Goldberg as soon as possible, you'll never find a better wife. I'm sure that's what you wanted to add," Albert said, and laughed.

"I didn't have to add that. That's already included in the meaning of the word 'content'," Marion said and took a big bite of her broiled chicken, satisfied by the conversation, and relieved that Albert didn't intend to abandon her. She was convinced that once he had time to mull things over everything would work out fine.

XII

1932

———

THE GREEN OLIVE AND THE black olive seemed to belong to different parties. They couldn';t agree. As soon as he choked one down, the other came up. They both tasted awful. The food here was for the birds. He had been told that Marseilles was almost part of the Middle East; certainly it was hot enough to be so, even though it was already October.

Slowly, Albert walked back to his hotel. The afternoon sun lay heavily on the houses and streets but it didn't seem to bother the people. They must be used to the heat. As for him, tomorrow morning he would be sailing to even hotter climates. Yesterday's excitement, the happy feeling of being free and unbound and venturing into something new, had been replaced by bitter thoughts. As bitter as the olives. No, he couldn't blame the food; it was completely his own fault.

"You're a bastard," Günther had told him.

"But there is no way I can take Marion with me to a wild and underdeveloped country like Palestine. I don't know how I will survive there myself." Those were the words Albert had used to cover up the true reason for his flight, his meanness, his crime. But he hadn't succeeded. Are there really people who can deceive themselves? He dropped down onto the inconsistently clean hotel bed and folded his hands behind his head. How had it all begun?

It had all begun with his father's illness. Until then, they had made plans and he had played along, though without great enthusiasm. Habit dulls the mind. All last year he had been travelling: twice more to England, then to Denmark, Sweden, and the Netherlands. Each time he returned home he felt more reluctance to settle down in Germany, more anger at the atmosphere there. Burning with outrage he had concocted wild plans, but Marion, in her quiet way, had always poured water on his fire. Dry and sober logic was always on her side but he still resented what she said.

After his father's funeral his mother clung to him. Of course he loved his mother, as was proper. But just because he was an only child he couldn't be expected to fuse his life to hers. Maybe that was heartless; certainly it was selfish. But didn't he have a right to be selfish? Nobody is owned by anyone else. We belong only to ourselves, not to a mother and not to any other woman.

"You now have heavy responsibilities, my son," she declared in her melodramatic way, making plans to live with him and Marion. She meant well. She meant well about everything, including her plans for him to run his father's business. It was not only one chain they planned to wind around his neck but three: the wife, the mother, and the business. It is harder to protect yourself against love than against hatred. You can build a wall against hatred, but you have to tear down a wall to protect yourself against love. He had done it, but he didn't understand how – or even why.

Günther had warned him. "All you're going to achieve is to feel lonely and to despise yourself." It was easy for him to say; according to Günther, Marion was the epitome of female virtue. But Albert hadn't been able to confess to his best friend the real reason for his restlessness: Marion was a wonderful person, but he was no longer attracted to her. The drive for adventure had been awakened in him again. And then there was the fear of living with his mother, his aversion to business and – more than anything – the bitter injustice of having to apologize for having been born in the dear fatherland. If it weren't for that, he wouldn't be going to Palestine, of all places. He could have gone to America or Australia or wherever.

Of course, Günther was right. He had behaved like a swine; he had wanted to be free from all shackles. But Marion's life wouldn't be destroyed because he had abandoned her. She'd find someone else, someone better than him. Too bad for Albert, who wanted to be free. Free to lie in a hot, stinking hotel room in Marseilles, not knowing what to do with himself.

Well, tomorrow it would be final; he would be sailing to the Promised Land. Perhaps he should have put an ad in the paper: Patriotic and loyal citizen, young and energetic, is looking for a suitable homeland. This was not as comical as it might seem; it was tragic, actually. If he hadn't already experienced life in Britain and Scandinavia, he might have believed he could fit in in those countries instead of being a foreigner twice over, both as a Jew and as a German. What irony: if his father had only lived long enough to see his son go to Palestine, he would have been overjoyed. Unlike Albert, who fell asleep in his clothes.

He woke up before sunrise, plagued by nightmares. Startled, he felt Marion's strong hands choking him, but it was only his shirt-collar. He washed and shaved and as soon as it was light enough, he went downstairs to eat breakfast. Then he ordered a taxi and went to the harbour.

It was much too early. He was the first passenger to plant himself and his bags in front of the iron embarkation gate. His steamer, the *Théophile Gautier*, lay before him in a light shroud of mist. Crates were being loaded upon it as well as baskets of fish and vegetables and all sorts of other things. Not in his wildest dreams could good old Théophile Gautier have imagined what kind of stuff fits into such a ship. Leave it to the French, he thought, to name ships after writers.

A bell rang and the *tricolore* was hoisted on the stern of the steamer. The day seemed to have officially begun. Albert's suspicion was confirmed when two policemen appeared, but the gate was opened only after other passengers assembled with their bags.

"Have your passports and boarding cards ready, please," one of the policemen called. The other attached a rope to the gate to prevent people from walking the wrong way.

Albert entered the passport control area.

"You have a German passport?" the officer asked, with obvious distrust in his voice. Apparently he found it suspicious that a young man who looked like a typical Provençal would try to leave France using a German passport. Albert wondered why policemen so often show distrust before finding out the facts, then remembered how unfriendly the conductor in Strasbourg had been when he entered France by rail. Who invented the fairy tale about the friendliness of the French?

"Et c'est à Berlin même que vous êtes né?" – You were born in Berlin itself? The policeman seemed surprised, and carefully compared the passport photo with the

original. To ensure that it wasn't the passport that was wrong but his suspicions, he interrogated Albert a bit more. Albert's answers came out just as angry as the policeman's questions, complete with the French pronunciation he had learned from Mademoiselle, a native of Orléans.

"I never knew that Berlin was situated on the banks of the Loire or that they speak French there. Live and learn," the policeman said. He told Albert to wait, and disappeared into his superior's office with Albert's passport. Albert was glad he had other papers as well as company letterhead in his suitcase in case he needed to identify himself. But it wasn't necessary. The policeman came back from his superior's office somewhat shamefaced and stamped the passport without further comment. His boss had explained to him that knowing how to speak French and looking Provençal didn't constitute criminal behaviour.

The British consular officer, too, had made things difficult, issuing a visa for Palestine after long consideration. Only the fact that Albert had inherited a well-established firm, for which he was officially going on a business trip, persuaded the consular officer to comply. The British were nervous, having been given the mandate over Palestine by the League of Nations because they promised to support the establishment and development of a Jewish national homeland, and now treating Palestine as if it were their own colony and doing everything possible to deny Jews entry. Ranjit's opinion of the British hadn't been as ungenerous as Albert had thought.

———◆———

"If this is second class, I'm glad I didn't book third," Albert told the steward who showed him to his cabin. Once Albert had stowed his bags, he took out the information the steward had given him about the ship, which included meal-times and lifeboat regulations. There was also a letter. Marion's regular, legible handwriting on the pink envelope hit him like a brick. He put off opening the envelope, worried about what it would say. Would she express bitter disappointment and the same reproachful thoughts he had himself, or the hope that he would return to Berlin, and to her?

With hesitation, his heart beating fast, he ripped open the envelope. The letter contained only a single line of text above her signature, the handwriting as clear and tranquil as she was herself. *Bon voyage and lots of luck*. She had written nothing else.

Albert leaned against the white metal wall of his cabin and looked through the open porthole at the black water of Marseilles harbour. If there really were a God, surely he would be punished for this, his biggest sin. A crime for which he would never be able to make reparation.

"A half-decent man doesn't leave such a girl," Günther had said.

"Erika and Manfred split up," he had defended himself.

"That's entirely different," Günther replied. "That's a horse of a different colour. Erika couldn't become a Jew and Manfred couldn't become a Christian. But you two don't have that problem, so the comparison is invalid."

As usual, Günther had been right.

Albert's freedom was confirmed by Marion's six words. He was free, and unsatisfied, and full of remorse. Would he ever be happy again? Would he ever be able to love another woman? Nonsense; he had loved Henja before he met Marion; someone else would cross his path. He mustn't carry these guilt feelings with him; he must look forward and not back. *Ex oriente lux*, the Romans used to say, and the ancient Jews said *MeZion Tezeh Torah* – the teaching comes from Zion, and from the Torah.

Albert tore Marion's letter into little pieces and watched as the pink shreds fluttered in the wind before disappearing into the water. Then he went up on deck where a colourful crowd had gathered. Fat dark-skinned men wearing garish neckties with thick gold rings on their fingers were probably Egyptians on their way to Alexandria. French army officers and their families must be going to Beirut. He wondered whether anyone else was going to Palestine besides the old Jew with his long beard and side locks. How unappealing! Albert would never be able to see such a person as his compatriot, especially in comparison to the tall blond young people on the other side of the room, Scandinavians perhaps. Among them were two pretty girls in scruffy clothes. He resolved to listen to find out what language they were speaking. Was it Finnish?

He was astonished to realize that they were talking Hebrew. One of the girls had clearly said *Ani lo rozah,* the phrase he knew girls use most often in every language: *I don't want to.* Albert didn't understand what the others said because they spoke so quickly, reminding him of his inability to comprehend English at first when he went to London. He moved closer to the group, feeling a little awkward.

"Shalom," he said.

"Shalom," the two girls replied.

The four young men looked him over critically. His elegant suit, the foppish spats on his shoes, and the way he wore the black beret at a jaunty angle made him look even more French than his face already seemed to indicate. *He's not a Jew*, the young people must have been thinking. *What does he want from us*?

Stuttering and with awkward grammatical errors, Albert said in Hebrew, "I assume you're going to Palestine too. So I thought I'd introduce myself."

All their faces showed surprise. "You're Jewish?"

"Of course."

"You're going up to Palestine?"

In spite of Mr. Werba's efforts to teach him Hebrew, Albert didn't know that one doesn't 'travel' to Palestine as a Jew. You may travel everywhere else but you 'go up' to Palestine, as if elevating yourself. Palestine: what a silly name! Of all the people who had ever lived there, the Philistines had been the only people who left nothing behind, neither words nor monuments. If they hadn't been mentioned in Jewish history, they would have been forgotten, unknown and unsung. Jews called and still call the land *Israel.* The Romans had called it *Judea.*

Albert had to think carefully before answering correctly: "Yes, I'm going up to the land of Palestine."

"Where are you from?"

"Berlin."

"Were you born there?"

"Yes."

"Kids, how do you like that? A genuine *yecka*, a German Jew, and he speaks Hebrew. Will wonders never cease!" They all laughed.

Albert wasn't sure whether they were laughing with him or at him, since he hadn't understood that last sentence. He forced a smile. "Please don't talk so fast. I want to understand what you're saying."

It had been a great effort to say those few words. He was laboriously translating from German. And he found it difficult to address these people, since *Sie*, the formal German *you,* doesn't exist in Hebrew. Even though the same fact had never bothered him in English, Hebrew was the only language he'd had to learn without enthusiasm and against his will. He'd enjoyed learning Latin and French, but having been forced to learn Hebrew, he found every little difficulty irritating.

His thoughts were interrupted by one of the young people. A muscular broad-shouldered fellow with light-blond hair and acute blue eyes, around Albert's age, extended his hand. "I'm Zalman."

Albert introduced himself. Zalman presented him to the other young men and the two girls. "I hope you'll join us," Zalman said. He now talked slowly, pausing after every word. "But do us a favour: take those white envelopes off your shoes, take off that pickled herring and open your collar. Otherwise we'll look like proletarians by comparison with so much elegance."

Everybody laughed. One of the girls said that Albert had probably understood only half the words. Albert recalled Manfred had once told him. *Women are attracted to helpless men, thinking they can teach them, mother them, order them around and what not.* The girl explained in broken German that the 'pickled herring' was his necktie, and the 'envelopes' were his spats.

Albert went back to his cabin and unbuttoned his spats. They would have been suitable in London or Berlin; here they were unnecessary. But he kept the tie on. "If it bothers Mr. Zalman and his friends, they can kiss my ass. Every society has its own unwritten laws but I believe they'll let me into Palestine with a necktie on," he said to himself. "Why does it bother them if I wear one? Open shirt collars with chest hair creeping out are more aesthetic? I'm much more bothered by the fact that those girls aren't wearing stockings over their hairy legs."

He straightened his tie before the little mirror in the cabin; the tie had become the symbol of his individuality. Then he went back up on deck. A tugboat pulled the *Théophile Gautier* out of the harbour while the ship's band played the 'Marseillaise'. The four men of the Palestinian group stood at the railing, watching the ship pull slowly away from the quay, but the girls had disappeared. When the ship began to move under its own steam, they came back. Now they were dressed as ladies. They wore stockings, and had changed into more elegant dresses and done up their hair with coloured ribbons. Albert smiled involuntarily at this provincial attempt to look sophisticated. *Bad examples spoil good manners*, he thought.

Zalman and his friends made no remarks about his changed appearance or the elegance of the girls. They went to the dining room amicably.

"Pardon, Monsieur," the steward said, "but this is the tourist-class dining room. Your second-class dining room is on the other deck."

"I want to stay with my friends," Albert said.

"As you wish," the steward shrugged, "but the food is better in second class."

Class differences didn't suit Palestine. *A la guerre, comme à la guerre*. However, Albert's new friends couldn't appreciate his sacrifice, since they didn't understand his conversation in French with the steward.

"Do you also speak English?" Zalman asked.

"Yes, much better than Hebrew."

"So we can talk English," Zalman said, with a strong American accent.

"Are you American?"

"I'm just returning from America. I was studying law there, but I'm from Jerusalem originally."

"Were the other five born in Jerusalem too?"

"Yes. But only one of the two girls was in America. The others were in Europe to visit relatives or to see a bit of the world."

"Are there other Palestinians on the ship?"

Zalman looked around in the dining room. "We're a small country and an even smaller people, but I don't know everyone, so I can't answer that question."

"What do the others do for a living?"

"One boy is a farmer and grows oranges; another is a carpenter. I don't know what the third does. The girl in the red dress is a chemistry student, and I think the one in the yellow dress works in an office," Zalman answered. Then he devoted himself to the noon meal. The advantage of a French ship, Albert noted, is that there are carafes of wine on the tables, and anyone can help himself. However, he was the only one at this table drinking.

When they went back on deck after the meal, the French coast was only a dark stripe on the horizon. The sea was greenish-blue, and the sky was cloudless. The ship was heading for the Strait of Messina.

"I never would have thought that I would sail like old Odysseus between Scylla and Charybdis," Albert said to the chemistry student who had lain down on the lounge chair beside him, but she only looked at him with wide eyes. She had never heard of Scylla and Charybdis. When he tried to explain Greek mythology to her, she cut him off abruptly. "There are easier ways to capture men," she declared. In one sense at least, Palestine was not as underdeveloped as Albert had imagined. Perhaps everything would be different than he'd anticipated.

He closed his eyes and fell asleep.

XII

ABDUL KADER MARAKA GOT UP from his low stool. "It is time to close the shop," he said to his assistant. Afternoon sunlight already fell upon the shirts and stockings in his display window, indicating it would soon be completely dark. It was already too late for him to do his accounts.

Abdul Kader's bookkeeping consisted of three tin cans. With their help, he had invented a system of absolute accuracy. The largest, which was round, in earlier but less lucrative years had contained English biscuits and now was full of cash. The second can was smaller and flat and formerly held chocolates. In it were collected unpaid invoices. When the weight of the big can indicated that the time had come to pay something to the landlord, his shop assistant, and the Armenian shoemaker from whom he bought the shoes he sold, the third can was called into service. The invoice came from the flat tin, the cash to settle it from the big tin; together they travelled to the third tin, which still smelled of the coffee it once housed. Abdul Kader's creditors recognized this aroma. When one of them visited his shop, he opened the coffee tin with a solemn face. If that individual's invoice was attached to an envelope containing the exact amount owing, he felt that he had won in the lottery. If the invoice and money owed were not yet in the coffee tin, Abdul Kader would shrug and convey his regrets that the payment had 'not yet come in'.

Everybody knew that Abdul Kader Maraka was an honourable man. When his hand went into the flat tin to pull out an invoice for payment, it did so blindly. He directed his head and eyes in the direction of the vaulted ceiling of his shop. No one could accuse him of being biased or preferring any particular creditor. Not Abdul Kader but Allah was responsible, and everybody was satisfied with that.

Everyone knew that even the unluckiest *schlemiel,* who seldom won this lottery, would eventually get his money.

Once a year, before the beginning of the great fast of Ramadan, Abdul Kader took all the invoices from the flat tin and probed deeply into the biscuit tin. Whatever remained there in coins and paper money after all the debts were paid was the money he had earned. Only that remaining money went into the leather bag he carried with him, firmly tied, in his pocket. From that bag he paid all his personal expenses and those of his three wives and fourteen children over the course of the year. From that bag he pulled half-piaster coins to pay for the Turkish coffee, the tobacco for the hookah, the dried and salted sunflower seeds and all the other little luxuries he allowed himself. He didn't touch the biscuit can for those. In this respect he differed most favourably from the big European and American merchants, who rarely distinguished between their biscuit tins and their leather bags.

The year 1311 in the Moslem calendar was a year of many expenditures but also of good revenue. The world was no longer the same. His two oldest sons, Fais and Hussein, were modern already. They called the year 1932 – the way the Nasrani, the Nazarenes, did. Everything was changing all around him; one could no longer sit in a doorless space selling merchandise. That was still possible only in the covered bazaars of the old city. Outside the Jaffa Gate, where every single day cars and buses full of tourists came by, one had to modernize like the shops in the new Jewish quarter which had windows of glass and charged much higher prices.

The Jews had also changed. There had always been more Jews than Christians or Moslems in Jerusalem, but when he was a boy, everyone else made fun of them. The Jews weren't shopkeepers then; instead, they mainly went to the Great Wall where they prayed and howled in their traditional costumes. The religious Jews were still there, but to their ranks had been added many other people indistinguishable from Englishmen. It all started in the Turkish period when the city wall was opened up. That was it. Abdul Kader had been fifteen years old at the time.

"They're breaking the wall of the city, those Turkish sons of bitches," his father had said.

"Why are they doing that?" he had asked.

"To allow the German Emperor to ride into the city. The old gate is too low and narrow for an emperor on horseback."

"Can't he go on foot?"

"Then he wouldn't be an emperor," his father had answered.

Abdul Kader smiled as he remembered the great day. The Kaiser had come in his colourful uniform. A white veil flew from the back of his helmet. On top of his helmet, the Kaiser had a stick of the kind a decent man would only have in his pants. His friends had told a lot of dirty jokes about the pointed helmet, shouting them loudly so that the veiled women could hear them too. They giggled a lot, especially about the rhyme they had all sung: "Kaiser Willem is a man every woman should love. When he can't do it below, he uses his stick from above." Back then, people laughed about that sort of thing. These days they ran to a doctor about it. Usually the new Jewish doctors his cousins all went to. Times had certainly changed.

Abdul Kader watched as his servant and the shop assistant placed heavy wooden shutters in front of his new glass window-panes and then ran a heavy iron bar across them. Abdul Kader locked the padlock and put the key in his pocket. Should he have a coffee at the low round tables of the coffee house next door and hear the news of the day? If only there weren't so much noise in the street!

Abdul Kader looked down the street, which widened into a square in front of the city wall. A cluster of people were assembled around a taxi. The taxi itself stood still, but its driver stood on the street, attacking a *fellah*. Four men were holding the excited cabbie by the arms and trying to calm him down. All were talking at the same time. Apparently the peasant, who had tied two wooden bread-delivery crates to his donkey's back, had been astride the skinny animal himself when it bumped into the parked taxi. One of the heavy crates had smashed a headlight. The taxi driver, prevented from using his fists, was forced to be content with calling the ancestors of the bread-carrier – particularly his mother, his sister, his mother's sisters and all other female relatives – questionable names.

The crowd was enthusiastic. Even the policeman, who had arrived in the meantime, seemed to be fascinated. With his *kalpak*, the fur hat of Turkish origin worn by the local police, the Cherkassian policeman towered over the laughing crowd around him. He had come with his Jewish colleague, since it had been suspected that there was some kind of dispute between Jews and Arabs. However as it was quickly determined that this was an altercation among Arabs, the Jewish policeman left.

The facts of the case were obvious. At a nod from the blue-uniformed guardian of the law, the taxi driver ended his tirade. The spectators were somewhat disappointed. The policeman turned to the poor *fellah,* who still sat on his donkey, trembling in his torn and ragged clothes. The man was close to tears. The Cherkassian took his notebook from his breast pocket, pulled the four-legged culprit by his long ear and asked in a quiet voice: "Which one of you is the ass?"

The crowd broke out in cheers. Rhythmically clapping their hands, they chanted the policeman's question like the refrain of a song: *"Miin min et-tneen hu eh-khmar, miin min et-tneen hu eh-khmar."* Still singing, the crowd accompanied the policeman, the bread carrier and his donkey to the police station.

Abdul Kader Maraka was happy with himself and the world. The day had ended on an amusing note. He didn't even want to go to the coffee house. Djamila, his third and youngest wife, the only one he still had relations with, would serve him a small cup of Turkish coffee at home. He hailed one of the horse-drawn buggies whose bells contributed to the street noise but also made it more pleasant. After all, a respected merchant had to be taken home in style. That was mandatory.

Abdul Kader sat down on the wide upholstered seat of the high-wheeled carriage, took out his *masbacha,* his Moslem rosary, and played with the thirty-three beads, letting them slide through his fingers. He wasn't all that meticulous about reciting the surahs of the Koran, but that was nobody's business but his.

XII

———

BLUE SKY, WHITE SUN, REDDISH-BROWN stones. Short streets, narrow lanes, little houses with thick walls. The light was so bright that it hurt the eyes. There was only shade close to the walls of houses. On wide window sills were round clay jars, dripping in the wind with condensation. The wetter they were, the cooler the water stayed inside.

No shade without trees. No trees without water. Not enough rain without trees. Without rain, not enough water. A vicious circle. There used to be forests here, the stout woman thought, cleaning the cistern of her house with a long broom. The first rain was expected soon, and the cistern from which she would draw water all year had to be clean. A merciless sun and hard labour had chiselled deep wrinkles into her face. The home-made dress she wore didn't fit her well and also made her look older than her age.

The underground cistern, surrounded by a low wall and a wooden scaffold, was in the middle of the cobble-stoned yard. A pail had to be lowered into it on a chain. All around the yard, the woman grew ornamental plants in clay pots. They were her pride and joy. The bougainvilleas, camellias, pereskias and other cacti and succulents, some with fleshy red flowers, grew and thrived under her small, labour-worn hands. She would have been surprised if anyone could have named all the plants under her care. She herself didn't know the names, and to her husband flora and fauna were of no interest whatsoever. To him a tree was only a thing you had to avoid carefully and not bump into at night. He wasn't the only one among the Jews of his generation to have lost all connection to and relationship with

Mother Earth through living in ghettos. For the same reason, he found manual labour unimaginable.

Of course there were tradesmen such as cabinet-makers and glaziers, tailors and shoemakers among the strictly orthodox Jews, but generally they were the simpler people. Like other learned men, her husband regarded scholarship as a lifelong immersion in the old books of the rabbis and Jewish philosophers. One couldn't feed a family or even provide three meals a day for oneself by studying, but why was there a God if not to ensure that rich Jews in Europe and America sent money to the pious *yeshivot* in Jerusalem? The donors believed that their benevolence would preserve not only the holy city but Jewish life in general, and that they would be well rewarded by God at his next accounting. The recipients regarded the donations as their right. Weren't they the ones who maintained close contact with the Almighty through their constant study? Rabbi Samuel Laski was convinced of it. From his hard-working wife he expected and received the respect he believed a man dedicated to God deserved. He wouldn't have understood it if someone had called him a parasite.

Rabbi Samuel would have regarded it as defamation had anyone suggested that he and his kind were more alienated from the Jewish faith than the atheists were. He would have called 'a product of a sick brain' the thought that he and his friends were committing sacrilege by creating a God in their own image. He and his co-religionists had created an image of the almighty which the God of Sinai, the God of Abraham, Isaac, and Jacob would not have recognized. For example, Rabbi Samuel Laski's God regarded it as sin for a married woman to show her hair or leave her arms uncovered. His God was offended if a knife with which meat had been cut approached a piece of cheese, and was concerned about the purity of pots and pans. And according to him, the creator of the universe considered lighting a match on the Sabbath sacrilege of the worst kind.

On the way from his yeshiva in the old city, where he had sat learning all day, Rabbi Samuel went through the Jaffa Gate past the shop of Abdul Kader Marakas. Then he slowly climbed up Jaffa Street to the new city. Disapprovingly he watched men with shaved cheeks and uncovered heads wearing short pants, and girls clothed immorally in short-sleeved dresses and bare legs. Those were the Godless, the

Zionists who wanted to beat the Messiah to it and build the Land of Israel. They hacked in the country's holy soil, they planted trees and carried stones like the *goyim*. They were worse than the Arab because the Arabs only worked to avoid starvation but these Godless Jews were turning work itself into a kind of religion. Such heresy was spoiling the young people. They hadn't come to Jerusalem to serve God the way he had done; their goal wasn't to die in the holy city and be buried on the Mount of Olives where the dead would rise when the Messiah came. His own eldest son even had the nerve to state that living Jews need resurrection more urgently than the dead! Rabbi Samuel thought of this son, and also of his eldest daughter, with distress.

Actually, it was his own fault that those two held modern views. Why had he sent them to the academic high school instead of putting the boy in a religious school and keeping the girl at home? That had been a mistake. He had been motivated by the neighbours' example, but he would have never imagined that under the influence of modern schooling they would defect from their faith. And now he had to allow the younger children to go the way of the older ones. He was embarrassed before his colleagues at the Yeshivah. They even suspected him of having progressive thoughts himself.

The fact that at his house Hebrew was spoken as an everyday language was another cause for their concern. In the homes of his colleagues, only Yiddish was spoken. Hebrew was maintained as the holy language of prayer and books. To them, that a child should tell his mother in Hebrew 'I have to go pee,' was a desecration of the holy language. It was almost sinful.

But nowhere in the ancient texts was it written that Jews should not speak Hebrew. His children and wife spoke Hebrew because *all* children who attended modern schools spoke Hebrew. He wasn't sure whether he had acted correctly, but one couldn't close one's eyes and refuse to see that the world was changing! It wasn't just the Hebrew language: the new houses, the new villages, a whole new city like Tel Aviv, water pipes and electricity gave the country a different face and a completely different life. He'd always thought that a wise man shouldn't struggle against the stream but swims along part of the way.

But now he had doubts. Who knew whether his eldest daughter, Leah, should be living with her aunt in Tel Aviv – was that a good environment for her? Rabbi

Samuel didn't think highly of his wife's sister. She was a vain, uneducated woman who judged people by their pocketbooks. But what can one do? When one can't give a daughter a dowry, one has to allow her to live where she can meet young men. The heavenly father will help, and what will be will be. Those were Rabbi Samuel's thoughts as he walked the long way home, looking neither left or right.

———

The problem child of Rabbi Samuel's thoughts sat in the yard, in the shade of the house, on a rather rickety chair, watching her mother clean the well. She was manicuring her nails. On a second chair lay a Parisian magazine in which a full-page ad by Coty offered precise instructions about the cosmetics a woman could use to make herself beautiful. She studied this carefully though she didn't depend on Coty because, with God's help, her slim and delicate body was crowned by a head whose fine lines might have illustrated the Torah – had the Jews permitted illustrations in their Torah.

"Why are you working so hard? You have running water in the house now," she said in the reproachful tone daughters use to cover up their unwillingness to help their mothers.

Her mother stopped scrubbing for a moment. She leaned on the broomstick and answered, with good humour, "I prefer to rely on the Lord rather than the Lord Mayor. So far, God has let it rain every winter, but the city sends water only twice a week. If we aren't careful, the tank on the roof is empty before the second water delivery, and then we are left high and dry. However the cistern fills up in the winter and provides water all summer long."

"We don't have those problems in Tel Aviv," Leah said.

"True. You have other worries there."

"What, for example?"

"For example, what to spend money on first, clothes or movies or concerts or theatre, or whatever."

"Personally, I don't have those problems since I have no money. But I was recently invited to a concert by the new Philharmonic Orchestra with Bronislav Hubermann," Leah said, with a certain amount of pride.

"And who is Bronislav Hubermann?"

"Mother, he's the world-famous musician who founded the orchestra. Don't you know that?"

"No. And he invited you?"

"Of course not. I was invited to *hear* him."

"I see. And who invited you?"

"Somebody," Leah answered, pressing her lips together, not ready to give more information.

"So now I'm completely in the know," her mother said, continuing to scrub the well.

"Rachel, Leah! A ladder, a chair, or something," Rabbi Samuel's voice broke in, his breathlessness conveying great stress.

"Where are you? What happened?" Mother and daughter both jumped up and looked around with great concern.

"Up here," Rabbi Samuel shouted, his head protruding over the eavestrough.

His wife looked at him in disbelief. "Are you completely *meshuggah*? What are you doing up there?"

Leah broke out in laughter. Her father's bearded face was covered in sweat, and his broad-brimmed hat was askew. He looked so comical that she couldn't control herself.

"Maybe Father wanted to learn to fly," she giggled.

"Don't make stupid jokes, just help me get down," the rabbi scolded.

His wife ran to the kitchen to carry the heavy kitchen table into the yard. Leah set the chair on which she had been sitting on top of the table, and the master of the house carefully dangled his feet toward the chair then slowly descended, first onto the table and then to the ground.

"Oy," he moaned. "Oy."

"What on earth were you doing on the roof?"

"The dog, a plague on him! The dog!"

The women had no idea what he was talking about, But after his wife gave him a glass of water to calm him down, it all became clear. The rabbi – who didn't mind walking alone through the narrow dark lanes of the old city, through hundreds of Arabs and Beduins — was afraid, like many ghetto Jews, of dogs. On his way home, not far from his front door, he encountered a member of the *Canis familiaris* species which, for some unknown reason, seemed to fancy him. When the rabbi walked away quickly, the dog accompanied him, barking. And that had caused the panic. The rabbi worried that the dog would jump on him the moment he put the key in the lock. With the strength of despair, he had jumped onto a protruding stone in the wall and pulled himself up onto the roof, away from the animal, who was still barking at him. Then the rabbi had crawled over the roof to the other side of the house.

His wife and daughter listened to this report with open mouths. It seemed like one of the greatest wonders of the world that Rabbi Samuel was still capable of such a physical effort. Normally he couldn't even bend down to tie his shoelaces. His wife had to do it for him.

"I would have never believed that you could climb onto the roof," his wife said, and she, too, broke down in laughter.

"When we're in danger, the Almighty gives us strength we don't normally have," the rabbi said with a big sigh.

"But where was the danger?" Leah asked.

"Quiet!" her father ordered. He stood up, walked inside with a dignified stride, turned to face the east, where Solomon's Temple had once stood, and began to sway forward and backward in prayer. In fervent incantation, his lips formed the prayer of thanks to God for his liberation from mortal danger.

"I hope the neighbours didn't see this, otherwise all of Jerusalem will be laughing at Father."

"Laughing? Why would they laugh? He really could have broken his neck," Rachel exclaimed. Shaking her head, she pulled the table back to the kitchen. This time, Leah helped.

X I V

———•———

"IF ONLY THE TEA WERE a little stronger, the bacon crispier and the toast cut thinner, this would be a first-class English breakfast," Inspector Donald Watson said. He and Patrick O'Brien, his colleague from the Palestinian Police, were being served by Ahmed, their house boy.

"Yes, if Ahmed understood more English and were cleaner, and if this damned house weren't in this damned country, and I didn't have to wear this damned uniform, everything would be first class," Mr. O'Brien said, draining a glass of orange juice in a single gulp. "Damn, this is sour."

"Of course it's sour. It was made from the season's first oranges. They're still green."

Inspector Watson had the advantage of experience over his Irish colleague: he had already served in Palestine for two years. He didn't share Patrick's opinion about the house in which they lived. He found its Middle Eastern style comfortable, although old-fashioned and somewhat dilapidated. But he understood that being a newcomer, Patrick might find it difficult to balance his considerable bulk while squatting over a toilet pan set into the floor. However, since such an installation, where one didn[t come in contact with the toilet seat, was much more hygienic in this hot climate than the European version, he had never bothered to change it. Since he resided in the Djabali quarter of Jaffa, he was resolved to live in the local style. The flies and Ahmed were part of it.

Ahmed ibn Hassan el Haurani was one of those fellows from Hauran in Syria who were attracted to Palestine like flies because here they found work and therefore put food in their stomachs. For a thief who had been caught red-handed, he hadn't done too badly. Had Inspector Watson known that the faithful fifteen-year-old whom he had saved from prison, and who he thought was devoted to him, spat at his master's bacon every morning before putting it in the pan, his opinion about Ahmed might have been somewhat less favourable.

"Why didn't you rent an apartment in Tel Aviv? There are some very nice houses there, and the city generally looks European." Asking this question, Patrick O'Bien devoured his sixth slice of toast and had a second cup of tea.

"Oh, there are several reasons."

"For example?"

"First of all, the Jews there don't like to rent to non-Jews. Secondly, Tel Aviv apartments are a lot more expensive. Number three is the risk of establishing social relationships, which is against the administration's guidelines, and number four is the fact that I, personally, don't like Jews. Should I continue?"

"Continue, Donald. As a citizen of the Irish Free State, it always interests me to hear English opinions about occupied territories," Patrick O'Brien said – not too clearly because his mouth was full.

"For my part, I can't understand why unreliable elements like Sinn Feiners are in His Majesty's service," Inspector Watson said impassively. Anyone not knowing that he had served with Patrick for years in Calcutta and in Kenya would have regarded his words as a serious provocation. Carefully stuffing a pipe while Ahmed cleared the breakfast table, he continued. "Now listen, my boy. You chose service here for the same reason I did. The Holy Land has a magnetic attraction for Christians like us."

"Since when do Protestants have the Christian spirit? But if you wish to return to the fold of the Roman Catholic Church, I'm ready to be your godfather."

"I'm being serious. But Patrick, you'll soon learn that things here are totally different than we imagined. The holy places always sounded so dignified—Jerusalem, Bethlehem, Nazareth, Gethsemane – we had respect for the names alone. But do you know what I had to do last Christmas at the Church of the Nativity, the holiest of all places in Bethlehem?"

"You didn't pray, you Protestant heretic, did you?"

"No, you Papish slave. Instead, I had to intervene with a truncheon and ten native Arab constables to establish peace between your Roman Catholics, the Greek

Orthodox, the Armenians and the Copts. Otherwise they would have torn each other to pieces. That was my 'holy night'!

"Yes, my boy, that's what it's like here. You stand near the Church of the Holy Sepulcher under the street sign that says 'Via Dolorosa' watching pilgrims from all over the world kiss the stone on which Christ is supposed to have set down his cross and a few minutes later, you watch a donkey piss on it."

"That can't be allowed!" Patrick interrupted, outraged.

"What can you do about it? Arrest the donkey? Just try to move a donkey while he is pissing. No, the sacred places of the past stay sacred only when life around them doesn't continue. You'll learn that just as I have. The more often you visit holy sites, the less holy they'll seem to you. It's like that with the whole country.

"Besides which, we're in the most complicated political situation you can imagine. Palestine is a crown colony, not a dominion, but a mandate territory with two nations, three official languages, and four religions – not counting all the unofficial sects. And our threefold mission here is impossible, namely to secure peace and order, to promote the development of the national homeland for the Jews, and to protect the interests of the Arabs. I wish someone could explain to me how those three goals can be reconciled."

"That is indeed a pretty kettle of fish," Patrick declared. His flushed face under an equally rosy bald pate, framed by fiery red hair, wrinkled with worry. "So what are we supposed to do?"

"Try to give this unfortunate place a decent administration. That means negotiating a kind of neutrality between Jews and Arabs that is somehow more sympathetic to the Arabs, and above all, by putting the interests of the British Empire first."

"Doesn't that contradict the official terms of the mandate?"

"Maybe, but who will object? The League of Nations in Geneva? Those gentlemen can kiss our behinds. The Jews keep complaining that we have impeded their immigration, but that's just not true. We issue about a thousand immigration certificates a month, besides which a lot of them come over on tourist visas and then settle here illegally. I caught one recently, and he had the gall to say that I was the one without justification here, not him.

"Only the Arabs have a certain respect for us. Not as much as the natives in Kenya did, but almost. The Jews, on the other hand, look down on us. Last month, I drove down to Rehovot. That's one of the older Jewish settlements in the south. A farmer stood in the middle of the road, loading grapes from his mule cart to a truck, blocking my way, so I got out of my car and told him to make room. 'Soon as I'm finished,' he answered. I told him a little more forcefully that I didn't have the time to wait for him. He replied, 'Mister, I waited two thousand years to grow vines on my own soil again, so you can wait three minutes for me to load my grapes.' What would you have done then?"

"I would have laughed and given him a ticket for violating the traffic regulations."

"That's exactly what I did. He wasn't thrilled."

"I can imagine. Do you speak the local languages?"

"I speak some Arabic, and you'll have to learn a little of that as well. We don't need Hebrew. Almost all the Jews speak some English, as long as it's about everyday things. As soon as a Jew comes in on an official matter or has to appear in court, he suddenly understands only Hebrew, even if his English is much better than his Hebrew."

"National pride, or what?"

"Something like that. Shylock always insists on his rights."

O'Brien scratched the fringe of hair framing his bald pate, leaned back in his chair and lit a cigarette. "You know," he said calmly, "the resurrection of Hebrew after two thousand years is quite an achievement. They're trying to revive our language in Ireland with much less success even though Gaelic has only been dead for two hundred years. And we've always sat on our own soil and weren't scattered in all directions like the Jews."

Inspector Watson tapped out his pipe. "You can't compare the situations because the Irish already share a common language: English. The Jews here don't, they come from all over the world, so they can't understand each other. Besides which, they want to establish a nation, which the Irish have already. In addition, the sons of Abraham have a great literature in their old language. But if we keep philosophizing we'll never get to the office, and we have to deal with two ships today."

"What do we have to do with ships?" O'Brien asked, putting on his cap.

"We have to check the passports of arriving passengers," Inspector Watson smiled as they left the house. "And I can already see the French ship at anchor down there."

"What's the name of that tub?"

"She's the *Théophile Gautier*."

"Who was that?"

"I hope you're not expecting me to know my way around Frenchmen too," Inspector Watson answered, cutting off all further questions. Silently and in step, they marched to the harbour of the old town of Jaffa.

X V

———

CLOSE UP, THE ROMANTIC MIDDLE Eastern scene that had looked so picturesque from the sea dissolved into dirt and squalor. The well-cut uniforms of the British police officers stood in contrast to the deteriorating walls and primitive wooden shacks of Jaffa's harbour installation. It wasn't even a real harbour; ships couldn't dock there. Only barges could negotiate the narrow inlet between almost invisible rocks. Albert had been required to jump from the steamer onto one such barge in order to be rowed to shore. Perhaps this symbolized his leap from Western civilization into a new world.

This was allegedly the harbour from which good old Jonah sailed to encounter the whale. Sea creatures were undoubtedly less dangerous than the animals Albert now faced on land. Arabian dock workers and carriage-drivers had fought so bitterly over the opportunity to carry his suitcases, it was a miracle that the suitcases – and he himself – had remained undamaged. The cabbie in whose two-horse carriage he now sat had saved him from the ruckus by driving his horses into the midst of the gang, cracking his whip on the left and on the right.

He had also cursed a lot, in Arabic, Hebrew, and Yiddish. Since the most juicy swearwords were in Yiddish, that must have been his mother tongue. Albert had never before met a Jewish carriage-driver. Looking at that broad back enclosed in a dirty jacket, he found it hard to summon up a feeling of community with the man. Nor did he experience the exaltation, gratification, joy, confidence and satisfaction he thought he would feel upon setting foot in the Holy Land. He wondered why he was so disappointed. What had he expected? There actually were a few palm trees, and three camels with matted fur following each other in single file. There were even veiled women, though they hardly resembled the oriental seductresses of popular imagination.

The carriage had turned into a wide road which seemed to be the main street of Jaffa. A sign read KING GEORGE AVENUE in three alphabets: English, Arabic and Hebrew. All the signs above the shops and stores were also written in those three languages. Albert pitied children going to school here.

He looked at the people. The women in black veils, only their eyes visible under garments that hid everything else, looked like walking pillars or headless nuns. He assumed that there must be some pretty Arab girls walking around without veils, and wondered how he could tell who was an Arab and who was a Jew. Men with red fezzes on their heads must be Arabs, but how could he have known his driver was Jewish? He resolved to try talking Hebrew to him.

"Is it far to Tel Aviv?"

The driver turned around and asked, "Far? What's far? If you're walking, it's far. For cars, may the devil take them, it's not far."

The driver's Jewish heritage had been revealed by his philosophical nature.

"Good, but I'm in your carriage. So how far is it to Tel Aviv by carriage?"

"It depends on the horses. If they're tired, it's far. If they're not tired, we're almost there."

"May I ask how your horses are feeling today?"

"Well, today, they're running like greased lightning. You see the yellow house over there? That's where Tel Aviv begins."

Albert hadn't imagined the modern city to be like this. This street with its low houses from which the plaster was crumbling, and along which workshops and little stores gave a dusty and disorderly impression, looked identical to the one before. One couldn't tell where old Jaffa ended and Tel Aviv began. It all looked equally poor and dreary.

Suddenly the carriage made a sharp left turn, and the scene changed. Some of the houses had two or even three storeys; they were in better condition, and the street was cleaner. Again they came to an intersection, and the carriage turned right into a wide avenue with a strip of lawn and flowering trees in the middle. Bright red blossoms against dark green. This was pretty. The street sign read

ROTHSCHILD BOULEVARD. Well, *boulevard* was a something of an exaggeration, but it could be excused. No shops or commercial establishments cluttered the thoroughfare; it was strictly residential. The houses looked nice, too. Albert admired them with interest. Most were built in a pseudo Middle-Eastern style, with curved windows, verandas supported by columns and stucco decorations. No house was attached to another and between all the houses there were a few metres filled with trees and shrubs. Not so bad, Albert had to admit.

"Here is your hotel," the driver said and put his foot on the lever that operated the signal bell of his carriage. The noise of the bell attracted a young man with oiled hair; the black bowtie on a collar that had once been white identified him as a waiter. He was in fact the waiter, receptionist, porter and concierge of the hotel, all in one.

"You have a room for me, I assume," Albert said. The hotel had been recommended by his friends on the ship, and he had wired from Alexandria, unaware that the hotel had never received a telegram before. In addition, he had composed it in English according to the international abbreviation code. The poor hotelowner could only find out what it said after he laboriously consulted with three of the four travel bureaus in Tel Aviv. That had made him angry. "For such a *schmuck*, such a dandy, I don't have a room," he had told his wife and his Boy Friday. "When he arrives here, tell him that the Ritz hasn't been built yet, but also tell him that in hotel code."

As a result, the waiter wasn't quite sure how he should behave. "I'm not sure whether we have a room for you, but I'll take a look," he answered.

While the driver lifted Albert's bags from the carriage and set them down on the sidewalk, the waiter, smelling of brilliantine, disappeared into the house, which differed from the other houses in the street only by the sign hanging over the entrance, with the Hebrew word *Malon*. Albert wondered why it had been necessary to invent a Hebrew word when every other language was happy with 'hotel'.

The waiter came back, beaming. The female *malon*-owner had looked at the guest through the window and overruled her husband's decision, as usual. They had a room. There were, in fact, eight rooms he could choose from. The hotel possessed ten rooms, and only two were occupied.

The waiter showed him to the room, which was painted white and furnished with an iron bedstead, a wooden table, two chairs and a clothes rack. The floor was made of white and coloured cement tiles laid out in a kind of carpet pattern. Instead of curtains, the two narrow windows had wooden shutters with permeable blinds. Their lower halves could be adjusted forward and backward to let more air into the room. It was possible to see the street without the sun shining into the room. The primitive simplicity of his first abode in the land of his forefathers gave Albert the same feeling in his stomach he once had when the elevator in the house on Wittenbergplatz in Berlin gave a sudden downward jerk.

When the waiter had finished piling his suitcases against the empty wall and left, Albert collapsed onto the hard bed. It squeaked under his weight, and that sad sound made his cup of misfortune run over. He began to cry like a little boy.

Although no one could see his tears, he was ashamed, arguing with logic against his own feelings. "First impressions mean nothing. Even though everything is very primitive here, it seems to be clean. One always has to meet the people before making a judgement. I'm not going to be living with houses and streets, but with people. So far I have hardly seen anything of this city, and nothing at all of the country."

However, these logical arguments didn't help him to overcome his depression. But he was hungry. The disembarkation in the morning, the formalities at the port, waiting for his bags, the customs check, and then the carriage ride, had combined to rob him of his noon meal. Now it was early afternoon and except for the meagre French breakfast on the ship, he'd had nothing in his stomach all day. He went to the hall to look for the bathroom to wash up. The cracked porcelain sink was clean, but no soap or towels were provided. Luckily he had his own. After a quick washing, he went into the street.

Although it was the end of October, he perspired in his light-weight suit. In Berlin, he would have been able to wear it only in the hottest summer months, and even then, he had never been too warm in it. Meanwhile all around him young people were dressed in shirts and pants and, except for an elderly man in a stained suit, he saw no one else wearing a necktie. He noticed that people were looking at him. Presumably they could tell that he was a foreigner, but he didn't care. He didn't have the slightest feeling of community.

He turned into another street that was relatively wide and had a lot of traffic. This one was full of shops and within a hundred metres, he counted four bookstores. He stopped before a window: Russian books, English books, German and French magazines, though most of the books were in Hebrew. He tried to read the titles but, to his regret, he realized that he didn't understand most of the words on the book covers or on the signs in the store.

He continued on his way, observing the people in the street. They might have all been Jews, but apart from their shapeless clothes, they didn't look different than people in any European city. Clearly all the racial theories so popular in Germany were nonsense.

He finally came to a restaurant. Before he entered, he tried to decipher the sign. *Mies* was the German word for miserable; he hoped that the food was better than the restaurant's name or appearance suggested. The owner, a fat woman with poor teeth and hands that were not too clean, greeted him with a friendly smile. She asked in Yiddish, "You're a new one?"

He understood, and answered in German, "Yes."

"Where are you from?"

Albert thought it peculiar as well as comical that a total stranger whose business it was to serve food asked him where he came from instead of what food he wanted to order. He didn't intend to give personal details, so he just responded abrasively, "I want to eat something."

Although the owner was a little insulted by his rough manner, she answered matter-of-factly. "Unfortunately I can't offer you a full meal, it's too late for that. But if you wish, I can make you an omelette with bread and butter and a glass of tea."

"Very well," Albert said and looked around in the restaurant. Six little tables, covered with oil cloth, and more chairs than were needed for the tables. Bare walls painted white, a hole in the back wall that apparently led into a kitchen and through which the food was passed, a sink beside it with a grey-looking towel. Those were the furnishings of the *missadah*. Only one other guest occupied the space. He was a rather good-looking man of about forty drinking a glass of tea and reading the newspaper at another table. More precisely, he had been reading the paper until Albert appeared, after which he only drank the tea and examined him.

I wonder how long it'll be before he talks to me, Albert thought. Immediately he heard the man say, "You speak German. Are you from Vienna?"

Slightly insulted, Albert answered, "Quite the contrary, I'm a Berliner." He wasn't sure why he had been insulted to be mistaken for an Austrian. For the first time that day, he laughed.

The other man laughed, too, and asked, "Is there really such a big difference between the two cities?"

"Frankly," Albert confessed, "I have no idea."

"I'll tell you something. I have never been to Vienna or to Berlin. But most of the people here who speak German tell me that they're from Vienna. You're the first person from Berlin I have met."

"How come you speak such good German then?"

"I went to a German school."

"Where? Here in Tel Aviv?" Albert was surprised, but then he remembered that the man didn't have to be born in Palestine. He could have come from a country where they had German schools. But the answer astounded him even more.

"Oh no, when I went to school, Tel Aviv didn't exist yet. I went to school in Jerusalem."

"What? There were German schools in Jerusalem? A Christian school?"

"Quite the contrary, as you said before. A school of the Benefit Society of German Jews. Have you never heard of it?"

Albert had to admit that he had never heard of the school or the existence of the society. He would have never believed that German Jews would bother about Palestine, but the man told him they had established schools and even a large hospital long before the Zionist movement had developed.

"Does the school still exist?" he asked.

"Sure. Only now, they also teach Hebrew. In my time, Hebrew didn't exist as an everyday language so we were taught everything in German. You know, I still know Schiller's *Glocke* by heart." He laughed, and began to recite the poem.

Albert considered how strange it was that German Jews had established a society to promote German culture in Palestine.

The omelette, bread and butter arrived at the table, and Albert occupied himself with his food. Listening to the man's flawless recital gave him the illusion that Schiller had known exactly what kind of a meal he was going be served in Tel Aviv. Just like the bell described in the poem, the omelette could have been 'solidly cast' and 'moulded in clay.' "That the work may praise the master, but the blessing …" the former pupil of the Benefit Society of German Jews was saying, though with regard to Albert's meal, only the bread deserved to be blessed. Still, he was so hungry that he had devoured almost everything by the time the recital ended with the last chime of Schiller's bell.

"That was beautiful."

"Once learned, never forgotten," the man said. Moving his chair over to Albert's table, he introduced himself. "My name is Cohen. I'm a chemist."

"Pleased to meet you. My name is Berg."

"And what's your profession, if I may ask?"

"I'm a merchant."

"That's not a good skill to bring to Palestine, Mr. Berg."

"Oh? Why not?"

"Here we need technicians, locksmiths, mechanics, cabinet-makers and engineers. And of course farmers. Merchants we can do without."

"Well, then I may as well go back right away," Albert smiled.

"I didn't mean it that way I only mean that you may have to adapt. Do you have other talents in addition to things commercial?"

"I can play the piano and drive a car," Albert joked.

Mr. Cohen was enthusiastic. "Driving is a wonderful skill. We need chauffeurs, and the bus cooperatives are looking for experienced drivers as well. Most people here come from small towns in Poland and Russia where there are no automobiles. You see? There you have an opportunity. You should think about it. When did you arrive in the country?"

"This morning."

"You only arrived today? Good God! I knew that you were a newcomer but I didn't realize you're that green. Do you have family here?"

"Not as far as I know."

"You came here all alone?"

"Yes. Am I too insignificant to contribute by myself?"

"Once again, you mistake my meaning," Mr. Cohen complained. "If someone doesn't have any relatives and friends here, he feels lonesome, and we have to take care of him a little." He rapped his water glass, and the owner, who had retreated to the kitchen, came running back, her fat jiggling. She rubbed her hands on her apron, releasing a strong odour of onions. Apparently she was preparing the evening meal.

Cohen said something quickly in Hebrew, which Albert didn't understand because of its rapid delivery.

"I want to pay my bill," he said to the woman.

"That's been taken care of," she replied.

"But how?" Albert protested. He hadn't seen any transaction, but Cohen's grinning face suggested something had taken place. The man probably had a monthly tab at the restaurant and told the owner to put everything on his account. Uncomfortable letting a complete stranger pay for his food, Albert insisted on knowing how much he owed.

The restaurant owner named a sum that seemed somewhat too low. On the other hand, the grub hadn't been worth much.

They left together. Cohen was a head taller than Albert. He asked, "Have you seen anything of Tel Aviv yet?"

"Very little. Is there much to see?"

"To be honest, there is nothing to see," he said thoughtfully. "You know, this is a city built for living in. There are no monuments, no public squares, no parks. Only a few commercial streets with stores and offices and a few residential streets with a bit of green. It was originally planned as a suburb of Jaffa, for a few dozen families who no longer wanted to live in the dirt and dust. But now we have more than thirty thousand people in Tel Aviv, so we've become a city with all the accoutrements – a municipal council, a fire department, our own police, garbage pickup and what not."

"Taxes, too?"

"Does anything work without taxes anywhere?"

Albert had the feeling it was time to say goodbye to Mr. Cohen. He wanted to do some sightseeing on his own and he had inconvenienced the other man long enough already. "I am really very grateful for your guidance, and I hope we will meet again if I stay in the country," he said, offering to shake hands.

Cohen ignored the outstretched hand. "If you stay in the country? You don't intend to leave, do you? A Jew must live in Israel. That's the only place he belongs."

Albert remembered hearing the same words from Mr. Werba, his Hebrew teacher, more than twelve years before. Outwardly there was no resemblance between tall, broad-shouldered Mr. Cohen and short, skinny Mr. Werba, but they had the same firm convictions. As a child, Albert had rebelled against such routine formulas. And he still rejected them.

"In my opinion, everybody should be allowed to choose to live where he feels comfortable – if he can afford that luxury, and if he's allowed to do so. It's not right to tell people: 'This is where you belong'. Each person has to decide that for himself. And there's no way I can make such a commitment after being here for only twelve hours."

Cohen had intended to invite the boy to his house the way he usually did with new immigrants. It was a good custom, and this form of hospitality was practiced by many other families. Mrs. Cohen was not thrilled at her husband's periodic announcements that a stranger was coming home with him but she never let the guest feel her dismay. It wasn't the extra work or even the expense she disapproved of but she hated to be seen by a strange man – or even worse, a strange woman – when she had just washed her hair or was wearing a shabby house-dress.

Cohen's enthusiastic feeling for the Jewish cause in Palestine made it hard for him to understand how a Jew who had already come up to the land could say he didn't know whether he would stay here. If he didn't have the proper dedication, why was he here in the first place? Just out of curiosity? He was glad the young man had paid his own restaurant bill. He didn't want to go out of his way for someone who was nothing more than a tourist.

"It was a pleasure to meet you. I wish you all the best. Shalom!" With those words, Mr. Cohen, shook Albert's hand vigorously and ran quickly to the other side of the street. His opinion of German Jews had plummeted.

Albert was glad to be alone again. Unaware though he was of Mr. Cohen's thoughts, he had come to the exact same conclusion himself: he lacked the proper dedication to be a Jew in Israel. He had never cared much for the religion, so in what way was he really a Jew? Because his environment had made him one? Palestine was as alien to him as China. He had become estranged from Germany because he was Jewish, but here he felt very German. Yet strictly speaking he was neither.

He walked down the street, deep in thought The sidewalk was becoming increasingly crowded with women and girls shopping after work. Albert wondered where the street went. First it bent and then it led downhill to the sea, where a red sun was about to set in its watery bed. He walked to the end where there was a railing overlooking a narrow sandy beach. He leaned against the parapet and watched the sunset. Anyone seeing him standing there so intent might have thought he had never seen the sun setting over the sea before.

———

Even when we sleep badly, we still sleep. The bed was hard and uncomfortable, with bulges and knots in a mattress that seemed to be filled with seaweed. In the evening, his hotel room looked even more dismal than it had in the daytime. The light came from a single naked bulb dangling from its own electrical cord. The only place where Albert could unpack a few things was the table. Twisting and turning on the awful bed, which squeaked at every movement, he produced a symphony of sounds like a broken pipe. In spite of his miserable mood and the noise, he fell asleep eventually and woke up only when the morning was already bright. First he thought it was the squeaking of the bed that had roused him, but then he realized that the sound he heard was coming from the street. He went to the window, opened the shutter, and saw a school band outside. Students marched by with drums and trumpets, their teachers acting like sergeants, trying to keep them in order. The young musicians tried as hard to maintain the beat as they did to keep in tune; occasionally they were successful. Other boys and girls, happy, healthy and sun-tanned, were singing the song the band was supposed to be playing.

Prussians may march better, Albert thought, but they have a lot less fun doing it. What might Papa have felt had he seen these uninhibited children: children who were not a minority in their school, who didn't have to worry what others thought of them, who didn't have to prove themselves, who had a personal connection to the curriculum and with the language in which they were being taught? Although he knew his father would have been extremely enthusiastic, he was not excited because he didn't feel connected to the children the way Papa would have been. He didn't identify with them, which was the key to his problem. He felt closer to his family's maid, Minna, or to his former classmate Borck than to his supposed nation. He wasn't even convinced that the Jews constituted a nation. But if he intended to settle here he had to become a real Jew inside and not just call himself one because others hung a sign around his neck.

Albert took a large terrycloth towel from his suitcase, grabbed a bar of soap and his razor and marched to the bathroom, whistling a melody from the *Threepenny Opera*: "You have to give a man his chance, for his chance is a man's God." Standing in the wobbly bathtub under a cold shower, he scrutinized at his naked body, especially the part which revealed him to be an honourable member of the club. "My dear circumcised friend," he said, "you only make me a Jew externally." He remembered what the poet Wilhelm Busch had observed: 'It's so easy to become a father, so hard to be one.' and paraphrased, 'It's so easy to become a Jew, so hard to be one.' Hell, it's not only hard to become a Jew mentally and morally; it's even more painful physically."

Suddenly the maid, a Yemenite Jew, came in to scrub the bathroom. Albert had forgotten to lock the door. She stopped dead on the threshold. Why was that young man standing naked in the bathtub laughing? She mumbled an excuse and quickly closed the door. Since her skin was brownish-black, like dark chocolate,

Albert couldn't tell whether she had blushed or not. He was supposed to have a shared culture and ethnic origin with her, but felt closer to Emma Krupnick or Edith the whore. His dear departed father's belief that Jews all over the world were a common nation was clearly insanity.

Albert towelled himself dry and stood before the mirror to shave. The cold shower and the appearance of the Yemenite girl had been enough to wipe away the last traces of his self-doubt. If a Jewish ethnic group didn't exist, Zionism was built on a wrong premise and this whole movement in Palestine was only a heroic attempt to prove an erroneous assumption. Rubbing cologne on his freshly shaven cheeks he imagined sending all these thoughts in a long letter to Günther. He could just imagine how his friend would reply:

"You're a cretin who is constantly contradicting himself. There is no such thing as absolute truth. Everyone sees truth only with his own eyes. You're just finding it hard to see your own truth because you're squinting too much and peering in all directions."

Albert put his things away and left the bathroom, reflecting on how very pretty the Yemenite girl had been.

———◆———

Albert hadn't come to Palestine for the purpose of discovering himself. He couldn't afford that luxury. He wanted to find a new home and a way to earn his living. His mother was now managing the Berg factory to which he had said farewell with a graceful bow. Hoping to find financial security in another country, he had brought along some samples of their products. Should he be able to sell a few orders, he would build up an import business here representing German manufacturers. He had already negotiated with a few other firms and received positive feedback.

Of course Palestine was much too small a market to support him, but if he could expand his sales to neighbouring Syria, Egypt, and Iraq, he could make a living. This assumption had been confirmed by an ad posted in the paper three months ago by a Lebanese company looking for German manufacturers of the same kind of articles he had in his sample case. The Gallides Brothers were expecting him to arrive in Beirut any day with his samples. The Fratelli Gallides wanted the sub-agency for Syria and Lebanon and for the Alawite State. He could give it to them. He would deal with Palestine himself and find a local agent in Egypt. There were no technical obstacles. The only issue was price On this beautiful cool day, his second in Palestine, a day which had begun amusingly with poor music and a chocolate-coloured surprise in the bathroom, he didn't feel the least remnant of the bad mood of the previous day. While there had been sunshine yesterday, today the sun was shining with a golden light and the sky was a shade of blue he had never seen before.

The hall outside his room was being scrubbed. He heard the splashing of water and the swooping of a cloth as well as the knocking of a broomstick. Stone floors in this climate were practical, he realized, since they were not only easy to keep clean but cool underfoot. The young Yemenite was singing a strange kind of song while she worked. It wasn't a melody in the European style but more like a series of monotonously repeated cadences. His musically trained ear discerned quarter and half notes in a minor key. She sang them in a somewhat nasal and muffled voice. So that was unadulterated Middle Eastern music! Not pretty, but interesting. The song had a slight, very slight resemblance to Grieg's *Peer Gynt*.

Albert pulled a light-weight light-coloured suit from his patented suitcase with the wrinkle-free guarantee. He'd had the suit made to measure for this journey. His mother thought it was too pale, since his year of mourning for his father hadn't ended yet, but he'd insisted that respect for the departed wasn't demonstrated by the colour of one's clothes. In spite of the suitcase's guarantee his new suit was very wrinkled, but he hoped that it would straighten out as he wore it.

He counted his money. He had to be careful now since, before earning any kind of revenue, he still had to travel to Lebanon and Egypt and have money left over to live on. As cheap and primitive as this hotel was, it would be too expensive for him in the long run. He would have to find a furnished room instead. Because the funds the German national bank allowed him to take out of the country were so limited, he had smuggled out some additional money. The thoroughness of the German border control made him he realize how foolish that was. He could easily have ended up in jail instead of in Tel Aviv.

More out of fun than as a precaution, he asked his mother to sew a little bag containing ten thousand-mark banknotes into the crotch of his underpants, close to the other little bag whose contents were even more important to him. When a customs officer had come into his railway compartment in Kehl and ordered him to empty all his pockets and take off his shoes, he'd started to worry. The officer made him stand up and raise his arms, then patted him down under the arms, around the hips, and even along the pant legs. But the officer's hand had only lightly passed the crucial area. The bulge there seemed natural for a man. Albert had been lucky.

Now he felt lucky again, having the extra money. He was sure he could change German marks at the foreign exchange shops. His program for the day would be breakfast first, then the bank, and then he would get to know the town and look for a room. He should also visit some old family friends whose addresses he had found among his father's papers. Perhaps those people would give him advice like Mr. Cohen yesterday, who suggested that he drive a truck or a bus. That idea seemed so ridiculous to him now that he started to grin. The chamber maid – whose name was Mazal – interpreted the grin quite differently and gave him a shy smile in return.

XVII
JANUARY 1933

———◆———

The heavy bus belonging to the Compagnie des Autos-Routières du Levant crawled up a hill that jutted out into the sea. The hill reminded Albert of the chalk cliffs of Dover, although there had been no sky so blue nor sun so bright in England during the month of January. Nor indeed in any other month.

The border with Lebanon was indicated by both the Hebrew name *Rosh Hanikrah* and the Arabic *Ras el-Nakura*: *the peak of the cut in the rock*. The drive from Haifa had taken less than an hour. Unfortunately, the bus only stopped in the ancient city of Akko for two minutes to let passengers board. Albert would have liked to explore this city of the Phoenicians and of the tribe of Asher. Titus had landed here to suppress the rebellion of the Jews. Roman legions had marched through its harbour into the town – both of which still looked as they must have two thousand years ago – on their way to the Galilee and to Jerusalem. Later the crusaders landed here. Marco Polo started out from here. This was the only place the Turks were able to ward off Napoleon, the only city he couldn't conquer.

Albert was amazed how much history was packed into this small city with the short name. But maybe having read so much about the past made him look for things that were no longer there. He was quite sure that his seed-cracking seat-mate saw nothing more in Akko than the lemonade vendor with the brass barrel on his back doing business with passengers. To fill a cup he simply bent over, and lemonade flowed through a long spigot running over his shoulder. If European barmaids poured beer over their shoulders like that their business would be booming.

The bus entered the border station, an open-sided structure flying the uninspired flag of the British protectorate on its roof. The flag's blue field sported a round white blotch inscribed with the word *Palestine*. The driver and his assistant emptied the baggage compartment of the vehicle and threw suitcases and bundles onto the customs counter. The border guards – two tall, thin, uniformed British policemen and their three Arab subordinates – didn't show much interest in their contents, since these people were leaving the country. They only felt a bag here and a grabbed a bundle there.

Albert asked one of the British officers why they bothered to check the baggage at all, given that there were no foreign exchange restrictions nor any kind of export bans in place.

"The law requires that we check, so we check," was his answer.

"But what are you looking for?"

"Why do you want to know?" the British officer asked.

"I'm just wondering."

"Oh, really? Please open your suitcase."

Albert regretted his curiosity. He didn't want to have to unpack and repack everything, and worried that his nice clean shirts would get dirty.

The officer examined the contents of the suitcase with a solemn face: shaving things, shirts and ties, two suits, underwear. Only a little green and purple-striped cardboard box evoked a comment. "Very hygienic for Beirut" he said. "However these things don't protect against infection as well as they do against pleasure."

Albert laughed. "Many thanks. Now I know what is being checked here."

The officer shrugged his shoulders and drew a chalk mark on the suitcase.

The passengers boarded the bus again and it drove down the north side of the mountain for a few minutes before coming to another barrier and a customs station flying the French flag. Here, the formalities took a little longer, and there was more talk, but finally they continued on their way. It was noticeably cooler than on the Palestinian side, almost cold, and the first raindrops fell from a suddenly dark sky. As they drove through Saida it began to pour. The rain lasted until they arrived in Beirut. The whole trip had taken slightly longer than three hours.

"Place des Canons," the driver called. Albert first thought he was cursing, but then he understood that it was the name of the square where they disembarked. One of the Gallides Brothers would be meeting him, so he looked around at the people standing near the bus. A short, slim young man with pale blue eyes wearing a red fez on his straw-yellow hair kept turning to his fellow passengers, asking them something before retreating. He looked like a tout for a hotel. Suddenly the man's blue eyes were directed at Albert.

"Pardon, do you happen to be Monsieur Berg?" he asked in good French.

"It didn't just happen. My parents were married." Albert smiled. The young man wearing the fez didn't get the joke so he added, "And you are Monsieur Gallides, aren't you?"

"Yes, I am the son. Welcome to Beirut. Of all the passengers who got off here, you were the only one I was sure was not Monsieur Berg."

"But why?"

"You look so local."

Perhaps this was his polite way of telling Albert that he looked Middle Eastern and not like a boy from Europe? Which was odd, because Albert himself was surprised to find someone from the Middle East with the Greek name of *Gallides* resembling a miniature Viking, despite his red fez. A somewhat older edition of Gallides was waiting for them in the hotel lobby. As it turned out, there hadn't been any Gallides Brothers for a long time, only this father and his son. It also turned out that the blond and blue-eyed gentlemen under the Moslem fezes were Sephardic Jews from Smyrna.

After exchanging the usual niceties and making arrangements for business meetings the following day, Gallides Senior said goodbye and Junior asked, "You're probably tired after your trip?"

Albert wasn't experienced enough to know that, in the Middle East, such a question is intended to evoke the answer "yes." In fact, it means "I would like to get rid of you." But Albert took the question at face value and replied, "It wasn't such a long trip, more like a very scenic drive. So I'm not tired at all; quite the opposite."

Jacob Gallides, called *Jacques*, was momentarily silent, then he accepted his fate and replied, "Then it will be a pleasure to show you some of Beirut's nightlife. You probably want to freshen up a bit and perhaps change your clothes, so I will pick you up in about two hours."

"That would be very nice," Albert said. Remembering his own good manners, he added, "May I invite you to have dinner with me this evening? I see they're already serving it in the dining room."

Jacques was a little embarrassed. "No, many thanks, but I'm not allowed to eat here."

Albert didn't understand why a citizen of the city shouldn't be allowed to eat at the hotel. Was it only for tourists? Only after the young Gallides had left did he remember that Sephardic Jews were strict in their eating habits and the hotel wasn't kosher.

Thank God it isn't Kosher! Albert reflected, as he dined alone, but with a good appetite, enjoying a delicious lobster and other food prepared in the best French fashion. He disliked Arab cuisine, finding it too heavy and spicy, while the Jewish food in Palestine had been simply inedible. If the French had done nothing else in Lebanon beyond introducing their cooking, they deserved the gratitude of the entire population.

Jacques showed up with three friends. One of them had a small French car. The rain had stopped, and it had turned a lot colder.

"I didn't expect a real winter in the Middle East," Albert remarked.

"It's already January 30th," one of his companions said. "The end of January till the end of February is the coldest period here."

They drove slowly through the streets of Beirut, which reminded Albert of Marseilles. Almost all the signs were in French and the better-dressed people were speaking French with each other. If it hadn't been for the drivers screaming at each other in Arabic, the illusion of being in France would have been complete.

The tour ended on the waterfront. not far from Albert's hotel, in front of a brightly lit white-washed establishment. A sign over the entrance said "Kit-Kat" in big letters.

"What's this?" Albert asked.

"A cabaret."

The Palestinian Jews had been much too puritanical for cultural institutions such as this. It seemed strange to him that five men would visit a place of entertainment on their own, without dates, but inside all the customers seemed to be men. The only females were onstage where ten girls, scantily clad, danced in a chorus line. They seemed truly bored, swinging their behinds and forcing their faces into fixed smiles. The dance troop wasn't just mediocre, it was miserable; nonetheless the girls all had good figures and shapely legs, which explained the applause they received. The customers in the place weren't very interested in the performance anyway. They just wanted to see half-naked bodies, breasts, and slender legs.

"They're from Paris," Jacques explained proudly.

"But the members of the jazz band are Palestinian," one of his friends said. "The sax player is excellent. His name is Menahem."

Albert had to admit that the band wasn't bad.

"You're probably glad you're living in Tel Aviv now rather than Berlin," another said, and then Jacques asked, "What's going to happen to your factory in Berlin? Do you think you'll be able to continue your business manufacturing and delivering?"

"Why not?"

"Don't you listen to the radio?"

"No, I didn't read the newspaper today either. Did something bad happen?" He'd had very little information from home in the three months that he'd been away, but doubted there had been an earthquake in the sands of Brandenburg.

"German President Hindenburg has named Adolf Hitler as Chancellor; the radio announced it his evening," the young men announced, almost in unison.

Albert gasped. That was far worse than an earthquake! How could such a lunatic have become Chancellor? Surely they were joking? But their faces were serious, and it was unlikely that all four of them had misunderstood the news.

"It's surely a temporary crisis," he explained, reminding himself that the Nazis were still a minority in Germany. "You have to understand: There are almost fifteen million unemployed in Germany, and that's a terrible problem. It confuses people. But the German nation is not a tribe of drunken savages. They'll come to their senses again soon."

"Now I know that you're a Jew. I didn't believe Jacques at first when he told me so," one of the men said ruefully.

I don't understand what you mean."

"You're an optimist. Jews are dyed-in-the-wool optimists. But they're not always right."

"Why are Jews always optimists?" another asked.

"Because in general, they've been so badly off everywhere that things can only get better for them."

"So let's hope that Monsieur Albert's opinion is the right one. After all, he comes from Germany, so he can judge the situation better than we can," Jacques said, raising a glass of arrack made cloudy by a splash of water. "This is the best arrack in the world. It's made in Zahle."

"Where is that?" Albert asked. He had never heard of Zahle, and it was also the first time he had encountered this sweet drink that smelled of anise. It went to his head quickly. He couldn't tell whether the sudden heat he felt came from the alcohol or the news.

"Zahle is a small town in the mountains of Lebanon," Jacques explained.

A group of acrobats was performing onstage. The Parisian dancers now functioned as bar girls. Some walked through the rows of tables hoping to join the patrons. Jacques apparently regarded it as his duty to offer his foreign guest something special, so when one of the artists slowly strolled by, he pulled out a chair and asked her politely to sit down and be comfortable. She immediately accepted the invitation.

"*Bon soir, Messieurs.*"

"*Bon soir, Mademoiselle.*"

There was a pause and general silence. The girl realized that she was expected to begin the conversation. She had a flawless body but cold grey eyes, dyed blond hair and a brutal mouth. Still, she was pretty in a vulgar sort of way.

"*La danse, ça vous a plaît?*" she asked. Her way of asking the question as well as her pronunciation seemed very strange to Albert. It was an odd form of *Parisien*. She had pronounced *danse* more like *dants*. The young men assured her loudly and enthusiastically that they had all loved the dance. But Albert added quietly in German, "I've seen better dancing. Where are you from?"

She turned around as if stung by a hornet. "From Dresden. You speak German?" She was so surprised that her big mouth stayed open. "Where did you learn German?" She must have assumed he was Lebanese, given his little black moustache, especially since there was a pile of fezes stacked on a chair at his table.

Meeting a *Parisian* hooker from Dresden who apparently regarded him as Lebanese helped Albert forget the bad news from home. He decided to continue the charade by replying, "I bought a book called *Teach Yourself German*." Before the girl could answer, he added: "But we must speak French now because my friends here don't understand a word of German."

This statement was true; in fact, since the other men hadn't understood any of the German conversation, one of them remarked, "*Alors, vous avez trouvé un compatriote.*"

Feeling she'd been made a fool of, the girl squinted her eyes and looked at Albert angrily. "Where do you really come from?"

"My angel, you should have already guessed it."

She pondered the situation briefly. Cheeky people are always from Berlin. "You must be a Berliner."

"Right. You're a smart girl," Albert said.

Appeased by this flattery, she devoted herself seriously to the job of entertaining the young men and encouraging them to order more drinks. In this capacity, she demonstrated the sense of humour usually associated with her native city as well as typically German thoroughness.

It turned out to be an expensive evening.

Albert took out his wallet. Jacques didn't want to let him pay, but Albert knew that the young men had only come to the cabaret on his account. Besides which – if it was true what they said about Hitler becoming chancellor – many things would have to change, including his personal plans. Jacques Gallides started arguing with the waiter with the result that some bank notes were returned to Albert, who had no idea what they were worth and therefore didn't know if he had actually contributed anything at all to the cost of the evening's entertainment. A combination of arrack and cognac and Lebanese wine had made him an incompetent calculator.

The foggy feeling didn't begin to diminish until he found himself on a path of paving stones and felt a sharp wind coming from the sea on his face. His beautiful hotel stood on a small rocky island opposite the city. A stone causeway connected it with the mainland, and he suddenly recognized that he was standing at the beginning of this causeway. With increasing clarity he also realized how his wobbly feet had conveyed him there. The girl from Dresden was holding him tightly under one arm. The last remnant of his tipsiness evaporated and sobering thoughts came to his mind.

"Thank you for your help," he said. "But why are you here?"

It was a rather brutal remark but she didn't seem to care. "In the first place, your friends asked me to look after you, and in the second place I haven't had an opportunity to speak German for over a year now. And thirdly … thirdly, as a matter of principle, I always go with the monkey who is paying the bill. It's safer."

Albert erupted in loud laughter. "Three reasons and one principle – enchanting!" His conscience told him he should send her away with a few pound notes, but he hadn't been with a woman since he had broken off with Marion. In the struggle between conscience and desire, conscience only wins the day after.

She seemed to know exactly what he was thinking. "It won't cost you much, because I don't feel like walking back to the flea-bitten shack where I live. What's your room number?"

"Room 132."

"Go to your room, but leave the door open."

"How are you going to get in? The St. George is very posh."

"Never mind posh. Please give me a five-pound note, or some smaller bills if you have any. I'll need them to grease the doorman's palm and then everything will be well-lubricated. 132 you said?"

"Yes."

"Bye."

Alone, Albert walked to the hotel lobby, still a little wobbly. He took the room key from the night porter. Since she had just relieved him so elegantly of five pounds, he was sure he would never see her again. Six Syrian pounds were equivalent to one Palestinian pound, which meant twelve marks. Five pounds were ten marks, so he hadn't got off too badly. He resolved to leave the door unlocked just in case, content whether or not she turned up. After washing up and undressing he lay down on his bed, intending to wait up for her, but the late hour and the alcohol won out and he fell asleep immediately.

He woke up because he was cold and pulled the blanket back over him, still half asleep. Then he bumped against something that woke him up completely. There was a second body in his bed! It took a few seconds before he remembered the events of the evening. He turned the bedside lamp on and looked at his companion. She was fast asleep, her mouth open, giving her an almost childlike appearance in spite of the streaks of eye makeup that had run across her cheeks. He felt sorry for her. It was a hard way of making a living. He decided not to wake her up, not relishing the thought of having sex with someone who probably serviced a different man every night. He turned the light off again, turned over, and fell asleep.

He woke up a second time, hearing something. The bed was empty and the grey light of dawn was already coming through the window. He looked at his watch: a few minutes to six. He heard water running in the bathroom. So the vendor of lust hadn't run away yet but was taking a bath in in Albert Berg's Public Bathroom. For some inexplicable reason he started laughing. She was taking quite a lot of liberties – for example, his suitcase lay open, with his second pair of pyjamas on top, wrinkled, but neatly folded. No wonder she had looked so familiar during the night. She'd been wearing his spare pyjamas. What insolence!

A figure appeared from the bathroom, wrapped in a large terrycloth towel.

"Oh, you're up. Good morning."

"Good morning, Miss. Now that we've shared a bed, it might be a good idea for me to know your name."

"Inge. You can say *Du* to me. You slept like a dead man, so I didn't want to wake you up when I got here. Do you want to now?"

"Do I want what now?"

"Don't act as if you didn't know." Inge dropped the big towel and stood before him naked. When he didn't make a move, she turned around and said, "So don't. At least it was a good bed. Such an elegant hotel does have its advantages."

Albert was tickled by her Saxon dialect. It always made him laugh the way peeling onions made him cry. He decided that he didn't want her to go.

"Inge, I didn't want to insult you, but I have to go to the bathroom first," he said.

She nodded knowingly and returned to the bed. He went to his suitcase, took out the little cardboard box the Palestinian customs officer had commented on, and disappeared with it into the bathroom.

———•———

Only when he closed his eyes and thought of Marion was he able to do his masculine duty. The shapely body lying beside him with her routine willingness hadn't excited him in the least. He imagined being in bed with Henja and Marion. When it was over, he was almost surprised to find an unknown creature who didn't mean anything to him. Silently he went back to the bathroom and cleaned himself. When he came back, Miss Inge from Dresden was already fully dressed.

"Well, was it good with me?" she asked, like a child who wants to be praised for her report card.

"Yes, very nice," he said. What else could he tell her?

She put her stockings back on. "All the men tell me that. They all say, nobody does it like Inge."

Albert had to smile. He had no experience with prostitutes, but suspected he had encountered a German phenomenon here. Prostitutes in all countries doubtless performed their age-old profession the same way, but only a German whore would develop professional pride. He would have liked to know why a girl from Dresden had come to the Middle East. Had she volunteered for the job? Was she a victim of the white slave trade? When he asked her how she had come to Beirut, she told him about the steamer and her sea sickness but not about her reasons for coming, so he decided not to probe any further. After all, she hadn't asked him any questions at all, not even his name. For her, he was the gentleman in Room 132.

He was embarrassed to ask her how much he owed her, but she simply said ten Syrian pounds, which equalled twenty marks. He gave her the money and she opened the door, looked down the hall to the left and to the right, and quietly said, "*Auf Wiedersehen*." Then she was gone.

Ships that pass in the night.

X V I I

"Even though driving through snow on icy mountain roads isn't easy, it was a good idea to rent this car, Jacques," Albert said. He carefully steered the 1929 Ford down the Antilebanon Mountains from Damascus to the plains before climbing up again into the Lebanon mountain range. The mountains were white with snow but the plains between them, which constituted the border between Syria and Lebanon, were as yellow and bare as a desert. There the formerly sinuous highway became perfectly straight.

Jacques kept trying to light a cigarette, first with a lighter and then with a match. When they closed all the car windows the windshield fogged up, so they had to keep one open in spite of the cold. The operation succeeded only when Albert rolled up the window briefly.

"If we had taken the train, we would have arrived in Damascus today and would only be back in Beirut the day after tomorrow," Jacques explained.

"But your father was against us driving on these roads."

"My father worries about his son," Jacques laughed. "I meant to ask, how did you like Damascus?"

"It's interesting, but I wouldn't want to live there. It feels as though nothing has changed there for two hundred years."

"Perhaps. But we made some good sales. It's lucky that you have merchandise ready and waiting in Tel Aviv."

"The goods are not in Tel Aviv but in the duty-free warehouse in Haifa. Still, they can be delivered within a week," Albert said.

"Great! But what's going to happen later? Do you think that political developments in Germany will cause any business problems for you?"

"I doubt it."

Jacques rolled down his window again and threw his cigarette butt on the road.

"Have you noticed that it's warmer here?"

"Maybe, but it's still a lot colder than I thought it would be in the Middle East. It was really cold in Damascus, and the charcoal stove in the hotel salon, where all the guests gathered, didn't provide much warmth. It just smelled bad."

"That's the odour of burning charcoal. We're used to it; that kind of stove is traditional here."

Albert blew the horn. A lone cyclist was riding his bike on the wrong side of the road. A *kefiyeh*, the white kerchief typical of rural Arabs, was wrapped around his head and neck, and his wide baggy pants billowed in the wind like balloons. He looked at them but stayed on the left.

"What do you call those stoves that are domed like mosques?"

"They're called *mangall*. Watch it! Oh my God!" Jacques called out because, at that moment, the cyclist decided to pass over to the right side of the road directly in front of their car.

Albert braked as hard as he could. The car began to spin and the left front fender smashed against the bicycle, throwing its rider off. His head hit the pavement on the other side of the road and he didn't get up.

Albert brought the car to a halt thirty metres further on and they ran back. The man showed no signs of life, but the desert around them revived. Although there had been no houses or bushes – let alone a living being – visible before, all of a sudden there were Arabs swarming everywhere, all running towards the scene of the accident.

"Monsieur Albert, run to the car! We must get away from here as fast as possible!" Jacques shouted.

"But we can't just leave the scene of an accident. That's an international law," Albert shouted back, instinctively following Jacques to the car.

"Which do you prefer?" Jacques panted, throwing himself in. "Obeying a beautiful rule or escaping without a knife in your belly?"

Albert turned the key in the ignition and the car started immediately. It shot ahead, not a second too soon. An Arab wearing an open sheepskin jacket, his *kefiyeh* blowing in the wind, was trying to hang on to the moving vehicle. But he failed because he only had one free hand; he was swinging a dagger in the other.

"What should we do now?" Albert asked, more to himself than to his companion.

"Get home as fast as possible. My friend has a garage where the fender and the headlight can be repaired. Nobody there will tell the police anything. That's how they make their money," Jacques said.

"I'm not going to do that," Albert declared categorically. "The accident wasn't my fault. That idiot was riding his bike on the wrong side of the road. I couldn't know that he would suddenly turn right ahead of us. So I have nothing to fear if I report immediately to the nearest police station."

"You don't know our police! Please listen to me. There was no traffic on the road; no one was behind us. And no one was in front of us either with the exception of the cyclist, and he is either dead or unconscious. The wild *fellahin* who would have stabbed us to death if you hadn't listened to me will take three hours to reach Chtaura and make a report. We can be in Beirut by then with the car stowed safely in the garage. Believe me, that's the best solution."

"Jacques, that solution goes against common decency. Besides, if the man is really dead, and the police investigate and they find out that I was the one driving the car, I'll probably go to prison. I don't look forward to spending time a Syrian prison, believe me."

"It would be a Lebanese prison because we're already in Lebanon." Jacques pointed his index finger at a dark spot still far away. "That's Chtaura over there."

Albert finally slowed down outside the town. He saw the police station a second before Jacques pointed it out, and pulled over.

"You're making a big mistake, Monsieur Albert, but ..." Jacques threw up his hands in a gesture of despair, sighed deeply, and followed Albert to the police station.

Outside the door, a policeman was busy fastening a stretcher to the sidecar of a motorcycle. Just inside a second policeman, with the stripes of a sergeant on his sleeve, sat at a table writing down a report he was receiving on the telephone. Both were uniformed from head to toe just like the French police.

"I want to report that I just had an accident, a collision with a cyclist," Albert declared in a voice that seemed hoarse to him.

"Oh yes. We already know about it," the sergeant replied, also in French but with a strong Arabic accent.

Jacques replied incredulously, "You can't, because except for us, no one could have reported it."

The sergeant stood up, stretching to his full height – which wasn't very impressive – and said, "Monsieur, you hit a cyclist who was proceeding in the same direction, but on the left side of the road. After you gave him a signal, he wanted to move over to the right side of the road. Since you drove faster than the sixty-five-kilometre-an-hour speed limit, the cyclist could not get to the other side quickly enough. You were driving a dark blue American car and left the scene of the accident without offering the injured man any assistance. You also fled without giving your name or licence number to the people who witnessed the accident. The licence plate was illegible because it was covered with dirt from the road."

The sergeant looked at the sheet of paper from which he had just read this text. "I will now delete the last part because, according to the law, you did *not* flee from the scene since you contacted the first and nearest police station immediately after the accident. We are the first and nearest police station."

Jacques was amazed, and shook his head to see whether he was dreaming. Albert was reminded of the magical tales of the thousand and one nights. How did the police know all this? No other driver, no house with a telephone, and no house or sign of civilization had been anywhere near the accident.

Albert cleared his throat. "Monsieur le Sergeant, we only fled because the witnesses at the scene came after us with knives. But it puzzles me how they could have given you this report so quickly."

The sergeant couldn't suppress a smile. "Telephone wires run along that road all the way to Damascus. Two hundred metres from the place where the accident happened, a man was sitting high up on the pole, repairing a line. He had a telephone, and informed us about what he saw."

While they were talking, two more gendarmes had appeared. The policeman with the motorcycle left, revving his engine loudly. The sergeant said a few words in Arabic to the new arrivals, and a second policeman left. Another motorcycle was heard before its noise abated as it drove off into the distance. When it had become quiet again, the sergeant said, "So now we'll compile a report. Your papers please. First your driver's licence. Are you authorized to drive a car?"

Albert handed him the brand-new driver's licence, which he had received from the Palestinian police in Jaffa just a month previously. Like all Palestinian documents, it was printed in the three official languages. Since he was travelling on a tourist visa he wasn't permitted to stay longer than three months. But if he travelled to another country, he could re-enter the country and stay for another three months, which is why he had scheduled this business trip before the first three months were up.

However, as a tourist, he was not authorized to apply for a Palestinian driver's licence. Albert had explained his problem to a taxi driver in Tel Aviv who had chauffeured him on his first trips around the country.

"What's the problem? Just dress in a sloppy way," the cabbie had suggested. He had gone to his driving test wearing a sweaty shirt and old torn khaki pants. The British policeman who gave him the test took a quick look at him, wrote his name and address on a form, drove around with him for three minutes and handed him the driver's licence. Suspicion that Albert wasn't local had never entered his mind. That was the driver's licence the sergeant was now holding in his hands.

"From Palestine? The driver's licence is recognized here, but do you have a visa for Lebanon?"

Albert pulled his passport from his pocket on whose brownish cover a black eagle spread its wings. The sergeant spelled out the words: *Dutches Reish,* then asked, "You're from Holland?"

"No, from Germany."

"But here it says '*Deutsch*' – he pronounced it *Dutch*.

"*Deutsch* means *Allemand* in the German language," Albert corrected him.

"Is that so?" The sergeant still had his doubts. He leafed through the passport and found a visa stamped by the French consulate in Berlin for the countries under

French mandate. That satisfied him. On a form he recorded passport number, visa number, names, date and place of birth, then returned the driver's licence to Albert while keeping his passport. Finally he stood up and said, "We need to drive back to the scene. I will come in your car."

Albert and Jacques left the police station walking behind the sergeant. The gendarme who had stood at the door the whole time without Albert noticing now walked along behind them. For the first time since he entered the station, Albert was worried. He turned to Jacques and said, "I feel like we have been arrested."

The sergeant heard the comment, turned around and said, "You're not under arrest. Not yet."

This gave Albert a bad feeling. He looked at Jacques questioningly. Jacques started to tell him something in Hebrew, but he had second thoughts about it and remained silent. Like almost all Sephardic Jews in the Middle East, Jacques Gallides spoke some Hebrew, but since Albert also wasn't fluent, they only spoken French with each other.

Albert drove slowly with two policemen in the car. But the sergeant, who sat next to him, asked him to speed up. "The marks will disappear if we don't get there soon," he explained.

"What marks?"

"Your skid marks. We need to figure out how fast you were driving. That will determine whether the accident was your fault or not."

"But listen!" Albert was gradually becoming angry. "The bicyclist was an ass. He drove directly in front of me. If I hadn't pulled the car over to the side and quickly hit the brake, I would have driven right over him. As it was, he only got a bump. Since he didn't bleed at all, I assumed he was only stunned."

The sergeant lowered his voice. Apparently he didn't want the other policeman and Jacques, who were sitting in the back, hear what he had to say. "I'm not interested in that fellow. As far as I'm concerned, he might as well be dead. One Moslem less. You're a Jew, living in Palestine. I'm a Maronite. The Maronite Christians in Lebanon are the greatest supporters of the Jewish goal in Palestine. We're natural allies. We're also the oldest nations in these two countries. Jews and Christians lived here long before these wild Moslems. The stronger the Jews become in Palestine, the better it is for us. So you must understand that I want to help you, but I must comply with the rules."

"Of course, I understand completely," Albert answered.

This was the first time in his life so far that it had been an advantage to be Jewish.

The motorcycle with the sidecar was coming toward them. On the stretcher was a motionless body. Albert instinctively braked, but the sergeant only gave his colleague a military salute and indicated that Albert should drive on. When they reached the scene of the accident Albert didn't know where to stop, but the police-man who had been at the police station earlier was standing on the road next to his motorcycle. On the side of the road stood a small group of Arabs wearing *kefiyes* and long jackets. Now they looked harmless.

First the two policemen walked around the car and looked carefully at the tires. Then they marched along the road to a place where there were tire tracks in the churned-up mud and melted snow. The imprints were repeated five metres ahead and then continued for quite a stretch like twin scars, becoming gradually fainter. They measured the skid marks in steps which were supposed to be a metre long each.

"I'm sorry, Monsieur," the sergeant turned to Jacques. "Your friend was in too much of a hurry. You drove at least seventy-five to eighty kilometres an hour, and that is against the law."

Albert shook his head. While he had been driving more than ninety, he was convinced no one could prove it, so he refused to admit it.

"Monsieur, it can be clearly seen where you braked for the first time. Then your car went into a spin, and finally you skidded when you let up on the brake. Now, unfortunately I have to bring you to the police headquarters." He stood at attention and declared in a formal tone of voice, "*Monsieur Albert Berg, au nom de la loi, vous êtes en état d'arrestation.*"

Jacques broke out in a torrent of protestations but Albert was much too agi-tated to say anything. The sergeant pulled a pack of cigarettes from his uniform jacket and offered each of them one. Now that the official part of the arrest was over, he became friendly again. They were pink cigarettes with bright red filters, probably intended for ladies. Albert thought he had recovered from his shock, but when he reached for the cigarette, he noticed that his hand was shaking.

"Do you think you will be able to continue driving?" the sergeant asked Albert. He must have noticed the shaking too.

Albert pulled himself together. "Of course," he said, and they all piled back into the rented car.

"How old are you?"

"Twenty-seven," Albert answered.

"Married?"

"No."

"Do you want to wait till you're old and impotent? I'm only two years older than you but I already have four children," the sergeant declared, obviously proud of his achievements. Albert wasn't in the mood to engage in small talk about the advantages of marriage and children. He had other worries now. He remembered Jacques's words, 'You don't know our police.'

Silently he drove along the wet road. The sergeant told him not to stop in Chtaura but to turn right. The road sign there said *Zahle*.

"Are we going to the town the arrack comes from?" he asked.

"Yes, the police headquarters is here. The hospital too, where the injured man was taken."

They were going uphill now. In the slush, driving was slow, but suddenly the town lay before them. It seemed to Albert that it consisted of only two streets, each with one row of houses. In reality it was a single road divided in the middle by a creek. The two lanes were connected by a stone bridge. They stopped in front of an administration building with a little courtyard in front and got out.

The sergeant, now all business again, asked Albert and Jacques to wait in the foyer. The other policeman sat on a chair next to the door, acting casual.

"I will announce you to the captain," the sergeant said.

"Now listen," Jacques said, after the sergeant had left. "Don't admit under any circumstances that you drove faster than sixty-five kilometres an hour. If the police captain wants to keep you here until the hearing, demand to speak to your consular officer immediately. They don't like dealing with the British consular officer but they aren't allowed to refuse. It always becomes a state affair."

"What does the British consular officer have to do with this?" Albert asked.

"He represents the interests of Palestinians in this country, just as the French consular officer represents the interests of Syria and Lebanon in Palestine."

"Jacques, you're forgetting that I'm not a Palestinian. I have a German passport."

"Oh yes, that's right. Luckily there is also a German consulate in Beirut."

Albert pondered this for a moment. Then he said with a bitter laugh, "Considering the latest developments in Germany, I suspect that the German consulate won't do anything to help a Jew. I can't use that card in my poker game."

"But you can bluff with it. They won't be up to date on foreign politics here," Jacques said.

A new policeman's face appeared in the door. "*Tafaddal, Effendi,*" the policeman said. With a gesture inviting Albert to enter, he added, "*Udkhul min faddlak, ya effendi.*" Was this overly friendly invitation only good manners, or was he ridiculing him?

The police captain was sitting at a desk whose baroque design and respectable age suggested it had already served in the Ottoman Empire. Monsieur le Capitaine himself had a constitution that would have honoured a nineteenth-century Prussian policeman. Looming between the files and papers on his desk and his head was a gigantic stomach. His small sharp eyes lit up in a full-moon face when the culprit and his companion entered. He beamed with enthusiasm, happy to enjoy a little diversion by interacting with a foreigner.

"Bonjour Monsieur le Capitaine," Albert and Jacques said almost simultaneously.

"Do you speak English? I don't speak French," the colossus said in English, and when Albert said yes, he added, "I hate the French."

Very frank, the police in Lebanon, Albert thought. *They tell complete strangers whom they dislike. The sergeant dislikes Moslems and the captain hates the French. I really wonder how this is going to develop.*

"I studied at the American university in Beirut, but this is the first time I have had an opportunity to speak English again since I came to Zahle. That makes me very happy."

Albert thought how beautiful and noble it was to make a man happy, although he wished his good deed could have taken a different form. The police captain, still happily beaming, declared, "So unfortunately I owe your visit in Zahle to the circumstance that you drove carelessly, as my sergeant has told me. What is your response to the charge?"

Albert quickly reflected. He had the feeling that his companion's advice might do more harm than good.

"Captain, you are completely right."

The captain's chair cracked from the sudden move the captain made, he was so surprised. Neither Jacques nor the sergeant, who stood at attention next to the big baroque desk, understood English, so Albert continued.

"I was driving at sixty-five kilometres an hour, which is permitted, but that was careless because I had failed to take two factors into account. One was the condition of the road after the snow, when the sand and the melted water make everything slippery, and the other was the cyclist's stupidity. That's why I admit that I am half to blame."

"Mister, don't be rash. It is for us to decide who is to blame," the captain said, laughing at his own joke. But then he said more seriously, "According to the law, the matter is as follows: If nothing happened to the man you hit, at least nothing serious, I can let you go, I mean if I accept your statement about the speed of your vehicle. My sergeant claims you were driving much faster than sixty-five kilometres an hour, but I admit that on a wet road, the skid marks can be longer even when you drive slowly. So that would be one possibility."

"And what would be the second?" Albert asked, curious.

"The second and third possibilities are something else. If the man was injured, we will confiscate your passport, and you will not be allowed to leave the French mandate territory before appearing at court, although you may move about freely within Lebanon. On the other hand, if the man is dead or if the doctor thinks the man will die from his injuries, I will have to take you to jail in Beirut."

Albert shuddered, and the captain hurried to ensure him that the jail in Beirut was very modern and comfortable.

"Do you know anything about the bicyclist's condition?" Albert asked hesitantly.

"No. As soon as we finish our coffee, we'll go to the hospital to see how he's doing." While the captain had been talking, an old man had arrived with a brass tray. At a signal from the captain, he served them all Turkish coffee in little cups. It was perhaps nothing but a traditional gesture, but Albert was deeply impressed. Not only because he really needed a cup of coffee, but also because of the unexpected way he was being treated. He couldn't imagine a European police officer offering a suspect coffee while warning him he might go to jail.

The hospital was on the other side of the connecting bridge. It would have taken only two minutes to walk there, but Monsieur le Capitaine insisted they drive. Since he occupied the entire back seat and the sergeant sat in front beside Albert, Jacques had to walk behind the car. Nevertheless, he arrived at the same time as the others.

An elegantly dressed gentleman, wearing a dark suit and red tie, with red handkerchief in his breast pocket and a red fez on his head, was waiting for them in front of the small, grey-painted building. He was the doctor. How he had known that he would have visitors was a puzzle, but Albert thought that Zahle probably held few secrets. The doctor spoke Arabic with the police captain and, for Albert's benefit, translated every sentence into French right away. A handsome man, he reminded Albert of Rudolph Valentino.

They all sat down together in the examination room. It was primitive but clean.

"The man is now conscious and complains about pain in his back. I couldn't find anything but a bump on the head, but can't certify that nothing else happened to him without X-raying his spine. He is also worried about who will pay for the damage to his bicycle," said the doctor.

The police captain pointed a finger at Albert. "I assume our friend here will look after any damage to the bicycle. I'm also certain that he will pay for the X-ray. So doctor, go and take a picture with your beautiful new X-ray machine."

Monsieur le Capitaine turned proudly to Albert. "You probably didn't expect that our hospital would have an X-ray machine, did you? We're not as backward here as people in other countries may think."

Albert expressed his admiration for the hospital and its modern equipment, despite his private opinion that it looked like a white-washed cow barn rubbed down with Lysol. He also confirmed his readiness to pay, but the doctor shook his head, apologizing. "Unfortunately we don't have any film for the X-ray machine. I have already ordered it from Beirut three times, but it hasn't come yet."

"How is that possible?" The captain was angry.

"The machine was a gift from the American university, but the Ministry of Health must provide the film and they are taking their time. Next week, next month, next year – who knows when supplies will arrive?"

Albert wondered whether he could send a taxi to Beirut to pick up the film, though he doubted any stores would still be open by the time it got there, given that it was already afternoon and considering the state of the roads. He was just about to voice his thoughts when Jacques Gallides, who had listened very carefully to both the Arabic conversation and the French version, spoke up.

"Can't you use the X-ray without film?"

Rudolph Valentino played with the stethoscope he was holding and thoughtfully looked at his hands before raising his eyes questioningly at the captain. Not a muscle stirred in the captain's fat face. The doctor also didn't bat an eyelash as he answered Jacques, "It could be done, but it would cost you a lot more money."

Parents who bring up their children according to the principles of truth and honesty sometimes do them great harm. The children may become adults who cannot cope with the realities of life. This is why it took a while before Albert realized what the doctor had meant. Then the blood rose to his face. How could anyone qualified to practice medicine, anyone who recited the Hippocratic Oath, agree to such a thing? It was a disgrace! And that jovial elephant, the police captain, was sitting beside him as a silent accomplice.

Jacques, on the other hand, had not only understood the situation immediately, but anticipated Albert's moral indignation and was very afraid he might express it. Overcome with emotion, he began speaking his native Ladino: "*Señor Albert, por la gracia de Dios*, keep your mouth shut now. Let me handle this, but give me your wallet." Then he retired with the doctor and the captain to another room for a little consultation.

Albert wasn't the only one who was outraged. The sergeant brought his fist down on his thigh. He was fuming with rage, perhaps also with shame. "*Koss*

Ummu, Koss ucht' abuhu," he exploded. Though Albert didn't speak a word of Arabic, the meaning of these curses, offering suggestions for the sexual satisfaction of the cursed person's mother and aunt, had already been explained to him. He didn't dare look the sergeant in the face. Through his own passive attitude, he had become an accomplice to bribery and corruption.

———◆———

The drive back across the mountains of Lebanon on a snow-covered road was so dangerous that Jacques – who had never learned to drive – was afraid to say anything about what had just happened in case he distracted Albert. It was ten o'clock at night when they finally arrived in Beirut, where there was no sign of snow. They were both hungry now. The events of the day had interfered with meals and also with their appetites. Supper was still being served on the wooden deck of the Lucullus Restaurant and although the place wasn't kosher, Albert was able to persuade Jacques to eat something.

"What did this affair cost me?" Albert wanted to know, after they had taken their seats at a table covered with a white cloth.

"The doctor wanted a hundred pounds but I negotiated him down to eighty. The police captain wanted fifty, and we agreed on forty. He claimed the money was really for the cyclist, but I'm sure the poor fellow won't see a piastre of it."

"At least I looked after him," Albert said. "The only good deed I did today. After you disappeared with the two gangsters and my wallet, I rummaged through my pockets and found a little over twenty pounds. I urged the sergeant, who was fuming with outrage, to accept the money and asked him to give it to the injured man, and that's what he did."

Jacques laughed. "I'm sure he kept it for himself, just like his superior."

"You're wrong. He put the money into the man's hands right in front of me. There are still some decent people over here."

"Would you call the doctor and the captain indecent? In my opinion, they are just reasonable people who know to take advantage of a situation," Jacques declared.

"How is it reasonable for a doctor to demand money to falsify a medical report? Or for a police officer to accept such a report knowing it's fake, and then for him to take a bribe for his complicity? You call that behaviour 'reasonable'? I call it corrupt, and I have never experienced anything like it."

"You haven't been in Palestine for very long," Jacques answered. "Are you saying there's no corruption in Germany?"

"Maybe there is, but I never heard about it."

"It's not reported in the newspapers here either," Jacques reminded him.

"But what if the sergeant or one of the other policemen reports the captain and the doctor? What happens then?"

"Then the sergeant will be fired." Jacques flung out his hand, which was holding a fork. A piece of *omelette aux champignons* flew all the way to the next table and into the lap of a middle-aged lady so stout it looked as though she could lift fifty kilograms with one arm. Albert was shocked by the accident, fearing yet another scandal. But it turned out that the lady was from the Netherlands and therefore not as prone to bursts of temperament as the locals. The problem was solved with an apology, a glass of hot water and a smile.

Jacques returned to his subject.

"The sergeant, you understand, saw nothing. He wasn't present when I paid the money, and neither were you. He can't prove anything and he can't cite any witnesses. Of course, I would deny everything, otherwise I would be liable to prosecution myself. So what can the good sergeant or any other subordinate do except grind their teeth in frustration? This is why the captain can get peacefully fatter and fatter and the doctor can continue buying expensive neckties, while those who are honest remain poor. That's life, my dear Monsieur Albert."

"Jacques, does this seem right to you?"

"I didn't invent the system, Albert. I just accept it. Sometimes, like today, it costs us a lot of money. We are importers. It sometimes happens that merchandise falls into an unfavourable customs category that a customs officer can change if he is willing. But the good will of customs officers doesn't happen by itself; it needs encouragement. Do you understand?"

"I understand very well, but I can't say that I approve of this system. Is it like this everywhere in the Middle East?"

"As far as I know, yes. You may call it corrupt. We call it elastic. And that's the kind of elasticity you have to build into business life here. Our officials earn very little money but they have a lot of power. The administration gives them the authority of Europeans but the salary of shoe-shine boys. The gap must be filled somehow. Have I made myself clear?"

"Monsieur Jacques, you have explained it perfectly. You should give lectures in economics. Unfortunately, I never heard anything like this when I studied the subject in university."

Jacques laughed and waved at the waiter. "Let me pay; you have already spent enough money today. I hope we will get it back after we make a few sales calls in Aleppo."

"I hope so. But you know, I can't drive anymore until we get that fender repaired," Albert said.

"We can do that right away. There is always a man at the garage till midnight. He'll take care of the car while we take the bus to Aleppo. By the way, Aleppo's not like Damascus. We don't deliver C.O.D. even to our biggest customers there. We have to give them sixty days after delivery to pay."

"Why?" Albert asked. "Are people in Aleppo more trustworthy then those in Damascus?"

"In Damascus, almost all the customers in our line of business are Armenians. There is a saying in Smyrna: 'A Jew can put ten Turks into a bag; a Greek is sharper than a Jew; but ten Greeks don't have a chance against one Armenian.' I can assure you, this is true. Which is why we only accept cash on the barrel head from the Armenian businesses in Damascus. But in Aleppo, our customers are mostly Jewish. They will never cheat you out of a piastre, and they pay their bills promptly. Especially when they're dealing with a Jewish supplier," Jacques added a little more quietly as he got up.

Albert also stood up to put on his coat. While one arm was still trying to find its sleeve, he asked, "Is it customary to categorize your clients – and their honesty – by race and religion?"

Jacques took the question seriously. "It doesn't have much to do with religion but with the nations in this part of the world. Every nation has its own system of ethics. The Turks are very different from the Arabs, although both nations are Moslems. The Greeks are different from the Armenians although they're both Christians. I don't have to tell you anything about the Jews since you know them, and also know what the commandment says."

"What commandment?"

"*Kol Yisrael arevim zeh lazeh.* All Israelites are responsible for each other."

Clearly Jacques – unlike Albert himself – had no doubt that the Jews were a people, a nation whose members had to be responsible for each other. And yet Jacques was not a Zionist, at least not in any active sense. This issue was still problematic for Albert, who had grown up regarding himself as German and could never see himself as belonging to any other nation. But Jacques and all the Jews here didn't identify with a particular nation; they didn't even have a common culture. In the Middle East, people were categorized not by where they currently lived but by their origin: the Armenians by Armenia, the Greeks by Greece, the Jews by their Jewish heritage, and so forth.

"Jacques, please show me the way to your garage," Albert said when they were back in the car.

"Of course. I will also take you back to your hotel afterwards; otherwise you'll get lost," Jacques assured him.

"You know what, Jacques? You're a good guide, and I mean that in more than one sense," Albert declared with deep conviction. "Many thanks."

X I I I

———

Berlin, the 6th of April, 1933

MY DEAREST BELOVED BOY,

I HAVE RECEIVED YOUR LETTERS and postcards from Syria and Lebanon. You write very well about what you see, but nothing about yourself and how you feel. You should know that your mother is more interested in that than in anything else. Do you feel at home yet, and have you made any friends? The photographs from Palestine you sent me are delightful. Your photos of the streets in Tel Aviv are very interesting, giving the impression of a small town full of horse-drawn carriages and hand-carts. And who is the young lady who appears in some of the photos? She has a very fine face and makes a graceful impression; is anything serious going on?

You should consider yourself lucky not to be here. Your aunt and uncle have decided to close their factory and will also move to Palestine shortly. I've decided to wait and travel with them; otherwise I would have left this week, as you advised me to do. Some of our customers have informed me that they regret that they must no longer deal with Jews. Some simply don't bother to pay our invoices, no longer finding it necessary to be honest. Nice people. But for now, I'm not giving away our business. Our manager, Miss Körner, would have liked to take it over. Her father was here and offered me a ridiculous price. I turned him down, and with a sarcastic smile he told me that I would soon have to give it away for nothing. I didn't say anything. I only sat in the office and cried. It's a good thing that Papa didn't have to experience this.

Other people came as well, like vultures, offering a few cents for the business your father and I built with so much effort. I would much rather lock the door than give our business away to people who want to get rich from our misfortune. Bruno suggested that I turn the business over to those employees who have been with us for over twenty years. Including Johannes, there would be nine of them. What do you think? We would only risk difficulties later when we wanted to get our property back. People seem to be convinced that this situation can't last long, but in the meantime, I'm losing my trust in humanity. People we used to help are passing me by in the street pretending not to know me. Other than that, however, I personally haven't experienced any abuse. A white-haired woman has an advantage over a man in that respect.

Oh yes, I almost forgot to tell you. Something strange happened last week involving a man I never would have expected. Major von Müller came to see me in the apartment. His two sons wear that abominable swastika uniform but still, he wanted to let me know that I should call him immediately if I had any problems. He said he would always protect me, and that he doesn't think highly of corporals who want to give orders to generals. He meant Hitler, of course. What do you think of that?

I was in Weissensee on Sunday. I went to say goodbye to our loved ones. They have even painted swastikas on the cemetery walls. Papa's grave is well cared for, but who will look after it when I'm gone? Our loyal servant Johannes has promised me faithfully that he will do so. But will he be allowed to do so? I arranged a small pension for him at the Dresden Bank and have given him all the suits you didn't take along, as well as those left behind by Papa. By the way, which of your books and things do you want me to bring to Palestine? Please write and tell me right away.

In Weissensee, I also visited the graves of your grandparents. You will laugh at me, but I had the feeling that our dead were aware of everything that is happening to us, especially your father. He is lying in German soil, which has never been a real home to him, while I have to leave my fatherland. At the cemetery I had the feeling that we were not turning our backs on our homeland but that it was running away from us, not knowing where it was going.

As much as I long for you and as much as I'm counting the days until I can embrace my only child again, I am also afraid of the future in a strange country. With your father at my side I wouldn't have had this fear; he would have adjusted quickly. But you and I lack his knowledge of Jewish customs. The fact that you haven't written anything about how you feel living in Palestine makes me worry.

I didn't intend to write about what follows, but since you sent me photos of you with that girl, I think it won't do any harm. Marion is getting married and will be going to South America where her fiancé lives. I thought it was extremely nice and well-mannered of her to come to tell me so, and say goodbye. Your friend Günther, on the other hand, is not in a good situation. His company has let him go because they no longer want to employ Jews. He has to look after his mother and doesn't know how. He intends to go to Austria to try his luck there. I am so sorry for him; he is such a decent person. However, I didn't dare offer him any financial help because we can no longer afford it. He says he hasn't written you because he's so mixed up that he can't concentrate. Your friend Manfred is emigrating, too. Guess where? To Palestine! You'll soon be able to continue your arguments about politics with him. That's all for today. It is late, and I'm tired.

Stay in good health, my boy, and a solution will be found for everything. I am already with you in my thoughts.

Kisses,

Your Mother,

PS: You should look for a small apartment for us.

Miss Leah Laski sat in her aunt's ornate living room, embroidering a picture in coloured wool. Mrs. Edelfels had decided that one wall of her dining room wasn't decorated enough and that another picture was required. It was cheaper to have her niece make such a picture than to buy one. The motif was a pretty corner of Jerusalem's old city. It was faintly traced on the linen that formed the background of the needlepoint. The choice of colours and shades was left to the creativity of the artist who, in this case, had good taste. She didn't use any bright colours and her work was meticulous.

Albert sat on a green velvet sofa at some distance from her. His own great-grandmother had done needlepoint, although by his grandmother's time it was already considered old-fashioned. He inched a bit closer on the sofa until Miss Leah threatened him with a dangerous-looking needle. He didn't want to die a hero's death.

They were alone in the apartment since Mrs. Edelfels had gone to a party, dragging her husband with her. Leah listened carefully as Albert translated his mother's letter into English for her. She didn't understand German and his earlier attempt to translate his mother's thoughts into Hebrew had failed miserably. He didn't translate every word into English, leaving out all mention of Marion and of his mother's interest in the young lady with whom he shared the sofa.

"I don't understand what your mother means when she says she has to leave her own country. Germany isn't her own country, is it?" Leah said.

"Why shouldn't Germany be my mother's country?" He asked the question despite knowing what her answer would be.

"The Jewish homeland is here," Leah said, predictably.

"Did you learn that in school?" he asked somewhat ironically.

"Yes. The same way we learned other facts, like two plus two makes four."

"We learned something entirely different in school. My mother, and her mother, and even my grandmother's mother learned that Germany was their homeland. I also learned the same thing, although I am no longer certain which – if any – of the ideas we were taught were true. Since I've come to Palestine and have travelled around the region, I'm not even sure anymore that two plus two makes four."

"Why not?"

Albert crossed his legs and leaned back. With his hands clasped behind his neck, he explained. "I have discovered that for people here, two plus two sometimes makes four, sometimes five and sometimes three, depending on which sum they prefer at the moment. I have also learned that the land which you see as belonging to the Jews is governed by the British, and that we Jews are actually in a minority here."

"Sure, for the moment, we're a minority," Leah admitted. "But we're the only minority that has achieved anything substantial in this country. When you came here, there was already electricity and water. There were refrigerators, houses and streets. Do you know who created all that? The Jews."

"Leah, my darling, did you build the roads as well?"

Again and again, Leah surprised him with her sharp mind. A girl with such an amazingly beautiful face had no right being so clever. On the other hand, he had never found any humour in her. Perhaps she had a different sense of humour than his but he hadn't discovered it yet. That's why he loved to tease her, taking pleasure in her serious replies.

"Many women carried stones although I didn't; I don't have the strength. But did you think these green fields and plantations just sprang up independently, or that the swamps drained themselves? The whole coast used to be a big breeding ground for malaria so no one was able to live here. We Jews made this place habitable. Only then did the Arabs come from Syria and from the Hauran or wherever to find work. Just look at the mountains of sand on the other side of the Yarkon River. That's exactly what Tel Aviv looked like before it was built. Nothing but sand! And in Haifa – look at all the trees on Mount Carmel. There wasn't a single tree before we came. Of course this is our country. A country belongs to the people who make it fertile. I could't live anywhere else."

"You can't know or say that because you haven't been anywhere else."

"I would like to travel to see other countries, but not to live in another country."

"Without ever having seen any other country, how can you be sure there's nowhere else you would enjoy living?" Albert mocked her.

"Because in a foreign country I would be among non-Jews. How could I feel comfortable?" Leah emphasized the word *foreign*. She was puzzled by Albert's lack of understanding. She knew that men often took longer than women to grasp important things but he was sophisticated, from the big city of Berlin. Was his exceptional slowness a sign of stupidity or of his upbringing?

Albert didn't know what Leah really thought about him. Though he was convinced he understood her very well, he suspected that she was incapable of understanding his feelings. So he tried to explain himself further.

"Can't you imagine that a Jew might experience Palestine as a foreign country, and that to him the local Jews might seem as foreign as Arabs? Can you sympathize if such a person realizes how little he actually has in common with the people who are supposed to constitute his nation, a nation whose flag he used to fly? Is it possible for you to imagine his gradual realization that there is no family resemblance at all between him and his supposed brothers?"

During this speech, Leah had stopped sewing and looked into Albert's face. Now she bent her head back over her needlepoint and answered slowly and thoughtfully. "I don't know how this fellow imagined Palestine before he arrived. It seems to me that he must have expected to find a kind of utopia here where everybody is an angel—"

"I only expected the girls to be angels," Albert interrupted and laughed.

But Leah didn't respond to his joke. She continued. "This fellow claims that he has nothing in common with the people of Palestine and that he can detect no family resemblance. I doubt it. Did you have more in common with people in Germany? Did you really feel a greater family connection with *goyim* and with anti-Semites? Be honest!"

Albert stood up from the sofa and began to walk around the edge of the oriental carpet. To think clearly, he needed some exercise. "I will be completely, even brutally, honest," he said. "In my opinion, if there were no anti-Semites and no Hitler in the country I came from, I would have much more in common with the people over there than I do here. That's truly what I feel."

"Then I feel sorry for you," Leah said. "What is it you don't like here? Or to be precise, what is it that makes you feel like such a foreigner?"

"I don't dislike anything. You're all very nice people, and there are an incredible number of idealists here. I have met people for whom I have great respect, and even people like your worthy aunt – whom I don't like and whom I criticize constantly – are hospitable and friendly. But I myself do not belong here."

"You still haven't explained why that is so. I think you're just imagining it," Leah claimed with conviction.

Albert scratched his head. "In a certain sense, all life is just imagination. Love is imagination. Hatred is imagination. Anger is imagination. But there are also things that are facts. For example, I walk through the streets of Tel Aviv and look at the street signs – Achad Haam Street, Gordon Street, Mapu Street, Bialik Street, Chernikovsky Street, and so forth. And I have no idea who any of these people are …"

"Authors," Leah said.

"I know that. I know that they are authors, but I'm not familiar with any of their books, and if I try to read one it means nothing to me, nothing at all. I have a German translation of a book by Sholom Aleichem. It's a very funny book, but the people in his stories, their environment and their opinions, are as foreign to me as those in a book by Tsao Hsueh-chin."

"Who is Tsausouchin?"

"An eighteenth-century Chinese writer."

Leah looked up. "So you're not familiar with Jewish literature. Do you think that everybody here is? Most of these books are just as meaningless to me as they are to you. Like all young people here, I have no experience of life in the ghettos of Europe. I can imagine it even less than life in London or Paris, which at least I see represented in magazines. But my lack of interest in Jewish writers doesn't make me feel like an outsider."

"That's not the only reason for my alienation; I only used it as an example of why I feel, walking around here, that my own heritage has suddenly become worthless. It's as if you had a bunch of banknotes in your pocket that were no longer accepted, and instead of being a rich man, you can't even buy a loaf of bread. It's the same with all the things I have studied. Names like Goethe and Schiller, Lessing and Herder are unknown here. Cicero, Virgil, Ovid, Horace, Plinius, even the Ancient Greeks are all people no one's ever heard of. But then I'm asked how come I never heard of the *Shulchan Aruch*. People assume I must be a very ignorant person since I can only translate it as *the set table*, and think it must be something to eat."

"You wouldn't find it easy to digest," a man's voice announced. Mr. and Mrs. Edelfels had come back into the house so quietly that neither Leah nor Albert had heard them. It wasn't clear how long they had been standing in the dark hall listening, but apparently Mr. Edelfels had heard a good part of Albert's speech. While his wife went into the kitchen to put on water for tea, he sat down in one of the upholstered chairs and continued. "The *Shulchan Aruch* is a book written by Yosef Karo in the sixteenth century. It is more or less a code of ethical behaviour for Jews. Excuse me for butting into your conversation, but I have to say that I think you're interpreting one thing in particular incorrectly."

"He isn't right about a lot of things," Leah insisted. "We have heard of Goethe and Lessing here …"

"Probably Lessing only because he wrote *Nathan the Wise* about Jews. You're all so chauvinistic," Albert interrupted her.

"Just a moment," Mr. Edelfels said. "Let me say something. Albert is right. We *are* chauvinistic here, and also provincial. With good reason. A people that wants to become a nation again cannot avoid a certain amount of chauvinism. But what I wanted to point out was that you are wrong to feel that your currency – as you put it – is worthless here."

"But that's the way it is," Albert insisted.

"No, that's not the way it is," Mr. Edelfels declared with great emphasis. "You're starting from the premise that education is important for its own sake. But I believe it is wrong to call a man educated just because he has names and dates and historical events in his head, or because he knows who wrote which books, or invented which things. The real purpose of education is to teach a man to think, and I mean to think independently. According to that theory, nothing you have learned is useless, neither here nor anywhere else. That's what I wanted to say."

Leah looked at her uncle with admiration. "I haven't heard you talk this much in a long time."

"I only talk when it's worthwhile."

"What is worthwhile?" his wife asked, returning from the kitchen in her pearl-studded black evening dress. "Did Leah at least offer you some tea and cake?" It was a rhetorical question because there were no cups or plates on the table.

"Yes, of course she did, but I didn't want any," Albert lied, to save Leah embarrassment.

Mrs. Edelfels was hard to fool. "I can't imagine that. You're a big cake-eater. In any event, you must try my cake now. Which do you prefer, tea or coffee?"

"Coffee, please."

"You'd better drink tea," Leah suggested. "We don't make coffee here the way you're used to, and you won't like it."

Mrs. Edelfels was surprised. "How do you make coffee in Germany?"

"In a percolator or with a filter. How do you make it here?"

"We take a spoonful of coffee powder, put it into a glass and pour hot water over it," Leah explained.

Albert shuddered involuntarily. "Then you must drink the grounds."

Mr. Edelfels laughed, "Go give him tea already. Otherwise the young man will have another reason to complain about Palestine."

Leah finally put her needlepoint away and stood up to help her aunt bring in the tea service and plates. Over her shoulder, she said, "The food here is one of Mr. Berg's greatest complaints. He claims we don't have any culture because to him, eating is an important part of culture."

Mr. Edelfels nodded. "And he is completely right." Turning to Albert, he said, "I lived in Paris for many years, so I can appreciate your love of gourmet cooking. But our women regard it as frivolous."

The tea and some very good home-made cake were brought in.

"What are your plans, Mr. Berg?" Mrs. Edelfels asked.

"What plans do you mean?"

"I mean what do you intend to do here? Leah told me that your mother is immigrating, too, and that you will most likely have to give up your factory in Germany. Is that right?"

"Yes, that's right. We hope to manufacture here instead, on a small scale initially, and still be able to supply our European customers as well as the local market."

Leah put her cup down on the table abruptly. "Does this mean that you have decided to stay here for good?"

Mrs. Edelfels nodded. "You don't hate it here that much then."

"You don't have to comment if you don't want to," Mr. Edelfels advised him, with a wink.

Albert gave a slightly embarrassed laugh, then sighed. "I don't have a choice now. The way things have developed, I can't go home."

"Home?" Mr. Edelfels repeated in a questioning tone.

Albert looked him straight in the face and said, "Yes."

No one said a word. Leah dropped her hands in her lap like someone giving up. Then she left the room. Mrs. Edelfels, and not Leah, accompanied him to the door.

"It always takes some time to get used to this country. Don't worry so much; it will age you prematurely," she advised him.

"Apparently people with different backgrounds don't find it very easy to communicate here," Albert said. It was obvious that Leah's reaction had surprised as well as depressed him.

Leah's aunt was not stupid; she understood immediately. "Nonsense, don't you worry! This will pass quickly. Boys and girls can always communicate when they're attracted to each other. They don't even have to talk to communicate."

"Sometimes not talking is better," Albert agreed.

"Good bye."

"Good bye and many thanks."

X I X

——•——

"ARE YOU A MEMBER OF the Zionist Association?" Mr. Finkelstein, officer of the Palestine Office of the Jewish Agency asked the young man with reddish-blond hair sitting across from him in his office on Meineke Street in Berlin.

"No, I have never been a Zionist," Manfred Neumann answered. Before he had even finished speaking, he realized how stupid he had been to tell the truth.

"Too bad. We have terribly few immigration certificates. The British won't allow us one tenth of what we require."

"And committed Zionists receive priority?" Manfred asked.

"I wouldn't necessarily say that, but Zionists at least have a moral claim. Couldn't you apply for a capitalist certificate? If you could prove that you have a thousand pounds the British consulate would give you a visa for Palestine in a flash, and you wouldn't need us anymore."

"Unfortunately, I don't have any money. My mother is a widow. But I could probably pay for the passage myself."

Finkelstein thought for a moment. A tall handsome boy. Good schooling. If only he had a suitable occupation, it might be possible to do something. But not this month. The certificates had all been given out. There might be something available for him in the May quota. But what about all those poor old people who had neither money nor a suitable occupation? Why didn't he try as hard to figure out something for them?

Aloud he said, "I see on your application form that you're an office employee. In what business?"

Albert had said that they needed tradesmen and mechanics in Palestine, not office workers. Manfred had often repaired water pipes and electrical things at home and he knew they would value that, so he decided to lie, hoping he wouldn't blush. "I am actually a plumber but became unemployed, so I have been working in an office."

"A plumber?" Mr. Finkelstein asked. "Not a bad occupation for Palestine. Tell me, Mr. Neumann, would you be able to pay for two tickets? If so, something might be possible."

"Why should I pay double the passage money? I don't understand."

Mr. Finkelstein bent across the desk, and lowered his voice. "I can't promise anything, you see, but it is possible we may be able to give you a certificate next month under the condition that you take a woman with you."

"But I'm not married."

"I know," Mr. Finkelstein said. "But certificates to Palestine include one for a married couple. Since we have a large number of single women wishing to immigrate, we can't afford to waste these. Do you understand me correctly?"

Manfred was afraid he did understand correctly. "In other words you expect me to take a complete stranger with me, pretending that she's my wife? But surely the British consulate will notice that we're not married, unless the woman is also named 'Neumann.'"

Mr. Finkelstein smiled. "The British consulate will demand a genuine marriage certificate, so her name will definitely be Neumann. You will have to get married, as hundreds before you have done. Of course this is a fictitious marriage; you don't have to live together in Palestine and not long after immigration you will get divorced again. As a man you are risking very little. It's a little more dangerous sometimes for the women."

"But this is terrible plan," Manfred protested.

Finkelstein became agitated. He had already spent a lot of time with this young man and his waiting room was full of other potential immigrants. "It's not terrible at all. Palestine is now the only country to which you can emigrate – if we can even get a certificate for you. Among the women are many who, unlike you, have been preparing to go there for a long time, who can already speak Hebrew, and who are at least as eligible as you are. Are you prepared to help one of them or not?"

Manfred nodded, then added, "Please give me time to find the money for the second ticket."

"Alright. Come back on Tuesday next week, and we'll introduce you to your *chaverah*."

"*Chaverah*? What's that?" Manfred asked.

"The exact translation would be *a female comrade*," Mr. Finkelstein said. "A *chaver* is a comrade, and a *chavera* is a female comrade, and that's how you have to look at her."

"Yes," Manfred said. "Many thanks, and goodbye."

"Shalom, *Chaver* Neumann."

———◆———

Miss Lewinsohn, seasoned clerk of the Palestine Office, sat opposite Mr. Finkelstein. Her forehead was furrowed. On the desk in front of her were index cards which she kept shuffling and sorting.

"It isn't so simple. Here I have a young woman, a Polish Jew, who was divorced last month. Her husband, a German Christian and a government official, divorced her so as not to jeopardize his career. He still wanted to live with her, but she no longer wants to. She wants to go to Palestine instead."

"Very Christian of the man," Mr. Finckelstein remarked. "How long were they married?"

"Three years."

"Why did a Polish Jew marry a German Christian in the first place?" Finckelstein asked.

"After she graduated from the Hebrew high school in Krakow she came to medical school here in Berlin. Apparently it was love at first sight for both of them."

"How old is she?"

"That's the problem. She is twenty-eight, and most of the boys we give certificates to are between eighteen and twenty-one. If we claim that she is the wife of one of those youngsters, the British may get suspicious."

"I have just the right man for her. He is twenty-seven but he will soon be twenty-eight. I told him to come back on Tuesday, so she should come then too. Does she have children by any chance?"

"No. She is a medical doctor, after all," Miss Lewinsohn giggled and took the next index card from her stack.

———◆———

Sonja Falkowitsch, formerly Mrs. Von Winter, sat in the dark, stuffy room she had rented in Augsburger Street. She looked at herself in the cracked mirror: broad cheek bones, long almond-shaped green eyes, and smooth, dark-blond hair that was difficult to set in waves. A thousand years ago Bulan, King of the Khazars, converted himself and his people to Judaism because Christianity seemed illogical to him. Shortly afterwards the Khazars lost their kingdom and their remnants mixed with the scattered communities of the Semitic Jews, but Sonja's cheek bones and her strong sinewy body were as Tataric as the women of the Khazars. Probably the Cossacks gave the blond hair and green eyes to one of her great-grandmothers.

A saying of her grandfather's kept running through her mind: "May God never burden us with as much as we can endure." Just a few weeks ago she was convinced that she couldn't go on living without Martin. But nobody dies that easily and today she wanted to live, although Martin himself was dead to her.

Dr. Martin von Winter had come home one day, given her a routine kiss, and said it would be necessary to make a small formal adjustment.

"What adjustment? To the apartment?" She had asked, naîvely.

"No, between the two of us."

"What do you mean?"

"Oh, my dear Sonja, given the circumstances it is necessary for us to get a divorce, but that formality doesn't have to change things between us. Do you understand? It will be just to satisfy the authorities. You'll stay here in the apartment and I'll get another address, but of course I'll still come here every night."

"Are you completely out of your mind? Or is this supposed to be a joke?" she had cried at the time. He tried to calm her down, though she no longer remembered exactly what he said. That he would be stripped of his position, which would endanger both their livelihoods, and things of that nature. She only remembered that she called him a bastard and a Nazi.

"You know very well that I'm not a Nazi and will never be one," he had said, outraged. So she hit him over the head with a chair. She didn't regret that at all. She was glad she was able to react so strongly before she collapsed into hysterical tears.

The court and the judges were happy to grant a divorce to a Jewish woman and her Aryan husband. Martin, who with his hooked nose, looked ten times more like an anti-Semitic caricature than she did with her small Tatar nose, which is why the judge had assumed that she was the Aryan and had treated Martin roughly and her politely. Only when he reconsidered his file did he change his tactics.

Martin hadn't dared to look her in the eye. Nonetheless, he proposed paying her a monthly allowance even though she didn't want his money. Her lawyer advised her to accept a financial settlement instead.

"Don't be foolish, Mrs. von Winter!" He still called her by the name she had given up as quickly as she had given up Martin. "Your husband must give you some money. You're entitled to it, because you worked just as hard for it as he did. Besides, whatever you decide to do now, you'll need capital. You don't want an allowance – alright. I don't think an allowance is advisable either, but for different reasons than you. It might be paid today but a law could easily be passed tomorrow that would outlaw such payments to Jews."

Now she was glad that she had accepted the settlement, since she had enough money to leave Germany, where she wasn't wanted. But where should she go? She considered her options yet again while combing her hair in front of the mirror. She couldn't go back to Poland for two reasons: her parents had disowned her when she married Martin, and there were few opportunities for women pediatricians to practice in that country. She had decided to apply to Palestine, given that she still remembered the Hebrew she learned in high school, but had been told that she was unlikely to be accepted as a single woman, especially one divorced from a Christian. She hoped that the message she had received from Miss Lewinsohn meant they'd had found a solution to her dilemma.

Hoping to make a good impression, she put on some lipstick and her most elegant grey suit. Dr. Sonja Falkowitsch grinned at her likeness in the mirror and left the room.

X X

"THE BATHROOM IS AT THE end of the hall. I can change there while you're getting undressed here. But there is only one bed although I assumed that there would be two. I'm sorry. Is that very uncomfortable for you?" Manfred asked, looking around in the small hotel room in Trieste. The afternoon sun shone through the window, making the simple place look almost pretty.

Dr. Sonja Falkowitsch, known as *Dr. Neumann* since the passport officer had entered her title and occupation into Manfred's passport, shook her head. "I know that you'll behave properly, and furthermore I'm not a little girl. I'm quite capable of defending myself."

Then she wondered why she was threatening a man as little to blame for this situation as she was herself. She ought to be grateful that he was prepared to take her along.

Manfred didn't resent her remarks. He took it as a compliment that she considered she might have to defend herself against him. *She is a pretty woman, my official wife*, he thought. *I've seen a lot worse.*

"You must understand. It was the only way," he said out loud. "First of all, I couldn't know that the ship wouldn't set sail until the day after tomorrow. Secondly, we have a joint passport, so the Italian booking our passage would have wondered why we wanted separate rooms. Thirdly, the people on Meineke Street insist that we must always behave like real married people – for our own sake and also for the sake of others – to prevent any suspicion about the certificate scam."

She appeared to be listening attentively and looking at him the whole time, so he wasn't prepared for her response.

"Manfred, did they take your tonsils out when you were a child?"

"Yes. How did you know?"

"I could tell by the sound of your voice." Sonja stood up, put a hand on Manfred's shoulder and pushed him into the chair she had just vacated. He was too surprised to offer resistance. "Open your mouth wide and stick out your tongue."

He stuck his tongue out, but then everything seemed so funny to him that he began to laugh and tried to turn his face away. But she had already grabbed him by the lower jaw with one hand. With the middle and index fingers of the other, she depressed his tongue.

Manfred laughed again, though it wasn't easy with Sonja's fingers in his mouth and his chin in her firm grip.

"Say *ah* again!" Sonja commanded.

"Ah," Manfred said, and began to struggle.

She let him go. "Exactly what I thought," she said. "The operation was performed very badly, and they have regrown. When we're in Palestine, I'll have to remove them again."

"You're a pediatrician," Manfred protested.

"That's precisely why I'm familiar with this kind of thing. You don't have to be afraid. Moreover, I think your adenoids should come out as well. To be sure, I'll have to get a mirror and another instrument out of my medical bag."

"What? You want to operate on me here? No way!"

"No, no, I only wanted to examine you, but if you don't want me to I won't. It's not urgent."

Half seriously and half in jest he said, "Now I won't be able to sleep all night for fear you'll perform surgery on me."

"Nonsense, Mr. Neumann, you're completely safe with me. Furthermore," she laughed, "we have another Jew here in this room who will protect us from each other."

Manfred didn't catch on right away. Only when he followed her eyes did he discover what she meant. Over the bed hung a picture, in gruesome and bloody detail, of the crucifixion of Jesus Nazarenus, Rex Judaeorum.

"Should I take that picture down?"

"Why? It doesn't bother me," Sonja said.

"Do you want to go get something to eat? I'm hungry. Aren't you?" Manfred asked.

"Can we afford to eat out, now that we have to pay for a hotel room? I have very little money because I didn't have the courage to smuggle anything," Sonja said, and looked through her wallet to see how much was left.

Manfred grinned. "I'm almost a millionaire, since I didn't have to pay for your passage. I still have lots of money which we can convert to Italian lire right away."

"But how did you get it out?"

"I used a method I learned from my friend Albert, who went to Palestine about a year ago."

"What method?"

"You may be my legal wife, Milady, but we're not yet so intimate that I can tell you that." Then he sat down on the bed and laughed until the tears came to his eyes.

What a big child he was! Hopefully his naivety wouldn't cause them problems. Sonja sighed, then she said, "Let's go get something to eat, Manfred."

"Aye, aye!" He jumped up, still laughing, and said, "Please excuse me for a moment. I must go to the bank to get my money," and went across the hall to the bathroom to retrieve it.Arm in arm, as befits a married couple, they walked past the smiling hotel clerk and through the streets of Trieste. Without admitting it to each other, they both appreciated the feeling of being out in public with a nice-looking partner whom other people admired.

"Manfred, I think we should use the informal *you*. We never know who might be listening to our conversation."

"I've wanted to do that for a while but was afraid you might misinterpret things if I suggested it."

"You underestimate my ability to make the correct diagnosis," Sonja said dryly.

Manfred couldn't come up with a clever quip in response.

Down at the harbour they found an inexpensive restaurant. It had a garden with little round tables from which they could watch the ships go by. All conversation stopped as they entered; it wasn't often that tourists were seen in this stevedore neighbourhood. The owner looked at Manfred, wiped his hands on his apron, opened the flap of the bar and came to their table. That kind of service was reserved for special guests and personal friends.

"What can I get you?" he asked, in an excellent Austrian accent.

"You speak German?"

"Of course. Austrians have been here in Trieste for a long time. I'm Croatian myself."

"Very interesting," Sonja said. She was afraid that Manfred would now engage in a long ethnographical conversation with the old gentleman. The group of young men in black shirts passing by reminded her that Italy, too, was a Fascist country where speaking freely could cause trouble.

"Can we get real Italian food here?" she asked.

"Of course. Would you like spaghetti or ravioli with a good glass of chianti?"

"Yes. Two ravioli please, and wine too."

"You could have asked me whether I wanted ravioli. Maybe I would have preferred something different," Manfred remarked, annoyed. He didn't really care what kind of Italian noodle in tomato sauce he offered his empty stomach, but was insulted by her high-handed manner.

She bit her lip. He was right. After all, they weren't really married!

"Please excuse me. I wasn't thinking, and fell into old habits. My previous husband was always very indecisive in restaurants and said, 'You choose for me. I'll eat whatever the doctor orders.' It won't happen again."

Manfred was mollified. "You know, I think I was only angry because with me it was the opposite. The girl I was with for many years refused to make decisions. If we went to a restaurant and I asked her what she wanted to eat, she'd always say, 'What do you think I should have? Order what you think is right.' It annoyed me."

"Was she a nice girl?"

"Yes." It was a quiet *yes*, without enthusism. For him, Erika was already so far away that he could think of her without any special feeling.

"Why did you leave her then?" Sonja said, immediately regretting her question. This boy was a stranger, and would remain one.

"We split up more than a year ago, even before Hitler came to power. Her brothers were in the SA and she couldn't make up her mind where her allegiances were. On the one hand, she had a close Jewish girlfriend and was going out with me; on the other, she echoed the anti-Semitic sayings she had probably heard from her brothers. One day I had enough of it, and I said 'Good bye, it's been nice knowing you'."

Sonja was surprised to realise that when he mentioned the girl and said that he had been with her for years, she had felt a sting resembling jealousy. Was she crazy?

The chianti and the ravioli came to their table served in more beautiful glasses and on better plates than those prepared for the diners at other tables.

"Isn't it strange?" Sonja reflected.

"What?" Manfred asked, with his mouth full. The food was excellent.

"We are refugees, we are beggars, we are heading into an uncertain future. The world has collapsed around us and we must build a completely new one, but we still have our fine expensive clothes and so of course we are regarded as people without the slightest worries, people who must be served chianti in crystal glasses. In any event, Manfred, *prost, l'cha'im*, cheers to both of us!" She raised her glass, and clinked it against his.

He was strangely moved. The few words she had spoken vibrated on the harp of his subconscious. He suddenly knew where he was and what his circumstances truly were. Until now, he had felt like a tourist on an interesting journey. But Sonja was right; he wasn't a traveller. He was a refugee who had lost his homeland and who was headed for a country he didn't know. The people in that country were strangers to him. His friend Albert was there, but could he provide any help? The Albert he used to know had been completely self-absorbed and was always finding himself in difficulties. But at least Albert spoke Hebrew, while Manfred was completely unfamiliar with that language.

"What's this called in Hebrew?" he asked, lifting up his fork.

Sonja was perplexed by the sudden question. It had come so unexpectedly. She smiled. "*Masleg.*"

"*Massleck,*" Manfred repeated.

"No, not *massleck*, but mas*leg*, with the stress on the last syllable."

"And what's a knife called?"

"*Sakin.* It's also stressed on the last syllable, like most Hebrew words," she added.

"*Sakin, masleg, masleg, sakin,*" Manfred repeated.

"At least now you'll always be able to eat." She was amused by the seriousness with which he absorbed his first lesson.

"How come you know German so well? You speak it without any accent. That's very unusual for someone who had a Hebrew education in Poland."

"I was in Berlin for ten years and studied at the university there. In addition, I had a very good teacher," Sonja answered.

"A private teacher?" he asked.

Sonja was quiet for a moment. Then she answered, "Yes, a very private teacher."

"I see," Manfred said.

They finished their meal and Manfred paid. When they were back on the street she took his arm again. What a firm gait she had, this woman doctor. He liked her better and better as time went on. During their long train ride to Italy they had hardly talked. The other people in their compartment had made private conversation impossible. Before their *wedding* they had been alone only once, in a café. Then, she briefly told him her history, but he had hardly listened because he was so unhappy giving his name to a stranger. It was as if he had sacrificed part of himself, and he was inexplicably terrified of her. Intelligent women with Asiatic features and almond-shaped eyes were not his type. The only consolation was she couldn't steal his fortune, since he didn't have one.

Evening had fallen and a warm summer wind was blowing from the Adriatic Sea. They were walking along the dark harbour road when Sonja asked, "Do you have plans for what you'll do after you arrive in Palestine, Manfred?"

"No, and I can't have any. I doubt I'll be able to work in my field there."

"What is your field, exactly? I only know that you were working in an office."

"Yes, in a firm that manufactured boats. I helped with the designs and also built models. But in all of Palestine there isn't a single shipyard nor any kind of boat-building company. They just use simple vessels for coastal fishing, and most of them resemble those built by the ancient Phoenicians. Still, I'm not too worried. I can do a few other things, like electrical installation. I'm not a professional but I'm sure I can improve."

"I'm sure you can," Sonja agreed.

"It will probably be easier for you," Manfred said. "Because you have a profession which is in demand. Plus you speak the language. It must be different arriving as a doctor than as a labourer."

"Maybe yes, maybe no." Sonja hesitated a bit before she continued. "I hope that I'll be able to work in one of the clinics in Palestine. Not only because I must earn my living but also because I love my profession very much."

"Oh yes, I noticed. My chin still hurts," Manfred remarked.

"I am terribly sorry, you poor man, But actually I want to say something else. I want to say that even after we end our fake marriage, I hope we can still be friends."

"Of course," Manfred said emphatically.

"For that reason, and also because I will always be grateful to you that, thanks to your willingness, and with your name, I was able to go to Palestine, I want to …"

Manfred stood still. "What do you want?"

"I want to insist that, should I earn money before you do, it should be regarded as joint income so that I can support you while you get ahead in your occupation. Do you understand? I have a profession in which I can earn money. Until you have one too, I want to help you. That's all I wanted to say. I hope you understand me correctly." She looked up at him, a bit worried that she hadn't chosen the right words. After all, she hardly knew him, and was worried that he might be offended by an offer that was entirely sincere and without ulterior motive.

"Oh yes, I understand you very well," Manfred said very quietly and then, without another word, he grabbed her around the hips and lifted her up. She didn't resist and she didn't cry out. He held her up in the air for quite a while. It seemed like an eternity. Then, just as suddenly, he set her carefully back down on the pavement.

She looked at him aghast, but his face was a stone mask. Very quietly and calmly he said, "You want to feed me, Doctor?" And then he shouted at her, making her recoil in fear, "But I have two arms and two hands, don't I?"

Overcome by a strange weakness, she rubbed her ribs which were still hurting from the pressure of his hands. She felt dizzy and instinctively leaned against him. More sobbing than whispering, she answered like a little girl, "Yes, Manfred, you have two arms. That you have."

They walked back to the hotel in silence, Manfred full of remorse for his silly behaviour. Why had he been such an idiot? He had hurt her, and was deeply ashamed.

Sonja blamed herself too, for hurting his pride, something she knew one must never do to a man. He was so angry he wouldn't even let her hold his arm anymore. Feeling she had ruined everything between them, she became dizzy again. But she didn't fall down; Manfred noticed her sudden unsteadiness and finally offered her his arm. She leaned against him with all her weight until the street stopped spinning. They said nothing still, but they continued walking pressed tightly together, each with a private feeling of guilt.

To the citizens of Trieste they no longer looked like a married couple. Far from it. The impression they made was that of a beautiful couple in the wonderfully delirious flower of first love. Italians understand this sort of thing, but neither Sonja nor Manfred noticed the well-meaning looks and the encouraging smiles of the people in the street.

—◆—

The night was very warm and the bed was exceptionally uncomfortable. It was deeper in the middle than on the sides, so they kept rolling towards each other. Sonja had been awake for a long time but Manfred was still asleep. She listened to the whistling of his breath, perhaps caused by the problematic adenoids she'd already diagnosed. She'd also noticed that his nose wasn't perfectly straight, and wondered whether he had ever been in a fight.

It was so strange to find herself in bed with a man of whom she knew nothing! Yesterday she had been more worried about her own desires than his, having come close to throwing herself into his arms. Would he have been able to control himself if he'd known? They might have actually consummated their fake marriage, like characters in a cheap novel. She hoped daylight would save her from that danger.

Carefully she pulled herself over the edge of the bed. On tiptoe, she looked for her toiletries, put on her silk housecoat, opened the door and shuffled along the hall to the bathroom. The doors of two other rooms stood ajar, their occupants probably hoping the draft would cool them down. In each room Sonja saw two single beds. She wondered if Mr. Manfred Neumann had deliberately selected a room with a double bed for them. But that was absurd; she had been standing right beside him when he had asked if there was a vacancy. He'd never mentioned how many beds they required; that decision had been made for them by the res-ervation clerk. It had never occurred to her before that a hotel employee could determine someone's fate.

The water pressure in the shower was poor; nevertheless she felt refreshed. Afterwards she stood for a long time at the not-too-clean sink and scrubbed her hands with a little nail brush. She wished her hands were less sinewy and her blood vessels less prominent. Had she grown her nails longer they might have been more attractive, but the children who were her patients were afraid of long pointed fin-gernails. She didn't want to give them another reason to fear doctors. Although it had been quite comical when Manfred was afraid of her yesterday.

She resolved not to mention that the other rooms had two beds each. She didn't want him to think she was complaining, even if it meant another uncom-fortable night. She combed her hair and applied her makeup, then shuffled back down the hall as quietly as before. The two other doors were now closed.

In their room, Manfred stood shirtless in front of the open window, exercising. He remembered Erika once advising Marion not to marry someone like him who exercised in the morning because it drove her crazy, his behaving 'like a windmill'. Marion had laughed and told her she was in no such danger with Albert, who disliked all physical effort except lifting spoons and forks.

Standing in the doorway observing him, Sonja was surprised by her desire to put her hands on his shoulders.

He smelled her perfume and turned around.

"Good morning, Mrs. Neumann. You're up early. Hmm, you smell good."

"Good morning, Manfred. You're full of energy early in the morning. Don't let me disturb your exercise. It's very healthy; I should be doing it too," She pulled her housecoat tighter and sat down on the bed. Manfred jumped across its width and planted himself beside her. The springs squeaked and the bed frame complained. She moved over a little.

"I was only exercising this morning to purge myself of a strong emotion," he said, grinning.

"What emotion is that?"

"My attraction to you," he said, and put both arms around her. He kissed her freshly washed neck. He enjoyed the feeling of her perfumed skin.

"Manfred, don't! Let me go!" she yelled.

He stopped kissing her but continued holding her tightly in his arms. "Damn it all, we're married, aren't we? I have the proof written down it in black and white."

She stiffened, fighting against her own desire with all the energy she could muster. She knew that if he didn't let her go she wouldn't be able to resist him much longer. Besides, they were legally married, so she couldn't even scream if he decided to rape her. The police would just look at their passports and laugh.

She said, "Manfred, don't be crazy. Please go back to your exercises and rid yourself of these thoughts. This won't work."

"What won't work?"

"This thing between us."

He released his grip and held her loosely, almost tenderly, in his arms. She was afraid that any movement she made to free herself would excite him.

"Why won't it work? Because I'm so repulsive to you?"

"On the contrary, my boy, but I'm ten years older than you."

"Sonja, I've seen your birth certificate. You know that's not true."

"A woman of twenty-eight is ten years older than a man of twenty-eight."

Manfred laughed and pulled her toward him again. "Did you come up with this calculation using Einstein's theory of relativity?"

She kept her composure and didn't give in. "It's a fact," she insisted.

"It's complete nonsense. On the contrary, men age faster and also die earlier. There are millions of couples the same age. Don't give me such baloney, especially when you look like a twenty-year-old yourself."

"Manfred, there is no point discussing this further. I'm a divorced woman, and not right for you."

Manfred released her and stood up. She also got up from the bed quickly and leaned against the wall. He looked at her almost sadly and said, "This has nothing to do with you being divorced. I believe that Madame Doctor doesn't want to get involved with someone who might become nothing more than a manual labourer. But don't worry. I won't give you any difficulty with the divorce – and none until then either."

She had turned as pale as the wall against which she leaned. She hadn't been able to control herself enough yesterday, so today she'd been holding back from showing him how much she liked him. It had never occurred to her that he might interpret her aloofness as a preoccupation with class differences! Troubled by her conflicted emotions, she hadn't noticed that tears were running down her cheeks.

"What are you crying about? I'm the one with something to cry about, not you," Manfred said, and indeed, he too was close to tears.

"Oh, Manfred," she sobbed. "What you just said is wrong, so terribly wrong." She ran over to him and threw her hands over his broad shoulders. Then she pulled his head down to her and kissed him full on the mouth. His first impulse was to reject her but the warmth of her kisses made that impulse go away as quickly as it had come. Wrapping his arms around her, he pulled her up to him.

"If you want me that much, then take me," she whispered.

Manfred thought of nothing except that he wanted this woman and none other. And he took her.

———◆———

"I could slap my own face," Manfred said.

"Why, in God's name, why?" She was appalled. Did he have regrets, now that she had admitted that she cared for him? Had her sacrifice been for nothing?

"Because I wasted an entire night lying next to such a delicacy without tasting her. I'll never be able to forgive myself."

She was relieved. She was happy. She had never been so happy. She laughed and threw herself over him and kissed the stubble of his reddish beard. "We'll make up for it, my dear husband. Now that you're really married to me, you won't get rid of me so easily. I'll scratch your eyes out if you so much as look at another women."

"You're a public menace. The tonsils, the adenoids, the eyes. What more do you want to rob me of? What do you have to say in your defence?" He tickled her, and they wrestled like children.

Then Sonja became practical. She slapped him on his flat stomach, which was hard as a rock, and commanded, "Get up and shave and make yourself beautiful. We must go see if our ship sails today. We don't want to be stuck here and miss the departure."

"First let's have breakfast," Manfred insisted.

"First you have to get dressed."

"Aye, aye, Madame Doctor!"

"Manfred, can you please stop calling me 'Madame Doctor', even in jest? There is only one person important enough for me to let him call me 'Sonja,' and that is my own husband."

Manfred jumped out of bed and bent over her. She protected her face with her hands, afraid of more kisses. But he only took her hands in his and said, "I thank you for the compliment."

"What compliment?"

"Didn't you even notice that you just declared your love for me? That you confessed that I'm important to you?" He pulled her up by the arms and she stood before him naked, as her silk housecoat dropped from her shoulders.

"Did I really declare my love for you? How could I have made such a mistake? But now that I've done it, I must keep my word," she said, laughing. A little more seriously, she asked, "Even though you finished those exercises, do you still love me?"

He wanted to say something witty, but couldn't think of anything. So he answered simply and truthfully, "Yes, Sonja."

She was almost ashamed of her own happiness and turned her head away. Her eyes fell upon the wardrobe mirror. She took Manfred by the arm and turned him towards it too.

"Adam and Eve," she said.

"After the fall from grace," he added.

"But still before paradise," she countered.

He laughed, turned her around in a circle and said, "If you insist on twisting the story of creation around, don't you dare take a rib away from me—"

"I only want to be your angel, not your God," she said, before he even had stopped talking.

"You always have to have the last word, don't you?"

She already had an answer at the tip of her tongue but she swallowed it and gave him a little push instead. "Now go make yourself presentable," was all she said.

After Manfred put his bathrobe on and disappeared in the direction of the bathroom, Sonja got dressed. Having been called many times to attend sick children at night, she was used to doing it quickly. Not only was she completely ready when he came back, but she had also packed their things and locked all four suitcases.

"You're the eighth wonder of the world," he said. "But where are the shirt and suit I have to wear today?"

"If you please, my Lord and Master," she said, opening the wardrobe where his suit and a fresh shirt and tie still hung. Clean socks lay on the shelf next to his shoes. "I won't always spoil you like this, but I wanted to be nice to you today. Besides, you were gone for so long that I had nothing else to do."

He laughed, grabbed her, and tried to kiss her again.

"Don't! I just put lipstick on."

"You can always reapply it."

"Where have you been? We have been looking all over town for you," said the nice old man in charge of the Jewish Agency for Palestine in Trieste.

"We had no idea we were supposed to report here," Manfred said.

"Of course you should have reported. Due to the unforeseen delay, your hotel stay is being paid for by the shipping line. The money to cover it is here with us."

"That's very good news," Sonja said. "We wanted to talk to you about our tickets anyway."

"They have been booked for tourist class; it's all been arranged."

"How many people are in such a cabin?" Sonja asked.

"Either four or six. Just a minute … Dr. Neumann, it says here. Is that you?"

"Yes, that's me," Sonja smiled, amused by the astonished face of the official, who continued, "For you we have a cabin with three other women, and Mr. Neumann … you're not a doctor?"

"No," Manfred said.

"For you we have a cabin with five other men."

"This is unacceptable," Sonja said emphatically, surprising Manfred almost as much as the other man by her tone.

"I beg your pardon, but that's the configuration of the ship."

"I don't care. We have paid for our own passage without using any public funds, so you have no right to separate a married couple," Sonja declared, and proudly lifted her head toward Manfred, who listened with his mouth half open.

"You're not, not … you know what I mean?"

"No, we don't know what you mean," Sonja said quickly, before Manfred had a chance to express what she called the 'German correctness phobia'. Despite her love for him, she suspected that he was afflicted with it.

The official hesitated. Perhaps this couple really didn't know anything about certificate marriages and, if so, he wasn't about to betray the secret. "I can't do much about this, unfortunately. You will have to discuss it with the Lloyd Triestino office."

"Can't you help us?" Manfred asked, the first time so far that he had opened his mouth. "The Jewish Agency is obviously a more important customer than we are."

The old man nodded. "I will certainly try. Please give me your tickets."

A few minutes later, they could hear an excited telephone conversation in Italian taking place over the phone. Then the official placed his hand over the receiver and asked, "Are you prepared to pay four hundred lire more?"

Manfred nodded. He still had almost a thousand lire in his pocket, apart from the German money which he hadn't converted yet.

The Italian conversation continued for a few minutes and then the official said, "Everything will be adjusted at the Lloyd Triestino office. But wait a minute. Before you go, let me give you your allowance for the hotel and meals."

Manfred thought for a moment. "Do you happen to have Palestinian pounds? I would prefer to take them so we have some local money when we arrive."

"It converts to about three pounds. Just sign here that you have received the money."

They thanked him and ran to the office of the line, which wasn't far away, where they were given their cabin number. The plan indicated that it was a tiny cabin for two, at the very front of the ship near the bow, and quite far below deck. Sonja pressed Manfred's hand when the grey-haired woman at the counter handed them their ticket. Instead of two separate tickets they now had one together, all the way from Trieste to Haifa.

"Boarding is at two p.m. tomorrow," the woman said, in fluent German.

"We'll be there," Sonja said. "You can be sure of that."

The woman followed the couple with her eyes, shaking her head at how strange Jews were.

Like two school children, Manfred and Sonja jumped on a bus and went to Miramare. There, in the beautiful landscape above the blue Adriatic, they enjoyed a four-hour honeymoon.

———◆———

The second evening after they set sail, they were sitting on deck. On the upper deck could be seen the bored faces of the first-class passengers, few Jews among them. But singing and laughing and even some dancing filled the tourist-class deck. Manfred felt a bit out of place, though Sonja made friends with many of the young people who were going to Palestine. Most of them came from Lithuania and Poland, and they all spoke Hebrew together. Manfred knew that Sonja had attended a Hebrew high school, but he hadn't realized how fluently she'd mastered the language.

"I was surprised myself that I'm still able to speak it so well," she told him, after a lively conversation with a group who belonged to a youth movement and intended to join a *kibbutz*. They had spent years preparing for it by working on a farm and learned to plough and to sow, to milk cows and to do all other kinds of farm work. Sonja called Manfred over and translated for him. The girls were proudly showing off the blisters and callouses they had earned when a voice over the loudspeaker called, "*Dottore Numane, Dottore Numane.*"

"I wonder who wants me?" Sonja asked. "Where do you go when you're called?"

"Upstairs, I think," Manfred said, and took her arm to lead her there.

A steward met them on the stairs. "Doctor Neumann?" he asked in German. "Yes."

"The captain requests that you to go to him." Then he lead them up another stairway.

Sonja looked at Manfred with questioning eyes.

"Maybe someone is sick," he said.

"They have a ship's doctor for that," she answered.

The white-haired captain welcomed them with a friendly smile. "I'm very sorry I must ask you for a favour," he said. "Our ship's doctor is busy attending a childbirth—"

"And you want me to help him?"

"No, he can manage by himself. But he can't get away, and we also have a very sick child here. The mother is desperate. That's why I looked at the passenger list and discovered you. You're a medical doctor, right?"

"That's right."

"Would you be so kind as to look at this child?"

"Of course."

Sonja turned to Manfred and said, "Please go to our cabin and bring me my black medical bag. It's under the bed."

Manfred was a little taken aback by her sudden bluntness. Sonja recognized how abruptly her manner had changed as soon as she switched into her professional mode and resolved to try to be more gentle in future. Aloud she asked, "How did your ship get transformed into a maternity ward, Captain?"

"The woman signed a declaration that she was only three months pregnant. It must have been a lie, although she wasn't showing very much. Still, I doubt she intended to give birth to her child just two days after setting sail. Her contractions must have been caused by the ship's vibrations."

"That doesn't seem very likely to me!" Sonja said. "Where did you acquire your excellent German, Captain?"

"My dear young lady, I've been sailing this ship since the *Lloyd Triestino* was still called *Triester Lloyd*, and the Austrian flag was flying where the Italian flag now flies."

"You're an Austrian?"

"I was," the captain said.

Manfred appeared with the case. Sonja threw him a particularly sweet and grateful look, which placated him. "My husband," she said, introducing him to the captain. "He is almost a colleague of yours. He builds ships."

"Oh," the captain said. "A ship-owner?"

Manfred laughed. "My wife is exaggerating. Not ships but little boats."

"In any case, vessels floating on the water," the captain said. "The steward will go with you, Dr. Neumann."

The steward took them back to tourist class. For a moment Sonja thought of sending Manfred away, but then she reconsidered. She wanted to include him in every aspect of her life now. She would find something useful for him to do.

"You didn't act like there was any particular hurry, and you probably would have continued chatting with the captain even longer if I hadn't turned up with your bag," Manfred said. "Is that appropriate behaviour in a medical emergency?"

"Well, our professor in Berlin once said that of a hundred children taking ill while travelling, only five have a serious illness. The other ninety-five just upset stomaches."

In the cabin to which the steward took them lay a nine-year-old boy with frightened eyes. His mother stood beside him moaning, "Oy, oy, my poor child!"

Sonja had learned from the steward that this family had Polish passports, so she addressed them in her mother tongue right away. Manfred didn't understand a word, which was fortunate. Otherwise he would have been astonished by his wife's rudeness.

"So who is sick here?" Sonja asked.

"Who is sick? The child is sick," the mother said. Her breasts were three stories high and her rear end provided a massive foundation for them.

"If it's the child who is sick, why are you moaning? You're only frightening him."

"When my boy is in pain, I'm not supposed to moan? I'm his mother."

"No one has any doubt about that," Sonja said, and opened her black bag.

"Who are you anyway?"

"I'm the doctor."

"A young thing like you? And who is that man then?"

"My husband. He's a doctor, too, though not for children. He's only here to ensure that I do everything right."

The woman, pleased to have the attention of two doctors, moved aside as far as was possible in the narrow cabin, considering her circumference.

Sonja sat down on the edge of the patient's bed and asked him gently, "Where does it hurt, my boy?"

"His stomach is killing him," the mother answered.

Sonja looked at the woman, sparks flying from her green eyes. She looked like a tiger ready to attack an elephant. "I asked the boy, not you. If you answer for him again we'll leave immediately."

The bastions of the material fortress quivered as though an earthquake had struck it. Since she had been slapped by her father when she was sixteen no one had dared talk to her like that. Her own husband trembled in fear of her, yet this young woman doctor had the nerve to reprimand her. Sonja's critical gaze made her afraid. She flushed and then turned pale, nodded her head, and waved at Sonja to signal that she should look after the child.

The little boy almost forgot his stomach pain, he was so fascinated by the duel he had just witnessed. The strange lady had defeated his mother, which was unbelievable. *Nobody* could defeat his mother. This gave him confidence in the power of the woman doctor and made him fear her as well.

She felt his stomach. He told her truthfully where it hurt, but was so afraid that he didn't even say "Ouch."

"Do you promise you won't eat anything more until I see you again in the morning? Do you promise?"

"Yes," the little boy said

"Good. You'll get some medicine soon and then you won't have so much pain anymore. Everything that doesn't belong in the stomach will come out."

Sonja stood up and told the woman, "The steward has to keep a toilet free for the boy. He will discharge a lot, and then he will feel better. But for God's sake, don't give him anything to eat."

"As you say, Madame Doctor." The mother had become quite meek. "But isn't it serious? Isn't it the appendix?"

"No. I wonder how he stuffed himself like that on the ship here. The portions aren't that big."

"He's a very poor eater," the mother said.

"I see. And as a good Jewish mama you're helping him along."

The mother nodded and smiled shamefacedly.

"If you love your child, don't do that please," Sonja said. She took two little pills from a box in her case. The mother went to the sink and filled a glass with lukewarm water.

"He won't take this," she said. "He never accepts medicine. He always spits it out."

Sonja was about to criticize her again but had second thoughts. "Why do you want to give him ideas like that?" she asked in a friendly voice instead. And to the boy she said, "You're not going to behave like a little monkey, are you? Monkeys spit things out, but big boys don't." She laid the pills on his tongue and held the glass in front of his mouth. He swallowed obediently. His mother's eyes widened and Manfred laughed. He hadn't understood the conversation, but it was clear what had happened. The big man's full-voiced laughter seemed funny to the boy in bed, and he started laughing too.

His mother threw her hands up in amazement. "He's laughing. My sick boy is laughing. He'll be well again soon."

"Stop calling him a sick boy. He's not sick. He just ate too much," Sonja said, her eyes flashing dangerously again.

"Yes, certainly. Forgive me, and many, many thanks."

As they were going back upstairs, Manfred said, "You know what?"

"No, what?"

"I promise you that you can treat my children, too. I liked what you did."

She stopped, and since she just happened to be two steps above him, she could kiss him easily. Laughing, she said, "You're going to entrust your own children to me? I would have never expected such generosity. But you know what?"

"No, what?"

"I have a slight suspicion that you have already entrusted me with one."

With that bull's eye she ran upstairs. Manfred only caught up with her at the salon door where the captain was waiting for her report.

They entered, out of breath, and from their hot, laughing faces, the captain could tell that he didn't have a dangerous infectious disease on his ship.

"Nothing serious, doctor?"

"No, only a little tummy with too much food in it."

"Thank God," the captain said. "The boy's mother acted as if he were dying."

"You know, Captain, it always seems miraculous to me that Jewish children manage to grow up in spite of their mothers."

Manfred and the captain laughed.

"Wait until you're a mother yourself, and then we'll see," Manfred said.

"I agree with your husband. Also, I would like the two of you to join me at my table in the dining room."

"But we're travelling tourist-class," Manfred remarked.

"As far as the meals on this ship are concerned, you're my guests for the rest of the journey," the captain said, and accompanied them into the first-class dining room.

———◆———

"I didn't imagine it would be this beautiful," Manfred said. "It's a fantastic sight."

Sonja was silent. She was much too excited to say anything. They stood at the railing with their arms tightly around each other as the panorama of Haifa came slowly closer in the cool early morning light. Eventually individual streets and houses could be seen. The golden dome of the Bahai Shrine flared in the sun. From there, a wide avenue led straight down to the sea.

"That's the famous Mount Carmel," Manfred explained, adjusting his camera for the distance. "The city climbs up the mountain. If only they had snow here, the sledding would be excellent."

"You have the craziest ideas," Sonja said. "Besides which, don't you think that every possible picture of Haifa from the sea has already been taken? You're just wasting film."

"But our arrival here must be recorded for posterity. Move over so I can get you in the picture."

Manfred took a few steps back and snapped Sonja with Haifa in the background. Then he pulled a little notebook from his pocket, wrote down the number of the film, and recorded: "Sonja in front of Haifa." Later he would copy the notes from his book onto the back of the prints. He kept precise records of his photographs so that at the age of eighty he would know exactly what was photographed when.

"What's today's date?" he asked.

"July the twenty-first."

Manfred cleared his throat. He had an important announcement to make. "Did you know that today is my birthday?"

Sonja stopped looking at Haifa and turned around. She placed her arms around his neck and gave him a ceremonial kiss. "I didn't know. Truly. Happy Birthday, and may you always stay in good health. The fact that we have arrived here on your birthday makes it even more meaningful."

Growing up, she never paid much attention to her own birthday. Few of her relatives in Poland even knew when their birthdays were. But ten years in Berlin had taught her that for most Germans, it's an important occasion. Usually the birthday child is given presents. Manfred was probably used to that. Unfortunately she didn't have a present for him, but she decided to arrange something so he wouldn't feel neglected.

When was her last birthday? About four months ago, when she had first been introduced to him. That made her four months older than her husband. It made no difference now, but in twenty years he would still be in his prime and she would be old. If forty-eight was old. She would probably be going through menopause.

These thoughts upset her, so she decided not to think about them for another ten years. She would have plenty of time to worry then.

"I have heard that the hottest time of the year begins now," Manfred was saying. "I'd hoped to get here sooner but everything took so long: the certificate, the wedding, and so on."

"Actually, it's lucky that it took so long." Sonja put her arms around him again. "Now we're here, and you have a wife, and I have a husband, and whatever may come we're not alone. Did it ever occur to you that we might not have developed this relationship if the ship hadn't had a defective screw? We would have boarded the ship directly in Trieste and each been assigned to separate cabins. We might have said *Good morning* and *Good evening*, but that would have been all. In a month or two they would have assigned a lawyer to complete the formalities of the divorce. Most likely we never would have seen each other again after disembarking."

"I can still do that," Manfred said in a Berlin accent, to make it sound humorous.

But Sonja didn't take it as a joke. "No, you can't. You can't get a divorce without my consent and that, my dear boy, I will not give you. Furthermore," she added, this time a bit less seriously, "I'm an exemplary wife who can satisfy her husband in every respect. Agreed?"

"Aye, aye!" said Manfred.

The deck filled with passengers. Everyone wanted to experience their arrival in Haifa Bay. At the bow of the ship the British Red Ensign was flying; it was inscribed with a round white disk upon which one could read the word PALESTINE. It was a rule that the flag of the destination country must be hoisted. What wasn't required was the second flag hoisted now: a white one with blue stripes at the top and bottom and a blue hexagonal star in the middle. The Italian line, whose main business in the Mediterranean was transporting Jewish immigrants, thought it advisable to show sympathy for its customers by flying their emblem. As the flag unfurled in the wind, the passengers spontaneously began to sing *Hativka*, the Jewish national anthem. Sonja sang along. Manfred only hummed the melody because he didn't know the words. Her eyes were wet, and she pressed his hand.

"Our country and our future," she whispered. He was emotional, too, and he had a solemn feeling, but didn't know whether he was already becoming a Jewish patriot or whether it was because everything was so new and unknown.

XXI

———⟐———

LIKE WOMEN, BUILDINGS CAN BECOME more beautiful with age. A very old house entwined with ivy can be beautiful; a Doric column remains beautiful even as a ruin, so that one assumes that it was equally beautiful three thousand years ago. That's how it is not only with buildings, but also with cities. They're not beautiful because they are old, but because they have remained beautiful even in age.

The same could not be said about the new city of Haifa. Haifa was a beautiful city thanks to three things that couldn't be created by any architect or city administration: the ocean in front, the mountains behind, and the sun above.

Sonja and Manfred were also surprised by Tel Aviv, though for different reasons.

"The city isn't as small as I had imagined," Manfred observed. "It will never be as beautiful as Haifa because it is flat, but it is a city under construction and the new smooth houses are very pretty. Still, something is missing. I don't know exactly what it is, but was also missing in Haifa."

"You know what I think?" Sonja replied. "I think nobody here, neither architects nor contractors, has given any thought to how the streets will look in fifty or a hundred years. I can't find a single building that has any kind of beauty in form or imagination that will endure many years from now. When the plaster peels off, it will all be very ugly. It is all simply modern and practical, but there is no style. That's my impression."

"Right," Manfred agreed, "and something else. There is no centre – a city hall or any public buildings – that look like something special. And there are no parks or squares. Why don't they build a beautiful big square and put a really decent monument in the middle? Also, I just realized something else. Despite the fact that Jews built these cities, I haven't seen a synagogue anywhere that is even one tenth as imposing as even the ugliest synagogue in Berlin. Do Jews lack history, or artists, or important architects? I can't understand it."

"Monuments are forbidden," Sonja said.

"What do you mean, forbidden?" Manfred's knowledge of the Jewish religion seemed to be as poor as his knowledge of Hebrew.

"The Bible commands that 'Thou shalt not make unto thee any graven image or likeness.'"

"But if I remember correctly, the commandment continues: 'so that you don't idolize it'. Surely, the danger that people will worship idols no longer exists in this day and age?"

"I'm not so sure," Sonja laughed. "The Bolsheviks have erected large statues of Comrade Lenin everywhere, which they worship. Exactly what our ancestors wanted to avoid."

"Maybe they could find something harmless to devote themselves to, such as Manneken Pis."

"Not everybody has the same taste as you, Manfred. Something like that would be indecent and would endanger the chastity of girls here."

"Does chastity even exist here?"

"More than it does in many other places. Definitely more than on Lake Wannsee, where you spent so much time."

"Sonja, that was a low blow. Strictly forbidden."

Sonja remembered this conversation as they made their way to the Kupat Holim, the health insurance agency of the Histadrut. The Histadrut in turn was the union of Jewish workers. Its office could be found at the Hadar Hacarmel, the second of Haifa's three levels. At sea level was the port city – the factories and warehouses of moving and wholesale companies, a mixed neighbourhood where Jews and Arabs lived and worked together in relative harmony. Halfway up Mount Carmel was a new Jewish residential area with beautiful streets and shops. Even higher up the mountain was the most elegant quarter, where only Jews lived.

Good leg muscles were needed to negotiate these streets and Sonja found it difficult to walk uphill wearing high heels. The most significant difference between these Jewish districts and those of other countries was that here, Jews weren't just tenants. They actually built everything themselves. The Histadrut saw to it that Jewish workers carried every stone and every bag of cement.

She wished someone would look after her as well as they did the construction of all these flat-roofed houses. They had been in the country for three months already and she still had no work. It wasn't proving as easy to find a job as she had imagined. She could always rent an apartment, hang out a sign, and wait for private patients, but who knew how long it might take to develop a practice that way? Her father, who was a doctor in Krakow, had advised her against this when she began to study. "First you should work in a clinic to become known as a good doctor. Word gets around fast, and then you'll be able to open a private practice," he had told her.

She didn't know Dr. Rosner, the new head of the health insurance administration. Last week she had dealt with his predecessor, hoping to find a position in one of the hospitals or clinics, but had been unsuccessful.

"We still haven't received your papers from head office in Tel Aviv, Dr. Falkowitsch," Dr. Rosner remarked.

"Neumann is my name now," Sonja said.

"Wasn't your diploma in the name of Falkowitsch?"

"When it was issued, I wasn't married."

"I understand. What does Mr. Neumann do?"

"He supports me," Sonja answered laconically.

"You say this as if you regret that your husband supports you. Isn't it the most natural thing in the world for a man to support his wife?"

"Sure," Sonja admitted. "And in fact, my husband is thrilled to be the head of the household. But I never expected to become a burden to him. In fact, I expected to find work here more easily than him since I speak Hebrew and he still doesn't. Also, I have a profession and he doesn't."

"What does he do then?"

"He works on construction at the port, where he earns a reasonably good wage. I mean considering the conditions here. But it's hard work, and I'm glad he has the physical strength for it."

Dr. Rosner played with his pencil. He hadn't asked these questions out of simple curiosity. He wanted to have a picture of her character. He still wasn't sure whether it was nothing but a wish to improve herself financially that had brought her to this office so often, as his predecessor had claimed.

"If I asked you to work on the paediatric ward without pay for a while, would that be acceptable?"

"I would accept anything you suggest. I'm the daughter of a doctor who mostly treated his patients without pay. I love children, and it gives me satisfaction to help them. It doesn't give me any satisfaction to sit in a furnished room all day and to do nothing but prepare food for my husband. I would be able to manage that even if I worked in the clinic most of the time," Sonja said, with some bitterness in her tone.

Dr. Rosner smiled. "In other words, you wouldn't make your husband suffer because you were volunteering here. Do you have children yourself?"

"No," Sonja said, blushing. She didn't want to make things more complicated. That's why she withheld the information that she was in the third month of pregnancy.

Dr. Rosner had come to a decision. This young woman was exactly what they needed: a doctor who was dedicated to medicine rather than business. Also, since she had graduated from the university in Berlin with *magna cum laude,* he knew that she was smart.

"I have another suggestion for you, an even better one. The Pinah Nidahat *kibbutz* is looking for a doctor to care for its own children and those of other settlements nearby. The place is somewhat isolated, and living conditions are quite primitive. But if we sent you there as our employee you would earn a modest salary and have few expenses. The *kibbutz* wouldn't ask you to pay for anything – neither the quarters in which you lived nor the food you ate in the community kitchen. You could save almost all your money—"

Sonja interrupted him. "Is it far from Haifa?"

"A drive of more than three hours."

"How could I do this with my husband?"

"A different option would include him," Dr. Rosner answered. "You could both become members of the *kibbutz* and he would work there like everybody else. In that situation neither of you would earn a salary, because no one in the *kibbutz* earns money or needs it. We would send your salary to the *kibbutz*, and it would go into the common kitty.

"Discuss both of these options with your husband and I'll talk with the people at Pinah Nidahat. Maybe we could even send you there for a trial visit, and if the comrades in the *kibbutz* find you agreeable, they'll give you six months to decide whether you want to become members or not. But I don't want to pull the wool over your eyes. It's not without danger there. The local Arabs are not friendly. They will bring their children to you to be treated for trachoma and bilharzia and syphilis, but you can't be sure that you won't be attacked by them anyway. The people in Pinah Nidahat have experienced quite a bit of hostility. Also, any doctor who works there must be prepared to treat adults occasionally as well as children. How are your surgical skills?"

"Like those of any general practitioner. I don't have many years of surgical experience," Sonja said.

"We don't expect that, because this isn't a job for an older doctor."

"This is a big responsibility you're offering me, Dr. Rosner, but it sounds exciting. I'm very tempted because it would be pioneer work, closer to what I had pictured Israel to be rather than the petit bourgeois lifestyle of the cities. But of course I must speak to my husband about it first. He is a person with strong opinions."

She stood up, and Dr. Rosner shook her hand. "It's good when a man knows his own mind, especially for the woman he's married to. But don't underestimate the cities. There is lots of pioneer work going on in them as well."

He showed her to the door and looked at her contemplatively. "You're a very sophisticated young woman, Dr. Neumann. It won't be an easy adjustment for you. Don't underestimate it. If you don't want to accept, I'll understand, and we'll find something else for you. The thing is, we may be able to accommodate you somehow in Tel Aviv or Jerusalem, but in Pinah Nidahat you would be needed."

"I understand. I'll call you," Sonja said, and almost ran through the door.

X X I I

———⟶———

"*Chaverim*, quiet please!" The secretary of Pinah Nidahat was trying desperately to turn the two hundred *kibbutz* members, who were mostly between twenty and thirty years of age, into a polite parliamentary assembly. Their meeting place was the large wooden hut where half an hour earlier they had finished eating supper. The tables had been moved outside, and were stacked unevenly under a starry sky.

"*Chaverim*, quiet!" the secretary repeated. It seemed that the less able its administration became, the more its responsibilities increased.

"Obviously we women can keep on talking," Daliah shouted.

"Why?"

"You only asked the men to be quiet, and that excludes me. Or do you think I'm a man?"

"Hear, hear!" other women joined in.

"Comrade Secretary mixes up more than his accounts; he doesn't know his Hebrew genders," another joker interjected.

The secretary was becoming frantic. "*Chaverim* and *chaverot*," he began yet again.

"Ladies should always come first," Daliah objected, winning loud approval from her friends.

Among the noise of chairs scraping on the floor, laughter and conversation, the secretary made a final attempt to control his audience. "*Chaverot* and *chaverim* or *chaverim* and *chaverot*, if you don't stop talking, I'll have to shut down the meeting."

It became a little quieter, and the secretary could finally lower his voice.

"We have to discuss some important issues. The first item on today's agenda is the orange harvest."

"You should say on this evening's agenda," someone yelled.

"We have to pick, sort, clean, wrap, pack and load the fruit."

"Such great news he's telling us," someone else snorted.

"I know it's not news," the secretary explained, "but perhaps one of you wise guys can tell me how we're supposed to get the fruit from here to Haifa on a three-wheeled truck."

"If Shmulik hadn't driven like a madman, the axle wouldn't have broken," somebody shouted.

"That wasn't Shmulik's fault," protested fat Nadia. She had her eye on Shmuel, the *kibbutz's* driver, mechanic and locksmith.

"*Chaverim*, please, it doesn't matter who or what caused the damage to the truck. We need to decide what to do about it," the secretary said.

"We'll walk," a voice piped up, to general merriment..

"Are you school children or grownups?" The secretary didn't wait for an answer to this rhetorical question. "To repair the truck would cost more than twenty pounds, which we don't have in our kitty, or we can rent a truck from the transportation cooperative for two pounds a day. We'll definitely have to get our truck repaired, it's only a question of when. So should we rent a different truck until we've sold the oranges and have enough money to repair our vehicle, or should we just borrow the money to repair our own truck right away? That's what I want you to vote on."

"I would like to speak to the first item on the agenda," the owner of a waving hand shouted.

"*Chaver* Eliahu has the floor," the secretary said, sitting down with a weary face.

A lean man of over thirty with the sunken eyes of a fanatic stood up. He was older than most of the other comrades, who respected him and usually let him speak, even though he sometimes got side-tracked into mysticism. A little *meshug-gah*, they said, but amusing. In the khaki pants and woollen sweater he wore over his open shirt, he looked like a soldier from World War I who had just survived a gas attack. They were all wearing sweaters or cardigans, for it was cold in the Galilee in November and the first rain had already fallen.

Chaver Eliahu cleared his throat and waited until it became quieter. He loved to speak softly. He found it made a special impression. "*Chaver* Amiel, I can't understand you at all. We didn't elect you secretary so that you would call general meetings about trivia. If you don't have the strength and the courage to make such world-shaking decisions on your own, you're not qualified to be a leader."

"Hear, hear!"

"Give it to him, Eli!" There was noise, laughter and protest.

"I'm always prepared to hand the office over to you," Amiel replied.

Eliahu continued. "Please understand me correctly. I'm not saying that Amiel is no good. He is good, only he is no good as a secretary. In fact the whole *kibbutz* administration has proven to be impotent—"

"Not true; Abraham and Susi have twins," someone shouted.

"*Shh*, let him finish talking!"

"I said I want to speak to the first item on the agenda," Eliahu continued, "and this is my point. The secretary should have raised more important issues for discussion, such as the question of night-time security and our shameful lack of guns and ammunition, or why the same comrades are always picked to be guards. There is the question of raising chickens in modern batteries and packaging their eggs. There is the question of purchasing a milking machine or the question of buying winter clothing for everybody, not just for the children. Then there is the little question of why the health insurance agency, to which we have been paying membership fees for years, cannot be persuaded to send us a decent doctor.

"*Chaverim* and *chaverot*," Eliahu raised his voice with a dramatic effect. "Isn't it enough that we have lost a child because we lack the most elementary medical provisions? Are there to be more victims? But that's not what our secretary and his committee wants us to deal with. A truck with a broken axle is more important to them."

Eliahu sat down. There was complete silence in the room. Everyone knew that his attack against the secretary, who was trying his best, was completely unjustified.

But no one dared to contradict Eliahu, not because he was one of the founders of the *kibbutz* but because the little boy suffering from diptheria who had died on the way to the hospital in Safed had been his own child.

A father who is still mourning for his child must be forgiven his bitterness. Amiel recognized that. In addition, he felt the tension among his comrades who were waiting for his reply and who were also feeling a bit sorry for him. Although they were hard to manage, being coarse and aggressive, they were generally fair.

He said, "Of course, Eliahu is right, but he didn't wait to see what else was on tonight's agenda. I therefore ask *Chaver* Shmuel, who was meant to speak at the end of the meeting, to tell us what he learned in Haifa yesterday when he was there to find parts for the truck."

"Not the damned truck again," someone shouted.

"But really, Amiel, this is incredible," another man yelled.

Shmulik came to the secretary's aid. He stood up, tall, broad-shouldered, and urgently in need of a haircut. "You idiots, you camels, listen to me. It has nothing at all to do with the truck."

"With what then?"

"With the doctor."

The room became completely still. Shmulik continued in his natural voice, which carried very well. "We have been offered a doctor. Perhaps even as a *chavera* of the *kibbutz*—"

Chavera Judith interrupted him. "How can a doctor become a *chavera*?"

"This is obviously a mistake," Hannah called out.

"No, I didn't make a mistake," Shmulik explained. "The doctor is a woman, who might—"

"No woman doctor will last here," one of the young people complained.

Amiel took a piece of wood and knocked on his table, the only one left in the room.

"I allowed you to interrupt me before, but now I demand that there be absolute quiet until Shmuel has finished speaking."

Shmulik took the floor again. "Before I went to Haifa, Amiel asked me to go to the health insurance office. There is a new director there, Dr. Rosner, and he welcomed me like a lost son. He said he had been trying to get in touch with us, to offer us a young woman doctor with excellent skills who is prepared to work here. She has only been in the country for three months, but she speaks the language. The director picked her because she is a pediatrician, which we need. Adults usually only require first aid, bandages and needles, and those can be administered by a pediatrician. The other way around would be much more difficult."

When he paused, a joker couldn't resist the opportunity to interrupt. "We'll only be allowed to have childhood diseases, and have to wash our behinds well before getting needles."

When the laughter had died down, Shmulik resumed. "I met the doctor and her husband."

There was movement and whispering in the hut.

"Yes, she is married. That's bad news for the bachelors among us but it can't be helped. They're coming for a visit on Saturday to look at the *kibbutz* and to meet us. By the way, I really liked her husband. He knows nothing about farming but a lot about plumbing and engines – the kind of technical issues I am the only one here to know anything about at the moment. We got along right away. I think we should welcome them nicely."

"Maybe we should pick flowers and hang up garlands?" fat Nadia declared ironically.

"Amiel, let me put a question to Shmulik," called a short man with lively eyes.

"Go ahead," the secretary allowed.

"What does the doctor look like?"

"She is a very beautiful woman, not tall but chic, and I believe she is a tough customer."

This got a reaction from the younger women, especially those who were not married yet. Daliah gave an audible sigh. "We are spared nothing."

"Where did she study and where is she from?" Hannah the kindergarten teacher inquired.

"I didn't ask her," Shmuel answered. "She spoke Hebrew with me and German with her husband. I also spoke German with him."

"Your German I want to hear." This time it was the secretary himself who was making jokes.

"Why? It isn't any worse than his English," another man retorted.

Amiel became serious again, knocked on the table and said, "Comrades, I believe that Eliahu has made it clear that we should try very hard to persuade this doctor to come here. We can't make Pinah Nidahat any more attractive than it is, especially for people who have only lived in the country for three months and are accustomed to the luxury of Europe. So far, we only have a single real building, and that is the children's house. It's decent, and our fifty-three noisemakers in there always look appealing, thanks to Hannah …"

Hannah jumped up and curtsied, which was followed by general applause.

"But," the secretary raised his voice. "All other living accommodations, workplaces and common rooms, even our library, are still only huts and barracks. Therefore," and Amiel emphasized the word, "we ask all comrades, and particularly the women, to make sure that the dining room looks neat. A few flowers on the tables wouldn't be such a bad idea. The tables here, the kitchen and the living accommodations should be cleaned—"

"If you want to build a fake Potemkin village to deceive her, you're crazy," a heckler shouted

"It would also be advisable," the secretary continued placidly, "not to wear your most patched shirts and pants on Saturday, and I suggest that Comrade Rafael try to shave for once, even though he finds it difficult."

Amiel waited for the laughter to die down. "What I'm asking is that we make an effort to make the place look somewhat civilized rather than resembling a nomadic Bedouin encampment. Those in favour, please raise your hands."

Two hundred hands went up.

X X I I I

———

MR. BEN-JAACOW'S DELIVERY TRUCK WASN'T very elegant, but it had a good motor. It needed a good motor because it carried loads of bolts and screws all week. Manfred was happy that he could borrow the truck, otherwise it would have been difficult to get to Pinah Nidahat on Saturday when there were no buses. "Go ahead and take your wife for a little drive. I won't need the truck on the Sabbath," Ben-Jaacow said, giving him the key and patting him on the shoulder.

Sonja had wanted to dress as simply as possible, but the only winter coat she possessed was trimmed with Persian lamb and, since she had to wear the coat, she thought she might as well wear the matching cossack hat as well. The truck's cab was greasy with oil, so she spread a towel over the seat to keep from getting dirty. Manfred was more suitably dressed in his wool-lined windbreaker. He could make good use now of the clothes he used to wear only on his boat.

They drove down the street from Mount Carmel and took the highway leading to Tiberias via Nazareth.

"This great plain is the Jezreel Valley," Sonja said. "Not far away must be Meggido, which was the Armageddon of the Bible. Everything was swamp here as little as twenty years ago. They have accomplished a lot. Look how green and cultivated everything is!"

Manfred murmured agreement. He had clipped a map to the dashboard and now studied their route.

"The round village down there is called Nahalal," he said.

"How do you know that?"

"It says so on the map," he explained. "It seems to be a *kibbutz* as well."

"If it's Nahalal, it is a *moshav* and not a *kibbutz*," Sonja corrected him.

"And what's the difference?"

"In a *moshav*, people work together and market their products together, but they each have their own households where parents and their children live together. In a *kibbutz*, the children sleep in children's houses so that their parents are free to work. They all eat together so no one has to run their own household. Adults don't need houses of their own, only individual rooms."

"Horrible! What about family life?"

Sonja hesitated before answering. It didn't seem that attractive to her either, but this was the first time she'd heard Manfred's opinion about life in a *kibbutz*.

"You know, this is only theoretical; I learned it from articles and lectures. I have seen as little of real *kibbutzim* as you have. In fact, we haven't seen much of the country at all apart from Haifa, Tel Aviv, and Jerusalem. So let's at least look at it first!"

"Well, isn't that why we're going there?" Manfred asked.

Sonja nodded. But she wasn't convinced the *kibbutz* would work for them. As much as she wanted to work again, it felt like a pipe dream. A man from a normal big-city environment couldn't adapt to a life like that. Most of the *kibbutzniks* had been ten years younger than her and Manfred when they committed to that lifestyle, and they did it with friends. It was all a big adventure. At eighteen, they weren't thinking about family life or building a home with someone.

If Manfred didn't like the *kibbutz*, there was no way she could accept a job there, even if she really wanted to. It was admirable that he found work only two days after their arrival, and was not ashamed of being a simple labourer even though he was so well educated. But there was no way he could keep doing such hard physical work forever. He was so tired every night. Besides which, he still needed to learn fluent Hebrew, and she would be having a baby in six months.

"I didn't expect the landscape to be so beautiful!" Manfred exclaimed, interrupting her thoughts. "Too bad I didn't bring my camera."

"It doesn't matter. Why do we need to photograph all this? And I'm hot. It's getting warmer, isn't it?"

"My colleagues at the port told me that we would experience three different climates during this three-hour drive. The coast has mild Mediterranean climate, Tiberias is two hundred metres below sea level and is almost tropical, and then we go on to the Galilee with its cooler mountain weather. Anyone who doesn't catch a cold here must be really healthy!"

Sonja looked at him with concern. "Unbutton your jacket. It is really warm right now and you don't want to get overheated and catch cold when the temperature changes. Manfred, I really think I have allowed myself to be influenced too quickly. You too, by the way. I suspect that this whole trip is for nothing. The more I think about it, the more certain I am that *kibbutz* life isn't right for the two of us."

"We're already more than half way there, my dear, so I don't want to turn back. Besides which, I'm interested in seeing this communist lifestyle."

"Sometimes I envy you."

"Why?"

"Because you were never a Zionist, and therefore you can look at everything without preconceptions. If you've come here without expectations, and haven't had any illusions, you don't experience disappointment. I envy you at the same time as I admire your ability to see things with such sober objectivity."

"Do you feel disappointed? You weren't a Zionist either, otherwise you never would have—"

She interrupted him. She didn't want to be reminded of her first marriage. "I know what you're implying. It's true. But I grew up in an environment in which we all felt like Jews. At my Hebrew high school all our classes had a Zionist orientation. My background was nothing like yours in Germany."

Manfred laughed. "You remind me of my friend Albert. I had discussions with him about this subject all the time."

"The half hour I spent with Albert in Tel Aviv was quite enough for me."

"Why?"

"He is an arrogant egotist who feels entitled for no reason. He admits that he wasn't happy in Germany, yet he doesn't like anything here either. Well, nobody invited him."

"But you also say that you're disappointed about many things."

"That's different. I'm disappointed in the vision I had for our life here, true, but not in Zionism itself. But Albert is disappointed in the country and the people. What has he done to earn the right to criticize everything? He's not getting his hands dirty trying to help. I believe it would never enter his mind to work the way you do."

Probably not, Manfred thought, reflecting that if a woman doesn't like her husband's friend, that's the end of the friendship. Well, it wouldn't be a great tragedy. Still, what Sonja had said wasn't fair, and he felt compelled to defend his old classmate.

"You don't know Albert as well as I do. In Germany, he thoroughly criticized the Germans, their politics, the government, and society in general."

"There was good reason for that back then, and even more reason today." Sonja interjected, but Manfred shook his head.

"You don't understand what I'm trying to say. The reason for his criticism was Albert's secret love of Germany. He would have loved to feel like a German – the way I did – but they didn't let him."

"Who didn't let him?"

"In the first place his father, who wasn't German himself, and then, of course, the way things developed. In my case it was very simple. I was a dedicated German patriot until the day that shithead Hitler came to power and declared that I was no longer a citizen. Not only that, but as a Jew, I was demoted to being a third- or fourth-class human being. So I told him, *kiss my ass*, and went to look for something else."

"Don't be so crude," Sonja remarked and pinched him in the body part he had mentioned.

"Ouch, it is strictly forbidden to touch the driver enroute," Manfred protested. "Where was I?"

"You said you went to look for something else."

"Oh yes. With Albert, it was very different. He was split into two parts growing up. His papa thumped into him that he was a Jew first and foremost, though he couldn't imagine what that meant since he grew up, as I did, with a German cultural heritage. At school, little Albert was expected to cheer loudly because the Germani chieftan Herman had beaten Varus and his Roman legions in the Teutoburg Forest, but at home his father and his Hebrew teacher told him that Herman's success in the Teutoburg Forest should mean nothing to him. The result was that Albert belonged neither here nor there.

"Of course, none of that explains why he is so uptight over here."

"I didn't know any of this before, but your explanations are wonderful. Psychologically, the case is quite typical. A child who is prevented from developing his natural inclinations and sympathies, including love of his homeland, will build his own fantasy world. Your friend's fantasy world was probably a Jewish state. Then he comes here and suddenly he is surrounded by Jews and discovers that reality corresponds very little to his ideal. Even worse, he feels that he doesn't fit into this reality himself; he only fits into the fantasy he has created.

"That's why he is angry. We're indeed much better off than Albert is. Since we weren't expecting to live in a fantasy world, we're happier about unexpected good things than we are annoyed about inconveniences. For example, as you said, we're able to enjoy this fabulous landscape."

They had crossed a mountain ridge and a deep valley lay before them. Manfred stopped the truck on the side of the road and they got out. Before them they saw the city of Tiberias sitting beside a large blue lake. The mountains beyond it shone with an almost violet light. A sign below them on the side of the road indicated that the lake and the city were two hundred metres below sea level.

The light green of fields after rain, the darker green of palm trees on the lakeshore and the white walls of the red-roofed houses formed a symphony of colour, light, and shadow against the background of the blue lake and the reddish-brown mountains on the far shore. Sonja relished the view silently. As always, Manfred was matter-of-fact. "If I saw something like this on a postcard, I mean in those colours, I would say it was kitsch. What's the name of this pond in the original language? It has about twenty-seven names in other languages, doesn't it?"

"You're exaggerating, but the Hebrew name is *Kinneret*. That means *a lute*. It was called that because of its shape."

"If we settled near this lute, I could go sailing again. It's at least four times as big as Lake Müggelsee," Manfred said.

Sonja took his hand. Manfred's asides were sometimes more informative than what he said deliberately. "Do you miss home a lot? I mean the sailing, tobogganing, skiing, and the other sports you're used to? Be honest!"

"No, I don't miss anything except for money and a decent job, but I'll get those eventually."

"For sure," she assured him, pressing her body against his. Remembering an inspirational line from the Polish national anthem, she intoned, "Poland is not yet lost," then led him back to the truck, laughing.

It was almost noon when they arrived at Pinah Nidahat. They were warmly welcomed by a friendly secretary with the body of a farmer and the high forehead of a statesman. First they had lunch together with the members of the *kibbutz* in the common dining room. The food was good, betraying the Czechoslovakian origin of the cooks. The complicated system of work-sharing among the comrades was explained to them, as was the *kibbutz*'s bookkeeping method. Then they toured the grounds, from the tractor and the cow barn to some of the private quarters. There they discovered how much their comfort depended on the character of each occupant. In spite of the simplicity and uniformity of beds, tables and chairs, some rooms looked nice and comfortable, while others resembled monastic cells of monks.

Sonja spent almost an hour in the children's house listening to the hearts and lungs of one little creature after another. She did it intuitively, not realizing that she was making a good impression on the people of Pinah Nidahat. One four-year-old boy was showing early signs of fever so she ordered him to bed, which the boy didn't like but his mother did. In the infant room, three young women were nursing their newborn babies.

Manfred hadn't come along, but Sonja told him about the children's house after she left it.

"It's the opposite of a cow barn," he said. "There the calf comes to the cow, but here the cow comes to the calf."

"Shame on you!" Sonja said. "Don't compare a young woman to a cow."

However, she wasn't sure whether she herself would be comfortable having the child she was carrying grow up in such a system. Sure, such children would be well-cared for and later the *kibbutz* would look after their secondary education – all things a family might find difficult to supply on their own. But she doubted it would suit her and Manfred. On the other hand, the young people here were the happiest they had met in Palestine. There was an atmosphere of joy, purpose and idealism in the *kibbutz*. And she was impressed by all the cultural activities they organized: reading groups, a theatre group, an orchestra. lectures and discussions. What other village so small could provide so much?

Worried that whatever decision they made would be the wrong one, she sat looking at Manfred, whose eyes were fixed on the road ahead, the steering wheel held tight in his big fists. She was prepared for a negative response from him, and resolved she would not argue but instead agree with everything he said.

"The bookkeeping system the brothers have over there is antiquated, and I would completely reorganize the labour distribution. With coloured index cards and a slotted board, the organization would be clearer and the work could be distributed better," Manfred said.

Sonja would have never guessed that he was preoccupied with the bookkeeping. The thoughts of a man, even one she believed she knew well, were unfathomable. What else would he say? She didn't have to wait long to find out.

"Their generator isn't connected properly either. It vibrates too much because they only poured a thin bed of concrete instead of a proper foundation. When I told the mechanic, his eyes opened as wide as those of Columbus when he discovered America. There are hundreds of other things that could be changed and improved, as I told the secretary."

"In German?" Sonja asked.

"Sure. He speaks German quite well, although with a Russian accent."

"What did he answer?"

"He said that he totally agrees with me and that I should regard it as my life's work to beautify and improve the *kibbutz*."

"It sounds as though they need you almost more than they need me. So what do you think? Would you like to go to Pinah Nidahat?" Her heart throbbed as she waited for an answer.

"That's entirely up to you."

"No, Manfred, it's up to you," she said emphatically. "The man has to decide in such matters."

"Since when?" he teased her.

"Since … Adam and Eve."

He grinned. "Quite right. Their change of residence was caused by Eve. Adam had no say in it. After all, she gave him the apple."

"Manfred, be serious for once! I don't want to be blamed for luring you there, apple or no apple. It must be your own decision."

"You have been luring me with two apples all along."

"Can you stop being vulgar for two minutes? This is a very serious decision we have to make," Sonja said, her voice sounding almost angry.

Manfred recognized how sincere she was about not wishing to influence the direction of his life, but he didn't want to make such a big decision about her future either. So he only said, "If you are asking me if I can imagine living and working in this *kibbutz*, I would say — why not? It is in a very scenic setting. It is a healthy way of life. There is company there that would be agreeable. But if you ask me whether I am ready to commit our future to the place, I can't answer until I've spent some time there. Does that make sense?"

"Yes, my beloved giant. So we'll try it." She leaned over and kissed him. The truck started to veer off the road, but he was able to hold the wheel steady.

XIX
1939

———

"WHY DON'T YOU CONVERT TO Islam?" Fais Maraka asked, as if it were the most natural question in the world.

"Since the Jews have been accustomed to their own religion for four thousand years, Fais Effendi, this is a rhetorical question. What would such a conversion achieve, in your opinion?" Albert asked. While his visit to the Marakas was purely a formality – they maintained excellent business relations and never had any problems – the conversation always turned into a political debate when Abdul Kader's oldest son was at the store.

"We would become a single nation, and then it would be no problem to kick the British out of the country. Meanwhile they're playing us against each other so they can rule over us," Fais explained.

"Not so loud!" Abdul Kader said.

Albert finished his cup of Turkish coffee and said, "Fais, let's not kid ourselves! As soon as the British leave here, we'll be fighting each other."

"Not if you become Moslems. We are related. You are like first cousins to us. Of all languages, yours is closest to Arabic. We're only divided by religion."

Abdul Kader intervened. "Fais, you're a fool. People don't change their religion like their shirts. And the Koran doesn't protect us against the hostility of other Moslems. You're young; you don't remember when the Turks were in charge here. They may have been Moslems, but I prefer the British. May Allah give them many more years!"

"My father doesn't find it advisable for us Arabs to govern ourselves," Fais told Albert. He didn't argue directly with his father, which would have been a serious breech of etiquette in the presence of a guest.

Abdul Kadar replied to the implicit accusation. "What do you hotheads know about government? Most of you can't even read or write! Ask Albert Effendi here whether he would allow your friends to govern him."

Albert laughed – a little embarrassed at being invited to pronounce on such a touchy subject. There was more to this conversation than the natural tension between generations, between the comfortable and the unsatisfied. Still, he was well aware that father and son weren't saying everything they were thinking. Middle Eastern politeness required that one only allow a guest to hear things that will not upset him.

"Albert Effendi has come to our country," stated Fais. "Those who visit a stranger's house must eat what the host offers. So the saying goes."

Albert extinguished his cigarette in the ash tray. "But this is not a stranger's house, Fais. For us Jews, this is the land of our ancestors. And since you have introduced the subject of religion, I want to suggest an alternative point of view. You're a Moslem today, and you feel like an Arab. But many Palestinian Arabs are actually the descendants of the Jews who lived here two thousand years ago. Many others arrived in recent years after Jews had begun to improve local conditions. It would be just as logical, therefore, for our Moslem cousins to convert to Judaism as the reverse."

Fais laughed. "Just because the Jews lived here two thousand years ago and the land belonged to them then, you want to lay claim to it now? Albert Effendi, you are an intelligent man. You must recognize how foolish that is, and that you will never succeed. On the other hand, it would make sense to establish an Arab state here, a state where a Jew might some day become a cabinet minister. With this proviso: there must be no further immigration. We won't allow you to become the majority here."

While his son was speaking, Abdul Kader kept nodding in agreement. Now, looking from one young man to another, he said, "Seeing the two of you side by side, you do indeed look like brothers. But there is one important difference, my son. You're enthusiastically talking about a future state and its ministers. But Mr. Berg here is setting up machinery in Tel Aviv and building a factory. There you have the matter in a nutshell. You may be an idealist, but he is practical. The Jews have the energy, the know-how and the money, which we don't have."

"Unfortunately, we don't actually have the money," Albert noted.

Abdul Kader shook his head. *Jews always have money* was clearly his opinion, as it is that of many people all over the world. "We only have to look at your colonies and at the city of Tel Aviv, and compare those buildings to the houses of simple workers. It is obvious that you have money. I don't regard this as something negative, however. The value of our land has increased twenty-fold and more because of it. Our *fellahin* can sell their tomatoes and eggs and no longer walk barefoot. The whole country is profiting, and I have nothing against that."

"Sidi," Albert said, using the Arabic way of address. "I assure you that the Sheik of Kuwait and King Ibn Saud have more money than all the Jews put together. Only they don't use it for the welfare of their people."

"That's true. I always say that, too," Fais said.

Albert continued. "The more real wealth you have, the poorer the people become. I have seen gigantic areas of unused real estate in Syria, in Iraq, and in Egypt. Syria and Iraq are under-populated. But here – in this little strip of land that has the worst and rockiest soil of them all – you're shown what work, diligence and modern technology can achieve, and suddenly you're all interested in this land. Before, you didn't even have a *name* for it. You called it *Southern Syria*. Fais Effendi, this land is no more southern Syria than Syria is northern Palestine. You Arabs may have come here for generations but it was never your land of origin and it never belonged to you. You are the last people who have the right to tell us whether we should be allowed to return. Where every stone is engraved with letters in our alphabet and every village is still called by its Hebrew name, even those you have tried to translate into Arabic."

"And you believe you can displace us because of that?" Fais laughed. "You just said yourself that we originated from you people a long time ago. Therefore our right to live here is inviolable."

"Agreed," Albert declared. "There is enough space for everybody. At least four million people will be able to live in this land once we develop it according to modern methods and an intensive economy."

"Impossible," Abdul Kader said.

"Why should it be impossible? There are countries in Europe about the same size with twice as many people. Belgium, for example."

"Belgium, Holland, Denmark," Abdul Kader said. "How can you compare them? Europeans are tens of thousands of years ahead of us in civilization."

"You know, Ya Sidi, I have never understood this point of view. In Syria and Egypt also I heard people insist that the Middle East could not be expected to be as developed as Europe. But in ancient times it was exactly the opposite. The Middle East was way ahead of Europe in development, and especially in science. It's hard to explain the slide backwards into feudalism, poverty, slavery and so forth," Albert said.

"Atatürk thought that the regression was due to religion. That's why he tried to reduce the power of Islam in Turkey. But I don't see the Turks making such great progress," Fais said.

Abdul Kadar shook his head.

"Fais, it has nothing to do with the religion of the Turks. Just look at the Jews. They have a religion. Compared with it, Islam is the epitome of progress. And still they're accomplishing something."

"Those who do, Ya Abuyi, are not the characters who stick to the commands of their religion. Albert Effendi doesn't wear a beard or sidelocks, and he doesn't wear a kaftan. He could just as well be a Moslem," Fais said.

Albert laughed. "My friends, I must go now. We began our discussion with religion and we end with religion again. Fais, I'm afraid we won't reach a consensus today, but that doesn't have to affect our friendship."

Abdul Kader and Fais loudly voiced their agreement.

Albert stood up. His legs hurt. He still found it difficult to sit comfortably on the low Middle Eastern stools. Abdul Kader got up too, and opened the door of the small back room where they had been sitting to see whether anyone in the shop might object that he was still maintaining friendly relations with Jews. Abdul Kader did not agree with the politics of the Muftis. Haj Emin Al Husseini, the Moslem Mufti of Jerusalem, was the instigator of attacks against isolated Jewish villages and sometimes against individual Jews. Among the Arabs, he was the originator of the boycott against Jewish industry. It had been going on for three years now, and who was being hurt by it? Only the Arabs. The Jews knew to protect themselves and to organize. If they decided to fight back, things could turn out even worse. In any event, Abdul Kader continued to buy merchandise from factories in Tel Aviv and Haifa, carefully removing all trademarks afterwards so no one would know. He was afraid of violent retribution from the Mufti and his gangs.

Peering out, he saw his assistant busy helping two slender Bedouin women pick out fabrics. With fingers hard and dark as wood, they were feeling the material. When they heard the door open, they turned around and gave the men provocative looks. Arab women were habitually veiled so as not to expose themselves to the eyes of men, but the Bedouins were not. They wore burkas decorated with small gold coins that dangled on their foreheads.

Abdul Kader was glad that Albert looked like an urban Arab, especially since he wasn't wearing a hat. Still, the Bedouin women didn't care about politics, so he wasn't particularly concerned about them recognizing a Jew in his shop.

"What do you think," he asked Albert. "Will there be war in Europe?"

"I don't think so," Albert said. "Hitler is achieving everything he wants without having to go to war, thanks to the cowardice of the British and the French."

"When you read the papers, it sounds like there's a lot of conflict," Fais said. He went to the front door to see whether Albert could leave without endangering the good name of the Maraka firm.

"I certainly hope there won't be a war," Albert declared. "We just had a baby."

Abdul Kader and Fais both congratulated him warmly. "*Mabrouk!*"

Then, "Boy or girl?" Abdul Kader asked.

"A little girl," Albert said.

A shadow darkened Abdul Kader's face. In his opinion, a man who only sired a girl was not very impressive, but perhaps it would be a boy the next time. "*Inshallah wa itshuf akhuha*," he consoled Albert.

Albert laughed. He liked this form of congratulation. "God willing, she will see her brother." Not a bad idea. "May peace be with you," he bid farewell in the traditional way.

"And may peace be with you," father and son replied.

Albert reflected on the sad fact that in Palestine, the only peace alluded to was in this greeting. Both coming and going, locals wished each other peace: *Shalom* in Hebrew, *Salam* in Arabic. But what was constantly on their tongues was not in their hearts.

He opened the door of his car and got in. It was advisable to return to Tel Aviv before dark, though he didn't look forward to going home. There were two problems: the baby cried so much there was no quiet place for him to be alone in the tiny apartment, and his mother and his wife didn't get along very well. His wife was smarter, but his mother was kinder, and suffered from the close proximity and the conflict. Unfortunately, he couldn't afford two households.

Albert drove slowly along Mamila Street. A few pretty young girls looked longingly at the big convertible and the elegant young man at its wheel. It was really a white elephant. An eight-cylinder Mercedes Nürburg fit into these narrow streets like a square peg in a round hole. It cost a fortune in fuel and repairs but was impossible to sell, being ten years old.

His mother had travelled out of Austria by train while her faithful chauffeur, Paul, drove the Mercedes loaded with her suitcases across the border to Basel. "Whose car is this?" they had asked him at the border. Paul had answered, "The Baroness of Berg." The car's registration was in the name of Berg and since it didn't sound Jewish, they had let him through.

The family name ought to have been *Birgaisski*, after the village of Birgais in Latvia where Albert's great-grandfather lived, but the Russian official who was compiling the census found it too complicated to spell and just wrote *Birg*. At least they hadn't been stuck with one of those names like *Pinkelstein* and *Wasserstrahl*, *Feigenblatt* and *Bügeleisen,* and similar witty inventions by humorous administrators! He wondered whether he ought to return to a Middle-Eastern kind of name like the Arabs had.

Albert accelerated. Having left the crowded Jewish quarter of Jerusalem, he was now driving downhill into the Motza Valley, and then uphill again in second gear via the hairpin curves called the Seven Sisters. Along the road, Arabs led heavily laden camels. A British military plane circled the summit, probably policing the area for possible attacks.

Albert recognized that there were no simple answers to the ongoing conflict with the Arabs. It didn't matter that Jewish immigrants had brought with them increased work and prosperity, hygeine and hospitals. The Arabs weren't impressed by such innovations. This wasn't a conflict between right and wrong, but between right and right. The most dangerous kind.

Driving the winding road in the Judean Hills past the green forest of Kiryat-Anavim, he saw the white houses and red roofs of a *kibbutz*. It reminded him of Manfred, whom he hadn't seen for five years. It was strange to think how en-trenched his former friend had become in that environment, how unassuming and satisfied he seemed, in spite of his wife's miscarriage. It was ironic that a doctor who managed to look after all the children in the northern Galilee had not been able to save her own baby. He wanted to be more sympathetic to Sonja but that woman really got on his nerves. Besides, she had made no effort to reach out to his wife, having seen Leah only once, shortly before they were married.

Albert often remembered the private conversation that had taken place be-tween them while Manfred was giving Leah a tour of the *kibbutz*, and probably quizzing her about her feelings for Albert.

"Do you really love this beautiful girl, Albert?' Sonja had asked.

Of course he had answered in the affirmative, then asked why she was inter-rogating him

"I don't know," she had said, "but I have the feeling you're living in a dream-world where you have fabricated certain ideals for your life. One of these ide-als might be to marry a woman of biblical beauty – the way you imagine Ruth or Esther in the Bible. The first girl you meet who comes close to this concept becomes your choice for life. But how can you be sure that you love her for her-self? And how do you know that you match each other in temperament? How do you know you'll be happy in bed? That's one of the most important things in a marriage."

"I agree," he had answered, "but in Palestine, you can't experiment before the wedding."

"That is indeed a shame," she had commented soberly. Sonja had been like a diviner standing over a hidden vein of water with a twitching rod. Like his wife,

Leah, she was keenly observant. Her scrutiny made him uncomfortable, and was probably the reason he had never visited them again.

Albert let the car roll down the last curves, which were not as steep as earlier ones. Through the opening of the mountain pass from the Judean Hills he entered the wide plain of Ayalon. The opening was called *Bab-el-Wad* in Arabic and *Shaar Hagai* in Hebrew, namely *gate of the valley*. Here were the ruins of an old caravan-sary where seventy years earlier, Mark Twain had let his horse rest. Incredible that a journey that took less than two hours today had taken two full days back then. In the past, even the moon was compelled to stop here, according to the Book of Joshua: "Sun, stand still over Giveon, and moon, in the Valley of Ayalon!"

Albert was so deep in thought that he almost failed to notice that someone was giving him a sign to stop. It was neither the sun nor the moon, but a British patrolman.

"Your driver's licence," said a police officer who somehow seemed familiar to him. "And please get out of the car."

When Albert made no effort to follow the English request, a sergeant repeated the words in good Hebrew.

Albert turned the engine off and got out. Three policemen and the sergeant descended upon the car, lifting up its seats and searching the pockets in the doors, while the officer went through the trunk.

Albert became angry, convinced they were singling out Jews for these searches, looking for weapons, which were their only means of defence. Meanwhile they gave Arabs free passage. To him, such hypocrisy made them worse than the Nazis. He gave the officer a hateful look and then remembered where he knew him from. He was the Irishman he had met at the Edelfels' home.

"Mr. O'Brien," Albert said, "aren't you ashamed of yourself?"

O'Brien looked at him carefully. "How do I know you?" he said, not in an unfriendly tone. The expensive car always instilled a certain respect.

"We met a few years ago at a party in Tel Aviv," Albert said. "At the time I would have never expected you would do something as malicious as this."

"Watch your tongue, mister. In what way are we being malicious?"

"By searching Jews for weapons and ignoring the Arabs."

"We examine every car regardless of the occupant's nationality, race, or religion. To accuse us of bias is an insult."

Albert wasn't a hero, but neither was he afraid of shiny buttons and authority.

"You may say that the British police are completely impartial. But if so, why don't they recognize that while a Jewish car might sometimes contain a single revolver for self-defence, Arabs camels loaded with weapons are never stopped because they cross fields rather than highways?"

Inspector O'Brien didn't answer, though he knew the damn Jew was right. The profession of neutrality by the British police was indeed hypocritical, but he was required to follow orders. Luckily he didn't have to prosecute the man, since he had nothing suspicious in his car.

O'Brien shut the trunk and waved his pudgy hand, indicating to Albert that he could drive on. He intended to ask him to say hello to Mrs. Edelfels in Tel Aviv, should he see her again, but Albert drove off without a backward glance. He was determined to show the policemen how unpopular their policy was.

Still, if war should break out in Europe, as Fais predicted, he would have to support the British. He liked his mother-in-law's formulation: "If the British fight against the Nazis, they should get the beating they deserve, but may God give them the strength to survive."

It was lucky that O'Brien and his people were not familiar with the Mercedes Nürburg, so they didn't realize that it came complete with an air compressor allowing flat tires to be reinflated right from the engine. Albert put the brakes on, made sure that no one was watching him, lifted the carpet and revealed the compressor. Hidden in the little sunken box was his Mauser pistol, firmly wrapped in an oil-soaked rag. He wondered how long it would take him to grab the weapon in an emergency. *I will have to practice*, he thought.

He lay the carpet back over the box and drove on. Just before Ramla, the only city in Palestine built by Arabs – all other cities and most villages dated back to the biblical period – a man and a woman in European dress waved at him. There weren't even any flowers to pick in the August heat. What kind of idiots went for a casual stroll in the vicinity of this nest of thieves and murderers?

He stopped the car.

"Do you happen to be driving to Tel Aviv?" the well-dressed gentleman asked him in poor English.

He had a strong German accent, so Albert responded in that language. "Yes. Get in."

"Look, Lottchen, a Mercedes," the man exclaimed to his wife, climbing into the back of the car. She said thank you politely and sat down next to Albert, who glanced at her covertly. This corpulent blond woman was no longer a "Lottchen" despite her smooth skin, but a grown-up Lotte in her late forties or early fifties.

"Professor Kramer," the gentleman in the back seat introduced himself. Albert countered with his own name. "We're very grateful to you for picking us up. You're from Germany?"

"But I have been in here for seven years now. You, on the other hand seem to be newcomers?"

"Does it show?" Lotte asked.

"Well, only newcomers would risk walking around here on foot. You were lucky that nothing bad happened to you. What in the world were you looking for outside Ramla?"

"We just wanted to explore the countryside. We only arrived last week," the woman said, and her husband added, "We like going on hikes, so we took the bus at random. When it stopped in this interesting town, we got off. The Arabs looked at us as if we were museum pieces, but I assumed that we look as exotic to them as they do to us."

"Hardly. They have been used to Europeans for a long time, and many of their wealthier people wear European clothes."

"Are you suggesting that it is dangerous to walk around here alone?" the woman asked naively.

"For a woman it has always been dangerous to visit Arab communities, but since the unrest began two or three years ago it has also become dangerous for men. Of course, most Arabs want to live in peace just like we do, but the Mufti has organized a number of murderous gangs. People say he is getting the money to attack Jews from Hitler. You never know where and when those thugs will attack you."

"You see, Siegfried, in a foreign country you should always inquire before undertaking anything on your own initiative," Lotte said.

Albert smothered a laugh at the man's name. If the woman had only been called Kriemhild, the couple could have staged "The Ring of the Nibelungs" in Ramla. Although Brunhild would be even more fitting for someone like her.

They drove down Ramla's only through-street. Because the pedestrians were so reckless Albert had to proceed slowly, so Frau Lotte was able to get a good look at the little, run-down, dirty houses. Large pieces of bloody meat hung in an open alcove that served as a butcher shop. They were surrounded by swarms of flies that refused to be driven away by a horse tail mounted on a small stick. The butcher was holding a long knife in his right hand and waved the horse tail occasionally with his left, but the flies showed more perseverance than he did.

"Is that pork hanging there?" she asked.

"Islam, like Judaism, forbids the consumption of pork. Those are legs of mutton and goat."

The professor leaned forward to explain. "Such customs are still quite foreign to my wife and me. She is not Jewish, you see, and I haven't had very much contact with things religious, although I still officially adhere to my heritage. It used to be completely unimportant before Hitler made it such an issue we had to go into exile. Please excuse me if I have touched on anything disagreeable. "

"What should be disagreeable about it?" Albert was honestly surprised.

"We have found that the Jews here consider it almost a sin when a German of Jewish descent has no knowledge of religious customs. Or at least that's the impression I got from some conversations we had in our hotel. But maybe I'm mistaken."

"No, not at all. When I arrived here seven years ago, I had the same experience, although I was better prepared than you are. At that time I was more preoccupied by the question of whether Jews can be said to be a nation when there are so many completely different types, from the dark-skinned Persians and Yemenites to the blond and blue-eyed Europeans. But a wise man told me a nation is whoever *feels* like a nation. Back home, Hitler determined that Germans of Jewish descent became Jews of German origin; here it is taken for granted that people of Jewish descent, no matter where they come from, must regard themselves as Jews first and foremost. If they don't, they are seen as traitors. People are not very tolerant in that respect."

"It is another kind of racial law," Frau Lotte said. "We have come out of the frying pan into the fire, Siegfried."

Albert felt sorry for the woman. She was going to have a hard time in Palestine, suffering not only the habitual intolerance of more knowledgable Jews but also their bitterness against the Nazis. As sturdy and broad-shouldered as the lady might be, she might not have the strength to endure it. If Siegfried had any brains, he wouldn't tell people that his wife wasn't Jewish. Especially since they had a son.

"Is your son a Jew, Professor?" he said aloud.

"Of course," Lotte answered, surprised. "His father is Jewish and therefore he is too."

"Not necessarily, dear lady," Albert said, surprised to realize how many details of Jewish law he had learned since marrying Leah. "Under Rabbinical law, only the child of a Jewish mother is a Jew. The father is unimportant. Which is logical when we consider that absolute proof of fatherhood is difficult to procure."

The professor was interested. "You're saying that my son isn't a Jew from the Jewish point of view?"

"Only if you had him circumcised after birth in accordance with Jewish ritual."

"My husband didn't believe in such a barbaric custom," Frau Lotte said excitedly.

Albert was distracted because they were now in the vicinity of Sarafand, the British army garrison. The military drivers here could be quite a hazard. Especially when they drove their ancient vehicles around corners at high speed when they were half-drunk, which happened often. But he had to agree with the woman that it was a barbaric custom. Which was why he had been delighted when his first child turned out to be a girl. His father-in-law, being a rabbi, would have insisted on circumcision otherwise.

He didn't envy this family trying to live here when the wife was a German *shiksa* and the son was uncircumcised. Presumably they had no other choice but to leave Germany, but they still had trouble ahead of them.

"May I ask you a question, Professor? What is your field?" he asked.

"I am, or should say I was, a professor of German," Siegfried Kramer said, and his wife accompanied this declaration with a small but discernible sigh.

"I keep telling my husband that a man with his knowledge and abilities should be able to earn a living anywhere," she declared. "I don't care what occupation he chooses. If I have to, I can work as a cook here myself. We just want to live in peace."

Unlike poor Lotte, Albert knew that this was not a country for people who wanted to live in peace. It was not a place of security and economic well-being. He remembered *The Divine Comedy* and cited aloud, "*Lasciate ogni speranza, voi che entrate.*"

"I beg your pardon?" Frau Lotte asked.

"Mr. Berg was reminding us that we shouldn't count on peace here," the professor paraphrased.

"I didn't mean external peace, but inner peace. Here, my husband will not have to endure the humiliation and ridicule and the indescribable injustice we had to suffer in Germany."

"That is true," Albert said, although secretly he saw only tragedy ahead for this family. It would not be as bad as the situation in Germany, but the man would still be ridiculed. As an assimilated Jew ignorant of religious rituals and customs, he would be called a *yecka*, a derogatory term to which an indecent ending was often added: *yecka pots.*

Ironically, no group of immigrants had achieved as much for the country as these ridiculed *yeckas*. It was true that Jews from Poland and Russia had learned to speak Hebrew better, and that Sephardic Jews were exceptional businessmen. But in the five years during which German Jews immigrated to Palestine in large numbers, the country had been transformed. They had real industry now; there were chemical laboratories, first-class mechanics and engineers. Well-qualified professors taught at universities and hospitals, which had become world-class. Houses and shops were well kept. The *yeckas* had even adapted to farming. The problem was that they didn't complain, which was why everybody else got away with criticizing them.

It seemed as though Lotte Kramer, standing by her Jewish husband when he was being driven from their homeland, had been the driving force behind this family's immigration to Palestine. She was logical and decent, resolving herself to adapt to a new country and learn a new language. But he feared that the reward for her decency would be icy rejection by everyone around her. Of course, it all depended on chance – on who their neighbours were, and how well she could adapt. She might even manage to become a better Palestinian Jew than her husband if he was unable to shake off his German ways.

Exactly the same thing had happened to Albert's dentist, who arrived two years ago with his Lutheran *housekeeper*, a woman Leah was convinced was really more like his wife. She adapted immediately, and learned Hebrew so well she acted as a translator between him and his patients. Albert found it hilarious. That woman was completely different from his own mother, who clung to her circle of old German ladies in an otherwise alien world. Social integration was clearly a very individual matter. He didn't think that the Kramers would have an easy time of it, but maybe their son would.

"How old is your son?" he asked.

"He is going on seventeen. Last year he was forbidden to attend high school in Germany. Even before that, he was terribly harassed in school."

"I can well imagine. How the Nazis are behaving is disgusting, yet the world is silent about it."

"We hope that he can graduate from high school here as soon as he understands enough Hebrew to follow the lessons," Professor Kramer said. "He is already learning some."

His wife laughed. "Our Heinz has great success with the young ladies with whom he went swimming today. They are very pretty girls. The young people are surprisingly beautiful, don't you think?"

"Yes, that's what people generally notice." Albert had already turned into the beginning of Herzl Street, the main road into Tel Aviv. "To what street shall I take you?"

"We can get out anywhere and then take the bus. We're at the Kaete Dan Hotel, but that is much too far away."

"It's not at all far by car, and I live near there. I'll give you my address. I'm sure my mother would be pleased if you visited us some time."

"We'd love to. Thank you for the invitation," Frau Lotte said.

Albert took his passengers to the hotel on Yarkon Street. It was small, but elegant by Tel Aviv standards. This was the last street before the beach, and the sight of the sea always pleased him. Heinz Kramer was waiting for his parents outside the hotel, still wearing his bathing trunks. For him, Tel Aviv was apparently a seaside resort. Albert could see why he was so successful with the girls. He was a well-built, handsome boy, blond like his mother. He had his father's eyes – marked by the fate of Jews – and his narrow nose. No one would have ever guessed that some of his ancestors had been Hanseatic seafarers.

Albert wondered what the girls on the beach would have thought had they – and Heinz himself – known that he was not, technically, a Jew. It was lucky that his swimsuit was not transparent.

Lotte and Siegfried Kramer got out of the Mercedes and waved their thanks to Albert. He said goodbye and went home to his three women.

———

On a Sabbath afternoon three weeks later, the Kramers came over for coffee and cake. Albert had told his wife and mother all about the professor and his family, leaving out the fact that Mrs. Kramer was not Jewish. He was afraid that Leah would regard a German Christian as an enemy and feel she was being forced to play host to a dragon.

The Kramers had made few friends yet, but they were still in good spirits.

"May I present my new identity: Chicken Farmer Kramer," the professor said.

"Oh?"

"Yes," Lotte laughed. "My husband ran into a former university colleague who has built a nice little house in a village called Kfar Offot where they produce eggs and vegetables."

"Do you know anything about raising chickens or growing vegetables?"

"I don't," Professor Kramer admitted, "but my wife does."

"My grandparents had a farm where I loved to work," Mrs. Kramer said. "We'll have to go heavily into debt, but the Jewish Agency is helping with a loan. It's the best solution for us."

Albert reflected that he probably should have done something like that himself instead of struggling with a factory, but Leah hadn't wanted to live in the country. At Rabbi Laski's house, chickens only had one purpose: to become chicken soup. Provided, of course, that they were killed in a strictly kosher way.

"The funniest thing about it is that the farmers in the village call each other 'doctor' or 'professor'," Professor Kramer said, "because most of them are academics, and the walls of their houses are crammed full of books."

The older Mrs. Berg was serving coffee and cake.

"You have a nice home," Mrs. Kramer remarked. "Were you able to bring all this furniture and the pictures with you from Germany?"

"Yes, although I gave most of our possessions away in Berlin. But even the few items we brought here are much too large for these rooms. Oh well, for half the year, we live on the balcony anyway," Albert's mother said.

Leah hardly participated in the conversation, feeling too insecure in German to contribute much. Professor Kramer looked at her profile with admiration. "You could have lived here two thousand years ago," he said.

Albert was proud of his wife's beauty but answered jokingly, "She isn't that old!"

"I didn't mean that," the professor replied. "Your wife doesn't speak German?"

"She has been forced to learn some because my old head refuses to learn Hebrew," Albert's mother explained.

"Is Hebrew her only language?" Mrs. Kramer asked.

"Yes," Albert said, "if you don't count English, French, Arabic and Italian."

Mrs. Kramer turned to her son. "Do you see, Heinz, how well educated people are here? You think you're so clever just because you can speak a little English."

While the others talked, Leah had only smiled politely and put another piece of cake on young Heinz's plate, but suddenly she raised her head alertly. She'd heard something they hadn't.

"What is it?" Albert's mother asked. "Is the baby crying?" Leah shook her head. She went to the window and listened again. Now the others could also hear the cries of the newspaper vendors. Yemenite boys, their side-locks waving in the wind like black pennants, ran down the street as fast as they could. Each carried a stack of extras almost taller than they were themselves. "Europe in flames," they cried. "Extra! Hitler marches into Poland." The fact that they couldn't pronounce *Europe* or *Hitler* or *Poland* correctly didn't prevent the Bergs from understanding what they said.

"What is going to happen now?" Albert's mother asked, wringing her hands in despair.

Everyone was silent. Finally Albert said, "I don't know what else is going to happen, Mother, but your son is going to become a soldier."

"There can be no conscription in a mandate territory," Professor Kramer argued.

"That won't be necessary. Everyone will volunteer if the British get involved."

Mrs. Kramer just looked at him.

"In that case, I will volunteer too," Heinz Kramer said.

"You are much too young! And besides, you're not going to fight against your own fatherland, are you?" his mother scolded him, no longer able to keep silent.

Heinz gave his mother a defiant look. "My fatherland is here," he said.

Leah turned to her husband. "You see? A half Jew has come to this conclusion faster than you, a hundred percent Jew. In your case, it took a few years." Since she said it in Hebrew, only Albert understood; besides, the comment was directed exclusively at him. He was amazed that Leah had figured out that Mrs. Kramer was not Jewish.

The little gathering came to a halt.

"This Hitler is a misfortune for the whole world," Mrs. Kramer said as they were leaving.

Leah remained polite and friendly until the door was shut behind the visitors. Then she turned and said to Albert, "That Mrs. Kramer may be a nice woman, but she was the first and will be the last German *shiksa* I allow into my home."

XXV

1945

———

THE LARGE MESS HALL BELONGING to the Palestinian Jewish regiments of the British army was packed. The soldiers gathered there could only be distinguished from those enlisted in the regular British Army by the word PALESTINE on their epaulettes and the blue and white squares on the upper sleeves of their tunics. All those on leave from the Jewish Brigade stationed in Italy and Holland had come, as well as Jewish combatants from the Royal Engineers, the Royal Air Force, and other services. Two full companies of the engineer corps had turned up. Even the young ladies who had volunteered two years ago for the Women's Corps of the Auxiliary Territorial Service had sent a contingent to the assembly, which was quite unorthodox.

Three officers were sitting on a small stage at the end of the hall where talented musical amateurs had often performed. The most senior in rank was Major Emanuel Na'aman. Of all those present, Sergeant Albert Berg was the only one who also knew the major as Manfred Neuman. Major Na'aman had earned a reputation for absolute fearlessness, as well as irrepressible humour, at the Italian front. Had he been an Englishman he would have already risen to Colonel, but the British army believed that promoting him to major was as far as they ought to go with a Palestinian officer.

"*Chaverim*," said Captain Ben-Korah. "We have gathered here today to find clarity about the road ahead. The war is coming to an end and victory is only a matter of time. All the other men and women wearing this uniform see this victory as their ultimate goal, bringing with it an end to their personal sacrifice. For us, however, this end will be just the beginning – the beginning of a difficult time.

"Fifty-thousand of us, more than ten percent of the Jewish population of the land of Israel, volunteered to fight in the British army. We did this despite being treated badly by the British, despite the fact that they had closed the borders of our country to our brothers and sisters and stifled the Jewish national homeland they were obligated to develop. Despite all this we fought in Greece and Egypt, in Libya, Italy, and wherever else we were needed. We don't expect gratitude, but we demand recognition of our loyalty. We are the only friends the Allies have in the Middle East. We will not allow them to pay us off with a kick in the ass—"

Resounding applause interrupted the speech. When it had died down, Captain Ben-Korah continued.

"In spite of our bitterness about British policy here, we did not hesitate to wear the British uniform. What was and still is most important to us is the destruction of the Nazi plague. What we didn't know about then, and what we still don't know the full extent of, is the incredibly cold-blooded murder of millions of our brothers and sisters. The human brain simply refuses to believe in this unprecedented dehumanization, this conversion of humans into beasts. It occurred not during a passionate battle for survival, but was ordered soberly, in cold blood, by the state. Only a nation that has lost its right to belong to the human race could accomplish such a thing. I don't believe there is a single person in this hall who hasn't lost someone dear to them, often in a gruesome way. We are an ancient people with a long memory. We will never forgive the Germans, never excuse them, and never forget."

All the men and women in the hall stood up, as if swearing a silent oath in response to a silent signal. Captain Ben-Korah took a sip of water, waited until they sat down again, then resumed his speech.

"When we became soldiers in the British army, we knew that the British had closed the borders and coasts of our country. What we didn't know was how much the Jewish nation, or unfortunately as we must say, its remnants, needs to have these coasts and borders opened to admit those of our tortured brothers and sisters who are still alive. But the British *still* refuse admission to those who have survived, though this goes against the most solemn promises of the Balfour Declaration, against the prerequisites of the Palestine Mandate, and against humanity. In doing so, the British have abandoned all decency, all righteousness, and even the smallest measure of compassion. I believe that we no longer owe the King of England any loyalty. I further believe that it is our duty to save the remnants of our nation wherever and however we can, which includes opposing the British if necessary.

"For thousands of years, we have been a tender and peace-loving nation, but we can afford to be so no longer. Not after what was done to us while the rest of the world stood by and did nothing. Those of us gathered here today know how to handle weapons, so we cannot afford to give up our arms when disarmament is called for. We may be few, but if the Allies, and in particular the British, think they can do with us what they want, we will demonstrate to them and to the world – including the Arabs, who were hoping for Hitler's victory – that they are mistaken.

"That is all I wanted to say. If anyone else wants to comment, please come up here and join me."

A commotion filled the hall, but no one objected to Captain Ben-Korah's speech. On the contrary, all the soldiers nodded their agreement. But Major Na'aman was not satisfied; in his opinion, it wasn't appropriate for a single officer to express the mood of the ranks. So when no one else offered to comment he stood up, adjusted the microphone to his height, and said, "What is the matter with you? Have you all gone blind?"

Everyone recognized that he had meant to say *mute* rather than *blind* and an appreciative chuckling was heard in the hall. Then Major Na'aman had an idea. "If no one else wants to talk, I will call Sergeant Berg to the mike. I know he always has something to say."

The faces of Albert's comrades betrayed their surprise. How did the major know Sergeant Berg? Berg was with the engineers while the major was with the brigade. Albert himself wondered how Manfred had spotted him among the mass of uniforms. Still, Manfred was now a superior officer. The army is the army and an order is an order. So he stood up and went over to the stage.

Albert thought for a moment that he would actually have to salute Manfred but he couldn't bring himself to stand at attention before his old friend, whom he hadn't seen in almost ten years. He simply stretched out his hand and Manfred took it, and with a sudden surge of mutual affection, the major and the sergeant embraced. They hardly heard the loud applause in the hall.

"Now you can screw the mike down to the height of a normal human being," Alfred said.

"*Chaverim*, I think I speak in the name of everyone present here, and also in the name of our comrades still in action, when I say that Captain Ben-Korah has expressed the thoughts and feelings of all of us. We have nothing to add. I'm sorry to disappoint Major Na'aman, but talking is not as valuable a gift as knowing when to be silent."

Albert took two steps to leave the stage, but Manfred held him back before returning to the mike, announcing the end of the meeting and singing the first verse of the national anthem in a deep bass voice. Everybody else joined in. The clear high voices of the women and the resounding voices of the men drowned out the loudspeaker from which Major Na'aman's bass was now barely audible. Then the soldiers filed out of the hall in earnest silence.

Albert said, "It was worth coming here just to hear you sing the "Hativka" with the proper Hebrew words."

"Yes, none of us would have ever believed that was possible. How are you doing, man? Where are your wife and child living these days? And my belated condolences. Last year in Italy I read a paper from here with your mother's obituary in it. She was a wonderful woman. How old was she when she died?"

"Seventy. It happened suddenly. A stroke. My wife and daughter are relatively well. Of course I had to give up the factory, and they're living in Jerusalem now. How are things going with you?" Albert asked.

They walked down the steps and left the empty hall. Out of old habit, they were talking German. Manfred remarked, "You know, in German, *going* isn't a reflective verb. Nothing IS going, unfortunately everything has to be done. At the moment, I'm convalescing because I had shrapnel fragments in both thighs, but as you can see, I'm walking again."

"Have you heard anything from your own mother?"

"No. I'm very worried. I'm so afraid those swine have murdered her. A refugee from Poland told Sonja that her entire family had been killed."

"How horrible! How is Sonja managing?"

"Now that I'm home for a little while, she is happy. She's waiting for me in Tel Aviv. Come back with me and we'll all have dinner together.""

"Unfortunately, I can't. I'm on guard duty tonight," Albert replied.

"It's so ridiculous! What is there to guard around here? Let's meet tomorrow or the next day. I can come to camp and pick you up," Manfred said.

"Give my regards to Sonja, please."

"Will do. And you say hello to Leah from me. We all must get together again some time. Otherwise, we'll lose track of each other."

"I agree. By the way, I can't help asking: How did you become an officer?"

Manfred stood still. It was obvious that walking was still painful for him. "In my opinion, the main reasons were my height and the fact that I can speak English."

They had arrived at the parking lot. Manfred carefully folded his legs into his khaki-coloured military vehicle. "See you soon, you old rascal." They shook hands again, then Albert gave Manfred a salute.

Back at the guardroom, Albert didn't recognize any of the four soldiers with whom he was on duty. Still, he was relieved to have this excuse not to sit next to Major Manfred's wife wearing his three sergeant's stripes.

X X V I I

HE LAY DOWN FULLY DRESSED on a narrow cot in the guardroom to rest up for the long night ahead. Insisting that soldiers perform guard duty so far from the front was a stupid game the British Army played. The time really had come for Albert to get out of this uniform.

At two o'clock in the morning, he picked up his flashlight and went to inspect the other guardrooms.

At four a.m. in complete darkness, he heard the sound of people walking. Since they were in military lock-step, it didn't seem suspicious. Even when he identified a large group approaching the guardroom he didn't suspect anything out of the ordinary. Then the door opened. Four young men and two young women wearing pants rushed in with drawn revolvers. They clearly weren't soldiers.

"The key to the gun rack, please!"

Albert's two men, who had been on duty outside earlier and were now resting, sat up on their cots.

"Are you crazy?" Albert said. He was as pale as a sheet. "You think you can steal guns from a military camp? You'll never get out of here alive."

It was clear to him these young people must be some of the rebels fighting the British in daredevil operations. Meanwhile, his two sleepy lads made no effort to get their own guns. He couldn't help wondering what happened to the other two who were supposed to be on guard outside, and why they hadn't sounded the alarm.

"Let us worry about whether we get out of here alive or not. Just keep quiet and give us the keys."

"No way," Albert declared. "We won't sound the alarm, so that you can get out of here in one piece, but we won't give you any weapons either. You don't need to wave your little revolvers at me; I'm not frightened. You can't fire them anyway, because at the first shot the whole camp will be up in arms and the British will capture you."

Albert's courage was aroused by his words. In his opinion, these extremists were using the wrong methods, but still, they were fellow Jews risking their lives for an ideal. If they were surrendered to the British they would probably be shot or hanged in Akko. Besides which he was quite certain that he and his men had nothing to fear from them, in spite of the revolvers.

Suddenly the two girls jumped him. He hadn't expected it. He hit back with his fists, but each one grabbed him by an arm and hung on with all her weight and didn't let go, no matter how hard he tried to shake her off. They were dark-skinned full-breasted girls, apparently Middle Eastern. Probably from poor families, themselves factory workers or domestics. While they held his arms one of the boys reached into Albert's pockets and pulled everything out: his lighter, cigarettes, handkerchief, and keys, among which was one with a tin tag. The boy ran with it to the green gun-closet. The key fit.

In a moment the boy had unlocked the closet and started passing guns to the others, who formed a chain to deliver them to their accomplices waiting outside. Albert got angry and became rough. He no longer respected the sex of the two rebels hanging on to him but started kicking them with his feet. He freed himself, so two of the boys abandoned their companion at the gun-closet and rushed over to hold him down. One girl put her hand over his mouth – a big red hand smelling unpleasantly of laundry soap. Now that he had attacked her, she didn't bother to be gentle.

Forty rifles, their magazines and ammunition crates were disappeared quickly while Albert's men sat passively on their cots as if the whole thing were none of their business. One of them even said, "There is also a machine gun back there. Since you're doing all this work already, you may as well take it too."

"Man, you're great!" said one young fellow, who seemed to be the commander of the group. He pulled the heavy machine gun from its hiding place. The three other boys had disappeared with the weapons and only the commander and the two girls remained in the guardroom.

They freed Albert.

"You can shout now, Sergeant, but I wouldn't advise it. I have a better suggestion," the fellow said. He couldn't have been more than twenty years old. "If you don't want the British to court-martial you, you'll have to declare that at least thirty people rushed through that door and, before you could sound the alarm, they had shoved cloths into your faces which knocked you out. When you came to, you had been tied up and couldn't move. That's when you started shouting, but unfortunately, you don't know anything else."

While he explained his plan, the girls unzipped their windbreakers and pulled out balls of thick cord, which explained both the size and the unusual firmness of their breasts.

"Sit down on that chair, Sergeant."

Albert obeyed. It wasn't a bad plan. How else could he explain what had happened? Quickly, with practiced hands, the girls wrapped the ropes around his arms, wrists, and legs, and around the chair. For better effect, the rebels tied up one of Albert's men in the corner behind a chair they had turned over silently. They displayed the other man trussed like a trophy in front of the empty gun-closet.

Then each girl pulled a bottle from her chest, uncorked it with her teeth and poured most of the contents over three cloths. They dropped these cloths on the floor beside each of the guards and splashed the remainder around the room, which immediately began to smell strongly of ether.

"You can start shouting in about an hour. Don't do it before then, because you would not have been able to regain consciousness so quickly. Lots of luck!"

With that, they disappeared into the dark.

Albert felt miserable. The ether floating in the air didn't make him unconscious, but somewhat foggy. The other two soldiers experienced the same feeling. Almost an hour later, when the British ordinance officer and two military policemen broke the door down with rifle butts – the rebels had locked it from the outside – the picture they encountered was completely believable.

"Holy Jesus," the officer shouted and ran to the telephone. The line had been cut. Those kids had thought of everything. He sent one of the policemen away. The other pulled out a big pocket knife and cut their restraints.

The brigadier conducting the interrogation arrived from headquarters. He was an older man with a gentle nature and a soft voice. His attitude was not very military, but Albert knew immediately that such a man was a much more dangerous opponent than any blustering type. Four other officers sat next to him: two colonels, one major, and one captain. They were all Englishmen with the exception of the captain. Patrick O'Brien was Irish, and already known to Albert. Albert had heard that O'Brien had been transferred from the police to the army but this was the first time he'd seen him in army uniform.

The ordinance officer presented his report. He had marched through the camp with the military policemen and had seen nothing suspicious. At 4:45 a.m. he had arrived at the guardroom, which that night had been under the command of Sergeant Berg. Surprised not to be addressed by the two sentries who should have been standing guard, he assumed they were inside, which was against the rules. That's why he had hurried to the door and started knocking. When there was no response, the two military policemen broke down the door.

The ordinance officer described how the guardroom had looked. He was shocked to find the sergeant and two other soldiers in a completely dazed state. He started looking for the missing sentries in the growing daylight. When reinforcements arrived, they were discovered locked inside a storage room of the adjacent troop kitchen. They were lying on a crate of tomatoes without weapons, without helmets and without their tunics.

The brigadier and the other officers listened silently to the report. Then the brigadier asked, "Lieutenant Parker, did you examine the guardroom and the area in front of it for tracks or any other evidence?"

"Yes, Sir."

"And did you find anything?"

"Only one object. It couldn't have had anything to do with the attack, although I don't understand what it was doing there."

"What kind of an object was that, Lieutenant Parker?"

"A lipstick, Brigadier."

None of the officers could repress a grin. Then ordinance officer placed the lipstick on the table and the brigadier picked it up thoughtfully.

"That is very interesting," he said. "Sergeant Berg, do you wear lipstick?"

"No Sir, Brigadier."

"Can you explain how this article came to be in your guardroom?""

"No Sir, Brigadier."

"You're a great help, Sergeant Berg. Can you at least tell us whether you or any of your men noticed this lipstick before the attack took place?"

"This is the first time I have seen it, Brigadier."

"Sergeant Berg, do ladies ever visit you in the guardroom?"

"I am married, Brigadier."

"That is not an answer to my question, Sergeant."

"I never have ladies visit me, Brigadier."

"Then there is only one explanation. A shiny object like this should have been noticed by at least one of the five men in the guardroom that evening. Since no one saw it, we must assume that it was not there before the attack. It follows that it must have been dropped by one of the attackers. It could be that one of the unknown men bought a lipstick for his wife. However, the condition of this object indicates something else. The lipstick has been well used. It follows, gentlemen, that there was a woman among the attackers."

The brigadier leaned back. The officers nodded their agreement, and all eyes were on Albert. For a few minutes, the brigadier thought with his eyes closed, then he bent forward with a jerk.

"Sergeant Berg," he said. "I have read your report. You write very well in English. Your report matches the statements of your men in all details. In fact, it matches the statements of your men too well. I have never before had the experience of three different people describing an event without contradicting each other on a single point. There are contradictions even in the Gospels. How do you explain this, Sergeant?"

"The contradictions in the Gospels, Brigadier?"

"Of course not. You would hardly be a suitable expert on that subject. I want to hear your explanation for the absence of any discrepancies in these three reports. Were the statements agreed upon beforehand between you and your men?"

"No Sir, Brigadier."

"Is it therefore the truth, Sergeant, that you can give us no information whatsoever about the identity or appearance of the group that attacked the guard building?"

"Yes, that is the truth, Brigadier."

"Then I want to formulate my question differently. I hope you will answer truthfully. As you know, we are not a court but an investigating commission. Captain O'Brien, please do not include my next question and the Sergeant's answer to it in your transcript. This is just, shall we say, psychological information. Sergeant Berg, let us assume, for the sake of argument, that you saw the faces of your attackers clearly and that you even knew some of them. In such circumstances, would you identify them?"

Albert hesitated for a few seconds. Then he told himself that he was going to be discharged in a few weeks anyway, and that furthermore, he could not be held responsible for his thoughts. So he answered in a loud voice: "No Sir, Brigadier."

The other officers almost jumped out of their chairs. Only the brigadier remained calm.

"That's what I thought. I thank you for your honesty, Sergeant. I want to ask you something else and once again, Captain O'Brien, this question and its answer should not be entered into in the record. If you had to choose, Sergeant, between your loyalty to the British army whose uniform you are wearing and your loyalty to your own ethnic community, would you prefer the interests of the latter?"

"Yes Sir, Brigadier."

"Did you do this last night, Sergeant?"

"No Sir, Brigadier. I was not faced with that decision."

"I'm inclined to believe you, Sergeant Berg. You can go."

Albert put his cap on, saluted and did an about turn.

The rebels had escaped from a British military camp without leaving a trace, with the rifles, the ammunition and the machine gun. A fantastic achievement. *But I have to hand it to the British*, Albert thought. *They have excellent manners.*

XXVII
1948

———

"FOR THE REVOLVER WE HAVE nine bullets. For the two Canadian rifles we only have Italian ammunition. It doesn't always fit, so you have to be extremely careful when firing. In a worst-case scenario, the hand grenades will be your best bet. We have seven of those."

The group commander of the Civil Guard, an insurance agent, spoke without hesitation or fear to the seven men serving under him. He had many years of experience in the Haganah, the self-defence organization that had served as the de-facto army of the Jews in Palestine before the State of Israel declared its independence. The British had tried to deny weapons to both the Haganah and the population it was designed to protect. Sometimes they even managed to destroy a hideout or two, but enough remained intact that the Jews were not completely defenceless against the bombs, bullets, and knives of the Arabs.

"Are we part of the regular army or what are we?" asked Mr. Shohat, a man of fifty-two who could only ply his trade as a warrior between seven at night and six in the morning. The rest of the time he had to look after his grocery store. He had almost nothing left to sell there except for a few questionable cans of sardines and a lot of hand soap, floor cleaner, and tooth paste. But as long as the bakeries still delivered bread, however limited the number of loaves, he had to be at his store to provide customers with the most important item on their ration cards. The laundry products could rarely be used because the Arabs had surrounded Jerusalem and cut off its water supply. Only the provident organization of cisterns and reservoirs and rationing the distribution of water to ten litres per household a day had saved the besieged populace from dying of thirst.

"Shohat, you make me laugh," Mr. Klein, a dental technician, said. "What difference does it make whether you're part of the regular army or not? What counts is that your hand grenade may be the only obstacle between a hundred thousand Jews here in Jerusalem and about forty million Arabs. Do you even know how to pull the pin and hurl the grenade?"

"They taught us that two weeks ago. But I assume that we're not the only defenders of the city and that there are other weapons as well," Mr. Shohat said emphatically.

"Don't be too sure about that," Albert Berg answered. "The other groups aren't any better equipped than we are. If the Arabs knew how poorly armed we really are, they would respect us less. Then they could easily trample us."

"Don't talk such nonsense," Reuben Mangani said. In civilian life he had been a piano teacher but he was now unemployed. "In the first place, there is a small troop of regular army nearby, and secondly, I myself helped construct a small mortar today."

"Can it be fired?" Klein asked.

"Yes. It doesn't hit the target very accurately but it makes a hell of a noise. The Transjordanian Legion had established itself near the railway station. That's where we tried it out, and the Legion gentlemen were so frightened that they all ran away. Now our people occupy the hill over there."

"That's good news," Albert said.

"I don't understand why you're so worried about weapons," Massoud Sharabi said. He was born in Jerusalem – as were Shohat and Mangani – but his dark skin and delicate figure as well as correct guttural pronunciation of Hebrew revealed his Yemenite origin. A silversmith, his slim dextrous fingers and sure eye made him the group's best shot, although just a month earlier he had hardly known what a rifle looked like. "We have the biggest and best weapon on our side."

"Oh? And what is that?"

"God," Massoud Sharabi answered, with unshakable faith.

Klein, the dental technician, cleared his throat. "Sharabi, I envy you your absolute confidence in divine providence, but tell me this: if we can safely leave everything to God, why did you kill two Egyptian soldiers last night?"

"Mr. Klein, you are a very wicked man. You don't believe in God's help? Praise be to Him! He has so much to do now watching over his holy city, and He needs our help. To fire the rifle was my job; his was to make sure that I hit the mark."

Albert signalled to Klein to be quiet. Massoud Sharabi belonged to a different world; the world of faith and prayer. Who knew which world was the real one anymore? Perhaps if so many Jews had not been convinced they were the chosen people and therefore deserving of divine help, they wouldn't have had the strength and confidence to keep on fighting for their own land. From what other source could they derive such unshakable courage? From a revolver with only nine bullets?

"We should hurry to get to our position. The others need to be relieved, and the thunder of cannon will start up again soon," Albert said.

Mangani looked at his watch. "We still have fifteen minutes. King Abdullah's British officers haven"t finished their tea yet."

Dental technician Klein shouldered his rifle. "At least one of those guys has my teeth in his mouth," he said.

"Now I understand why they're firing at us," architect Gedalja declared, joining the conversation.

"The behaviour of the British is no joke," Shohat objected. "First they declare they can't handle the situation here and take it to the United Nations. But when it is decided that the only solution is two states – one for the Jews and one for the Arabs – the British reject the UN's decision, blockade our entire coast, and openly support the Arabs. It is simply incomprehensible."

They had almost reached their post. Albert put on his helmet before replying. "What do you not comprehend, Shohat? It's very simple. The British want to get out of Palestine as much as mice want to get out of cheese, but they mustn't admit it. So they're counting on the Arabs to butcher a few hundred thousand Jews, so that they – the British – can come back to save us, in the name of humanity, with the administration they have waiting at this very moment in Cyprus. But because our own Palestinian Arabs won't fight against us, the British have been forced to recruit troops from the Arab kings in surrounding countries. Half a million Jews against forty million Arabs seems like good odds to them, since they don't care if the holy city of Jews, Christians, and Moslems goes up in flames in the process."

"The world won't allow it," Klein said indignantly.

"The world doesn't care either. Just as it didn't care about the six million Jews killed by the Nazis. We're the only ones who won't allow it unless Massoud's right—which I hope—and God won't allow it either," Mangani said.

Massoud Sharabi was a few steps ahead of them. Now he turned around. His eyes gleamed and his white teeth were bright in his brown face. "Praised be His name. Amen."

Albert gave Klein a kick and whispered to him, "I was with the British military for almost six years but soldiers like him are something new to me!"

He released the safety catch of his revolver and carefully slid down the slope to their position, which was a freshly excavated ditch on the southern slope of a suburb of Jerusalem. Beneath them in the Ein-Karem Valley an Egyptian infantry company was positioned, armed to the teeth. The Egyptians didn't lack ammunition, as the constant whine of bullets demonstrated. Albert hardly took note of which kind of guns were being fired since they were drowned out by the noise of the Transjordanian artillery commanded by the British. Apparently tea-time was over.

The trench was poorly protected by sand bags. A depression surrounded by rocks and boulders ran directly from it to some houses on the outskirts of town. Being visible from the valley, this depression was the most dangerous area for the Jewish combatants and claimed the most victims. The only protective cover was provided by a few trees that had been planted with much effort and loving care between the rocks, and those trees had been splintered by gunfire.

"Finally!" a woman's voice cried from the trench. "We thought you wouldn't get here at all tonight."

"Since when are we in the company of ladies here?" Mr. Klein wondered.

"Since today," a girl's voice answered. "The section commander thinks that we shouldn't rely entirely on you old guys, so he sent us here to take care of you."

"You've got a lot of nerve calling us old guys!"

The men in the company were all about fifty years of age; Albert himself was only forty-two, young enough that he ought to have been in a regular combat unit.

But since he had already served as a soldier and therefore had useful military experience, he had been deployed to supervise a group of civilian guards in Jerusalem instead.

"I'm Rachel, and this is Zivia," the cheeky young lady introduced herself and her comrade. "We've been assigned to you because some action is expected here tonight."

"Got it. Where are the others we're supposed to relieve?"

"We sent them home when we arrived here half an hour ago," Rachel said. She saw the revolver in Albert's hand and asked, "Are you the group leader?"

"Yes. And I have to say, it was extremely irresponsible to let the whole daytime group leave. If an attack had come during the half hour you were waiting for us, how would you two girls have held the position all by yourselves?"

"We assumed you would come any minute, and we felt so sorry for the men. They had hardly eaten all day. Furthermore, we have a small surprise for the Arabs."

"Of course, you would be a surprise all right. A pleasant surprise," Albert answered.

But Rachel opened her coat and showed him a submachine gun she was protecting against the damp evening air.

"What's that? A sten?"

"Something like that. A home-made affair from Tel Aviv."

"And why don't we have one of those too?" Mangani was furious.

"Because you have no experience with them, I assume. We took a course. I can take this thing apart completely and put it back together in three minutes." Rachel was obviously proud of her achievement. A tall woman, she wore men's pants and had pulled a wool stocking over her hair. Albert could make out her broad freckled face in the growing dark, and he didn't find her attractive. But he had to admit that she was vivacious.

Zivia's face couldn't be seen, only her back. During the whole conversation she had been standing behind a sandbag, directing her eyes at the valley. She didn't turn around now either as she asked, "Could somebody please relieve me for an hour? I must run home quickly to see whether my children are in bed."

Albert remembered his duty. "Klein and Sharabi, take the first watch."

The two men placed their loaded rifles into the furrows of the parapet. Sharabi fixed his eagle eyes firmly on the valley below, where there was continuous gunfire. They were under strict orders not to waste ammunition and to shoot only when something moved toward them and even then, only if they could expect to score a direct hit.

Albert thought about what a strange war this was; a war in which some soldiers ran home to put their children to bed and others believed that their bullets were guided by God. A war in which fully equipped armies battled poorly armed and inexperienced civilians. A war in which a newly born state with a legitimate birth-certificate had to fight for its life against other states that only recently gained their own independence.

He felt that the Jews had no choice. Either they stood their ground or they would be slaughtered – at least here in Jerusalem. Things were not quite as bad down in the lowland. He shuddered when he thought of his two children and his wife Leah, lying on mattresses in the cellar where they would be safer from grenades than upstairs. He wondered how far it was from this miserable trench to his own home. Sholat's store was about three hundred metres away, which meant it was four hundred at the most. How horrible to realize that his family was living within reach of a gunshot from the front!

And all he'd been able to feed them today was lentils. That was all that was available; a few lentils and some rice cooked over the wood of the ravaged trees. If only he could find milk for the children, but there was no milk to be had. Most of the cows in the outlying districts had already been killed by enemy fire. At least they'd provided meat at the end of their lives.

Albert promised himself he wouldn't let his family starve to death, and that he and the men under his command would hold out until relief arrived from the coast. For her part, Zivia waited a few more minutes until it was completely dark then crawled boldly up the gully. Somehow seeing her shadow disappear around the corner of the nearest house made Albert feel better.

"Mangani, will you take Zivia's submachine gun while she's away? Or don't you know how to handle it?" he asked.

"I have experience firing a sten, so why don't you give it to me?" the architect said.

"Suits me," Mangani declared in an insulted tone. "Let Gedalja have fun with it."

Red, white, and green flares, like stripes in a futuristic painting, permeated the black night sky. Then came the yellow reflection of an exploding mine and the bluish-white light of bursting shrapnel. It was all accompanied by music: the castanets of machine guns, the howling clarinet tones of flying artillery shells, the kettledrums of mines and mortar fire, and the piccolo whistling of rifle bullets.

"Something is happening in the old city," Shohat said.

Sharabi fired once, twice. An Arabic expletive was heard, not very far away, then it was quiet again. The others pressed their heads against the parapet and tried in vain to detect something through the darkness.

"Sharabi, what did you see?" Albert whispered.

"A shadow was moving," Sharabi whispered back.

The rocky boulders at night overstimulated the imagination. Were those just stones, or were Arab soldiers crawling uphill on their stomachs?

"The stone up there just moved," Klein whispered hoarsely. "There, to the left, below the tree stump."

Nothing could be seen, but suddenly there was the flashing of gun barrels before them, on a rather broad front. Bullets hit the sand bags and whistled above their heads.

"Fire!" Albert shouted.

Rachel pulled the trigger of her weapon and drew an arc from right to left. Gedalja, five metres from her, did the same.

The firing from the hill ended, so Albert gave Rachel a sign to stop shooting. Gadalja had already quit.

"Can you hit anything with this thing?" he asked Rachel.

"Yes, at sixty metres."

Apparently the Egyptians hadn't expected automatic gunfire so they moved downhill, and the defenders, now more accustomed to darkness, saw their shadows departing. Sharabi was in his element. He took careful aim and fired. After every single shot, another shadow disappeared.

Klein fired too until Albert grabbed him by the arm. "Don't waste the ammunition, Klein. But Shohat, lift yourself up. You can now stand above the edge of the trench without danger. You have the best hurling arm of us all. Quickly, throw a hand grenade down there."

Shohat took a swing. An arm that normally had to lift heavy crates and sacks of potatoes was also a good lever for the grenade. It flew in a high arc and landed between the shadows crawling downhill. Lightning was followed by an explosion. They heard the bang of bursting metal, felt stones and earth splashing up, and then heard a terrible screaming that ended quickly.

Some poor *fellahs* sent to a foreign land by King Farouk to fight a war that meant nothing to them had just lost their lives for nothing. Their own country was neither in danger nor was it being attacked. There would be a few women without a husband and probably a few dozen children without fathers in the Nile Valley. Albert felt sorry for them.

Sharabi must have had the same thoughts. "*Jerachem Hashem*," he called out. May God have mercy.

"We should have a few hours of peace now," Gedalja said.

"Yes," declared Klein, "but you know what I feel now?"

"No."

"Hunger. Real hunger. Couldn't our army equip us with a few sandwiches?"

"Where from?" Mangani asked him.

Shohat dug into his shoulder bag. "I have some leftover bread today. The people who were supposed to pick it up, the Lichter family, you know them … The wife died yesterday in the bombardment, and the children are in the hospital with severe injuries. I thought you might need something to eat so I made sandwiches – sardines, with a bit of oil and salt."

Everyone pounced on the sandwiches except Sharabi. "I can't take bread from dead people," he said.

"Nonsense, Sharabi. The bread wasn't near the poor woman at all. These are just sandwiches like all the others in my store."

"I am not hungry," the Yemenite insisted.

"You talk to him!" Shohat said.

"Shh!" The music teacher's extraordinary hearing had picked up a sound. Sand and small pebbles were rolling somewhere. Then they heard a load or a body being dragged on the ground behind them.

"It's Zivia," Rachel said.

It was indeed Zivia, cautiously rolling into the trench. Excitedly, she told Rachel, "You really missed something!"

"What?"

"We almost had visitors," she said, laughing, "but our welcoming committee was prepared for them."

Gedalja shook his head. Zivia was having too much fun. He wasn't at all comfortable with women fighting beside him; it was simply unpleasant. On the other hand, they wouldn't have had enough fighters if they'd refused to let women participate. He had to admit that Rachel at least was quiet and disciplined. She only fired when she received an order and then she did so with confidence. These *Sabras*, these Palestinian-born Jewish women, were a breed apart, Gedalja told himself. He handed the submachine gun back to Zivia and sat down on a wooden plank that ran across the trench.

"Sharabi, come take a rest now," Albert said. "I suspect that we'll need you again later."

Sharabi, Shohat, Mangani and Zivia all sat down with Gedalja. Klein and Rachel remained on guard. Albert went over to the seventh member of his group, who had been crouching in a corner of the hole all this time.

"Mr. Goldenberg, I can know, everyone knows, that you are very concerned about your safety. May I recommend therefore that the next time we are under fire, you lie in front, directly under the sand bags. It is much safer than here where everything is exposed."

"He's right," Mangani said.

The other were silent. They had always regarded Goldenberg's cowardice as a blemish on the group. In the presence of the two women it made the men even more uncomfortable. Goldenberg was a writer, mainly of children's books about biblical heroes. It was a shame that his enthusiasm for the heroic deeds of the Maccabis didn't inspire him to copy them himself.

Albert watched Gedlja stuff his pipe, envious. He suffered more from the fact that neither cigarettes nor tobacco could be had in the beleaguered city than from any other deprivation.

"Where did you find tobacco? Do you still have a supply at home?" he asked.

"This isn't tobacco, it's camomile tea," the architect said.

"You can smoke that?"

"Yes. Of course it doesn't taste like tobacco, but it isn't too bad. The pharmacies still sell powdered camomile tea. Do you want to try it?"

"Unfortunately I don"t have a pipe with me, but tomorrow I'll try your recipe."

The sky had brightened since a full moon had risen, which made their watch a little easier.

It was almost bright enough to read a newspaper, had one been available. Instead, Albert studied Zivia's face. Judging by her voice and figure he had imagined her to be young, in her early twenties like Rachel. But Zivia was a mature woman. Late thirties, he guessed. A pretty face, energetic chin, beautiful eyes. What was she doing here?

"How did you get to be in the home guard, Zivia?" he asked. "They generally don't take a woman who has children."

"I was in the Haganah before I was married and also after, before I had children. My husband is down south with the army, and I simply can't sit alone at home. I believe we owe it to our children to do something to protect them. Especially since I have had training."

Goldenberg shrank even more noticeably.

Shohat asked, "And who is minding your children now?"

"Their grandmother."

There was murmuring in the trench.

"What's the matter, Klein?"

"Nothing. I'm only quoting Heinrich Heine. Berg, do you know this? 'O brave land of Westphalia, may God bless your crops, save you from war and glory, from heroes and heroism,' and so forth?" Klein was reciting it in German.

Albert laughed. "The others don't get the allusion. The two of us are the only *yeckas* here."

Gedalja bravely drew on his camomile tea. "The tooth mechanic is a crazy guy," he noted. "Klein, how is your appetite? Are you still hungry?"

"No, but now I'm cold. I could use a hot cup of coffee. Tea would satisfy me too."

Mangani goaded him. "Klein, you have become such an old man. You're standing next to a young girl. You haven't had it so good for a long time but all you can do is complain that you are cold."

"Enough silly talk. We should try to sleep for a little while so we can relieve the others later," Albert said.

Everything was quiet except for the sound of Shohat's snoring. Sharabi just leaned against the wall of earth, his eyes closed. The hours passed without further incident. They took turns on watch, even Zivia, who insisted on relieving Rachel despite the protests of the men. At midnight the gunfire began again. Shots came both from the valley below and from the Egyptian position. Luckily the bullets either fell short or whistled over their heads. Nothing was seen on the slope which was bathed in bright moonlight. Still, they all stood against the parapet, even Goldenberg. Better safe than sorry.

Then they heard steps. Not creeping or crawling. Steps that sounded like a small elephant stomping downhill.

"Halt! Who's there?" Albert shouted.

"Don't shoot, kids, it's me."

"Who is me?"

The little elephant came around the corner of the house above and turned into the gully. It was a short rotund man whose big beard covered half of his body.

Shohat recognized his neighbour, Rabbi Rosolsky. "Rav Rosolsky, are you *meshuggah*? There is shooting here."

"So what?" the rabbi answered and continued towards them. He didn't even crouch down; at his age, and given his physique, that would have been impossible. Meanwhile Egyptian bullets kept whistling along the gulley and there was no way they could save the old man from them. Nine pairs of eyes watched his progress, aghast.

The rabbi arrived safe and sound, carrying a market bag. He pulled out a package wrapped in newspaper and two large thermos bottles. "I brought you some hot tea and some cakes. The people watching over our neighbourhood at night deserve something warm to eat," Rav Rosolsky said, as if it were the most natural thing in the world.

"That's why you're risking your life?"

"At my age, it doesn't matter what method the Almighty chooses to call me to Him. I'm only sorry that I'm too old to do anything else for our defence. But tea I can bring you." The rabbi sat down on the wooden plank, spread the cakes out on the newspaper, and poured tea into the thermos cups. They ate and drank in turn.

"Now Sharabi has one more reason to believe in divine miracles," Klein whispered to Gedalja.

The rabbi heard him. "So? What's the miracle?" he asked.

"That you arrived here in one piece," Klein answered.

Gedalja added, "Actually, to my colleague here, the tea is the miracle. Because he had just wished for some."

Rav Rosolsky appeared to smile under the beard that covered most of his face. "I'll tell you what the miracle is. Not the tea, but the water for the tea. The miracle is that we have water."

"On that subject, opinions vary," Klein said. "Of course we couldn't survive for two days without water, and that's exactly what the Arabs counted on when they cut it off. But the fact that we are supplied with water for weeks or even months, we owe to Doctor Benjamin's retention and distribution system."

"Maybe to him, too," admitted the rabbi.

"Not a very pleasant man, this Dr. Benjamin," Mangani said.

"Energetic men who push through all obstacles are seldom pleasant," Gedalja said.

"Do you mean that as an explanation or as an excuse, Gedalja?" Klein asked him, with a fake look of innocence.

The architect remained serious. He was interested in the subject. He continued, "Is Ben-Gurion pleasant? Is De Gaulle pleasant? Is Stalin pleasant?"

The rabbi butted in. "I protest! You can't name Stalin and Ben-Gurion in one breath. Our Ben-Gurion might be an instrument of divine providence."

Klein laughed. "I hope you won't tell him that, Rav Rosolsky. He already seems to think so himself."

Sharabi became angry. "Oy, this man is such a heretic, Rabbi! They all believe nothing here. They call themselves Jews but they have no religion. It's bad, very bad." He shook his head and went back to the parapet where Albert and the two women were standing, eyes toward the enemy but ears attuned to the conversation behind them.

Rav Rosolsky didn't take this charge of heresy too seriously. "Yes, religion is a strange thing," he said. "Did you ever wonder why most Jews and Christians don't follow the commandments of their religions while the Moslems are true to theirs?"

"No," Gedalja said. "Why is that?"

"It's because the characters of Jews and Christians cannot be reconciled with their religions. We Jews have a strong religion, we might even say an intolerant religion, but we're a soft and tolerant people."

"I'm not at all convinced of that," Albert interrupted him from the edge of the trench.

"Yes, yes," the rabbi insisted. "We have harsh laws but soft hearts. If a woman commits adultery, our law declares that she must be killed. But have we ever followed this law? No one can persuade me that throughout the thousands of years of our history no woman ever cheated on her husband. Certainly Jewish women have been unfaithful to their husbands now and then, but not one was sentenced to death. Why? Because the harsh laws of our religion don't fit the character of our people.

"It's the same with the Christians, but the other way round. Can you imagine a sweeter, milder, or more gentle religion than Christianity? If an enemy strikes your cheek, offer him the other, they are instructed. But just try striking a *goy* and see what happens! They won't stand for it, because the Christian character is much more ruthless than their religion.

"It's different with the Arabs, and with Moslems in general. '*Din Muhammad fi'l seif,*' They declare; Mohammed's faith is the sword. The sword suits their character, so the people keep their religious commandments."

"Well, you learn something every day," Mangani said.

"Rabbi, you have given us much pleasure."

"That was my intention, to give you some pleasure," the old man said, putting the thermos bottles back into the market bag. He also folded up the newspaper to take home. Even old paper was valuable these days.

"Wait! We will help you get back up," Albert called. It had become quiet now. There was no shooting from below.

Shohat and Klein each took one arm of their dignified guest and Albert pushed from behind, but before he was all the way out of the trench the rabbi turned around again and declared, "I forgot to tell the young ladies something. I hope you didn't misunderstand me. The fact that women are not sentenced to death in spite of the law doesn't give them permission to cheat on their men."

Zivia and Rachel laughed. Rav Rosolsky turned around the corner of the house with short, measured steps. It was almost two a.m. Not an hour for an old man still to be on the road.

"He is fabulous, this old gentleman," Zivia said.

"Yes," Rachel agreed, "but in order to find out whether I can follow his advice, I will have to get married first."

"That shouldn't be hard for you," Albert said.

She looked at him and sighed. "I have bad luck. I only seem to appeal to men who are either too old or too short for me, or they're already married."

Klein burst out laughing. "Berg, you have been given a three-fold rejection. You meet all three of these criteria."

"You would think we are at an amusement park," Mangani complained.

Shohat answered. "As long as we can laugh, we still have the strength to overcome hardship."

Albert looked down into the valley with concern. The moon was in the west. The landscape looked different with diagonal shadows crossing it. "It's too quiet for my liking. I think they'll start up again soon, and in greater numbers."

His prophecy turned out to be true. The attack came at four in the morning, beginning with a heavy mortar bombardment. Then two planes started dropping bombs. The missiles landed far behind their position but the men were still worried they might hit their homes.

"It's getting serious," Gedalja observed.

There was movement in the valley. They couldn't see exactly what was going on but assumed that the enemy soldiers were breaking into smaller groups to climb up the slope in several different places.

"We won't be able to hold them back," Mangani said. "And we can't split up. If they come at us from different directions, we're done for."

"Everyone in Jerusalem heard that bombardment. Probably they'll send us reinforcements," Albert declared, with a confidence he didn't feel. Their side had an inadequate number of combatants, besides which he knew only too well that this sector was of negligible value. Headquarters didn't regard the Egyptians and the Arab irregulars coming from the southwest as a serious threat. They'd always believed that the real danger was east of the city where the only disciplined Arab force, the Transjordanian League, was stationed, so the best troops were sent there.

He knew their ammunition wouldn't last very long but, if necessary, he had exactly one bullet for each of his people left in his revolver. He was determined that they not fall into Arab hands alive, especially the girls. That would prove worse than death for them. He also wondered whether his own wife and children would be able to flee to the city-centre in time.

"As soon as you see a target, begin to fire," he called to the others.

Sharabi began to sing Psalm 83 in the monotonous ancient melody of the Yemenite Jews. Klein protested quietly against the nasal music. "There are enough unpleasant noises here already without our friend Sharabi's contribution," he whispered to Albert. But despite himself, he listened to the words of the Psalm and realized that although they had been written a few thousand years ago, they fit the current situation precisely.

They saw the first Arabs approaching from thirty or forty metres away. The submachine guns of the two women clattered, the rifle shots cracked, and Shohat hurled two hand grenades, one after the other, into those dark clusters of bodies. Suddenly bullets whistled above their heads from behind. From both sides of the trench, dark figures in military boots rushed down the slope. Drawn bayonets flashed in the poor light, and a voice yelled, "Kids, you can rest now. Stop firing, otherwise you'll hit our people!"

It was incredible. The Arabs didn't have the nerve to fight and ran from the flashing blades of the bayonets. When dawn broke, the valley was empty. The Egyptians had withdrawn and the irregulars had fled. The assault squad that had saved the home guard's lives as well as those of the residents of the suburb they were defending disappeared as quickly as it had come.

"You don't think you're the only tea party we have to attend today, do you?" the commander declared. "We're a travelling music show that plays for the Arabs wherever they want to dance. That's why they believe we must be at least a full army division. We don't want to disillusion them."

Now that the danger had passed, Zivia collapsed on the wooden plank, shaking. A similar delayed reaction to tension, fear, and fatigue affected almost everyone. Everyone but Sharabi. For him, being delivered from peril was the natural consequence of singing the Psalm. He would have never expected anything less from his God.

When a new group of guards came to relieve them, Goldenberg didn't move. They had let him sleep in the corner of the dug-out. Klein was shaking his arm to wake him up when he saw, to his horror, that the man wasn't asleep. Goldenberg was dead. There was a small jagged hole in his temple, apparently from a shell fragment. He had hardly bled.

No one else had suffered so much as a scratch. Of all people, the only coward among them had become a hero.

"His poor wife," Zivia said.

They carried him up top and asked a few old men to look after the body and to notify his family as well as the authorities. There they discovered that the Egyptian planes had scored only one direct hit: they'd demolished the only building thought to be completely bomb-proof – a big house on the corner. Six mothers carried the bodies of their children from the rubble of its deep cellar, where they had put them to bed that night.

Fear choked Albert's throat until he saw his own wife approaching him holding the hands of his children. He was so grateful they had survived the onslaught that he forgot momentarily about the misfortunes of others.

Meanwhile, the daytime group of defenders had planted a pole between the sand bags that lined their position. From it, the Israeli flag flew proudly in the spring wind and glowed in the morning sunshine.

XXVIII

1951

————

CRACK! RED IN THE FACE, Mrs. Kramer stood in the kitchen of her home and broke one egg after another on the edge of the bowl. She separated the egg whites and yolks, pouring each into a separate bowl. The cake would have tasted better if she could have made it with whipped cream, but none could be found these days. She had to use egg whites instead.

She didn't look like her sixty-two years, but her husband had aged a lot. The professor and chicken farmer stood at the kitchen window, surveying his garden and the long sheds behind it. "Soon I won't be able to stand eggs and chickens anymore," he declared. "Live chicken, dead chicken, boiled chicken, roast chicken, chicken fricassee, raw eggs, soft-boiled eggs, hard-boiled eggs, fried eggs; I'm sick and tired of them all."

His wife laughed. "Be happy that we have chickens now that there is no other meat, and everything else is in short supply as well. Because of rationing, the poor people in the city only get two eggs a week. For them, chicken is a luxury item traded on the black market."

"Life here has become very difficult," the professor admitted. "What did Albert Berg say to me? 'We waited for our own state for two thousand years, then all this had to happen in my time.' By the way, did I tell you what happened on the bus to Tel Aviv?"

Mrs. Kramer shook her head. "No, you never tell me anything."

"Really? I feel like I tell you everything! Anyway, the day before yesterday, I was on the bus next to Mrs. Mendelsohn. I was wondering why such a spindly little granny suddenly had a huge bosom. I must have looked at her breasts a little too conspicuously. She noticed and—" …"

"That is not at all like you, Siegfried. Shame on you! And at your age!" his wife interrupted him.

"You don't have to keep teasing me about my age, Lotte. But anyway, like I said, she noticed me staring and said, 'You would probably like to know what I have here, right, Professor?' I answered, 'Mrs. Mendelsohn, frankly, I'm not that curious,' but she wanted to confess, perhaps so that I wouldn't think that she had suddenly become a nursing mother. She told me that she had a chicken on each side and fifteen eggs in the middle. She was taking them to her nephew so that his children would have something to eat.

Then just before Tel Aviv, near Ramat-Gan, the bus was inspected. Policemen boarded it and looked everywhere, even under the seats. We all had to get up. An egg fell out of the old lady's bosom and broke. One of the cops asked whether women in the Holyland now laid eggs. In the end, the old lady had to get off the bus and go to the police station to be searched by a female officer."

"How did it turn out?" Mrs. Kramer asked.

"I don't know," the professor said. "I assume they confiscated all the food and ate it themselves. Surely she won't go to jail for something so trivial? Of course, the police can't be blamed either. They can't tell when something is being smuggled in order to feed a family and when it is destined to be sold on the black market."

"Well," Mrs. Kramer said, "it's not a nice state of affairs. But given how many new immigrants need to be housed and fed, it is necessary to resort to rationing. Actually, I think it's admirable how well it's been organized."

"Yes, and also how little is to be had. You can't buy an onion in Tel Aviv! Every time Doctor Salomon next door puts another piece of cauliflower schnitzel on his fork he says, 'Yet another Moroccan.'"

"I don't understand," Mrs. Kramer said.

"What's so hard to understand?" the professor answered. "Salomon means that with every privation he suffers, another black person can immigrate to the land of Israel."

Mrs. Kramer remained silent. The professor wandered from the window to the refrigerator to pour himself a glass of orange juice. He emptied the glass slowly in small sips, deep in thought. "And now we're going to have a black addition to our own family. I could never have imagined such a thing," he finally said.

His wife stopped beating the eggs. "Esther is a very nice girl, and if it doesn't bother your son that her skin is somewhat dark, it shouldn't bother you. Furthermore, your friend Dr. Salomon told me himself that Yemenite women are exceptionally clean and make very good wives. He said that he really likes Esther."

"So let *him* marry her if he likes her so much!" the professor said wearily. "Heinz is a man of thirty, and I can't tell him who he should marry. But I'm not going to be at their wedding, I promise you."

"Siggi, don't say that. You mustn't even think it!" Mrs. Kramer was very aggravated now and raised her voice. "To hear this for the second time in my life! I would have never believed it. And especially not from you."

Professor Kramer was surprised. "What do you mean 'the second time'? I have never had occasion to say anything like this before."

"Not you," his wife said and gave him a steely, almost hateful look. "The last time I heard a man declare he wouldn't be attending a wedding was almost forty years ago. That man was my father, when I told him I was marrying a Jew. So now you know how I feel."

Siegfried stood there, frozen on the spot. Then he left the kitchen silently, ashamed of himself. Mrs. Kramer took her egg beater into her strong hand and whipped the egg whites furiously. The tears rolling down her cheeks mixed with the foam. A little salt wouldn't hurt the cake.

———

Heinz Kramer's arrival could be heard far in advance. His mother knew the clamour of his motorcycle. She quickly wiped the tears from her face and opened the door.

"Good day, Mr. Karmon," she said with fake joviality. Heinz had changed his name to Johannan Karmon since he had become a public servant. *What a good-looking man he is*, his mother thought, holding out her cheek for a kiss. "Two cakes are already prepared, and I'm baking the third one now for the ceremonial visit of Esther's family," she said.

But Johannan hardly listened and gave her only an automatic kiss. He was upset about something; she could tell. "Where is Father?" he asked.

"In the living room, if he isn't with the chickens. Why? What's up?"

"Nothing," her son said.

"You seem disturbed. Is anything wrong? Did you quarrel with your bride?"

"Oh, everything is fine. I just have to discuss something with Father," Johannan said in the offhand way in which spoiled sons talk back to their mothers.

"And I'm not supposed to hear it?" Mrs. Kramer had suspicion in her voice.

"It's better if you don't. It's a man-to-man thing," he answered, smiling at her in a conciliatory manner. Then he went to the living room and closed the door behind him. His mother's face indicated both concern and reflection.

Professor Kramer was sitting at his desk, head in hands. He was studying the *Jewish Lexicon*. That moral slap in the face from his wife had really shaken him up. That's why he wanted to read what good old Georg Herlitz had to say about Yemenite Jews. Maybe they weren't the primitive desert-dwellers he'd imagined.

When his son entered the room suddenly, he looked up. Johannan didn't even wait for his father to greet him but immediately declared, "We can't get married."

Even half an hour ago, those words would have been music to his father's ears. Now, he was no longer so sure. "What happened?" Professor Kramer asked quietly.

Johannan planted himself on the sofa. "I went to the rabbi's office to arrange for the date of the wedding and of course they asked me for the names of my parents. I told them, not thinking anything of it. Then the rabbi asked whether my mother was Jewish and I innocently told him the truth. The old man asked, 'But surely you yourself have been brought into the Covenant of Abraham?' It never occurred to me that what he was referring to was circumcision. Trying to be witty, I replied that I didn't need to join any religious clubs since I had fought in our war of liberation and was a reserve army officer."

Johannan paused, and his father asked, "So how did that go over?"

"Not well. The rabbi handed me back my ID and declared that I wasn't permitted to marry a Jewish woman since according to Jewish law, I'm not a Jew myself."

"You can go to Cyprus and have the wedding there. Then you'll be recognized as a married couple in the State of Israel after you return," Siegfried Kramer declared, amazed to hear himself suggesting alternative ways for his son to marry a woman he objected to.

"I can't do that for two reasons. First of all, I can't afford it on my public service salary. And secondly, how am I going to explain to Esther why we can't get married at home?"

"She knows nothing about it?" his father asked.

"No, of course not. I'm even afraid that when she finds out why we can't get married here legally, she won't want to marry me at all."

Professor Kramer couldn't suppress a little smile. From his perspective, that wouldn't be such a calamity. But he said aloud, "How could you have imagined that your wife wouldn't notice that you're not circumcised?"

"I thought it wouldn't be so important after we were married and besides … besides, she has no experience on which to base a comparison."

Professor Kramer couldn't hold back any longer and laughed out loud. His wife heard the laughter from her place in the kitchen and stopped worrying.

"Really, Heinz, I wouldn't have thought you'd be so naïve. A young Yemenite woman like Esther might enter marriage as a virgin, but do you really believe she has never seen a boy taking a pee? How many brothers does she have?"

"Four. Of course you're right. I'm so mixed up, I don't know what I'm saying. But what do I do now? You're my father, and it's all your fault. So maybe you can give me some advice!"

Siegfried Kramer became serious. This really wasn't a joke for his son. It was disastrous, and would have been equally so whoever he wanted to marry. He considered the situation and then said, "You know what I do whenever I have a personal problem? I discuss it with your mother and she usually finds a solution."

"There is no way I can tell Mama about this. She already has a complex because of her German origins," Johannan protested.

"I didn't mean you should talk to her. But what your mother has always been for me, Esther should be for you now. Talk openly with her. Then you'll see, we will *all* see, what stuff she is made of. If she is as wise a person as you say, she'll help you find a solution. What time will she be arriving with her family?"

"In about an hour," Johannan said in a very depressed tone.

"So take her aside and go for a walk with her. We'll talk with her parents in the meantime. It is better anyway if a young couple isn't present when their parents meet for the first time," Professor Kramer explained, indicating that he considered the conversation to be over.

But something else was bothering his son. "Whatever else happens, please be nice to Esther's parents. I know you're not very enthusiastic about mixed marriages, but it isn't their fault Esther and I fell in love."

"My boy, don't worry about that. I will behave as pleasantly as I can. Your mother has already made sure of that." He stood up, smiled, and patted his son on the shoulder encouragingly.

When Johannan had left the room and Professor Kramer had stuffed his pipe, he went back to his desk and involved himself in reading the encyclopaedia article on Yemen and its Jewish population. Apparently, King Solomon was right. Everything on earth repeats itself. Everything has happened before. And the Prophet Jeremiah was also right when he said that the sins of the fathers are visited upon their innocent children.

———————

Although it might have appeared to the other passengers on the bus that half a village was travelling together, the group comprised only Esther Amrami's closest family. Her father, her mother, her grandmother, her father's first wife, the two brothers from that marriage, already grey-haired, along with their wives, her two younger brothers and her two sisters. Including Esther, they were thirteen in all; not such a large family. Thirteen was an auspicious number among Jews, though considered unlucky by Christians, Esther reminded herself. Johannan would be surprised. She was sure he hadn't expected her whole family to accompany her on this visit.

Esther was proud of her family, especially of her father. Although the age difference between them was about two thousand years, she had a much more harmonious relationship with her own parents than many *modern* children did with theirs. She was aware that she and her younger siblings had managed the transition from the biblical lifestyle of her parents to the atomic age in a single leap. To be able to do this required both the intelligence they'd inherited from their ancestors and the honesty tolerating no compromise with which her father ruled the family.

She also recognized that, along with an iron religious discipline, they'd been brought up with the limitations of out-dated customs. She and her siblings had a long way to go to become the equals of the Ashkenazi Jews in technology and science. Her little brother had demonstrated how big the gap was just the previous day. He had declared proudly that the father of his classmate Zeharya worked at the Weitzman Institute of Science. It turned out that the man was actually employed as a cleaner and laboratory guard. "It will take a few generations before a Yemenite Jew can work there as a physicist or biologist," Esther thought. "But at least I know what physics and biology are, even though my parents don't."

Still, it would have never occurred to her to have contempt for her parents because they weren't educated, or because they believed that the earth was created in six days, or because they insisted on wearing traditional garb. She found the European clothes of her brothers far less dignified than the full-length gown of heavy striped silk and the round felt cap her father was wearing. But she had no illusions about how he would be perceived by others. She knew Johannan's parents would be shocked to see so many people in Middle-Eastern clothing. Her own new dress and matching shoes, both in the latest style, wouldn't help. But it was important to her that they realize where she came from. It was better for them to find out sooner rather than later.

She looked through the bus window at the dark green of the olive plantations, the white houses and red roofs of the villages they passed, but she saw nothing. Her thoughts were still preoccupied with Johannan and his parents. She got along quite well with his mother but not with his father, despite the fact that people always say that mothers don't like their sons' wives while fathers fall in love with them. Maybe the common wisdom couldn't be relied on. Could she win Johannan's father over? Her narrow hands with their long fingers and naturally rose-coloured nails, now carefully manicured, gripped the little suitcase she held on her lap. She wondered whether her plan to please Johannan's father would work; perhaps it wasn't a good idea to stage such a surprise today of all days. He would be surprised enough as it was.

She looked at her hands, reflecting that her awareness of them had changed radically since they had been praised in a newspaper review of her third concert. Every word of that review was engraved in her memory: 'While Esther Amrani's hands are telling the story of her songs with expressive grace, her full, soft voice sings the melody.' This had been followed by a few more sentences of praise in the grandiose style typical of music critics. Since then, she had started earning more money than Johannan. She had been turning her salary over to her father, but soon her husband would be entitled to it.

Deep in thought, she only realized where they were when the bus pulled in at the Kfar-Offot stop. She quickly gathered her family and appeased the driver – who had already become annoyed – with the beautiful smile she had learned at music school; a smile which she'd practiced in front of the mirror over and over again, like all artists. It wasn't easy to get her grandmother off the bus. It hadn't been easy to get her onto it in the first place, but once they were on the way, the old lady liked the ride – her very first – so much that she protested loudly when it was time to disembark.

Esther took her youngest brother by the hand and walked ahead of her family. It wasn't good manners, but she had to show them the way. Her father followed at a distance in order to give a respectable impression, since the usual custom was that a father should walk ahead of his children and not the other way round. Obadyah Ben Ezra Amrani, his striped silk gown reaching down to his sandals and blowing in the wind, walked proudly along the dusty dirt road between a corn field and a banana grove. He was followed by his sons in order of age with their women at the rear. Esther, who had gone ahead, was waiting for them in front of a beautiful house at the end of the road, a house with wide glass windows and sliding doors. Then the tall figure of her betrothed appeared.

The sharp eyes of the old man saw with satisfaction that the young couple wanted to kiss, but respect for him held them back. *In my day,* he thought, *it would have been impossible for a bride and groom to see each other without their parents' supervision. And in my day, a daughter would never have dressed like Esther does, with bare arms and an uncovered bosom. In my day, a man would have had to pay the father of his bride an appropriate dowry. But everything has changed. You're not allowed to marry two women anymore, even though God commanded us to be fruitful and multiply. How can anyone fulfill this commandment with only one wife?"*

Obadya Amrani saw another man and a woman coming out of the house. The woman was tall and broad; broader and heavier than both his wives and his mother put together. Even Esther, who was quite a bit taller than he, only reached her bridegroom's chest. He reminded himself that they were completely different people than his family and lived in a completely different world. He bent down and took a handful of the reddish sand. Another world and another time, but the land remained the same. The feeling of the good earth in his palm gave him strength to withstand the insecurity that had suddenly overcome him.

"Oh my goodness," Professor Kramer said. His groan sounded like a death rattle.

His wife turned pale. She took her husband's arm to support him, but she was also unable to take another step. "Our boy, my only child, in such company," she whispered. "Siggi, we mustn't allow this."

"Now you say so. But when I tried to explain the situation to you before, you became upset. Still, a certain technical problem stands in the way of their marriage, so let's hope nothing comes of it."

"What are you talking about? Quickly, tell me?"

"Later. They're all coming up to the house now."

Siegfried Kramer had already regained his composure, but his wife kept leaning against the stone wall that surrounded the patio. She had filled large wooden planters on top of the wall with carnations and the flowers were in full bloom, glowing in a variety of colours. Frau Lotte's face was as white as the white carnations and as stony as the wall. In her motionless state as well as in her stature, she resembled the monument of the goddess Hammonia in her native city of Hamburg.

"Blessed be those who are entering," Professor Kramer recited. He had practiced the traditional greeting a few times to ensure that he could say it correctly.

"Blessed be those present here," Obadya Amrani answered, according to form. It was much less effort for him.

Esther stood by her father's side introducing every member of her family. Mrs. Kramer pulled herself together and with a strenuously forced smile intended to signal polite friendliness, managed to utter, "Please, do come in." She hoped that no one had noticed her reaction to Amranis' arrival. It was a futile hope. Esther recognized immediately how unwelcome they were and it tore at her heart strings. She hoped that her father was oblivious to the rebuff, but that hope was also in vain. The sharp eyes and the even more acute sensibility of the old Yemenite didn't miss a thing.

His acuity was demonstrated by the instructions he gave to his crew immediately upon entering the living room. "Sit on chairs!" he called out in the Yemenite dialect the Kramers couldn't understand. Obediently, the family sat down on the chairs in the large room – all except for the grandmother. Granny looked at the beautiful oriental carpet, searched for an agreeable pattern, and then crouched on the floor in her customary manner, legs folded under her. She pulled her skirt up a bit to show off the long dark-red pants she was wearing underneath, tied at the ankles and adorned with embroidery. Then she placed her dark-brown bony hands on her knees. She didn't see why she should be uncomfortable.

"On a chair? Really? Do you expect me to ride a bicycle next?" she asked her son.

He couldn't order his mother to do anything. No one, not even she herself, knew her exact age.

Strangely, it was the natural behaviour of the grandmother that changed the mood in the room. Against her will, even Mrs. Kramer had to laugh. "You can no longer bend your legs, Siggi, the way this ancient woman can," she told her husband.

Then Johannan sat down on the carpet as well. "We can't leave Granny sitting all by herself down here," he said. Everybody laughed when he tried to twist his long legs into the same position as hers.

Meanwhile, Esther had disappeared with her little suitcase, although only her father noticed. Mrs. Kramer, who spoke much better Hebrew than her husband, asked, "Which one of you ladies wants to come in the kitchen with me to get the cake and tea?"

All the women jumped up. "Oh, for God's sake, I don't need that much help. One person is enough!" Mrs. Kramer protested.

For the first time since they had come, Simha, Esther's mother, opened her mouth. "I think I should do this," she said quietly.

Mrs. Kramer nodded.

Simha adjusted her kerchief adorned with small coins, straightened out the three-quarter-length, gold-trimmed dress she wore over her long baggy pants and followed the woman of the house. Next to expansive Lotte, slender Simha looked small and fragile. Professor Kramer considered the women and reminded himself that though they represented two different worlds, even two different eras, both were mothers and therefore had the same feelings at this moment.

Obadya Ben Ezra Amrani had similar thoughts.

Professor Kramer tried to begin a conversation with the potential father-in-law of his son, but it soon became apparent that the Hebrew language was insufficient to build a bridge between them, thanks to his German accent and the many mistakes he made. They had to be satisfied with exchanging smiles and lifting their cognac glasses. Grateful he could fortify himself with liquor and astonished at how much the old man could drink, the professor poured his guest another glass.

The return of the ladies with refreshments broke the deadly silence that had prevailed in the room. There was the clattering of dishes and cups, and the guests started to move again.

Suddenly they heard the beating of a drum. Esther stood in the wide doorway leading to the next room dressed head to foot in traditional Yemenite clothing. The gold coins around her neck and scattered across her kerchief were a little shinier than those of the other women, her fabrics more costly and their colours brighter because this was one of her stage costumes, but every stitch was authentic. A clay drum lay in the crook of her left arm. It was shaped like a water jug with a calfskin stretched over its open bottom. With incredible speed, the fingers of her right hand played a drum roll on the calfskin, then slowed down to short rhythmic beats.

That was the surprise she had planned. She had brought the costume and the drum along in her suitcase. Everybody was as surprised as she had anticipated; indeed, Mr. Kramer dropped his tea cup and Mrs. Kramer stared at her open-mouthed. She had never seen Esther dressed this way and couldn't help but wonder if the girl was trying to remind them that despite the elegant Paris fashions she wore, she was not a European.

But that wasn't Esther's motivation at all. This was what she had been wearing when she met Johannan, a long time ago. She had been very young and very shy, singing in front of several hundred soldiers. He, the nice friendly officer, had first encouraged her and later courted her. She regarded this costume as her talisman. She hoped it would bring her good luck.

The room was so quiet everyone could hear Esther inhale before she began to sing a wordless melody. It grew louder and louder until she finally sang the words with her full voice. The beating of the drum and the sharply measured pauses between phrases gave the melody an exotic rhythm. It wasn't a new song. It wasn't an old song. It was a timeless song, the most beautiful song of erotic love that has ever been written.

Esther was singing "The Song of Solomon" in the language and perhaps even the melody of the original author. With slow dancing steps and a controlled swaying of her body she approached Johannan, who had jumped up to embrace her, then she darted away. Over her smiling lips came the three thousand-year-old text: *"Dodi li va'ani lo, haroeh bashoshanim"* – "My beloved is mine, and I am his; he feedeth among the lilies."

The Amranis forgot that they were supposed to make a good impression. Rhythmically clapping their hands, they supported the drum. Even Obadya Ben Ezra sang the traditional refrain, which in the ancient manner lets the singing of the soloist bounce back like an echo. His not very melodic efforts couldn't dampen the enchanting impression left by Esther's voice. Mrs. Kramer had tears in her eyes, and the professor didn't dare to blow his nose, although he needed to very badly.

With a short double beat of the drum and a last twirling rotation of her body, Esther ended the song and fell into the arms of her young man. Johannan performed his first sensible deed of the day. He lifted her up and carried her out of the room in his arms. The audience clapped enthusiastically.

Johannan set his beloved down on a concrete block that held a water pipe a few spans above the ground. Standing before this romantic seat, between rows of tomatoes and cucumbers, fanned by the fragrance of chicken manure, he revealed the terrible truth he'd been hiding from her and the consequences he had finally realized at the rabbi's office that very morning. He didn't look at Esther, but paced up and down nervously, his eyes on the ground, his hands clutched behind him. When he had finished speaking he finally turned around and looked at her. Esther was holding her hands in front of her face and her body was shaking. Gold coins jangled with every tremor of her shoulders.

"Esther, Estherke, my darling, please don't take it so tragically. We're sure to find some way out of this," he said and embraced her. With much tenderness, he pulled her hands from her face and almost had a heart attack.

Esther was laughing so hard that tears ran down her cheeks.

"Oh Johannan Habibi, what a *yecka* you are!" she erupted through her laughter. When she saw the blank look on his face, she pulled herself together. "Are you a Jew? Do you feel like a Jew?" she asked briskly.

"Of course," he said.

"Then I don't see why you shouldn't suffer just like all little Jewish boys must suffer – even twenty-nine years later."

He had never thought of this particular solution. "At my age, Estherke, it would be a painful operation."

"I guarantee that the first son I present you with will give me greater pain." She was smiling, but he was well aware of the steel underneath. And he knew she was right. His mother had frequently commented that if men had to endure childbirth, the human race would have died out a long time ago.

"Of course you're right, though immediately before our wedding isn't the optimal time for such a thing. Why on earth did Ben-Gurion sell the freedom of our citizens to the orthodox rabbis? Couldn't he have found another coalition partner without having to make concessions to those hypocritical bigots ... at my expense?"

Esther laughed. "If your Majesty is afraid to enter the kingdom of your marriage with a somewhat sore sceptre, I promise to wait in all humility, love and patience. Besides ..." Esther paused. She had never even thought of such indecent things before, let alone expressed them. But she knew that Johannan needed cheering up. Every true artist has a sixth sense for the mood of her audience.

She took another approach. "Besides," she repeated, "every sick child one nurses back to health, one learns to love even more."

Johannan laughed and embraced his bride, then whirled her around. A few tomato plants standing in the way lost their valuable fruit. Professor Kramer saw Esther's colourful Yemenite costume fluttering around his son – that pillar of the Israeli Foreign Office – and started humming "The East is God's, ti ... ta ... to ... The West is God's, em ..." He hoped that the spirit of Schumann would forgive him.

"You two haven't eaten anything." he said. "That's why Mother sent me to bring you cake and lemonade." First he placed a small tray on the concrete block, and then a large bouquet of his wife's most beautiful carnations in Esther's arms. Esther understood this gesture immediately. Johannan's parents had finally accepted her in spite of her family – or perhaps even because of it. A girl coming from such a background who had become what she was must have both brains and character. She saw it in her father-in-law's friendly smile. He seemed almost bashful.

Automatically slipping back into the submissive role of a Middle-Eastern woman, she lowered the long-lashed lids over her beautiful eyes, bent forward, and kissed his hand.

Johannan was uncomfortable with this behaviour but his father was deeply touched. He gently stroked her coal-black hair. "You are a very good and intelligent child," he said, in surprisingly correct and understandable Hebrew. Continuing in the same language, not to give the impression he might have secrets with Johannan, he told his son with satisfaction, "It seems like your old father might have been right after all. Your girl found a solution to your difficulties, didn't she?"

Esther had regained her balance and with it, her modern confidence. "Yes," she answered, giggling. "The answer was with him all along, only he hadn't thought of it." She stroked Johannen's arm and added, "He's a little slow on the uptake, my lord and master."

Professor Kramer nodded in agreement. "True. That's why he is a diplomat in the service of the State of Israel." Laughing at his own joke, Professor Kramer walked ahead of the young couple, back into his house and to the company of his exotic guests.

———◆———

"Oy," Mrs. Kramer said, when they were in bed. "That was some day! As much as I like Esther, there's no way I can relate to her family. Did you see the old grandmother eating with her hands? The other women tried to use the cake-forks and teaspoons but you could tell how little practice they'd had with them."

"If we'd known ahead of time," Professor Kramer said, "it would have been more polite not to set out forks at all. You should never make your guests feel ashamed."

"That's really not my fault. I had no idea how uncultured they were," Mrs. Kramer said.

"It has nothing whatsoever to do with culture. Civilization and culture are completely different things, as the example of the Nazis has clearly shown us! These people have their own culture. For example, Mr. Amrani can read from all sides – from the top or the bottom, from left or right, he reads everything at the same speed. I happened to notice because he was reading a newspaper that Heinz had left lying on the table upside down."

"How did he learn to do this?" Frau Lotte asked.

"One of the older sons explained it to me. He told me they have very few books in Yemen. The Arabs there are illiterate and only the Jews can read and write. But with only one book for about thirty children or more, they can only learn if they sit in a circle with the book in the middle. They keep changing seats so that every child learns to read from all directions. You see, Lotte, that's an example of what I call culture."

"But the women of the older generation can't read at all. Thank God, Esther had good schooling."

"Yes," Mr. Kramer said, "and she is also intelligent. And I am quite convinced that Heinz will have a very faithful and devoted wife. She won't look at another man once she is married."

"I'm not a Yemenite and I didn't look at another man after our wedding. On the other hand, I'm not so sure that you have always been faithful to me." She sat up and gave her husband a scrutinizing look.

Mr. Kramer smiled. He was flattered.

"Tell me honestly, Siggi. Have you ever cheated on me?"

The professor's bald head flushed a little. Why was she asking this now that they were old and such things were no longer important? "Lottchen, honestly, I have always been faithful to you ... except for once. When you sent me to Westerland alone, to recuperate, some twenty years ago, and I had a little affair there."

Mrs. Kramer's face darkened though she said nothing.

"Lottchen, you're not mad at me, are you, after all these years? It happened only that one time."

"I'm missing that one time now," Mrs. Kramer said, switching off the lamp on her night table and turning her back on her husband.

XXIX
1954

———

"The heat outside is almost intolerable, but it's nice and cool here inside your house," Dr. Sonja Neumann said, sitting down on the sofa. The living room was big, spacious and very elegantly furnished. Wide sliding doors connected it with a patio leading to the garden. The fresh westerly wind from the sea brought with it the flagrance of jasmine blossoms.

"Yes, we were lucky with this house," Mrs. Leah Berg answered. "Albert always has something to complain about, so he says it is too far away from the factory, but I think he likes it too."

"Did you suddenly inherit money? If I didn't know that there's no lottery in Israel, I would have assumed you were a big winner! Not so long ago you were still living very modestly, weren't you?"

"Yes, you're right. We were still living in Jerusalem, we moved there when Albert joined the British military. After the war we stayed on when he became a public servant. We never had any money, because Albert gave the factory to his partner during the war and only kept one quarter as his share."

"I remember Manfred telling me about that," Sonja said.

"So what happened to us really was like winning a lottery. About a year ago, a building contractor from Tel Aviv showed up asking whether Albert's father had been called Max. He needed to purchase some parcels of land in order to complete a new project, and the land registry indicated that they belonged to someone named Max Berg with an address in Berlin."

"This is just like something in a novel!" Sonja exclaimed.

"It gets even more fantastic." Leah said. "But before I tell you the rest of the story, let me get you something to eat and drink."

"Just a drink, please; soda or lemonade without ice," Sonja said.

While Leah disappeared into the kitchen, Sonja looked around in the living room. It was just as she would have imagined it, all the pictures hanging perfectly straight and everything fanatically clean, even the ashtrays, which must be hard on chain-smoking Albert.

Leah came back and set two glasses of lemonade and some cheese sandwiches on the coffee table. "Let's get comfortable. The children are at school, so we still have a few hours of peace and quiet. Are you staying overnight in Tel Aviv? If you do, you would be welcome to join us this evening. We already have guests coming over."

"It depends when Manfred is done with his meetings in the city, but it isn't easy to get out here without a car."

"Oh, it's not more than twenty minutes from Tel Aviv, and I'm sure Albert would be happy to pick you up and take you back."

"We can discuss it when Manfred gets here," Sonja said. "Meanwhile, tell me more about that building contractor."

"Well, as I said before, the man had an address in Berlin, so first he sent a letter of inquiry there. Of course the letter came back. The street doesn't even exist anymore."

"He must be a real idiot," Sonja interrupted. "He should have known that somebody who owned land in Israel …"

"He knew. But he was hoping that neither the person who bought those lots almost thirty years ago nor any heirs would be alive, so that he could get the land cheaply. But the officials at the land registry office wanted absolute proof that no one had a legal claim to the property, so the search for Max Berg didn't end there.

The contractor didn't count on German efficiency; as Albert always says, the Germans might eradicate their consciences and exterminate human beings, but they will never get rid of official papers. So a copy of a document came back from Berlin from what they called the 'resident registration office' stating the date of my father-in-law's death as well as the date of Albert's departure from the country. 'Son Albert, born such and such a date, deregistered for the purpose of travel.' It also included the date my mother-in-law 'deregistered.' After the war, with half of Berlin in ruins, some conscientious bureaucrat was still able to locate this information."

"It must have been Martin," Sonja laughed.

"Who is Martin?" Leah asked.

"An old acquaintance, a very pedantic and dutiful Prussian official I once knew."

Leah glanced at the other woman, hesitated for a few seconds, and continued. "At any rate, to make a long story short, the man realized that he had to try to find either the son or the wife of Max Berg. Of course, they could have been in America or in Australia, but meanwhile he went to the tracing bureau for family members in Jerusalem and explained he was looking for a man named Albert Berg. The secretary sent him to an office three doors down the hall. 'You mean they can give me information there?' The secretary answered: 'No. That's where you'll find Albert Berg. It's his office.'"

"This story is so incredible, no one could have invented it," Sonja said. "So then you sold him the land?"

"It wasn't that simple. First, Albert had to prove that he was the genuine heir of Max Berg before the lots could be re-registered under his name. He still had a copy of his father's will, but it said nothing about land in Tel Aviv. It only said that his father left him all the real estate he owned. However the lawyer who drew up the will was still alive, and he clarified things. Then Albert wanted to sell, of course, but I stopped him."

"How did you become so rich then?" Sonja waved her hand, taking in the room and its beautiful furnishings.

"We're not rich; the things you see here are not expensive. Eventually I came up with a plan to get the most out of that land. Money keeps losing its value here, but real estate is always worthwhile. And when immigration is high, its importance increases. So I told the building contractor that if he wanted our three lots in Tel Aviv, he would have to give us some cash plus at least six new lots of land in an undeveloped area.

We ended up settling for four lots. We built this villa on one of them with the money we got for a different one; we still own two but I don't want to sell those yet. Albert invested the cash in the factory, so he owns fifty percent again. The work doesn't suit him, but to be honest, he's never enjoyed any kind of work. I believe what he would like best is to be retired."

Sonja listened silently and with interest. She couldn't help thinking that if women like she and Leah didn't guide their men, they would never get very far. Aloud she said, "Albert's father could never have dreamt that a few square metres of sand would be worth so much one day."

"You're right," Leah admitted. "He only bought real estate here in order to have some land in Israel. He was a great idealist, Albert says. Unfortunately I never knew him. But now you have to tell me what made you leave your *kibbutz* after so many years."

"It wasn't an easy decision. I struggled for years both with Manfred and with myself. When Major Emanuel Na'aman came back from the military—"

"I forgot that Manfred has a Hebrew name."

"Well, I can't get used to calling him 'Emanuel'. I called him 'Mannie' once but that made him angrier than I've ever seen him. It must have brought back unpleasant memories."

Leah seemed distracted, so Sonja returned to the main topic of the conversation. "As I said, when the major came back from the war and they told him he had to work in the cow barn the very next day he didn't say anything, but I knew something was wrong. When my husband isn't telling jokes, he is either seriously ill or deeply unhappy. So I immediately started looking for a job as a physician some place else where we could have a private life. To be honest, the big *kibbutz* family was getting on my nerves as well."

"For me, such a life would have been totally impossible," Leah said.

"It's a matter of temperament. Some people are very happy there," Sonja said. "But for us, there were two additional factors that affected our decision to leave. They were building those camps for new immigrants everywhere, the *ma'abarot*, with their wooden barracks. Have you ever seen one?"

"We have one near here but I've never gone into it."

"I went in. Three times a week. From barrack to barrack, treating children. It was indescribable."

"The papers talk a lot about them," Leah said.

"What the papers tell you is nothing like the truth. The misery, the dirt, the neglected children – you've got to see it all with your own eyes."

"But it's only a transitional stage, isn't it? They're making every effort to build better housing for those people. And we're giving them work too. My own household help comes from the camp near us," Leah said.

Sonja shook her head. "The founding idea of Israel was definitely not to create a proletariat of new immigrants to scrub floors for the long-established upper classes."

Leah felt personally attacked. "You're being unfair. Most of these new immigrants have no education and no marketable skills. They can't all become bankers overnight. The most important thing is that they earn their keep rather than being supported by the state through our enormously high taxes. In Albert's factory, almost all the workers are North African women."

"My comment was more of a regretful observation than a criticism. In a capitalist society, such people are at least partly absorbed and given employment. Our *kibbutz* on the other hand, like all *kibbutzim*, failed completely at integrating them. We could accept very few new members, and to give people pay for their labour was against our socialist principles. To do so was held to be exploitation of the workers.

"Manfred has a very clear mind and the hypocrisy that this attitude entailed really upset him. We were sitting in our little room at Pinah Nidahat one day when he said, 'As a state, Israel is of historical significance, but the moral obligation of this state is to give the Jewish nation a homeland and to accept all those who want to come. If the *kibbutz* doesn't accept this obligation, the *kibbutz* has outlived itself and has lost its justification. I'm not interested in working in the cow barn just to protect the interest of its members.'

"That's when I knew it was time to act. I went to Haifa and negotiated a contract with a private clinic on Mount Carmel. I only told Manfred about it when everything was signed, sealed, and delivered. He was just returning from a general meeting, terribly angry about how party politics continued to divide the *kibbutz* on important issues. He was clearly upset, and cursing his head off. So I simply said, 'Don't worry about these things anymore. Next week we're moving to Haifa.' Then I told him what I had arranged."

"And how did he react? Albert would throw a fit if I did something as important as that without even consulting him!"

"Manfred was silent for a while, but then he said something very typical of him." Sonja laughed. "He said, 'You see what a smart man you married, a man who knew exactly what kind of a woman to look for?' I must tell you, Leah, it almost felt like a second honeymoon when we found our apartment on Mount Carmel."

"And now he's working for a shipping line. Albert calls him 'my friend the admiral.'"

"Yes, Manfred is very satisfied. Whenever he can be involved with ships, he is in his element. He's good at it too because one of the directors said recently, 'Man, Na'aman, where have you been hiding all this time? We could have used you a long time ago.'"

"That's nice. That sort of thing encourages a man."

"It encouraged him to make one of his bad jokes. He answered, 'Where have I been hiding? Behind the skirts of my wife.' Well, the director reaches about to his navel, so he responded, 'In that case, your wife must need quite a lot of fabric for her skirts.' He probably thinks I'm a monster."

"If that's the extent of your worries, you should be happy," Leah laughed. Then someone rang the door bell furiously.

"That must be the children," Leah said.

Sonja pulled herself together, put on a smile and waited for them to burst into the living room. She didn't envy Leah's big house or her pretty face, but she did envy her having children. Fifteen-year-old Nava, already taller than her mother, was Leah's spitting image. She held her eight-year-old brother Jossi by the hand and Sonja saw immediately how closely the boy resembled his father. Leah introduced them.

"This is Sonja, the lady you've heard so much about. She is a doctor."

Well-mannered Nava, already a young lady, stretched out her hand, but Jossi stuck out his tongue as far as he could and said 'baah'.

"Jossi, that is so rude! Is that how you welcome a guest? I'm ashamed of you!" Leah scolded him.

Nava defended her brother. She always protected him, even when he didn't deserve it. "Eema, you told him that Sonja was a doctor. Every time Jossi goes to the doctor he has to stick out his tongue and say 'aah'. So he thought that's what you're supposed to do."

Sonja smiled. "He is quite right. Come on, Jossi, show me your tongue again. It was so beautiful."

But now Jossi was embarrassed. His mother had yelled at him even though he had meant well, so he couldn't be motivated to open his mouth again.

The next time the bell rang Nava went to answer the door. Manfred had arrived to pick up his wife. He was wearing an elegant suit and Leah, who had only seen him in *kibbutz* clothes, was amazed to realize how much clothes can change a man's appearance.

"Leah has invited us to have dinner here tonight," Sonja told him.

"It turns out I have to stay in Tel Aviv until tomorrow afternoon, so we'll be glad to come," Manfred replied. Then he gave Jossi a very long look. "You know what, my boy, when your father was your age, he looked exactly like you. He also made a face just like that."

"How do you know?" Jossi asked in an unfriendly tone.

"I know because I'm an old friend of your father's."

Jossi didn't respond but on the way to the bathroom, where he was sent to wash his hands, he could be heard telling his sister loudly, "That's a lie."

"Shush, Jossi, how can you say something like that?" Nava scolded him.

"There is no way a big man like that could have been Abba's friend when Abba was little!"

"Don't be silly! He wasn't a big man then; they were *both* little."

Jossi shook his head. Not only did he resemble his father physically, he had also inherited his sceptical character. It wasn't easy to make him change his mind.

The adults in the living room had overheard the conversation and were greatly amused. Leah said, "Sometimes I have the impression that my son, who was born in Israel, is an even greater *yecka* than his father."

Manfred laughed and pointed at a large oil painting in a heavy gold frame. He remembered it from the Bergs' home back in Berlin. "Maybe it's the influence of that scribble over there," he said.

The picture, depicting a landscape on the Havel River which included the city of Potsdam, hung impassively above them all.

X X X

———◆———

MRS. KRAMER TOOK HER SHOPPING bag from the hook, wondering if she remembered to write down everything on her mental list. Since Heinz no longer lived with them they needed so few groceries. She put on an old straw hat since the sun was too strong for her and walked down the dirt road through the fields, waving at her husband who was watering his vegetables.

He looked so lonely standing there. They both were increasingly lonely now that most of the original families had left the village and they didn't get together with the new ones. She didn't know them, but they all knew who she was because she was a German, and no one associated with a German. If Salomon, the old bachelor, weren't such good friends with Siggi, and if old Mrs. Mendelsohn wasn't so good-natured, she and Siggi wouldn't even have been able to enjoy a card game in the evening once in a while.

With these thoughts in mind, she arrived at the store on the main street. She was still amazed to see so many beautifully packaged goods in the window, reminding her of life back in Europe. The rice and the sugar were white again. Things appeared to be falling back into place.

There was a new sales clerk in the store, a thin woman who walked with a slight limp. Mrs. Kramer put her glasses on and read her shopping list out loud. The sales lady didn't move. Mrs. Kramer stared at her.

"Don't you want to give me my things?" she asked, before she noticed that a number was tattooed on the woman's bare arm. In blue ink, the way cattle are branded or pieces of meat are marked. She was shocked. She had no idea what to say, imagining what the poor woman must have suffered in the concentration camps.

The sales lady just stood there like a monument made of stone. Finally she spoke. "I don't serve Nazis. Get out of here!" she snarled between tightly pressed lips, her chest heaving.

In spite of her age, Lotte Kramer could have knocked the other woman down with a single blow, but she only trembled, understanding all too well what she was feeling. She fled the store like a thief, then walked back home slowly, blinded by tears.

"Siggi, oh Siggi," she hugged her husband, crying. "Siggi, I want to go home."

He knew what she meant. Here was her garden, and the house that had given them sanctuary through all the difficult years. But it had never really been home for Lotte no matter how hard she tried. *Not even for me, and I'm actually Jewish,* he thought.

"Yes, Lottchen, we should go home," he said out loud. "My professorship is available for me again."

X X X I

ALBERT CAREFULLY EASED HIS SMALL English car into the garage and switched off the engine. The radiator was overheating again. This wasn't surprising, given the weather outside. He wished he could walk around in nothing but his underwear rather than dressing up for company tonight. He wasn't in the mood for entertaining customers, but he had to. They were visiting from America.

He locked the garage and went into the house.

"The children have already eaten and now I have to make another meal for you. Couldn't you have come home earlier? I'm not running a restaurant here," was how Leah greeted him when he entered the kitchen.

"Sorry I'm late. It was only thirty-four degrees in the shade, so I had to go dancing with a dozen girls to warm up after work," he answered angrily.

Leah was sorry that she had snapped at him. Why did she always get so agitated and say things she later regretted? "Did anything special happen at the office today?" she asked, in a conciliatory tone.

"All my enemies should be forced to run factories in Israel," Albert said, sitting down at the table.

"What was the problem this time?" she asked, bracing herself for his daily quota of complaints. She really should be used to it by now

"I had visitors from the Histadrut. They want me to provide higher hourly wages, a pension fund, paid holidays, health insurance, etcetera, etcetera. Otherwise there'll be a strike. By the Histadrut itself, mind you, not by the people who work for us! How the government thinks it can attract foreign investors this way is a mystery to me."

"But Albert, there are unions in every civilized country in the world."

"Who says Israel's a civilized country? We have high wages and low productivity, yet we're creating legislation appropriate for a welfare state. What's the result? Higher prices. But such high prices make it impossible for us to have a successful export trade, so as a result the government has to subsidize our exports. Who ultimately pays for everything? The taxpayer. Taxpayers are the only productive people in the country. Long live socialism!"

"Would you like it better if people who've just lived through a war also had to work for low wages, Mr. Albert Berg, factory-owner? I don't think so. Anyway I'm sure our elected politicians don't know less than you about these issues," Leah said, placing a bowl of salad on the table in front of her husband.

"I'm not worried that they know less than me, but that they don't know *more* than me. They prove that every single day."

"Really?" Leah asked.

"I'm convinced of it," Albert declared. Then he devoted himself to his meal.

Leah sat down across from him. "I also had visitors today. Manfred had some business in the city so Sonja spent the afternoon here. She really liked the house. I invited the two of them to join us later."

"OK. Do I have to go pick them up?"

"No, Manfred's company rented a car for him. He seems to be a rising star there. Sonja is also very happy at her new clinic."

"I'm not surprised. They are both such competent people."

"Yes, that's true. So tell me, Albert, was Sonja married to someone else before Manfred?"

His fork stopped halfway to his mouth. "What makes you think that?" he asked, surprised. Manfred had asked him to keep Sonja's first marriage a secret, and he had done so.

Leah pressed on. "And was the husband a German a public servant, a *goy* named Martin? And did Manfred himself have a wife or girlfriend before Sonja who called him 'Mannie'?"

Albert put his glass of cold water down so hard that the ice cubes jumped. "How the devil do you know all that stuff?"

"I didn't know it, I just suspected it from a few comments Sonja made in passing. But from what your face tells me, my deductions were correct." Leah smiled. She put some salad on her own plate. "I was always quite good at math," she added.

Albert was speechless, and that seldom happened.

———

"Turn the radio off! That noise is making me nervous. How can you stand it?" Leah complained.

"You're so old-fashioned, my love. This is modern music; you must learn to develop a feeling for it. Let me at least listen to the news before our guests arrive."

"You call that wailing of cats the news?"

"The news is coming on next. But if you have no desire to update your musical knowledge, we'll pick another station in the meantime."

A hysterical voice started shrieking over the radio instead.

"That's even worse! We don't have to listen to hateful diatribes from Arab stations," Leah said angrily, but Albert lifted his hand for quiet and listened intensely.

"This Zionist peril … Jewish world domination … want to expand from the Nile to the Euphrates … to destroy Islam … to attack peace-loving Arabic people … bridgehead of imperialists …" Albert turned it off, his face grim.

"They whip up hatred among their people with those terrible lies. And that's what you wanted to hear?" Leah said.

"No, what I wanted to hear was the voice. You know whose it was? My old friend Fais Maraka."

"I thought he liked Jews!"

"He used to. Especially Jewish girls. This pathological hatred of his is inspired by injured vanity. Like so many other Arabs, he can't forgive us for the fact that they couldn't defeat us last time. So they want bloodshed again. It makes me want to puke. If it weren't for this Arab fantasy of revenge we could all live in peace, and they would lead better lives themselves. If there were peace, I would have been able to invite Fais to join us tonight, and you could have watched him embrace me."

"Possibly. If there were peace. But in the meantime, he would rather cut your throat," Leah said, sighing. Then she changed the subject. "Apropos of invitations, I hope you asked those American customers to bring their wives along?"

"On the contrary. I asked the customers to bring their husbands along. With Americans, the women are in charge."

"I see," Leah said, reflecting that women were really in charge everywhere; it just wasn't as obvious to him.

Albert looked at his watch. "Our guests are taking their time. Maybe the Americans are having trouble finding the house. You know," he continued, "they made me upset, in spite of the large order they placed, because they refuse to admit importing our goods is profitable. Instead, they make a big fuss about what a favour they're doing us. 'We have to support you brave Israelis; after all, you are such great idealists', Mrs. Rothstein said. It was hard for me to smile gratefully and keep my mouth shut."

"Yes, I'm sure it was a big sacrifice for you," Leah said. "I hope you will manage to maintain the same decorum in your own house."

Albert wanted to respond, but the first guests, the engineer Kalman and his wife Rachel, had arrived. They lived in the neighbourhood. Soon after that Manfred and Sonja showed up, and then Johannan Karmon with Esther. The Karmons had just returned from their first foreign posting and were waiting for a new assignment.

Rachel Kalman had become heavier since he'd first met her in the trenches outside Jerusalem. But she still had a lot of freckles and a big mouth. Albert was glad they'd run into each other one day when he was out walking with his children. She had recognized him and yelled across the street, "Hey you; Comrade Revolver!" This was the first time he'd met her husband. Noticing that the man was shorter than Rachel, Albert couldn't resist teasing her. "You didn't remain faithful to your three principles," he said.

She laughed. "If you can't jump over the barbed wire, you have to crawl under it."

Neither the engineer nor the others understood what they were referring to but Leah just looked at them and nodded. She solved the riddle instantly. Albert was beginning to realize what a dangerous person his wife was.

Then Albert's American customers arrived. The Rothstein and Perlman ladies shook hands with the other guests while Mr. Rothstein looked around in the room. Mr. Perlman made a beeline for the liquor cabinet where Manfred had appointed himself bartender.

"We must all speak English now," Leah said, forgetting that Sonja would not be able to follow the conversation.

"I didn't picture Israel like this at all," Mr. Rothstein said. "Despite being a poor country that depends on our financial support, you live the way only millionaires do back home!"

"Would you have preferred to find us living in tents?" Rachel asked – luckily for Albert, because it saved him from letting slip the pointed comment that was on the tip of his own tongue.

"No, certainly not," Mrs. Perlman assured her, "but we've always had a certain image of the fighting heroes of Israel, and instead we are confronted by well-dressed women and elegant homes and hotels. They don't make a particularly heroic impression."

"I am so sorry to disappoint you," Manfred said, bringing her a glass of brandy with soda. He was walking with a slight limp. The humid weather made his shrapnel wounds act up.

"Yes," Rachel called out her boisterous way. "For us Israelis, it isn't possible to become heroes. Isn't that right, Albert?"

Johannan Karmon didn't seem to be really present. The day's heat kept making him re-experience the moment he had pulled his gunner from a burning tank. He shook himself back into awareness of his surroundings. They were talking about heroes.

"How do you make heroes?" he asked.

"Esther will explain it to you," Manfred answered. "You make heroes the same way you make cowards."

"Good one, Manfred," Albert said, "you always know how to save the situation."

"You can count on me, Albert. Even with a bare ass." The two men started shaking with laughter like little boys. Nobody else knew what they were talking about, but the Americans just assumed it was an Israeli joke.

The door bell rang again.

"I'm so sorry we're late," said Mrs. Gunther, the wife of the American Ambassador. She introduced one of her husband's new colleagues and his young wife.

"The nearest neighbours are always the last to arrive," Leah remarked.

"This time it was because my husband was listening to the Bible lecture on the radio. As you know, he is a Bible fan."

"But the lecture is in Hebrew," Albert said.

"I like to have the Gideon Bible in front of me in English while I listen to the Hebrew. It helps me learn the language and also appreciate the beauty of the original text."

Engineer Kalman smiled, and said, "You remind me of a Russian diplomat who told me that since he learned English and began reading Shakespeare in the original, he has realized that Shakespeare is almost as good as Pushkin."

The Americans laughed heartily.

"It must have been quite an effort for him to admit that," Mrs. Gunther said.

"How do you like it here?" Leah asked the new couple from the embassy. She hadn't caught their names but was flattered that the Gunthers felt comfortable bringing other guests to her house.

"We're pleasantly surprised by Israel," the very tall man declared. "What you have achieved here is fabulous."

"We seem to surprise everybody, and each from a different perspective," Johannan Karmon said, as though making an important political statement.

Manfred looked at him. "Man, Karmon, I know your job is to represent the Foreign Office, but don't behave like such a Prussian."

"Leave my husband alone, or I'll remember my own Middle Eastern temperament," Esther said.

Manfred pretended to cower in fear, and Sonja told him, "I'm glad that somebody knows how to shut you up!"

"Have you seen much of the country yet?" Leah asked.

"Not yet," the young American woman said, "but this weekend we want to go on a grand tour."

"When there are no buses or trucks on the roads, you can get places a lot faster," Mrs. Gunther observed.

"Actually, I don't understand how a modern state can survive without public transportation on Saturdays. The trains don't operate, no telegrams are delivered, and everything is closed: shops, movie theatres, and so on," the new man from the embassy said.

"True," Manfred said, "and the port is closed as well. No ships are loaded or unloaded. It costs us a fortune."

"Poor people who can't afford taxis can't even go to the seaside on the only day of the week they have off," Sonja said, who was always aware of the social cost of public policy.

"Unfortunately, our calcified clerics don't remember that the Sabbath was created for man and not man for the Sabbath," Albert sighed.

Gunther raised his long bony finger and said, "Watch out, Mr. Berg, those are heretical thoughts. Another Jew spoke those same words two thousand years ago and he too failed to convince his countrymen. His name was Jesus and he came from Nazareth, where we'll be going tomorrow. That sentence is in the Gospel of St. Mark."

There was embarrassed silence in the room. It was only broken when Manfred said, "I was always of the opinion that you should be crucified, Albert."

"For God's sake," Sonja said quickly, "you can't do that to Leah. She would have to clean up afterwards, and she can't stand dirt and disorder."

Rachel laughed, and the others joined in.

—•—

"Did you notice that the Rothsteins and the Perlmans didn't say a word in front of their non-Jewish compatriots?" Leah asked after their guests had left,

"Yes, I did. Apparently the invisible ghetto persists. Even Jews from the great republic of America are self-conscious and shy in Christian company."

"But here we are not self-conscious, because having our own flag on our own soil makes us feel equal to everyone else. Even you, my love, despite all your bellyaching, have to admit that you are proud to be a Jew and an Israeli."

Albert had become thoughtful. "Being a Jew and being an Israeli are not the same thing the way they were in biblical times. Jews who fought for the modern land of Israel and worked hard to build their country have become different people because of that country. We're now a nation, with all the flaws and virtues of other nations. Therefore the same plus the same equals different. Explain it to me. You were always good in math, Leah."

"This has nothing to do with math. It is pure philosophy, and that's where you *yeckas* are the experts." And with that declaration, she went to the kitchen to do the dishes.

———————

Esther Karmon linked arms with her husband. "I'd like to keep walking for a little while. It's healthy exercise in my condition."

Johannan took her carefully by the arm. Her pregnancy made him treat her like a fragile vessel.

"We were given a lesson today about how to make heroes," he said, laughing.

Esther replied quietly, "I would much prefer to make a little coward. If we all gave birth to cowards there would be peace in the world."

Johannan sighed. "Peace seems to be a luxury we can't afford here in Israel."

THE END

page number

1. The statue of Baron vom Stein in Dönhoff Square: Vom Stein (1757-1831) was a Prussian statesman whose reforms paved the way for the unification of Germany.

4. Low German (Plattdeutsch) was spoken in northern Germany. High German (Hochdeutsche) was the dialect spoken in Berlin; it derived from the biblical translations of Martin Luther in the 16th centuries.

8. The Iron Cross (Eisernes Kreuz): a German military honour given for extreme bravery in battle.

9. A shtetl is a small Jewish village in eastern Europe.
   The *Talmud* is the great and comprehensive commentary on Jewish laws and rituals.

11. "Gymnasium" is the German term for an academic high school or grammar school (Grades 5 to 12).

14. Wilson's "Fourteen points": President Woodrow Wilson's speech explaining the reason for the US entering World War I, which declared that the objective was not simply retaliation for the German sinking of American ships but "to vindicate the principles of peace and justice in the life of the world."

Prince Max of Badenout: Maximilian Alexander Friedrich Wilhelm, Prince of Baden (1867-1929), served as Chancellor of the German Empire in October and November 1918, overseeing its transformation into a republic with a parliamentary system.

The German ("imperial") flag was black, white and red. It was replaced by the black, red and gold flag of the Weimar Republic.

17.	Schopenhauer: Albert Schopenhauer (1788-1860) was a German philosopher famous for his pessimistic view of the universe and of human nature; Spinoza: Baruch Spinoza (1632-1677) was a Jewish philosopher whose view was essentially optimistic since it posited that God and Nature were the same, and that it was possible for man to behave ethically.

Shiksa is the Yiddish word for "a non-Jewish girl".

18.	Meshuggah is the Yiddish word for "crazy".

21.	Old High German looks and Brandenburg attitude: In distinction to Albert, who is very conscious of being conspicuously short, dark and Semitic, red-haired Manfred is extremely tall and blends in with other Germans. Brandenburg, whose capital was Potsdam, was the centre of a very cosmopolitain culture that drew people from across Europe.

21.	Zionist:"Zion" is another name for Israel; Zionists are those who believe in the right of the Jewish people to return to their traditional homeland.

22.	*Walter Rathenau:* a German industrialist, politician, writer, and statesman who served as Foreign Minister of Germany during the Weimar Republic.

	Kashubian: a west Slavic ethnic group from Poland;

	Wendish: also known as "Sorbs," another Slavic group, this one from the north.

25.	Christian Morgenstern: A German poet (1871-1914) whose work satirized scholarly writing through wordplay and nonsense

43.	"Ave Maria" (literally "Hail Mary") is the popular name for "Ellens dritter Gesang"(Ellen's Third Song), by German composer Franz Schubert

(1797-1828). It is ironic that Edith, who is a prostitute, plays it, since it is the prayer of a virgin for help from the Virgin Mary.

45.   Mishpoche is the Yiddish word for "family."

55.   Tochuses; singular tochus: Yiddish word for "the buttocks".

64.   The Balfour Declaration: was a letter (dated 2 November 1917) from the UK's Foreign Secretary Arthur James Balfour to Walter Rothschild for transmission to the Zionist Federation of Great Britain and Ireland. It stated that "His Majesty's government view with favour the establishment in Palestine of a national home for the Jewish people, and will use their best endeavours to facilitate the achievement of this object, it being clearly understood that nothing shall be done which may prejudice the civil and religious rights of existing non-Jewish communities in Palestine, or the rights and political status enjoyed by Jews in any other country."

67.   Max Reinhardt was an actor; Erwin Piscator a theatre director; Leopold Jessner another director; Bruno Walter a pianist and composer; Leo Blech an opera conductor and composer; Kurt Weill a composer. All these figures were associated with experimental and intellectually challenging work.

76.   Der Stürmer:(literally, "The Attacker") was an anti-Semitic weekly tabloid published by Jules Streicher; the Völkischer Beobachter (literally, "The People's Observer) was the official daily newspaper of the Nazi Party.

79.   Heinrich Heine (1797-1856): A German poet, journalist, essayist, and literary critic, heis often considered the last Romantic.

Chancellor Stresemann: Gustav Stresemann was a German chancellor in the Weimar Republic. Brüning: Heinrich Brüning, a Roman Catholic, was Chancellor of Germany during the Weimar Republic from 1930 to 1932.

82. Emperor Franz Joseph: The significance of this remark is that Czechsolovakia was part of the Austrian Empire until 1919.

    Galicia: The Battle of Galicia, also known as the Battle of Lemberg, was a major battle between Russia and Austria-Hungary during the early stages of World War I.

82. Gruppenführer: A sarcastic reference to a very high rank in the SA (Stormtroopers), equivalent to a Lieutenant General.

83. The Sudetenland: Part of Bohemia, it was populated mostly by Germans rather than Czechs. It belonged to the Austrian Empire until after World War I, when it became part of Czechoslovakia.

98. Disraeli: Benjamin Disraeli (1804-1881) served twice as British Prime Minister.

    Ramsay MacDonald: A member of the Labour party, whereas Disraeli was conservative.

106. Et altera pars auditur: Latin for "Let the other side be heard from as well."

118. Mahatma Gandhi (1869-1948): The leader of non-violent resistance against the British occupation of India.

124. Ex oriente lux: Latin for "enlightenment comes from the east".

125. Yecka: Slang Hebrew term for "a German Jew".

128. Odysseu is the hero of Homer's Odyssey, a Greek warrior trying to sail home after the Trojan War who is delayed by many adventures. One of them involves trying to pass between two dangers in the strait of Messina, Scylla and Charybdis, the first being a six-headed monster, the second a whirlpool.

130. Schlemiel: Yiddish for "a foolish or inept person".

131. Fellah; plural fellahin: Arabic for "peasant".
     Cherkassian: An ethnic group from the northern Caucassus.

134. Yeshivot; singular yeshiva: Hebrew for a school of religious study.

135. Goyim; singular goy; Hebrew and Yiddish for a "non-Jew".

146. Schmuck: Yiddish for "a contemptible person"

148. Missadah: Hebrew for "restaurant".

149. Friedrich Schiller's ballad, "Die Glocke" (Song of the Bell) is a very long poem containing dozens of expressions which have become part of the German language.

154. Threepenny Opera is a famous piece of musical theatre described as "an opera for beggars" with lyrics by Bertold Brecht and music by Kurt Weill. Albert's allusion to it is ironic, since he's smuggled out so much money, but he still feels like he's lost everything.

156. The Alawite State was a French mandate territory on the coast of Syria from 1920-1936.

177. Tafaddal, Effendi: Come in, Sir; Udkhul min faddlak, ya effendi; Do enter please, Sir.

191. Sholom Aleichem: Literally, "Peace unto you, friends" was the pen name of Yiddish nauthor Solomon Naumovich Rabinovich (1859-1916).

201. Until World War I, Trieste was part of the Austro-Hungarian Empire, then it became part of Italy.

225. Manneken Pis is a famous Belgian fountain in which a bronze statue of a boy urinates into a basin.

248. Mabrouk! Arabic for "congratulations."

249. Pinkelstein and Wasserstrahl, Feigenblatt and Bügeleisen: These names would mean "Piss-Stone", "Water Jet", "Fig Leaf" and "Pressing Iron".

254. "The Ring of the Nibelungs": In Wagner's opera, Kriemhild is supposed to be a pretty young woman while Brunhild is performed by a singer who is more formidable. Hence the irony of someone like Lotte's having a husband named Siegfried.

258. The Hanseatic League was a large northern European trading and shipping association in the late Middle Ages

293. Georg Herlitz and the Jewish Lexicon: The German-language Jewish encyclopedia called Jüdisches Lexikon was first published in the 1920s and 30s by Georg Herlitz in several volumes. New editions were published in recent years

303. "The East is God's": Robert Schumann's Talismane, Op. 141, No. 4, with lyrics by Johann Wolfgang von Goethe, begins "The East is God's!/The West is God's!/Northern and southern lands/ rest in the peace of his hands."

ABOUT THE AUTHOR

LEON LEVIT LIVED THROUGH THE events of his novel. Arriving in British Mandate Palestine in 1932 he continued his family's textile business and started a family. He served with the British Army in Palestine, and later participated in Israel's war for independence in 1948. He served as Israel's Economic Attaché in New York for 7 years, following which he was posted as Charge des Affairs to Turkey.

Upon his retirement from the Foreign Office he dedicated his time to writing this manuscript – in German, his mother tongue

Not expecting the book to be published in Germany, he always hoped it would be translated into English for a wide readership. He died in Tel Aviv in 1974. Through the help of his daughter Daphna Levit, *A Mercedes in the Sand* was published in German in 2002 and is still available under the title *Ein Mercedes Im Sand*. At last, *A Mercedes in the Sand* is available in the English translation.

OUR FATHER

—●—

OUR FATHER COULD READ, SPEAK several languages – including Latin and Turkish. He was an easy going unpretentious man who enjoyed the play of words and loved to laugh. He created many funny songs, skits and parodies that were preformed within the diplomatic missions in which he worked.

He possessed a thorough and complete knowledge of world history, geography, literature and music and was a constant source of information and inspiration to us in our formative years. He constantly pointed out the opposing view of any issue, which he was quick to analyze and understand with humor and honesty.

A patient listener, he gave his children unending love and encouragement, and many moments of joy, laughter and music.

Ruth (Levit) Miller – Ottawa 2016

ACKNOWLEDGEMENTS

———

To Ms. Susan Glickman – Ph.d.

My heartfelt gratitude for her encouragement and editing of the German translation of the Novel.

To David Sachs – best selling author of "The Flood" for his assistance and constant help in enabling the publication of this book..

To A.J Sykes – Author and Editor – for his enthusiasm, encouragement and editing skills.

To Martin Gomez – for his original and effective concept and design of the book cover.

To my husband Arnon - for his belief in this project and constant support throughout.

Ruth (Levit) Miller –Ottawa 2016

71944982R00209

Made in the USA
Columbia, SC
08 June 2017